The PLANT HUNTER

The
PLANT
HUNTER

T. L. Mogford

WELBECK

Published in 2022 by Welbeck Fiction Limited,
an imprint of Welbeck Publishing Group
Based in London and Sydney
www.welbeckpublishing.com

Copyright © T. L. Mogford, 2022

The moral right of the author has been asserted.

A CIP catalogue record for this book is available from the British Library

Hardback ISBN: 978-1-78739-936-5
Trade Paperback ISBN: 978-1-78739-937-2
Ebook ISBN: 978-1-78739-935-8

Printed and bound by CPI Group (UK) Ltd, Croydon, CR0 4YY

10 9 8 7 6 5 4 3 2 1

For Ali

He that dares not grasp the thorn
Should never crave the rose.

Anne Brontë

PART ONE
August 1867 – London

Chapter 1

The day which was to change Harry Compton's life for ever began like most of the others this past year. His eyes snapped open — as they usually did — a good ten seconds before Mrs Pincham's brisk knock at his door. How did his mind manage to wake him so efficiently? Harry wondered yet again. Was it chalking off the hours as he slept?

'Master Compton?' came his landlady's harsh London vowels.

'Awake, Mrs Pincham,' Harry groaned. 'Wide awake.' He lay there a moment longer, staring up at the damp stains that spread across his ceiling like dark, unexplored continents. Then he rolled out of bed and carried his chamber-pot downstairs, trying to avoid the fierce eyes of his landlady as she cracked eggs one-handed at the kitchen range.

Slops disposed of, Harry hurried back up the stairs to his bedroom, where he dressed as quickly as possible. Flannel shirt and trousers, twill waistcoat, flatcap and boots — comfortable clothes, the clothes he'd worn in his former job. Unlike the other salesmen at the boarding house, Harry preferred to complete his ablutions at work, and as he caught sight of his unshaven face in the glass, he realised how much older he looked since he'd arrived here from Battersea last summer. Dark eyes tired, and a touch wary; the little cleft at the base of his square jaw blackened by stubble. It was a handsome face, he'd been told more than once, and it had been both his fortune and his curse. For without it, he'd never have landed this strange new job in the first place . . . Turning away, Harry ran down the stairs and into the dining-room, where the landlady was already laying out the chafing trays.

'First down again, Master Compton,' Mrs Pincham said. Her keen gaze took in his unkempt appearance, then flickered away.

Within a few minutes, Harry knew, Barrington, Ratcliffe and Drinkwater would make their appearance — preening and strutting, resplendent in their freshly-brushed frock-coats, beards carefully clipped, hair gleaming with pomade. They were always 'Mister' to Mrs Pincham, despite the fact that two of them were even younger than his own twenty-one years.

'The early bird, Mrs Pincham,' Harry said, using the tongs to lay a poached egg between two triangles of cold toast. There was no danger of spilling the yolk, he knew, as the landlady liked to steam the things until they had the consistency of India rubber. Having washed his down with a cup of hot, strong tea, Harry headed for the front door, just catching the first bars of 'Mr' Barrington's tuneless voice issuing from the stairwell behind him.

It was a fine summer's morning, Harry found to his delight. In the open countryside at the end of North Street, the sun was rising over the fields of Fulham, and in the misty distance he could just make out a ploughman steering his dray horse, digging furrows for his next crop of potatoes.

After crossing the humpbacked slats of Stamford Bridge, Harry skirted the railway line above Chelsea Station. In the cutting below, the stationmaster was standing outside his ticket hut, clay pipe cupped in one hand, scarlet cravat knotted jauntily around his neck. The man raised an arm to Harry, well-used to seeing him pass at this time of morning, and Harry waved back.

Turning away from the railway line, Harry wove between a network of market gardens. August had been warm this year, and, judging by their wilting tops, all those carrots, turnips and runner beans could use a drink of water. The scrubby grounds of St Mark's College appeared to his left, and Harry followed its fencing for a time, then drew to a halt, feeling that little heart-clench of excitement which always accompanied this part of his walk to work. For just a few yards ahead of him lay the King's Road, Chelsea.

The moment Harry joined the road, he was struck once again by the magnificence of Mr Weeks's stovehouse. Something in the way that it rose so dramatically from the pavement, a fantastical cathedral of white-painted iron ribs and gleaming plate glass. Within those domes, a lush jungle of exotic plants pressed against the panes, flaunting their charms, enticing one to enter.

Harry's attention was caught by one of Mr Weeks's undergardeners, who was setting up a pavement sign outside the nursery with a new poster fixed upon it. '*Madonna Lily Bulbs!*' the lettering screamed. '*Lifted fresh from the Plains of Syria! Only three sovereigns a half-dozen!!*'

'*Only* three sovereigns?' Harry said.

The undergardener glanced up. Boulter, his name was – Harry had met him once or twice at the Man in the Moon.

'Cheap at half the price,' Boulter said, baring his snaggle-teeth. 'You ain't seen nothing like these blooms, Harry. And the fragrance . . .' He fanned a hand against his chest like a swooning lady. 'Fuck me ragged.'

Harry threw Boulter a doubtful look, then continued past the next stovehouse, where a team of window-cleaners was busy polishing the glass, trying to attain a sheen that could compete with that of Mr Weeks's. Behind lay Mr Veitch's Royal Exotic Nursery, with its neat rows of greenhouses running between here and the Fulham Road; then came Mr Wimsett's stockground, acre upon acre of beds and borders stretching all the way down to the Thames — musk roses, monkey-puzzle trees, forsythia. Was there anywhere else on earth that hosted as many valuable plants as the King's Road? Harry wondered. The plains of Syria? He doubted it.

He continued along the elegant, gravelled thoroughfare — reserved for the monarch's exclusive use until 1731, as the most direct route from St James's Palace to Hampton Court, but now a hive of private enterprise. Flower-sellers from Hammersmith were setting up barrows of peonies, hoping to capitalise upon the prestige of the plant nurseries. Harry knew a few of them by name, but they were too busy secur-ing the best pitches to greet him. Next came the gates of the Cremorne Pleasure Gardens, padlocked shut now, a couple of smashed flagons outside suggestive of last night's festiv-ities. A beggar in tattered clothes sat amidst the earthenware shards, head bowed, upturned cap laid out before him. Harry dropped a four-penny piece inside, and the beggar nodded without looking up. Sometimes, Harry wondered if the man waited there especially for him, as he was usually gone the

6

moment that he passed. Not that it mattered — one thing Harry wasn't short of these days was spare change.

He reached the dogleg of the King's Road, where the publican of the Man in the Moon was busy sweeping the horseshit off her section of pavement. 'Morning, Ma Potts,' Harry called out, and the old woman swivelled her hatchet face his way, leaning heavily on her broomstick.

There'd been more plant nurseries on the King's Road once, Harry knew — as many as twenty, at one point — but London's steady creep westwards had proved unrelenting, and a few of the weaker operations had been sold off for housing, or for shops catering to the new residents — tobacconists, tea-sellers, chophouses. Only past the squawking cacophony of Mr Baker's pheasant dealership — *'Exotic Fowl to the Royal Household!'* — did the nurseries begin again: Colville's, Tuck's, Little's. This last had a placard outside. *'Just 4 miles from London,'* it proclaimed. *'Omnibuses from the Bank every ¼ of an hour.'* Nice idea, Harry thought — lure in the City boys to Chelsea village. If you could still term it a village, he reflected, seeing a fine new terrace of houses sprouting from the green grass of Markham Square.

But as he reached the most ornate stovehouse of them all, Harry felt his spirits ebb. Raising his head, he read the words *'JM Piggott's Plant Emporium'* detailed in curly wrought-iron above the door. Josiah Piggott, he thought — my Lord and Master . . .

Mr Piggott had been a foundry-man once, Harry knew — a pig-iron manufacturer from Bow. But then he'd got wind that the tax on glass was to be dropped in 1845, and had purchased these premises from an ailing nurseryman. A canny choice, as the price of glass had duly plummeted, and Piggott had poured all he had into constructing his new stovehouse. A touch smaller than Mr Weeks's, it was true, but a good deal showier, its combination of sinuous curves and rectilinear glass panes calling to mind the Crystal Palace of the Great Exhibition. Just the thing to draw the eye of the well-heeled punter. The only catch was that its owner knew next to nothing about horticulture.

Taking a steadying breath, Harry turned off the King's Road into Anderson Street, and knocked on the nursery's backdoor. 'Name?' came an aggressive voice from the other side.

'Harry Compton, sir.'

The door opened to reveal Decimus Frith, Mr Piggott's nursery foreman, and the man tasked with securing his operation from espionage and theft. Mr Frith was a short, thickset man in his mid-fifties, with sandy hair and a pair of washed-out blue eyes that seemed always to be smiling at some private joke. According to Jack Turner, Harry's old friend from Cultivation, Frith had served as an officer in the Crimean War – killing twenty Russians in a single day, Jack claimed – and the yellow stripe he wore down the sides of his worsted trousers still lent him a faintly military air.

Frith peered up at Harry, hard eyes crinkling in amusement above his waxed blond moustaches, which protruded from the sides of his face in sharp, elegant spikes. 'Why do you always arrive alone, Compton?' he asked. 'Too good to keep company with the other chaps from Mrs Pincham's?'

'I like to take my time, sir. See the King's Road wake up.'

'*Things* don't wake up, Compton,' Frith drawled, waving Harry into the backyard of the nursery. 'People do.'

Harry gave a flat smile, eyes sliding inexorably to Frith's ulster coat. Whatever the weather, the man always wore it, leading Jack Turner to claim that there must be a pistol concealed beneath its skirts. 'A fair few of Frith's fancy-friends died in the Charge of the Light Brigade,' Jack had vouchsafed to Harry once. 'Learnt him the dangers of being unarmed, so now he always carries a barker . . .'

'Run along now, Compton,' Frith said in his cut-glass accent. 'Get your gladrags on!'

Harry rounded the hoardings that shielded the nursery's customers from the sights Josiah Piggott did not want them to see. The brick outhouse containing the boiler that heated the stovehouse – a smoke-belching, pot-bellied beast that some underpaid stoker was constantly feeding with coal. Then came the coalstore, and the potting shed, where the nursery's head gardener, Mr Jarvis Siggers, propagated the rarest and most valuable plants Piggott owned – those bought from the curators of botanic gardens, or from auctions following the deaths of private collectors. That was where Harry was meant to be working by now – that was what had been promised him – but no, he had to walk on by, around the stinking heap of manure and into the cramped little hut set aside for Piggott's salesmen to change their clothes.

Harry pulled closed the warped door, then lit the paraffin lamp, the ammoniac reek of horse manure still stinging in his nostrils. At least there was no one else inside. His outfit still hung from the peg where he'd left it at close of business on Saturday. Quickly, Harry undressed, then slipped on his white linen shirt and fawn-coloured trousers, and changed into his frockcoat. Silk lining, velvet collar,

9

double breasts of the softest black cotton — how well he remembered having that coat fitted on Jermyn Street! It had been Mr Frith who'd taken him. Three years Harry had been working in Cultivation by then — until Piggott had spotted him one morning whilst touring his nursery's growing grounds in Battersea. 'He looks about right,' Piggott had remarked to Frith, and Harry had been thrilled to be plucked from obscurity; honoured that the master had seen some talent in him. But it had not been that at all, Harry had learnt, for he'd been promoted for his good looks, rather than his horticultural abilities — chosen to work not in the potting shed, but in the stovehouse, where his handsome face might help flog an exotic plant to an undiscerning client, most of whom were wealthy women of a certain age.

Sinking down on to the bench, Harry stuck a fist into one of his Oxford brogues and began to buff the leather with an ostrich-feather duster. If Jack Turner and the boys from Cultivation could see him now . . . Shoes polished to the requisite gleam, Harry tied a cotton bib around his neck and set about shaving at the washstand. Having towelled himself down, he fixed on his wing collar and reached for the pot of bear's-grease pomade. And then there it was, the face that had sold a thousand pot plants. Harry winked sardonically at the mirror, then fixed on the ash-grey topper that set off the costume so fetchingly. No other nursery dressed up its salesmen like toffs. It was Piggott's way of standing out from the crowd.

Back in the yard, Harry saw that Mr Siggers had arrived in the potting shed, and was busy transferring a batch of slipper orchids into ornamental terracotta pots, readying them for sale. The man didn't even turn his head as Harry passed.

On the other side of the hoardings, Frith was opening the back door to Harry's fellow salesmen — Barrington, Ratcliffe and Drinkwater — who swaggered in like dandies, vanity stroked by all the admiring looks they'd drawn on the King's Road in their Piggott's frockcoats. All they would need to change in the hut was their footwear.

'I'll outsell you this week, Compton,' Barrington called over. 'You see if I don't!'

Harry made no reply, just followed the cinder path between the petunia beds towards the rear door of the stovehouse.

Sales were brisk that morning, even by the nursery's usual standards. Harry spent the first part of his day outlining the soil requirements of the insectivorous pitcher plant to a blonde woman in a poke bonnet and low-cut bustle dress. The woman kept wafting a fan across her swelling bosom, saying, 'Do you not find it rather sultry in here, young sir?' In the end, she'd ordered six of the plants, then slipped Harry a calling card and told him to drop by Cheyne Walk next week to 'cast an eye over their progress'. Next had come a more serious-minded customer, a high court judge with a soupstrainer moustache, seeking a gift for his wife. He'd listened to Harry's passionate discourse on the differing scents of the Australian pittosporum, before choosing the least aromatic variety, which his clerk would return later to collect. Harry was just in the process of telling a very pretty lady with a pink parasol why ferns needed no pollinators, as they could reproduce themselves alone by means of spores, when the door of the stovehouse flew open, and in came Josiah Piggott himself.

Harry peered uneasily between the fronds of tropical foliage. Everything about Mr Piggott was oversize, as though he'd spent too long in his stovehouse glutting on bonemeal and leafmould. Some six foot two inches tall, with a barrel chest and bushy silver sideburns that spread across his jaw like climbing ivy. Springy brown hair flecked with grey, a few sprays of which protruded from a sable top hat, fashioned by the same tailor as Harry's. A garish red-and-green tartan waistcoat peeking from beneath his morning coat, a nod to some specious Caledonian ancestry that Piggott had cooked up to appeal to the increasing number of Scots buying plants in Chelsea. As usual, he carried his gold-knobbed cane – though he had no problem walking, despite his girth and advanced years – and when he spoke it was in a permanent bellow, those East End vowels just audible beneath a dreadful approximation of the Queen's English.

'Finest stovehouse on Her Majesty's King's Road, though I say so meself,' Piggott roared, embracing with one tree-trunk arm his companion – a nervous-looking potential client whom Piggott must have swept up along the way. 'You want rhododendrons for your new pile in Hertfordshire, sah?' Piggott went on. 'Then you'll find 'em out back – and more competitively priced than at Veitch's or Weeks's, by Jove! But this is the showroom where I keep me crown jewels, so to speak, and these fine fellows' – Piggott indicated his team of salesmen with a sweep of his cane – 'are just the chaps to show you what's what!'

The fact that Barrington, Ratcliffe and Drinkwater knew as little of the vicissitudes of horticulture as their master was of minor importance. They all stared at Piggott, practically drooling like dogs, fully alive to his hint that there was money to be made here: for if a man were building a new country house, then he would be buying large-scale and long-term.

But Piggott was heading for Harry. 'This here's Harry Compton,' he called out, 'our most knowledgeable salesman. Ain't nothing young Harry can't tell you about botany — though he's so pretty most folk want to stick him in a Ming vase and keep him in their conservatory!'

This image seemed to discomfit, rather than encourage, the customer, so Piggott — remarkably alert to others' reactions, despite all appearances to the contrary — changed tack. 'But I see Harry's tied up with this exquisite young creature' — the lady with the pink parasol blushed the colour of her appendage — 'so I'll steer you instead to Rex Barrington, who'll provide you with all the assistance you need.'

Once the customer had been dispatched, Harry excused himself from the lady with the sunshade, and sidled over to Piggott. 'Sir?'

'What is it, boy?'

'I've been a year now in Sales, and—'

'Not *now*, Compton,' Piggott hissed, then strode away through his stovehouse, sweat oozing from his ruddy brow — despite all the time he spent in here, he never seemed to acclimatise to the humidity.

'Tree ferns?' came a meek voice.

Harry turned to find the lady with the pink parasol standing beside him. 'A joy to behold, ma'am,' he replied, 'but a tad slow-growing. Personally, I'd favour the hart's-tongue fern . . .'

The day wore on. The salesmen all took their lunch on rotation, repairing one by one to their wooden hut, where a basket of food would be waiting, purchased from one of the local tradesmen. When it was Harry's turn, he pulled shut the door to minimise the reek of manure, then sat down to eat his slices of beef tongue, wondering yet again if he should resign right now, or stick it out in the hope he might one day be allowed to join Mr Siggers in the potting shed.

Suddenly, there was a knock at the door, and Harry stood up to open it. Peering around its frame was a moon-faced youth with a head of ridiculous red curls.

'Jack!' Harry exclaimed. 'What brings you up this way?'

'Just dropping off some seedlings,' Jack Turner replied. He glanced over one shoulder, then beckoned Harry closer. 'I've news! There's plant hunters in town.'

Harry's eyes lit up. If nurserymen were the gallery owners of the King's Road, then plant hunters were its artists. Wild and reckless, and with the self-regard to match.

'There's a few of 'em mustering tonight at the Man in the Moon,' Jack went on. 'Some of the boys from Cultivation are going down to take a gander. Want to come?'

'Too right,' Harry said. 'What time were you thinking?'

'Seven o'clock?'

'Perfect.'

Jack winked. 'You do look dashing in that get-up, old stick,' he said in his Cockney accent. 'Give Beau Brummell a run for his money.'

Harry cuffed his old friend on the shoulder, then a shout went up — 'Turner!' — and Jack threw him a quick salute, and retreated.

Harry sat back down to finish his lunch. He knew what Jack and the other lads would be after — plant hunters needed hired hands, and there was big money to be made if you were chosen to join an expedition. Not that such a commission was easily achieved. Plant hunters risked life and limb on their expeditions to find rare plants: they needed people with them whose gifts extended to survival and fearlessness, as well as to botany.

Harry checked the time and headed back out to the stock-ground. Beside the rear gate stood the handcart of wisteria seedlings that Jack would have dragged over Battersea Bridge. *Wisteria floribunda*, Harry saw — Piggott had been buying them on the cheap from his rivals' catalogues for years; Harry must have germinated thousands in his time in Cultivation.

By the back door, Decimus Frith was patting Jack down, checking his pockets for pilfered seeds. 'Enjoy this, do you, sir?' Harry heard Jack ask. 'Must remind you of looting on the battlefield . . .'

Chuckling to himself, Harry fixed on his topper and prepared himself for the busy afternoon trade. Seven o'clock at the Man in the Moon, he thought, as he set his face into a solicitous smile. He'd be there — with bells on.

Chapter 2

The pub was rammed with drinkers. Harry sat at a corner table, with Jack Turner on his right, ginger curls dewy with sweat. Opposite sat Tony Banks, a bull-necked Scot who'd arrived in Cultivation just before Harry had left. The others — Pugh, Tonks and Davies — were all new to Harry, and they regarded him with a marked scepticism, he felt. Perhaps it was the residue of bear's-grease pomade in his hair, or the clean-shaven gleam to his face. Either way, Harry was glad to have Jack Turner by his side, treating him as though he'd never left Cultivation at all.

'Over there,' Jack called above the hubbub, pointing to a louche, rangy man standing by the bar. 'That's Paxton Crosse, ain't it? And look who's creeping up on him!'

Sure enough, the small, fussy figure of James William Wimsett was edging across the taproom, preparing to make his pitch. A conversation started up, the famous plant hunter leaning nonchalantly on the bar, the nurseryman gesticulating imploringly with open palms. Eventually, Wimsett nodded at Ma Potts, the publican, who refilled Paxton Crosse's glass of porter, before the two men repaired to the snug. As they passed close to the corner table, Harry took in the plant hunter's sunburnt face and crooked, knowing smile. The things that man must have seen on his travels . . .

'It was Crosse who brought back that purple crabapple from Kazakhstan,' Jack went on. 'The one Colville's are selling. What's the name again?'

'*Malus crossii*,' Harry replied.

'Smart-arse,' Banks muttered.

'What did you say?' Harry asked, meeting the Scotsman's eye.

The table fell silent, and Harry could sense Jack glancing uneasily between him and Banks. Jack had seen Harry's temper before; knew there was a flint edge beneath all that charm.

'You Sales boys all know the name of a plant, don't ye?' Banks goaded. 'But no how tae grow one!'

'Lads, lads,' Jack Turner intervened. 'Harry here's a plantsman to the tips of his toes. When he was in Cultivation, he germinated seeds none of us could get a breath out of. Remember them gingko seeds, Harry? Everyone said they was rotten, but you cleaned 'em up, sowed 'em in three inches of loam – and blow me down, a glossier set of seedlings you never did see!'

Banks gave a begrudging nod and looked away.

'Thanks,' Harry said stiffly, and Jack answered with one of his winks.

'Over there,' Pugh called out, the first time he'd spoken. 'That's Niven McCabe, ain't it?'

They all looked round to see a burly, scar-faced man emerge from the snug, deep in conversation with the owner of a Southfields nursery. He looked more like a gamekeeper than a plant hunter to Harry, with his tweed breeches and deerstalker hat.

'I thought he'd been eaten by cannibals in Guatemala,' Pugh said.

'And that's Donald Moncrieff behind him!' Davies put in. 'I'm sure of it.'

'Why do they all have to be Scottish?' Tonks complained.

''Cause we Scots is as hard as fuck,' Banks said with a nonchalant sniff.

Harry smiled, and the atmosphere seemed to lighten.

'I heard Moncrieff was just back from Syria,' Pugh said. 'Wonder what he collected there?'

'*Lilium candidum*,' Harry replied.

Everyone turned to look at him.

'Three sovereigns a half-dozen at Weeks's,' Harry added.

Davies shook his head. 'It's like tulip fever all over again. What was it that Dutchman did in Amsterdam? Swapped his mansion for a single bulb?'

'They'll be doing that on the King's Road next,' Tonks muttered.

'Paxton Crosse charges two thousand guineas an expedition now,' Jack said.

'Piss off!' Banks exclaimed.

'*Excluding* expenses.'

'I wonder how much he pays his hands,' Pugh reflected, and the group turned again to gaze at the bar, where McCabe and Moncrieff were enjoying sherry cobblers that someone else had paid for.

Harry wasn't sure if Jack was right about the plant hunters' fees, but there was no doubt that the way the King's Road did business was changing. Until recently, plant hunters had worked exclusively for august academic institutions such as Kew Gardens, the Chelsea Physic Garden or the Royal Horticultural Society at Chiswick. But nowadays, aware of the massive profits being made by the commercial nurseries, they were taking their work private — and reaping the rewards.

'I'm going over,' Banks said, unable to restrain himself any longer. He heaved himself to his feet and shouldered his way to the bar. A couple of undergardeners hopped out of his path, affording Harry a view of a small table nestled under the panelled staircase that led up to the few modest rooms the Man in the Moon offered for rent. Sitting alone at the table was a short, dark man with a straggly brown beard. A tatty billycock hat rested on the table before him, and the man's head kept bowing down to it, as though in prayer. His arm lay beside the hat, trembling slightly, creeping ever closer to a pitcher of wine that sat precariously close to the edge.

Turning his gaze to the bar, Harry saw the publican, Ma Potts, eyeing the man with dour interest as she twisted open a jar of pickled whelks. She gave a sharp nod, and a moment later, Edwin the chucker-outer appeared, a massive bear of a man with a Malmsey nose, who Harry knew took great pleasure in cracking heads. 'Watch him,' Harry saw Ma Potts mouth, before the scene was lost from view.

'He's off down the Cremorne later,' Banks said, throwing himself back down into his chair.

'Who is?' Pugh asked.

'Paxton Crosse, you greasy divot!' Banks retorted. 'There'll be a fair few painted lassies about at that time of night. If we approach Crosse when his guard's down, maybe he'll give us a place on his next expedition.'

'You've got it all mapped out, don't you, Tony?' Davies laughed.

'We'd best not bring Harry to the Cremorne,' Jack threw in. 'You should see how the ladies make a beeline for him. Crosse'd never get a look-in!'

Frowning with embarrassment, Harry signalled for another round.

'Well, you ain't cheap, Harry,' Davies said, 'I'll give you that.'

Harry shrugged off the compliment, if that was what it was. It seemed the least he could do, given that Sales were paid twice what Cultivation got. And then there was the subsidised accommodation he received . . . The drinks arrived, and conversation switched to Old 'Pie-Gut' Piggott, and whether he would ever be found in here trying to recruit a plant hunter. 'Too tight by half' was the unanimous conclusion.

They all fell silent again as Paxton Crosse sauntered past their table, trailed by a long line of nurserymen ducking and scraping like courtiers. Then came McCabe and Moncrieff, the latter limping slightly, a shimmering blue feather tucked into his hatband, no doubt plucked from the tail of a bird of paradise.

'Drink up, lads,' Jack called out. 'That's our cue!'

Looking over to the table by the stairs, Harry saw the small, dark-skinned man shaking in his seat, eyes rolling back in his head. Harry put down his tankard and got up. He knew that look only too well; remembered it from his childhood with a horrible clarity. As Harry approached his table, the man slumped forward, and his arm knocked the ceramic jug to the floor.

'That's it!' Ma Potts shouted. 'Edwin!?'

The chucker-outer made his move, but Harry stepped in front of him and said softly, 'There's no trouble here, Eddie.'

The chucker-outer glanced back at Ma Potts, who pursed her lips, eyes roaming appreciatively over Harry's face. Eventually, she turned away, calling back over one shoulder, 'Well, it's still two shillings for the jug!'

Harry handed the chucker-outer the payment, then looked down at the swarthy man. He was lying face-down on the table, making little popping noises with his lips. Harry took off his jacket, rolled it up, then slipped it under his head.

'What're you playing at, Harry?' Jack Turner hissed as he walked past, heading for the door.

'I'll come and find you later at the Cremorne,' Harry replied. 'After I see this fellow right.'

'You're a soft touch, Harry,' Jack said, shaking his head. Then he fixed on his flatcap and followed his friends into the night.

The man had stopped shaking now, Harry saw. His blood-shot eyes fluttered open, and Harry crouched down next to him. 'You had a bit of a spell, sir. A fit.'

The man pushed himself up into a sitting position and leant his head back against the wainscot. 'Don't you think I know that, boy?' he said in a thick accent. 'Now pass me my drink.'

Harry had half-expected a Spanish lisp, so tanned was the man's skin, but the intonation was different, something Harry couldn't quite place. He slid the cup across the table.

'Roight up to me mouth,' the man urged. 'Me arms ain't steady yet.'

Irish, Harry thought, lifting the cup to the man's flaking lips. He sucked at the contents, breathing quickly through his nose. Over by the bar, Ma Potts was watching them closely, her expression hovering somewhere between fury and pity. Harry remembered seeing a 'NINA' sign in the window once, when she'd been advertising for a position – 'No Irish Need Apply'.

'Thanking you,' the man said.

Harry lowered the cup. 'Breathe deep and slow. In through your nose, and out through your mouth.'

The man looked up at Harry with weary eyes. 'You know the affliction, then?'

Harry nodded. 'My mother.'

Gathering up his jacket from the table, Harry put it back on. Ma Potts was coming over now, strong sinewy arms folded across her apron. 'You work at Joe Piggott's place, don't you?' she snapped.

'Harry Compton,' Harry said, holding out a hand.

Ma Potts ignored the gesture. 'Your friend's lodged himself in one of my best rooms. He's paid in advance, but if you could ask him to make this his last night, I'd be grateful.'

Harry nodded, and the publican turned away to start clearing empties from the other tables. Now that the plant hunters had left, the taproom was quieter. In one corner, the chucker-outer sat alone, smoking a cheroot as he gazed mournfully into the middle distance.

'Help me upstairs, will ya, boy?' the Irishman asked.

Harry held out an arm, and the man used it to push himself to his feet, then hooked one hand around Harry's shoulder. With his other, he picked up his hat and wedged it on to his matted brown hair. 'Up we go,' he said cheerfully.

They tottered away from the table, and Harry kicked open the swing doors to the staircase. The Irishman's arm was looped over both his shoulders now, and up close he smelt oddly fragrant, a blend of stale cologne and toffee. Harry was just starting to wish that he'd ignored his conscience, and followed Jack and the boys to the Cremorne, when they reached the landing. 'Well, this is me,' the Irishman said, fumbling in one pocket.

Out came a large iron key, which the man prodded against the door, missing the lock by a good three inches. Was he really cursed with seizures, Harry wondered, or simply drunk as a lord?

'Here,' Harry said.

The Irishman relinquished the key, and Harry inserted it into the lock. It twisted to the left, and he pushed open the door and stepped back.

But the Irishman remained where he was, leaning against the wall, staring at Harry with eyes of bright, steely blue. He was younger than Harry had thought — no more than forty-five. 'You've the patience of an angel, boy,' he said, looking at him in wonder. 'And the face.'

Harry frowned.

'Don't you worry, lad,' the man added with a grin, 'I'm not one for the sins of Greece. Never have been, despite all offers. Lorcan Darke,' he said, extending a hand.

Tentatively, Harry took it. The man's grip was firm and dry, his gaze unwavering. 'You'll come in for a dram, Harry?' he asked.

'How d'you know my name?'

'Sure, you told it to that harridan downstairs! Come on – lend you some Dutch courage before you join your pals at the Cremorne.'

Harry wondered how the man could have known that, too. When his mother had come round from her convulsions, she would remember nothing of what had occurred. So much the better, Harry had often thought.

Darke pushed open the door and, in the light thrown by the landing sconce, Harry had a sense of a room crammed with more possessions that might have been usual in rented lodgings.

'You'll forgive the mess, I'm not much of a housekeeper,' Darke said, indicating a chair by the bed. 'Take a pew.'

Harry picked his way through the clutter and sat down, as the Irishman addressed himself to the gas-lamp. At length, the room flooded with light, and Harry could discern its contents more clearly. On an occasional table in the corner lay some kind of tobacco pipe, with a candlestick and some little pots of unguents scattered around it. Three leather trunks were stacked side by side against the wall, one of them covered in a dustsheet. Laid beside them was a bedroll and blanket. It seemed that Mr Darke had been sleeping on the floor, rather than in the bed, which Harry could see now was covered in little squares of ochre paper.

Stooping to pick up one that had fallen to the floor, Harry's eyes widened to find a daguerreotype of a naked woman leaning over an ottoman, her head angled back to the camera. The woman's face was dark and alluring, her eyes like a cat's, and she wore a curious necklace of coiled silver around her throat.

'Beautiful women,' Darke said with a wry chuckle. 'My greatest weakness – and my greatest joy.'

Harry passed the image back, cheeks burning, and Darke turned and started rummaging in one of the trunks. 'Ah!' he exclaimed, holding up a half-drunk bottle of whiskey. 'A taste o' home.'

Darke stood there for a moment, motionless in the glow of the lamp, suddenly fixed in time like some ancient chieftain or idol, bright blue eyes gleaming in his saturnine face. Then, as he stepped forward, one boot caught on the dustsheet, and Harry saw that it wasn't covering a piece of luggage at all, but a wooden crate topped with a pitched, glazed roof.

'Is that a Wardian case?' Harry asked.

Darke glanced round. 'So you're a plantsman, are you?'

'I am,' Harry muttered under his breath. 'Or was . . .'

'This case was built by Dr Ward himself back in 1852,' Darke said proudly, tapping a black fingernail on the glazed gable. 'The year he was elected Fellow of the Royal Society.'

Harry nodded. Most people in Chelsea knew the story of the lucky Dr Ward. A medical man with a keen interest in the natural world, Ward had stumbled on his discovery quite by accident, whilst making a study of the life-cycle of the caterpillar. Having left one of his subjects in a soil-filled jar overnight, Ward had been astonished the next morning to find a baby fern sprouting inside it. He'd realised then that inside a small sealed glasshouse, a plant could thrive without water, or even fresh air. Ward's patented contraption had soon become indispensable to botanists, used to transport live plants from one part of the world to another. Harry had seen one once — conveyed in triumph up the King's Road towards Mr Weeks's nursery, verdant with exotic foliage — but it had been hard to get a close look past all the crowds.

'*Sláinte*,' Darke said, passing Harry the grimy toothcup he'd found in his trunk. 'Help yourself.'

Harry poured himself a modest measure of the amber-coloured liquid. Now that his eyes had adjusted, he was able to identify more of the botanical equipment that lay scattered about the room. The stacked wooden frames of a plant-press. A varnished box and viewfinder that could only constitute a daguerreotype camera. A cylindrical container with a hinged lid and shoulder strap that Harry knew to be a vasculum — a sort of reinforced satchel that horticulturalists used to carry plant specimens without crushing them. On its front was a plaque engraved with the name 'L. R. C. Darke'.

'Are you a plant hunter, then?' Harry asked.

'I am . . . or was,' Darke echoed, with the ghost of a smile. He took off his rough tweed coat and laid it carefully on one of the trunks. 'Now get on and wet your beak, Harry! You're making me nervous.'

Harry obediently sipped his Bushmills as Darke set about lighting the candle on the table. A moment later, the man's small hands began to flit back and forth with a dexterity Harry wouldn't have imagined possible just a few minutes earlier — plucking up a glass jar; scooping out some black paste with a teaspoon and placing it on a ceramic plate; using the flame of the candle to set the paste alight. Soon, Harry smelt the sweet, herbal reek he'd caught in Darke's clothes, and realised that this must be opium, and that the man's entire being was saturated in it. How could such a raddled specimen as this be a plant hunter, Harry wondered, thinking again of the swashbuckling heroes he'd seen downstairs in the taproom.

'Ever partaken?' Darke asked, using the teaspoon to transfer the burning syrup into the bowl of his pipe.

Harry shook his head.

'Wise man,' Darke said, lips clamping on to the teat of the pipe as he drew the pale fumes deep into his lungs. 'There you *are*,' he murmured, as though greeting an old friend. Then he was silent for a time, his pink-rimmed eyes half-closed, so that Harry wondered if he'd fallen asleep.

'What brought you here?' Harry asked.

Darke's eyes flickered open. 'Finish your drink, boy, and I'll tell you,' he said, setting down the pipe, the smouldering bowl resting on the side plate.

Harry did as he was told, gasping at the heat of the whiskey, then looked up at Darke expectantly.

'You'll have heard of Lord Kinlathan?' Darke asked.

Harry shook his head.

'Rich man from County Meath,' Darke said. 'Decent sort, all told, and imbued with an insatiable appetite for exotic plants. Sent me on a number of expeditions to the Far East — China, Japan, Malay.' Another of his dry chuckles: 'He's got an estate that he likes to fill with the brightest new

27

trinkets. Or *liked*, I should say, for he died last year, and his son and heir, in his infinite wisdom, has refused to pay me for my last expedition. A slug in the Lord's vineyard, that's what I call the likes of him! So I caught the boat here instead. To try my hand at Chelsea.'

'Did you manage to sell your stock?' Harry asked.

Darke smiled. 'The right question, young Harry. Everything I collected made it safely home to Ireland. Over the South China Sea; through the Indian Ocean, across the South fuckin' Atlantic!' Darke reached for his pipe and drew on it angrily. 'But one wee crossing of the Irish Sea and I lose the lot. Take a closer look at that Wardian case, would you? Go on!'

Harry examined the miniature greenhouse. One of the glass panes at the back was missing.

'A storm not twenty miles from Holyhead,' Darke said. 'Seawater all over my cuttings. Seedstock ruined. Bulbs poisoned. Everything lost.' He let out a mirthless laugh and sucked again on his pipe. The reek of opium filled the room now, making Harry feel a little nauseous. Surely there was a danger of it seeping under the door, drawing the attention of Ma Potts, or worse, her chucker-outer . . .

'Ah, don't look at me like that, Harry,' Darke said, 'like a wrathful angel! You can't begrudge me my pipe. It steadies the seizures.'

'You sure it doesn't cause them?'

Darke grinned. 'So your mother suffers with the same affliction?'

Harry nodded, not bothering to correct Darke's use of the present tense.

'I had my first seizure last year,' Darke went on. 'Caught the blackwater fever in Hunan province, and it brought the condition on.' He put down his pipe and looked at Harry, his eyes seeming to penetrate deep into Harry's innermost thoughts. 'It's an interesting region, Hunan,' he continued. 'Full of undiscovered flora. You've heard of the icicle tree, I'll wager?'

Harry knitted his brows. 'That's just a legend.'

'A legend, says he!' Darke exclaimed. 'Well, Alexander the Great thought it real enough! As did Marco Polo. The most beautiful tree on God's green earth, people say. Gorgeous pinnate leaves. Lacy and deciduous – a bit like *Pistacia sinensis*. Know what that is?'

'The Chinese pistache?'

'Good lad,' Darke said, the creases in his sun-browned cheeks deepening as he smiled, as though his lips were set in parentheses. 'The foliage alone would commend it, of course. But the blooms – sweet Mary Mother of God.' Darke shook his head: 'As clean and white as an icicle bathed in frost . . .'

'Like a horse chestnut?'

'Horse chestnut my arse!' Darke scoffed. 'This tree makes *Magnolia grandiflora* look like a roadside weed! The flowers are like frosted daggers, Harry. Exquisite in every way. And the tree's temperate. And *hardy*. Imagine that. What a showstopper! It'd be in every garden in the Western World . . .'

Harry shrugged, and Darke widened his eyes, which were moist now, their pupils like chasms. 'Ah well, another disbeliever,' he said. His eyes began to close then, his lips moving soundlessly.

'I should leave you to your rest, Mr Darke,' Harry said, climbing to his feet.

'Human kindness . . .' Darke murmured.

'Excuse me?'

'The rarest of treasures. Harry Compton . . . human kindness . . .'

Harry caught Darke's shoulders just before he hit the floor. Dropping to one knee, he supported the Irishman's slender frame, then lowered a hand to his ribs and eased him down on to the bedroll.

'Thank you,' Darke said, as he curled up on his side. 'You're a kind boy, so you are.'

Harry pulled the blanket up over him. 'Ma Potts has asked that this be your last night here,' he said, and to his surprise, Darke responded with a nod, meek as a child.

Having checked that the opium pipe was fully extinguished, Harry turned down the gas-lamp and snuffed out the candle. 'Well, good night, Mr Darke,' he said, receiving nothing in return but a slow, rasping snore.

Thankfully, Harry made it out of the pub without encountering either Ma Potts or Edwin the chucker-outer. The King's Road was quieter now, the only sounds a few distant cheers from the Cremorne Pleasure Gardens. Harry set off towards them, still feeling strangely unsettled by his encounter with Lorcan Darke. So this must be the seamier side of planthunting, he realised – the failed, lonely aspect that no one spoke of, as far from the strutting peacock of a Paxton Crosse or Donald Moncrieff as could be imagined. He rounded the dogleg of the King's Road, thinking now of how Mr Darke had seemed able to stare into his heart, to read his hopes and ambitions. The man had something mystical about him . . . Harry stopped and shook himself. Darke was an opium-eater, a pipe-dreamer. And as for that trove of Oriental erotica . . .

A pair of dandies came swaying through the shadows, leather soles clipping the cobbles. 'They've shut up shop,' one of them declared. 'Doxies all taken. You're too late!'

Sure enough, the gates of the Cremorne were locked with a chain, two beefy men in bowlers stationed outside, each brandishing a nightstick. 'Fuck off out of it, pretty boy,' one of them said, and Harry felt a great wave of lassitude wash over him, as though the whiskey and opium fumes were only now taking effect. He would just have to catch up with Jack Turner and his pals another night, he thought, pulling his coat tight around his shoulders and steering his steps in the direction of Mrs Pincham's boarding house.

Chapter 3

'Master Compton?'

Harry wondered if he was dreaming. The insistent knocking at the door suggested not.

'Master *Compton*!'

Harry flicked open his eyes. He was in his room, stretched out in bed. 'Awake, Mrs Pincham,' he groaned.

'You said that half an hour ago!'

Harry swung his legs out and sat up. A dagger of light was shining between the curtains, hurting his eyes. 'I'll be down presently.'

As the landlady's ponderous tread creaked away across the landing, Harry forced himself to his feet, reached tentatively for his clothes and pulled them on as fast as he could bear. Then, after rinsing his face at the washstand, he dipped his toothbrush into the pot of alum powder and began to scrub vigorously at his molars, trying to eradicate the flavours of Irish whiskey and opium fumes that still coated his tongue.

'Last down for breakfast,' Mrs Pincham said, as Harry came into the dining-room. 'That's not like you, Master Compton! I've nothing for you, I'm afraid,' she added gleefully, gesturing at the empty chafing trays, and the three used plates where Barrington, Ratcliffe and Drinkwater had breakfasted earlier, apparently in some style. 'I could poach you an egg, I s'pose,' she conceded, but Harry shook his head and poured himself a cup of tea. It was tepid, which at least meant he could drink it fast. He poured himself another and drank that too, unmilked.

'At the tavern, were we, Master Compton?' Mrs Pincham said, tilting her pouchy face his way.

'Mr Piggott kept me late,' Harry lied, suddenly feeling an urgent need to use the pail privy outside.

It was nearly a quarter to eight when Harry finally made it out of the small terrace of cottages on North Street and over Stamford Bridge. There was a freight train rolling down the tracks, but no sign of the friendly stationmaster with his scarlet cravat. On the King's Road, the nurseries were already open for business, a series of wasp-waisted women directing servants to where they should drag their handcarts of exotics next. No beggar awaited him this morning at the dogleg of the road, just an omnibus marked 'Bank' unloading passengers from the bench seat fastened to its roof.

Harry skirted around the wagon towards the Man in the Moon. A rickety horse-cart was parked outside, its blinkered nag munching away at a nosebag. A few yards on, staggering out of the front door of the pub Harry saw a pot-bellied man in a crooked top hat. 'Watch your head, John,' the man said, and as he emerged further, Harry realised that he was holding the wooden handles of a stretcher.

Whoever lay upon the stretcher was motionless, draped in a grimy linen shroud. A second man – John, presumably – appeared, sweating under the weight of the other end. 'Hurry up before you drop it!' John rasped, as the two men shuffled down the pavement towards their cart.

'Wait!' Harry cried, running after them.

The two undertakers halted, and the shroud slipped down a little, revealing the face of the dead man.

'I know him,' Harry said, feeling his head reel.

The two men glanced at one another, then lowered the stretcher to the ground. With shaking hand, Harry drew back the rest of the shroud. Lorcan Darke was dressed in the same scruffy tweeds that Harry had left him in, puny arms folded across his chest like a stone knight on a triumphal tomb. There was a faint smile on his lips, and his face was still so swarthy that . . . 'Are you sure he's dead?' Harry asked.

The two undertakers grinned. 'Quite sure,' one of them said. 'Topped himself with opium, didn't he? Place stank of the filthy stuff.'

Harry stared down at Mr Darke's face, wondering how someone who'd seemed so alive only a few hours ago could suddenly be gone.

'That's enough now,' John said, losing patience. He reached down to re-cover the body, then he and his colleague heaved the stretcher back up.

'Where are you taking him?' Harry asked.

'Guy's Hospital. A gift for the students. Unless you're a blood relative, of course . . .' John glanced hopefully at Harry.

'Just an acquaintance,' Harry said.

The two undertakers muttered an oath and moved away. Then a cry went up from the tavern — 'Oi!' — and Harry turned to see Ma Potts standing by the door. She gestured to him with her broom, and he hurried over.

'You've saved me a journey,' Ma Potts said with a wink. 'That Irishman's left something for you.' She ushered Harry into the taproom, redolent now of stale tobacco and burnt sherry. Reaching under one of the benches, Ma Potts hoisted up an object on to the table. Harry recognised it at once: it was Lorcan Darke's vasculum, but instead of his name on the lid, there was a scrap of paper marked with the words 'HARRY COMPTON'.

'He left it outside his door,' Ma Potts went on. 'But don't think you've a claim on anything more. Costs money to get a corpse removed, you know!'

Harry stared down at the vasculum. The paper marked with his name had been stuck on with a dab of what looked like opium paste. Harry peeled it off and stuffed it into his pocket. 'D'you think . . .' he began, looking up into the publican's hard black eyes. 'D'you really think he killed himself?'

'So the carrion-hunters said, and that's good enough for me. God forgive his cursed soul!' Seeing Harry's face fall, Ma Potts gave a sigh. 'Look, the door was bolted from the inside. Poor Eddie had to kick it in.'

Harry turned to see the melancholy chucker-outer sitting at his favourite table, trying to lift his spirits with a glass of hot milk and gin.

'Well, go on,' Ma Potts urged. 'Take the bloomin' thing if you're going to!'

The vasculum was surprisingly light for something made of sheet metal. Hooking its strap over one shoulder, Harry thanked Ma Potts and headed outside. The undertakers' cart was gone now, its space on the road already occupied by well-to-do plant-buyers. Harry wended between them in the direction of Sloane Square. As he passed Mr Baker's pheasant dealership, he adjusted the shoulder strap of the vasculum and felt something rattle inside. He stopped and shook the thing again. There was definitely something in there. The hell with it, Harry thought. He was late as it was − might as well be hanged for a sheep as a lamb − so he ducked on to Royal Avenue and sat down on a bench.

The curved, hinged lid of the vasculum lifted away easily. Reaching inside, Harry found a sheet of wax paper folded to create two paper pouches. Slipping a finger into the first, he drew out a sprig of dried foliage. Eight small, pinnate leaflets on either side of the stem, just like the leaves of a *Pistacia sinensis* . . .

Feeling a faint quiver of excitement, Harry investigated the second pouch and found a pressed flower inside. A bright white flower, long and tubular, with five spreading lobes at the base. 'He actually found it, the old rogue!' Harry murmured, cradling the dried icicle tree flower in one palm, marvelling at the intricacy of its structure, at the shocking gleam of its white petals. A few passers-by were eyeing him now, but Harry paid them no heed, lost in the beauty of the plant, and in his admiration for the late Lorcan Darke's accomplishments. Then, very carefully, he returned both leaf and flower to their paper pouches, and replaced the sheet in the vasculum.

But as he withdrew his hand, Harry felt something else. A small square of folded paper. Gently, between thumb and forefinger, he drew it out and opened it.

Sketched in pen and ink was a map. In its centre was a landmass, labelled in Mr Darke's looping hand as 'INLAND

CHINA'. This landmass was bisected by an uneven line marked 'YANG-TZE RIVER'. Then came a few more marks, perhaps indicating towns or villages, each labelled with what Harry assumed to be words in Chinese.

Harry's gaze roved around the map, then stopped. Just south of the 'Yang-tze River' was a small black cross. Using his forefinger, Harry traced the line from the cross to the corner of the map. This label was in English. 'Icicle tree,' he read.

Harry looked up at the sky, feeling his heart shift in his chest. Somewhere out of sight, a military band was playing 'Rule, Britannia!' Harry needed to think very carefully about what he would do next, he realised. His first instinct was to turn around and cross the river to Battersea. Go and find Jack Turner; see what he made of this strange turn of events. But then he imagined Banks, Tonks, Davies and Pugh all crowding around, pressing him: 'Why not do this, Harry . . . No, *we* have to do that . . .'

No, Harry needed time to contemplate his options; to work out how best to proceed. Getting to his feet, he continued up the King's Road, aware of people staring at him now, their attention drawn by the odd cylindrical satchel on his shoulder. Should he go back to the boarding house and hide the thing? No, better to keep it close.

Piggott's was doing a galloping trade, scores of customers already inside, misting up the windows. Harry passed the stovehouse, then turned down Anderson Street and knocked on the back door. It took a while, but then he heard Decimus Frith's patrician voice, 'Name?'

'Harry Compton.'

The door opened. 'Man of extremes, aren't we, Compton?'
'I overslept.'

Harry stepped inside, then felt a stinging cuff to the side of his head. He spun round to find Frith eyeing him contemptuously. 'That was a warning, Compton — there won't be a second.'

Harry raised himself up to his full six-foot height. He wanted to smash a fist into Decimus Frith's grinning, moustachioed mouth, but forced himself instead to keep walking, his left ear still hot and ringing. 'What's in the lunchbox?' he heard Frith call after him as he rounded the hoardings. 'Tea and crumpets?'

Jarvis Siggers was hard at work in the potting shed, Harry saw as he passed, using a rabbit's-tail brush to extract gladiolus pollen in the hope of creating a new set of hybrids. He turned and shook his head at Harry through the glass-paned door. The only time the head gardener deigned to notice him was when he arrived late.

Harry entered the hut and slammed the door. Once he'd shaved and dressed, he felt a little more like himself, and could almost have convinced himself that Lorcan Darke's colourful life and sordid death were nothing but a dream. But then he saw the vasculum lying on the bench. What if Frith came in and opened it? Or Barrington, Ratcliffe or Drinkwater on their lunch hours?

Harry undid the hasp of the vasculum and took out the map. The small square of paper slotted neatly into the inside pocket of his frockcoat. The herbarium specimens he could risk leaving for now, he decided, reclosing the vasculum and stashing it under the bench.

Having fixed on his topper, Harry headed outside. All eyes turned to him as he entered the stovehouse. His fellow salesmen he could ignore, but no, there was Old Pie-Gut, lurking beneath the hanging baskets, buttering up another customer. A moment later, Piggott was making his way over, gold-knobbed cane swinging. 'You're late, Compton,' he hissed, plucking a snail from the leaves of a giant hosta and crushing it in one fist.

'I'm sorry, sir.'

Piggott's ruddy face grew ruddier. 'Sorry don't sell my plants!'

Harry steeled himself to meet the man's eye. 'I need to talk to you, sir. In private.'

'If this is about Mr Siggers and the bloody potting shed . . .'

Harry shook his head. He could sense the other salesmen all staring at him, willing on the inevitable explosion, and Harry's imminent expulsion from Eden. 'It concerns the nursery,' Harry said, suddenly aware of the sweat sheeting down his back.

Piggott studied Harry coldly for a moment, as though he were some strange weed that had seeded itself in his stovehouse.

'I have a proposition' – Harry swallowed: he knew his next words were crucial – 'that I believe may be of value to you.' He lowered his voice: 'Considerable value.'

Piggott sucked his teeth, as though weighing up how best to proceed. Then he raised one bushy eyebrow and reached for his fob pocket. 'Well then, young man,' he said briskly, handing over an ivory calling card, 'you'd best come by my house tonight. Eight p.m. sharp.'

Harry pocketed the card as Piggott strode away. His heart was going like a jackhammer, but somehow, when he turned to the client beside him — a willowy woman rendered taller still by the purple ostrich feather protruding from her hat — he managed to control his voice. 'How may I help you, ma'am?'

The hum in the stovehouse started up again, the usual conversations and sales patters resuming.

'It's about your water lilies,' the woman said.

Harry nodded, plucking his shirt away from his flanks, hoping that his sweat wouldn't soak through the material and smudge the map. 'Amazonian,' he asked, 'or Himalayan?'

Chapter 4

At 7.45 that evening, Harry found himself walking up
Sydney Street in the direction of South Kensington. He
was still dressed in his frockcoat and topper, but in this
part of town, he blended in seamlessly with the crowd.
Evensong at St Luke's Church had just ended, and a procession of bluff old boys and richly attired women thronged
the pavements.

On reaching the Fulham Road, Harry turned right, in
the direction of Pelham Crescent. He'd been up this way
once before, when despatched to Onslow Square to apologise to a client whose begonia collection had been decimated
by whitefly. But he'd never made it as far as the 'Pelhams',
and nothing could prepare him for the elegance of the
houses he found there – storey upon storey of snow-white
stucco, partitioned by green-painted railings and neat box
parterres. Even the servants' quarters in the basements
looked immaculate, their façades as bright as the icing on
a wedding cake.

Harry stopped to check the calling card. '*J.M. Piggott, Esquire,*'
it announced in heavily embossed letters. '*Nurseryman and
Seedsman to the Royal Family. 114–118 King's Road & No. 5 Pelham Place,*

London'. This royal connection was news to Harry — no doubt another of Piggott's self-aggrandisements.

Hearing a sudden crash from the pavement ahead, Harry gave a start, but it was just a coalman emptying a sack down the chute into the cellar of one of the houses. Harry stood there a moment, trying to calm his nerves, then skirted the coal cart to find Pelham Place extending on the corner.

If anything, the houses here were even more impressive than those of the Crescent. Broader and better proportioned, and with larger front gardens. There was no mistaking which was number five, even without reading the number stencilled in black by the door. A huge arbour of stained teak soared from the front garden, with an array of the nursery's finest climbing roses growing up it — *Rosa acicularis, Rosa virginiana, Rosa arkansana* . . .

Harry creaked open the iron gate, suddenly appreciating the immense quantity of money Piggott must be making from his nursery. He was the sole owner of the enterprise; any debts he'd taken on to build his stovehouse must have been paid off years ago. Day after day, week after week, a river of gold was flowing into his personal coffers. No wonder he could afford to live in such style.

Normally, on entering a house like this, Harry would have headed straight for the tradesmen's entrance, but tonight he bounded up the Yorkstone steps to the front door and tugged the bell-pull. A loud jangle came from inside the house, and Harry felt himself start to sweat again, despite the coolness of the air — for the summer's heat had fallen away now, and there was a first hint of autumn in the breeze. You can do this, Harry told himself, as he cleaned the soles of his brogues on the iron scraper. This is your chance . . .

At last, the front door opened, and who should be behind it but Decimus Frith, wearing his usual militaristic attire and expression of self-satisfaction. 'Just can't stay away from me, can you, Compton?'

As Harry passed, Frith swung a mock hook at the side of his head, and Harry instinctively ducked down. 'On your toes, boy,' Frith chuckled, as he watched Harry take off his hat and hang it on the stand. 'You're in the General's tent now.'

The hallway floor was of chequerboard marble, highly polished, bisected by a magnificent staircase of dark mahogany. To Harry's right was a closed door, behind which he heard faint peals of female laughter — there was a Mrs Piggott, he knew, though she'd never been spotted at the nursery. Perhaps there was a Miss Piggott too — as tough and overbearing as her father. But Frith was signalling to Harry now, so he walked past the roomful of unseen women and made his way upstairs.

At the top of the first flight was a bathroom, its door ajar. Harry peered inside as he passed, his mouth dropping as he made out the varnished oak base of what could only be a built-in 'water closet'. Harry had seen sketches in the papers, but this was . . .

'Up, man, up!' Frith urged, climbing the stairs behind him.

Clustered on the staircase walls were oils of various bucolic scenes, interspersed with lithographs of rare and exotic plants. Harry wondered who had overseen the decoration. Mrs Piggott? Or a designer tasked with creating a show of horticultural sophistication?

He'd reached the second landing now. On the staircase above, he caught sight of a yellow chamois leather flitting in and out of the spindles – some unfortunate housemaid, working late into the evening. Opposite him was a doorway, and as he stepped towards it and knocked, a voice he knew only too well boomed, 'Come!'

Harry entered the drawing-room. Ahead, between two French windows, stood a glass-framed bookcase, the leather tomes within it entirely untouched, Harry suspected, pages still uncut. Turning towards the fireplace, he found Josiah Piggott ensconced in a wingback armchair, clad in a smoking jacket and cap, slippered feet warming by the hearth. A silver salver of glasses and decanters had been laid out on the coffee table before him.

'Oh, it's you, Compton,' Piggott said, as though surprised by Harry's arrival. His demeanour now was of a benevolent professor receiving an unexpected call from a wayward pupil. Perhaps this was the manner Josiah Piggott affected at home, Harry thought, marvelling again at the man's love of performance; at his ability to dissemble.

'Sit down, boy,' Piggott said, indicating the wicker-seated chair on the other side of the table. 'And do come in, Decimus. No need to lurk outside like a garrotter.'

Frith gave a sly, upcurving smile as he closed the door. Harry's chair had been positioned facing one of the French windows, and as he sat down on it, he made out the carved wooden top of the arbour rising from the garden below.

'Some Madeira?' Piggott asked, before adding in a lower voice, 'Decimus . . .'

Frith stepped towards the drinks tray and poured three measures into the crystal goblets. There was something rictal in the man's grin now, Harry thought, knowing he'd be paying later for this minor courtesy.

'Now then,' Piggott resumed, warming his Madeira glass between his palms, 'you wished to talk to me. Presumably about the little pilfering problem we've had at the nursery of late?'

Harry tilted his head.

'Out with it, boy!' Piggott commanded. 'And it's not just seedstock I'm talking about, there's the copper piping too.'

'I don't know anything about any pilfering, sir.'

'If you're trying to protect your pals in Cultivation,' Piggott pressed, raising a finger in warning, 'you should know that they've been treated too kind for their own good — fed on lollipops . . .'

'*Sir*,' Harry said, and to his surprise, Piggott held his tongue and sat back. 'I wonder, sir, if you've heard of the icicle tree?'

Piggott gave a puzzled frown.

'It's considered one of the most beautiful trees in the world,' Harry went on. 'Maybe the most lovely of them all. Marco Polo searched for it, and—'

'Yes, yes,' Piggott said, waving one rubicund paw through the air. 'But what's your point?'

'I know where to find it.'

Piggott turned in wordless astonishment to Frith, who responded with a surly shrug.

'But I shall need a backer, sir,' Harry continued. 'Someone to finance my expedition.'

Piggott drew in a long, shuddering breath. 'You're asking me to fund a botanical expedition to find an exotic tree — with *you* as my plant hunter?'

Harry squared his shoulders. 'I am.'

Piggott stared at Harry for a moment, then let out an explosive guffaw. 'Do you have any *concept* of what it takes to be a plant hunter?'

Harry opened his mouth to answer, then quickly shut it again.

'You've heard of David Douglas, I presume?' Piggott asked.

Of course Harry had: every man and boy on the King's Road knew of the thrilling adventures of the plant hunter who'd discovered the Douglas fir — and given it his name.

'Think he just walked in off the street, do you?' Piggott went on, exchanging a ribald glance with Frith. 'No! He did a seven-year apprenticeship at Scone Palace, didn't he? Then a spell at a private school in Perth to consolidate his learning. Then Valleyfield House in Fife, then the Botanical Gardens in Glasgow. And all that before Hooker even took him as *assistant* on his first expedition.'

The man was enjoying himself now, Harry could tell.

'Then, when he finally got to the Americas, Douglas joined a group of fur-trappers on the Columbia River. The men were on horseback, but Douglas stayed on foot, the better to gather his seeds. When the group was attacked by a grizzly bear, the trappers gave up and retreated to the nearest town, but Douglas carried on. Fell into a gully and injured his foot — had to cut open the wound himself to let the blood! Then, when he reached the pine forest he'd been searching for, he couldn't climb to gather the cones so he shot them down with a gun. Died a couple of years later in Hawaii, when he fell into a pit trap, and was gored to death by a bull.'

Seeing Harry still sitting there in silence, Piggott clicked his tongue. 'And what are your qualifications, boy? Cultivating a couple of hyacinth bulbs down in Battersea?'

A wave of despondency washed over Harry. The King's Road was teeming with men far more accomplished and experienced than him. Yet here he was putting himself forward as a plant hunter . . .

'I think we're finished here,' Piggott said. 'Mr Frith? If you'd kindly show my guest out . . .'

But Harry's fingers were in his inside pocket now. 'Perhaps you should have a look at this, sir,' he said, holding out the specimen sheet. 'Before you come to a final decision.'

Something in the sheen of the wax paper seemed to pique Piggott's interest. 'What is it?' he snapped, boarish eyes gleaming. 'Bring it here!'

Following Piggott over to a cherrywood writing desk by the wall, Harry laid the specimen paper on its leather top. A green smoked-glass lamp was set to a low burn above. Piggott twisted the neck of the lamp to strengthen the light, then watched, breathing noisily through his nose, as Harry removed first the sprig of foliage, and then, more carefully, the pressed flower.

'Fetch me my glass, Decimus,' Piggott said.

Frith moved to the cabinet on the other side of the room and came back with a mother-of-pearl magnifying glass. Snatching it out of Frith's hand, Piggott raised the glass above the pressed flower, one eye closed, greasy mutton-chop side-burns glinting in the lamplight. 'My word,' he murmured, switching the glass to the foliage, then back again to the flower. 'My *word*,' he repeated, those East End vowels stronger now. 'Come and have a look at this, Decimus.'

Piggott stepped back from the desk to make way for Frith, a greedy speculative look in his eyes. He seemed to have forgotten Harry was there.

'Very fetching,' Frith said.

'Is that all you have to say?' Piggott shot back. '*Fetching?*' He broke off and turned to Harry. 'Where did you get these?'

Harry felt the blood rise in his cheeks. How best to explain?

'He must have stolen them,' Frith said.

'I did not!' Harry protested. 'They were . . . bequeathed to me.'

'And they're real?' Piggott asked.

'Quite real,' Harry said, then dropped his eyes coyly. 'Perhaps I could take them to Mr Weeks, test *his* appetite for showstoppers . . .'

Piggott held up a palm. 'Steady, boy,' he said, his great block of a face coming ever closer to Harry's, so close that Harry could smell the Madeira on his breath. 'Why don't you take a seat, eh? Whilst I discuss the matter with Mr Frith.'

Harry returned to his chair and picked up his goblet, as Frith and Piggott retreated to the other side of the room, where a tall sash window gave on to the house's back garden and stables. There was some kind of reference library there, Harry saw; Piggott took down a volume, then both men hunched over it, sending the occasional furtive glance Harry's way.

Harry took a first sip of Madeira. It tasted smoother and more delicious than anything he'd ever known, no doubt aged for decades in some Portuguese cellar. He glanced back to see Piggott at his desk now, wielding a pair of silver tweezers. He poked about at the specimens for a time, then returned to his conclave with Frith.

Harry drank some more, wondering if he might have underestimated Josiah Piggott's horticultural expertise. It had been two decades, after all, since the man had taken up nursery work. He must have picked up a thing or two in that time – he certainly knew his plant hunters. Perhaps the Queen really *had* awarded the nursery the Royal Warrant, and—

Piggott was back now, looming large over Harry's chair. 'You say you know where this icicle tree grows?'

Harry nodded. 'I've a map, sir.'

'Well, let's see it.'

Harry forced a smile. 'I thought we might strike an agreement first. Agree on a fee, then put it in writing.'

'No flies on this one, eh?' Piggott said, exchanging another glance with Frith.

Harry looked Piggott straight in the eye. 'You taught me well, sir.'

'Harrumph,' Piggott replied. There was a pause, then he went on, 'So you have a map, you say?

'Not on my person.'

'But in safe keeping?'

'Of course.'

Slowly, like the tide washing over ridges of sand, the tension in Piggott's expression was smoothed away. 'Well, I like the sound of this, young Harry!' He paused by the decanter, one hand grasping its crystal stopper, a smile playing on his thick lips. 'But you'll have told your pals about it, I expect? Those ruffians in Cultivation?'

Harry shook his head.

'One of your colleagues at Mrs Pincham's guesthouse?'

'Not a soul,' Harry said.

'Not a soul,' Piggott repeated. 'Then let's drink to your good fortune, boy!' he exclaimed, picking up the decanter and filling Harry's glass to the brim. 'Before we talk shop.'

Behind him, Harry heard a soft click, and turned to see that Decimus Frith was gone.

'I've always recognised your ability,' Piggott was saying as he retook his seat. 'Ever since I first spotted you in Battersea. You know that, don't you?'

Hearing the squeak of the front gate, Harry picked up his glass and walked over to the French windows. Down on the street, he saw Decimus Frith emerge from the arbour, then head quickly up Pelham Place.

When Harry turned back, Piggott was standing right behind him. 'Where has Mr Frith gone, sir?' Harry asked, feeling a small worm of anxiety twist in his chest.

'You told me you wanted a contract drawn up,' Piggott smiled, 'so he's gone to fetch the notary.' Piggott sat back down. 'You're a rising star, Harry. *A man of parts*. I can see that now.' He took a gulp of Madeira, and a tawny droplet slid down his chin. 'A future plant hunter!'

'I'd want two thousand guineas,' Harry said.

Piggott wafted a hand through the air, as though the sum represented a mere bagatelle, and Harry felt his anxieties deepen. He knew he should be pleased, but this was not excitement he felt running through his body, but fear. As though some atavistic instinct had sensed something that his mind did not want to grasp.

Harry put down his glass on the coaster. 'Was that a flushing water closet I saw downstairs, sir?'

Piggott glanced up in surprise. 'Venetia and I just had one installed.'

'May I?' Harry asked. 'With all this wine . . .'

'Be my guest,' Piggott muttered, turning to pick up the decanter.

Harry moved towards the door. As he neared the desk, he paused.

'Well go on, boy,' Piggott urged, and as he leant forward to refill their glasses, Harry seized his chance. Lunging forward, he snatched up the dried specimens from the desk. He half-expected Piggott to call out some reprimand, to rush at him. But he didn't. All Harry heard was the neat clack of the decanter being replaced on the salver, and then he was through the door and out on the landing.

Slipping the specimens into his coat pocket, Harry hurried downstairs to the W.C., hearing more women's laughter drifting up from the ground floor. He paused outside the lavatory door, suddenly concerned that he'd misread the situation. But then his resolve strengthened. Everyone knew that Piggott was as mean as hell; for him to have accepted such a fee without demur must mean something was wrong.

Turning away from the lavatory, Harry crept down to the hall, eased open the front door and stepped outside. *Rap, rap, rap,* came a sharp noise from above, and he glanced up to see Piggott knocking at the French windows with his signet ring, his face a mask of baffled fury. But Harry ignored him and started running down Pelham Place, then on to the Fulham Road and away through the fields of Chelsea Park. The autumnal moon shone bright above, plump and waxen, lighting Harry's short cut between the market gardens. He'd left his top hat at Piggott's house, he realised, letting out a burst of nervous laughter as he sprinted around the premises of St Mark's College, then past the terraced houses of North Street.

Harry slowed, chest heaving, one hand massaging the stitch in his side. The nagging sense that he'd behaved irrationally was growing stronger. Perhaps Piggott had meant him no harm. Perhaps Frith really had gone to fetch the notary, and by running away, Harry had just ruined his one chance of fame and fortune – and jeopardised his job! But he'd made his choice now, he resolved, hurrying up the steps to the boarding house.

The front door was on the latch – it was not yet nine o'clock – so Harry pushed it open and entered the hallway, so mean and narrow compared to that of Pelham Place. In the sitting-room, he could hear Mrs Pincham jawing away to one of the other salesmen – no doubt boring him with tales of her son, Caleb, who'd joined the Royal Fusiliers and was currently doing battle with the Fenians in Ireland.

'Only me, Mrs Pincham,' Harry called through the half-open door. 'I won't stop – I'm off up for an early night.'

'Need one, I 'spect,' Mrs Pincham replied with a cackle.

Harry ran up the stairs into his bedroom, locking the door behind him. Turning up the gaslight, he dropped to his knees. There was the vasculum still safe beneath his bed, just where he'd left it, with Lorcan Darke's hand-drawn map neatly folded inside.

Harry closed his eyes and shook his head, imagining the mortifying scene when Frith and the notary arrived back at Pelham Place to find Harry gone. Perhaps it was not too late, after all. He could go back — tell Piggott that he'd decided to fetch the map for him; hope his strange behaviour hadn't made him change his mind about the expedition.

Sinking down on to the bed, Harry took the dried specimens from his coat pocket and placed them on the counterpane. What an idiot he'd been! Unprotected by their wax-paper pouches, the flower had lost its petals. And a leaf had crumbled into dust.

Hearing a noise outside the door, Harry froze. Then it came again: the soft creak of a foot on the stairs. Quickly, Harry got up and switched off the gas-lamp, then moved to the door and stood beside it, back pressed to the wall.

The noise came again, closer now, followed by a different sound, the tinny scratch of metal inside a lock. Then the scraping stopped, and, in the shard of moonlight coming in through the window, Harry saw the door handle start to turn.

Harry suspended his breathing. Outside the door, the floorboards gave a low groan, as though someone were adjusting their standing position. Then the handle twisted again, and the door began to inch open.

Taking hold of the vasculum, Harry raised it high above his head. Silently, in the moonlight, he saw the moustachioed profile of Decimus Frith enter his room. Frith turned, just managing an expression of utter bewilderment before Harry brought the metal base of the vasculum crashing down on the crown of his head.

Frith dropped to the ground instantly, like a marionette whose strings had been cut. The sound he made when he hit the floor seemed immense — one stocky shoulder, then the side of his face, smacking down hard against the bare boards.

Harry stared down at Frith's prostrate body, dizzy with panic. Tossing the vasculum on to the bed, he crouched down by Frith's side and fumbled with one hand beneath his ulster coat. Sure enough, something cold and hard protruded from a leather pouch buckled to his belt. A moment later, Harry was holding a small but surprisingly heavy pistol.

Harry got to his feet, weapon still in hand, unsure what to do. Then his bedroom flooded with light as the landing sconce was lit, and Mrs Pincham appeared in the doorway. 'What the blue Moses . . .' she began, glancing from the revolver in Harry's hand to the motionless form of Frith on the floor. Then her eyes widened in terror. 'Help!' she cried. 'Help!'

Instinctively, Harry cast the gun away from him. It landed with a clatter by the washstand, and exploded, blazing orange and emitting an ear-splitting crack as the bullet hit the ceiling, sending down a shower of plaster powder.

'Help!' Mrs Pincham screamed, crouching down and covering her ears. 'Murderers!'

'Mrs P?' came a concerned voice from downstairs.

'Fetch the peelers, Rex!' Mrs Pincham shrieked. 'Harry Compton's gone berserk!'

The sulphurous reek of gunpowder brought Harry back to his senses. Grabbing the vasculum from the bed, he just had time to register the trickle of blood dripping out of Decimus Frith's left ear before he ran out of the open door, and down the stairs.

Rex Barrington was standing in the sitting-room doorway, his open mouth framed by his silly black beard. Harry sprinted past him on to the street as Mrs Pincham shrieked, 'The police, Rex! Quick as you can!'

Then, without looking back, Harry ran down South Street and out into the dark, open farmland of Fulham.

Chapter 5

Dawn was breaking as Harry made his way along the river-bank at Battersea, head lowered and collar pulled up to his ears. Out on the Thames, the first of the sailing barges were pushing into the wharves of Chelsea, delivering timber, coal and hay. An enormous paddlesteamer chugged between them, her thick black funnel billowing out clouds of smoke that dissipated in the misty air. Harry stood for a moment on the shingle, watching as her engines switched into reverse and she started to moor at Cadogan Pier. Perhaps she was returning from some distant corner of the Empire, he thought, with a plant hunter aboard, bringing in a fresh haul of exotics to sell to the nurseries of the King's Road.

Shaking his head in bitterness, Harry continued up the riverbank, nose wrinkling at the sharp reek of effluent wafting up from the water. Bright red worms slithered in the mudbanks below – bloodworms, feasting on the sewage. Above him stretched the boundary wall of Battersea Park, newly planted with ornamental shrubs and saplings, most of which had been bought from Piggott's. Twenty yards ahead, sloping down to the water, ran the concrete slipways of Battersea's many manufactories – the white-lead works, the candle-makers, the saltpetre yards.

By and by, the stone wall of the park ceded to scrubby undergrowth, and Harry turned his back on the river and started to clamber up the bank, pushing between reeds and nettles until he reached a path banked by hawthorn hedges. Thirst and hunger were starting to trouble him now that his fear had given way to fatigue, and he paused for a moment, staring out at the island of Battersea, cut off at its southernmost end by the moat-like River Heathwall, watching as a ragged girl – no more than eight – gathered bunches of watercress to sell on the streets.

Harry gave a shudder as his mind drifted back to the strange, dreamlike events of the previous night. Was Mr Frith alive, he wondered? Or had he killed him? Harry still wasn't sure, but like a coward he hadn't waited to find out, sprinting away through the darkness until his lungs were fit to burst, desperate to put some distance between himself and the boarding house. Only once he'd reached the ploughed fields of Earl's Court had he stopped to formulate a plan, deciding that his best chance was to take the rutted path of the Old Brompton Road, then skirt around the outer streets of Chelsea until he could cross the Thames at Chelsea Bridge.

He'd managed a few, fitful snatches of sleep at the eastern edge of Battersea Park, before being woken by a cabman relieving himself by the roadside. The man had cursed Harry for a vagrant, which was a fair assumption given his dishevelled appearance. Peering down now, Harry saw his Oxford shoes caked in sludge and horseshit; his silk waistcoat striped with lichen and moss. He combed a hand through his hair and felt it bristle with twigs. The dried herbarium specimens were lost, he knew – left behind at the boarding house – but at least he still had Lorcan Darke's map stowed in the vasculum.

The bells of St Mary's, Battersea, pealed, telling Harry it was a quarter to seven. Time to go, he thought. Cautiously, he continued along the hawthorn hedge towards the gates that protected Mr Piggott's growing grounds from intruders. Opposite rose a convenient thicket of elderberry shrubs; Harry withdrew to its cover to await the arrival of the first Cultivation workers, catching the vile but familiar smell that told him the night-soil men had made their deliveries. At the growing grounds, the manure used on the plants was human, rather than equine.

Harry crouched down low as Bill Hartley, Head of Cultivation, sauntered past the thicket. A moment later, Pilbrow, the night-watchman, opened up the gates for him, then bid his master good morning and went home to his bed. It was Bill Hartley who'd given Harry his job here, when he'd first arrived from the South Downs with nothing more than an eager face and a letter of recommendation. Bill was looking a little hunched now, Harry thought, and those wire-framed spectacles suggested that his time at the growing grounds must be nearing an end – in this business, a man whose sight was failing would soon be put out to pasture.

Next came the apprentices, boys of just twelve or thirteen. The first undergardener Harry recognised was Tony Banks, still rubbing the sleep from his eyes, haversack slung over one shoulder, dibbler in hand. Then came Davies, followed by Tonks and Pugh . . . but where the hell was Jack Turner? What if Jack didn't turn up for work today? Harry was just considering if he should approach Banks instead when he caught sight of a familiar shock of red hair.

58

'Jack!' Harry hissed.

Jack Turner glanced about him in puzzlement.

'*Jack!*' Harry repeated, and finally Jack peered more closely at the elder thicket, and saw Harry lurking within.

After checking behind him, Jack pushed his way through the bushes until he was face to face with his old friend, his worried eyes taking in Harry's filthy clothes, the stubbled jaw rigid with strain. 'Jesus, Harry,' he said. 'What's happened to you?'

'I'm in trouble, Jack,' Harry replied in a low voice. 'I need money. Enough for passage home.'

Jack nodded. 'You're awful pale, Harry. When did you last have something to eat?'

'Not for a while.'

Jack swung his bag off his back and pressed it into Harry's hands. 'I'll be back soon,' he said, then ran off through the gates.

Harry sat down on the mud and sank his teeth into Jack's eel pie and half of a Banbury cake. Rarely had cold, cheap fare tasted so delicious. Uncorking the flagon, Harry drained its contents, feeling his head reel as the small beer worked its effect. There was birdsong in the trees now, a mistle thrush by the sound of it, and in the far distance, Harry could hear the creak of the iron hinges as the cold-frames were opened to the morning air.

Perhaps he'd slept then, as it felt like moments before Jack was back, shaking him by the arm, one hand in his pocket. 'Had a whip-round,' he said, pulling out a fistful of coins.

Feeling a lump rise at the back of his throat, Harry looked away, hoping Jack wouldn't see his lip tremble.

'What did you do?' Jack asked, pointing to the vasculum on Harry's shoulder. 'Rob a plant hunter or something?'

'Worse than that, Jack,' Harry said grimly, as he stuffed the coins into his frockcoat.

Jack tilted his head, and a couple of corkscrew curls sprang free and dangled over his brow. 'I don't believe a word of it,' Jack said. 'Not you, Harry.'

A skein of greylag geese passed above them, their powerful wings beating the air.

'You are coming back, aren't you?' Jack asked.

Harry looked at him. 'Not for a while.'

Jack nodded, then held out a hand. 'Well, I'll see you when I see you, then.'

Harry squeezed his friend's warm, calloused palm. Then they smiled at each other, and Jack hurried away. Only once Jack had disappeared inside the growing grounds, and the gates had been locked behind him, did Harry emerge from the thicket and rejoin the path.

Two hours later, Harry was standing on the platform of Battersea Station, vasculum looped over one shoulder, ticket for the London, Brighton and South Coast Railway clasped in one hand. His eyes felt heavy with fatigue, but he forced himself to keep alert, in case Piggott should suddenly appear on the platform, perhaps accompanied by a peeler, spinning his wooden rattle to raise the alarm. But there were only labourers about, heading home to Wandsworth after a night shift at the cigar and tobacco manufactory.

Harry felt his head start to loll. The prospect of going home — of seeing his father — offered such a wonderful sense of comfort that . . .

A bell rang at the end of the platform, and Harry's chin jolted back up. Stepping forward, he glanced to his left to see the great iron horse rolling over the bridge from Chelsea Basin. Eventually, with much snorting and clanking, the train drew to a halt, and Harry checked his ticket for the right carriage. He could have afforded a First Class berth with all the money Jack had given him, but he'd thought it wiser to keep something in reserve, so had gone for Second instead.

The train doors started to open, and a smattering of passengers descended. Carriage B, Carriage B . . . Harry headed towards it, checking all about him for familiar faces, but there was no one but—

'Morning,' he heard, and spun round to see a bearded man in a peaked cap standing behind him. It took a moment before Harry registered the scarlet cravat looped around his neck. Of course: the friendly stationmaster he knew from his walks to work.

'Off somewhere nice?' the stationmaster asked.

'I'm . . . ah . . .'

The man's eyes dipped to the moss and mud stains on Harry's trousers. 'Well, enjoy yourself,' he said, his manner somewhat altered. 'Perhaps I'll see you tomorrow.'

Harry muttered a quick farewell, then climbed aboard the train. As soon as he'd taken his seat in the compartment, he turned to look out of the window, seeing the stationmaster still watching him, drawing on his pipe, brow furrowed. But then the train pulled away, and Harry sat back and closed his eyes, not intending to open them again until they were well outside London.

Chapter 6

It was early afternoon when the train stopped at Pulborough Station. Harry got off and hurried across the iron footbridge that spanned the tracks. He was just emerging from the little stationhouse, relieved to have made it to his destination unaccosted, when . . .

''Arry?' came a thick Sussex voice. 'That you?'

Harry whipped around to find a small, portly man standing behind him on the verge, wearing a coat even more badged with stains than his own. Next to him stood a scrawny white mare, the halter of which he held in one hand.

'Davy . . . Grigson?' Harry said, the man's name coming to him just in time.

'The very same. Here to see your pa, I 'spect?'

Harry nodded.

'Then you'll be wanting a mount.' Davy stood back and presented the horse with a flourish of one arm. 'This here's Winnie.'

The mare glanced from her master to Harry and — evidently impressed by neither — bent down to crop the grass.

'Three shillings a day,' Davy went on, 'and a swifter steed you'll not find in all of Pulborough.'

Harry smiled, despite himself. Davy Grigson had been working as a potwash at the coaching inn the last time Harry had seen him, but he'd evidently broadened his horizons.

'Tempting,' Harry said, 'but I think I'll walk.'

'Suit yourself,' Davy replied with a good-natured shrug. But then his eye was caught by Harry's vasculum. 'I've seen a few bee orchids up on the coombe lately. P'raps you could take Winnie up there tomorrow — collect a few?'

'I haven't ridden in years,' Harry said. 'But I hope you find a taker for Winnie on the next train.'

'God willing!' Davy said cheerfully, glancing back at the empty stationhouse as he drew a hipflask from his pocket.

Harry bid Davy farewell, then continued on towards the village, memories flashing before his eyes like sparks struck from flint. There was the square-towered church at the top of the hill, with the one-room parish school where Harry had studied until he was fourteen. '*If Harold Compton spent half as much time on his penmanship and scripture as he does on collecting wildflowers, he would head the class by now . . .*' There was the post office, behind which Harry had stolen his first kiss with Joyce Calder, the bookbinder's daughter. Where was Joyce Calder these days? She'd been a few years older than him, as Harry recalled. She'd be Joyce Someone-Else now. There was the coaching inn — the Oddfellows Arms — less busy since the railway had come, but still with a few farmhands milling about outside, no doubt thirsty for an early pint of Harvey's.

Not wishing to risk bumping into anyone else, Harry left the High Street and walked down the grassy slope out of the village. As he clambered over the stile that led to the river, he paused to admire the view of the Arun Valley, a picture-book illustration of the English countryside: rolling fields of corn and pasture, copses of ancient woodland, chalky escarpments purple-flushed with rampion flowers . . . *home*.

Harry set off along the north bank of the river. The water was high for late August, swirling in fat eddies around the meanders – they must have had rain up in Horsham. Those pools would be stuffed with sea trout, Harry knew, but you'd have to wait for the river to drop to have a chance of catching them. Passing a circle of field mushrooms, he bent down and snapped them off at the base, brushing the dirt from their caps with one thumb and eating them greedily as he walked.

It took him a good twenty minutes before he had sight of the cottage. Once the servant quarters for a manor house which had burnt down in the mid-1700s, the cottage had been a gift from his mother's family on the occasion of her marriage. Sufficiently far from their ancestral seat in Hampshire that they could have nothing more to do with the young couple after their wedding . . . Harry checked himself. His father had taught him not to be bitter about the way his maternal family regarded them. Harry's mother had suffered from a condition that would have landed her in an asylum had his father not taken her off their hands. 'More luck you and me,' as his father always said. 'We had her to ourselves!'

Harry stepped over one of the stub-ends that scarred the landscape around here, traces that told of the opulence of the original manor house. A section of garden wall, sprouting with fernlets; a collapsed, igloo-shaped ice house festooned with old man's beard; a marshy overgrown depression that had once been a carp pond. Harry's maternal family had sold off the surrounding fields decades ago — though they still owned the fishing rights where their land had abutted the Arun.

A thick beech hedge surrounded the cottage's grounds. Harry pushed open the kissing gate set within its branches, eyes moving instinctively to the brick and flint barn on the other side of the courtyard, which his father had converted into his workshop. The door was closed. Perhaps his father was taking a rare day off.

Harry approached the cottage, reassured by the plume of woodsmoke rising from the chimney. He rapped twice with the knocker, then heard a volley of barking, followed by the sound of footsteps. A moment later, the door opened, and a small piebald creature forced its way through the gap and leapt up into Harry's arms.

'Geddown, Wilberforce!' Harry heard his father say, though it was hard to discern much with a Jack Russell terrier licking the dirt off his face.

'Come in, come in!' Michael Compton urged, plucking Wilberforce out of Harry's arms. 'What brings you home, son?'

As he followed his father into the cottage, Harry was relieved to find him as well turned-out as ever. The same neat twill coat and trousers; the same thinning brown hair swept back from its widow's peak. Michael Compton had always had a beaky nose, though it was a little redder now, and his smile was more lopsided from so many years trying to conceal those gappy teeth he didn't like. 'Thank God you get your looks from your mother, son,' as he liked to say . . .

The range was lit, Harry saw, a vat of soup simmering away as always. Clamped to the edge of the kitchen table Harry recognised his father's fly-tying vice, with a few cases of feathers and hooks alongside that reminded him of Lorcan Darke's opium paraphernalia. Harry's face must have fallen then, as his father asked in a worried voice, 'There's not something wrong, is there, son? To bring you home?'

Harry chewed the inside of one cheek, unsure where to begin. Then he felt his father's kind eyes searching his face, and a gentle hand squeeze his shoulder. 'You look tired, son,' he said. 'Why don't you get your head down for an hour? We'll talk later.'

'It's still early, Pa.'

'And what of it?' Michael Compton said with a smile. 'Up and sleep.'

Harry swung the vasculum over his shoulder and made his way up the cramped staircase. However much older Michael Compton grew, he never lost the ability to sense what other people needed, nor the desire to help them achieve it. Harry wondered what he would say when he found out what his son had done . . . Banishing that dark thought to a corner of his mind, Harry lifted the latch to his bedroom door, the motion as familiar to him now as it had been on the day he'd left home for London.

The bed was made up, he saw, as though his father had been expecting him home at any moment. Harry drew the curtain across the poky casement window, then peeled off his grimy frockcoat. On his desk, beside a pile of old editions of *The Gardeners' Chronicle*, sat a notebook. Harry opened it up and found the nature diary he'd kept as a boy, dried flowers and leaves still gummed into its swollen pages. Flicking through, Harry saw the seasons change before his eyes. '*Ranunculus ficaria*', he read, with a line pointing to a shrivelled brown celandine. 'Brighter yellow this March than last. Ask Miss Baines if an example of "Natural Selection"?' Harry smiled, remembering his endless questions about Charles Darwin and the natural world. It must have driven his teachers mad.

He turned away from his desk, hearing a faint scratching at the door – Wilberforce's claws, he realised. Harry was just about to let him in when he heard his father's footsteps outside, followed by the sound of his mild chidings as he carried the little dog away.

Seconds later, Harry lay down on his childhood bed – narrow feet poking over the end now – and fell into a deep and dreamless sleep.

It was still light when Harry awoke. At first, he thought he must have slept right through to morning, but then he checked his pocketwatch and saw it was only 6 p.m. Rummaging through his wardrobe, he found some old clothes, then got dressed and headed downstairs.

His father was sitting at the kitchen table, half-moons wedged on the end of his nose as he tied a fishing fly. He occupied the same place Harry's mother had liked to sit when she'd given him extra lessons, insisting that his rather rudimentary education be supplemented with more esoteric subjects like Latin, history, poetry and botany.

Over by the range, Wilberforce was lying on his side, eyes closed, docked tail knocking on the stone floor.

'Feeling better, son?' Michael asked as Harry approached.

'Much,' Harry replied.

'Help yourself,' Michael said, gesturing with his whiskery chin to the pot on the stove.

Harry filled his bowl, seeing leeks and sorrel in the broth, but only a meagre amount of meat. Every month for the past year, Harry had sent his father half his wages. The man must be spending the money on fishing tackle . . .

'Good?' Michael asked, as Harry spooned the soup into his mouth.

'Very.'

Michael smiled, then twisted some black cotton around the hook of the fly. A Stoat's Tail, by the look of it. 'Why have you come, Harry?' he asked, without looking up from his work.

Harry swallowed, then patted his thighs, and Wilberforce stretched his arthritic joints, and leapt up on to his lap.

'Something's happened, Pa,' Harry replied as he stroked the little dog's back. 'Something bad.'

'I see,' Michael said. 'Well, you'd better tell me about it, then.'

So Harry told him — about his encounter with Lorcan Darke, and the gift of the map. About his meeting with Josiah Piggott, and the fear that he was being double-crossed. About hitting Frith over the head, and the gun going off before he'd run away into the night.

'Was he dead, do you think?' Michael asked matter-of-factly, as he wove another feather into his fly.

'I don't know,' Harry said miserably, remembering the blood dripping out of Frith's ear. 'But he wasn't moving.'

'And it was your satchel that you hit him with, was it?'

68

'The vasculum, yes.'

'Away and fetch it for me, would you?'

Harry did as he was told. When he returned, his father took it from him and tapped it against one strong palm. 'And it was like this? Empty?'

Harry nodded.

'Then you can't have killed him, son! The thing's made of tin — not lead! You'll have knocked him out, nothing more.' Michael put down the vasculum and looked at Harry shrewdly. 'The real question is what you do next.'

'I thought I might find a position in the Lea Valley,' Harry said. 'There's a number of nurseries there now. Perhaps—'

'May I see this map of yours?' Michael interrupted.

Harry took it out of the vasculum, and Michael squinted down at it. 'China, eh?' he said. 'Your mother had a cousin out in China.'

'Pa . . .'

'Runs some kind of trading company in Shanghai.'

'I'm a salesman, Pa,' Harry protested, 'not a plant hunter! I must have been bung-eyed when I suggested it to Piggott.'

Michael got to his feet. 'Come on, son,' he said, turning for the door, Wilberforce at his heel.

It was still light outside, the South Downs unfurling into the distance like a patchwork quilt, the faint burble of the Arun melding with the soft coos of roosting woodpigeons. Harry followed his father across the courtyard to the work-shop. Reaching a hand above the lintel, Michael took down the key, and unlocked the heavy oak door.

But inside, all was not as Harry remembered. His father usually worked on at least three sculptures at a time: angels and Madonnas and weeping mothers; occasionally the bust of a dignified-looking gentleman, commissioned to sit upon a family tomb. But today, all that stood on the floor was a single block of limestone, a few half-hearted chisel marks on one side revealing just a hint of the figure within.

'You're not working, Pa?' Harry asked, seeing his father's tool roll discarded in one corner, next to a pile of grey blankets.

Michael turned and held out both hands. The joints of his fingers were red and puffy. 'Rheumatism. That's why I keep on with the flies. Trying to get some of the feeling back.'

'How long?' Harry asked.

'Six or seven months. But we're not here to talk about that.' Beckoning for Harry to follow, Michael shuffled to the back of the workshop where, growing in two crude earthenware pots beneath the skylight, Harry saw a magnificent pair of ornamental trees.

'Look,' Michael said, cupping a hand beneath the branches of the nearest tree. Resting on his palm Harry saw a perfect, glistening orange.

'Well, I'll be damned . . .' Harry murmured. How well he remembered planting those trees! He must have been eleven years old. He'd gone with his father to deliver a cemetery sculpture to a wealthy old man in Stopham. His father had let him drive the cart, and when they'd reached the old man's house, Harry had been worn out from working the reins. The man had had a bowl of oranges in his dining-room, purchased from Covent Garden Market and brought down on the train that morning. Seeing Harry's flushed cheeks, he'd tossed him one. Harry had relished the fruit, of course, but he'd also kept every pip, cleaning them with a rag, soaking them in riverwater overnight, before planting them in pots fashioned from crocks of gin scrounged from the Oddfellows Arms. That had been not long after his mother had died, and Harry had become obsessed; had thrown everything into the ridiculous endeavour. Five of the seeds had germinated. Three of the seedlings had died, but the surviving two Harry had grown on, keeping them on his windowsill on warm nights, then closer to his bed as the weather became colder. It had been his success with these orange trees that had secured Harry his job at Mr Lazenby's yew nursery up on Codmore Hill. And it had been Mr Lazenby who'd recommended Harry to his old friend Bill Hartley in London.

'Oranges,' Michael was saying, 'on the South Downs! Would you credit it?' He turned to Harry. 'You've a gift, son, and this is your chance. Don't you see?'

For one joyous moment, Harry felt himself carried along by his father's enthusiasm. He did have a particular skill when it came to growing strange and exotic plants, he reminded himself. Time and again in Cultivation, Harry had cast an eye over seedlings that no one knew what to do with, and had predicted what changes would need to be made if they were to thrive. 'That's overpotted,' he'd tell Jack, or, 'That one needs more acid in the soil,' and nine times out of ten his instinctive observations had proved accurate. Surely this sixth sense would stand Harry in good stead when it came to collecting, then transporting, a new genus of tree? But then those prickles of doubt began again . . .

'Old Lazenby,' Harry asked. 'Is he still alive?'

'Lazenby?' Michael echoed. 'What's he got to do with the price of fish?'

'He found me the job at Piggott's, remember? What if Frith contacts him, and learns where you live . . . ?'

'Lazenby sold up years ago,' Michael said. 'What, you think this Mr Frith is going to chase you all the way down here?'

'He wants the map.'

His father ignored him. 'You forget about Frith, and Piggott, and the whole bloody lot of 'em. You can do it for yourself, son! You told me once how much a rare bloom can fetch on the King's Road. Imagine if you had the only stock of this icicle tree, or whatever it's called!' Michael stared at him. 'Portsmouth's not thirty miles from here. There's boats go to China every week.'

'How could *I* afford passage to China?'

'You let me worry about that,' Michael replied.

Harry sighed. 'What if he was just a crank?'

'Who?'

'The plant hunter — Lorcan Darke.'

His father put both hands on Harry's shoulders and shook him. 'Where's your pluck gone?' he asked, searching his son's face with burning eyes. When Harry said nothing, he turned with a sigh and walked away.

Harry stood motionless for a moment, thinking about what his father had just said. Then he stepped forward to the orange trees, and reached up a hand. There were still a few overblown flowers on the upper branches, and their scent reached him now, sweet and warm, like the fruit of some distant land.

Hearing a playful growl, Harry turned to see Wilberforce chewing at one of the grey blankets that lay in the corner of the room. Bending down, he tugged the blanket from the little dog's pin teeth, then threw it back on to the pile and followed his father outside.

Supper was a sombre affair. Harry knew that his father was nettled by his lack of ambition, but was too soft-hearted to say. Even when subdued, though, there was still something soothing about Michael Compton's presence. It was what had first drawn Harry's mother to him, Harry knew. Ada Serocold had been the middle daughter of a noble family from Romsey — 'Mad Ada', as she was known about town, on account of her seizures. She'd met Michael at the parish church where his own father had been sexton. One Sunday, before the Eucharist, Ada had had one of her episodes, and the young Michael had helped her out into the churchyard. Something in the tender way he'd cared for her had calmed Ada, and soon, Michael Compton was the only person she'd wanted by her side.

Ada was as clever as she was beautiful, so Michael couldn't believe his luck when her family had agreed to his marriage proposal, and had offered to set the young couple up in a cottage near Pulborough. Michael had been apprenticed as a mason then, but there was abundant stone to be found in the ruins of the old manor house, so he'd seized the opportunity to elevate his profession to carver. They'd all lived happily and quietly together, trying to push Ada's illness out of their minds, until her seizures had become so frequent that her body could take no more . . .

'Son?'

Harry looked up at his father's worn, gentle face. The face of a man whose life had been made by his wife, and ruined by her death.

'You had enough?' he asked.

Harry nodded. They'd finished their usual dessert of bread and treacle now — as elaborate as puddings got since Ada had died.

'Then get yourself up to bed.'

'But . . .' Harry protested, eyeing the dirty plates.

'Go on,' his father said.

Wilberforce's stumpy tail beat a brisk tattoo on the floor as Harry got to his feet.

'Sleep well,' Michael called after him. 'It'll look brighter come the morning.'

Chapter 7

Harry awoke to the sound of voices. Opening his eyes, he found his bedroom window awash with sunlight, a porthole into an ocean of gold. He stretched, then checked the time — already ten o'clock!

But then the voices came again, and a jolt of panic speared Harry's stomach. Slipping out of bed, he inched open his bedroom door.

'Very well,' Harry heard his father saying downstairs. 'If you insist.'

'So I can see him now?' came a condescending drawl that made Harry's palms instantly start to sweat. For there was no mistaking it: Decimus Frith was downstairs in the kitchen, talking to his father!

'I told the boy to sleep it off in the barn,' Michael said. 'Didn't want him in the house, to be honest, the state he was in.'

Then came a low, threatening growl.

'Don't you mind old Wilberforce,' his father said with a chuckle, 'he ain't used to strangers! Now follow me. It's this way.'

Harry heard the front door open, then the crunch of boots crossing the gravel yard. Straight away, Harry ran out of his room and over the landing to his father's bedroom, taking in the bed with only one half disturbed; his mother's walnut dressing table, empty now save for a single photograph in a silver frame — Ada Compton, staring back at him, her rich brown eyes and high cheekbones so eerily similar to his own.

Harry hurtled over to the window, then gave a gasp. It was Decimus Frith all right, a white bandage twisted around his head, covering his left ear. Harry looked over to the corner of the yard. A pale, raw-boned horse stood tethered to the apple tree — Winnie, the mare Harry had seen offered for hire by Davy Grigson.

Michael was almost at the workshop now. Suddenly, his gait stiffened, and Harry knew that he must be doing some fast thinking. A moment later, Michael turned to Frith with a smile, and pointed up at the ancient yew tree on the top of the hill, no doubt regaling Frith with his favourite story about the Druids who had worshipped there before the Roman invasion.

How could his father behave so collectedly, Harry wondered. But then he thought of the hundreds of times he'd seen his father calmly tend to his mother as the convulsions had struck — laying her flat to stop her injuring herself; prising her teeth apart so she wouldn't bite through her tongue; changing her clothes when she lost control of herself. Michael Compton had faced far worse than Decimus Frith, Harry realised, his admiration for the old man growing stronger still.

As Frith turned to look at the yew tree, Michael darted a hand above the lintel, then snatched up the key and slipped it into the lock. 'Son?' Harry heard him call into the workshop as he opened the door. 'There's a man from London here to see you . . .'

There was no reply — self-evidently — so Michael gave an apologetic shrug. 'My boy's a heavy sleeper — especially after a night at the Oddfellows.'

Frith glared at him. 'Is that a fact? Well, I'll soon wake him up!'

As Frith pushed past him and disappeared inside, Michael swiftly locked the door behind him. Then, moving as quickly as his old joints would allow, he set off back for the cottage.

Harry ran out of the bedroom and bounded down the stairs. He met his father in the kitchen.

'Frith's here!' Michael hissed, face contorted with fear. 'Alive and well, and mad as a snake!'

'I know, and—'

'No time to talk, son.' Flinging open the dresser, Michael grabbed a wooden cigar box. 'This is all the money you sent me — I never spent a farthing of it. There's some of your mother's gems in there too.' Michael pressed the box into Harry's hands, then snatched up a sealed letter from the sideboard. 'An introduction to your mother's cousin in Shanghai. The address is at the top.'

From outside, they heard the sound of thumping as Frith began to kick against the workshop door.

'Get your things,' Michael went on, 'and put some clothes on, for pity's sake!'

Seeing Harry's expression as he suddenly realised he was standing in the kitchen in his drawers, Michael let slip a chuckle, and for a moment his tired old face looked twenty years younger. 'You find that tree, Harry,' he said. 'Swear to me you'll try?'

'I promise,' Harry replied, then ran up to his room and chucked his vasculum and some clothes into an old leather valise, along with his favourite copy of *The Gardeners' Chronicle*. Then he threw on his frockcoat and trousers, almost tripping over his braces as he hurried back down the stairs.

He found his father out in the yard, standing guard by the workshop door, a coal shovel clutched between his painful, misshapen hands. The banging was deafening now, and Wilberforce was barking in a frenzy, dashing towards the door, then doubling back and barking again.

'Take his horse!' Michael called to Harry. 'I'll hold him off!'

'But, Pa!'

'Your mother would've wanted you to have your chance, Harry,' his father cried. 'Now go on. Get out of here!'

So Harry screwed up his courage and ran over to the mare, who stood swishing her threadbare tail against the flies, entirely unmoved by the commotion. Slotting an unlaced shoe into the stirrup, Harry threw one leg over the saddle and took hold of the reins, desperately trying to remember what little he knew about horses as he steered the mare's bony head towards the gate.

Amazingly, the horse began to advance, but then an explosion came from inside the workshop – the report of a shot! – and whipping his head around, Harry saw the door fly open.

'Stay where you are, boy!' Decimus Frith called out, his face drenched in sweat, a revolver clutched in his hand. 'All I want is the map. Throw it down, and I'll leave you in peace.'

'Don't do it, Harry!' his father cried, gripping the shovel more tightly.

Frith's eyes crinkled in irritated amusement. 'It's stolen, you know. Your good-for-nothing son stole it from Josiah Piggott!'

'You're a liar, Frith,' Harry called back. 'A liar and a bully.'

Frith stared at Harry for a moment, then widened his stance and took aim at his face. The Lord's Prayer had just begun to rattle through Harry's head when Wilberforce flitted across the courtyard and sank his sharp little teeth into Frith's calf.

'Fucking Christ!' Frith bellowed. He shook his leg free, then kicked out viciously, catching the dog squarely in the stomach, so that he flew into the air, landing several feet away.

'Go, Harry!' Michael yelled. 'Now!'

Harry squeezed his heels into the horse's flanks and, with a neigh of displeasure, she set off towards the kissing gate, halter dangling from her bridle. The old mare was moving faster than Harry might have hoped, but not fast enough, it seemed, as looking back over his shoulder, Harry saw that Frith was taking aim again.

As he waited for Frith to pull the trigger, Harry heard a kind of war cry, and saw Michael charge at the gunman, coal shovel raised above his head. The bullet, when it came, hit his father in the chest with a sickening clump, like an axe striking a dry log.

Harry gasped in disbelief as his father buckled at the knees. Drawing in the reins, he saw his father's face as pale as paper. 'Go . . .' Harry saw him mouth, his eyes glassy, his jaw slack, blood oozing between his lips.

Ears still ringing from the gunshot, Harry looked back and saw Frith busy with his revolver again, loading fresh cartridges. Sprawled on the ground just a few yards away lay Wilberforce, struggling to get to his feet. Without thinking, Harry removed a shoe from the stirrup and reached down to the dog. He almost slipped from the saddle, but then his fingertips got hold of the scruff of the little dog's neck, and he hauled him up, drawing him tight to his chest as he jabbed his heels back into the horse's flanks and geed her on.

'Come on, come on,' Harry said, wishing he had a riding crop to hand. But then there was another crack, and Harry felt something fizz past his ear. The horse reared up, then soared over the gate, Harry almost losing his seat as they landed heavily on the other side.

'I'll find you, you little prick!' he heard Frith yell behind him, 'And when I do, I'll kill you!'

As the horse galloped away down the riverside path, Harry gripped Wilberforce so tightly that his arm began to hurt. But it was only as they neared the village that the pain became almost intolerable, and Harry realised that it wasn't sweat soaking through his shirt, but blood.

Chapter 8

Three days later, and Harry was sitting alone in the garret bedroom of a dockside inn, looking out of the grimy window on to Portsmouth Harbour. Now, as at every hour of the day, the waters between here and Gosport were overloaded with a complex medley of ships: freighters and men-of-war, steamers and schooners, smaller fishing boats weaving in and out of them. The scene seemed utterly chaotic to Harry, but rather than try to understand it — to seek some order — he just gazed at the comings and goings as though watching some mysterious, incomprehensible dance.

Laid out in one corner of the room was his counterpane, on which Wilberforce slept, his breathing laboured. Harry was still unsure as to the extent of the little dog's injuries, but they were more serious than his own — his being a mere nick from Frith's final bullet, as though he'd snagged his coat on a nail. Which was exactly what he'd told the doctor who'd called on him yesterday — at vast expense, naturally, in keeping with everything else in this godforsaken place.

There was a sudden barrage of yelling from outside, and Harry looked up to see one of the schooners pushing too close to a Royal Navy warship. Having watched absentmindedly as the smaller boat put up its sail and tacked rapidly out of the harbour, Harry lay back down on the bed, his mind wandering back to how he'd come to be here in the first place.

It was as though he'd lost time, Harry thought, like his mother during one of her fits. One moment he'd been fleeing the cottage on horseback, the next cantering along a country lane towards Petworth Station, some six miles distant. How he'd managed to handle a horse with an injured arm, he would never know. He'd been in a daze, he supposed, unable to comprehend what had happened. He still wasn't sure now . . .

He remembered the pain, though, the hot steady throb in his shoulder as he'd dismounted. Uncertain how severe the bleeding was, he'd used his belt as a kind of tourniquet, then put his jacket back on to cover the red stain. All the while, Wilberforce had lain at his feet, licking busily at his stomach, as though there were some kind of delicious nectar contained within his fur.

Finally, having hitched the mare to a tree with plenty of grass beneath to crop, Harry had placed Wilberforce inside his open leather valise, and walked into the station.

There was a train to Portsmouth at the top of the hour, the stationmaster had informed him, so Harry had bought a ticket and proceeded on to the platform, where he'd collapsed on a bench to wait.

And it was only then, as his breath had begun to steady, that the truth had hit him. His father was gone for ever, murdered before his eyes. His hands had begun to shake then, and he'd felt the blood drain from his head like sand from an hourglass. Then, before he'd known it, the bile had risen in his gorge, and he'd thrown up all over the paved floor of the platform, vaguely aware of passengers tutting in disapproval as they passed. Then he'd buried his head in his hands and wept.

Harry had been in Portsmouth since Thursday, and had done little more than sleep. It was as if a black fog had descended upon him, and all he'd wanted to do was lie in that room with the curtains drawn. His wound was dressed, it was true, but that was the only useful thing he'd achieved. He hadn't told the police about his father's murder. And he hadn't enquired after passage to China.

But today would be different, Harry promised himself. It had to be — he couldn't stay here for ever. Rolling over, he forced himself off the bed, feeling Wilberforce's sad eyes follow him as he crossed the room to where his valise lay. The little dog was dying, Harry suspected, another victim of the havoc he'd caused since his ill-fated encounter with Lorcan Darke.

Opening the cigar box that his father had pressed upon him, Harry counted seven five-pound notes still left inside. The way that Michael had stacked the bills so neatly brought tears to Harry's eyes once again, so at first he didn't see the little velvet bag tucked into the far end of the box.

Of course — his mother's jewellery! Unknotting the silken cord, Harry tipped the contents on to the bed. An amethyst brooch, a gold cross pendant, a silver locket . . . Opening this last, Harry found a tiny daguerreotype of his mother, taken before her marriage, judging by her elegant dress. She'd been a strikingly beautiful young woman, he saw, with her glossy black hair and searching, intelligent gaze. He kissed her image, then looped the chain around his neck, wincing a little as he crooked his arm. Wilberforce let out a whimper too, so Harry got up and nudged the tin bowl of water closer to his muzzle. To his surprise, the dog's pink tongue flickered out to taste the water. 'That's it,' Harry said, stroking the little patch of white between the dog's eyes. 'That's the way.'

It was the first time Harry had felt hopeful since arriving in Portsmouth. Eager to capitalise upon the sensation, he left the inn and headed out into the maze of cobbled streets behind Camber Dock. Here, as in the rest of the city, the air was full of rotten fish — a revolting stench that penetrated his clothes and made him want to gag. Above him, the seagulls wheeled in the salty breeze, laughing their horrible cackle, a fitting accompaniment to the whining and clanking of the ships' masts.

Harry had been told by the innkeeper that there was a pawnbroker's shop nearby, but there was a whole row of them, he saw now, easily identifiable by the mark of their trade — three golden balls suspended from hooks below the eaves.

Choosing an establishment at random, Harry pushed open the door, hearing the feeble tinkle of a sprung copper bell as he stepped inside. Perched at a desk at the end of the shop, hunched over a ledger book, sat a thin man with a scrappy ginger beard — grown, Harry suspected, to obscure the smallpox scars that pitted his cheeks like the surface of a crumpet. The man glanced up at Harry, monocle clasped in one eye like a rubber ball in a bony fist. 'Can I help?' he asked in a thick Portsmouth burr.

Usually, Harry would have been uneasy at the prospect of such a transaction, but now he was careless of what others thought of him; he had no desire to please, nor even to avoid giving offence. 'How much for these?' he asked, holding up the little velvet bag.

The man beckoned with one long finger, and Harry made his way through the cluttered shop, the shelves around him groaning with much-loved curios and heirlooms that hard times must have prised from their owners' hands – carriage clocks, toby jugs, ships in bottles, chipped Delft-china figurines.

'Show me,' the man urged, taking a roll of black velvet from under the desk and unfurling it with a practised flick of the wrist.

Harry tipped the items of jewellery unceremoniously upon it. 'I've the time to visit all your colleagues along the road,' he said, 'so mind you don't try to swindle me.'

'*Swindle* you?' the man echoed, as though such a thing were unthinkable. Slipping a pendant magnifying glass from his fob pocket, he held it close to the amethyst. 'But these are rather fine, sir,' he said, his manner a little less supercilious. 'I can give you four sovereigns a piece.'

That'd barely buy a Venus flytrap on the King's Road! Harry thought. Shaking his head, he reached for the velvet bag.

'One moment,' the man said, releasing his monocle so that it fell through the air and caught on its chain. His eyelashes were as pallid as his hair, Harry saw, giving him a peculiar, rather startled look. 'If I might offer you a little advice, sir,' he said with an obsequious smile. 'Most of the other brokers on this road have connections to . . .' The man raised his eyes Heavenwards. 'How might one put it delicately? The bluebottles.'

'Bluebottles?' Harry repeated, crossing his arms.

'The peelers, sir.' The man batted his faded lashes. 'There's folk, you see, who aren't shy of coming to Pompey with goods they might not have . . . shall we say . . . earned for themselves. They'll pawn 'em, then get themselves off on a boat to somewhere far away. Now, the peelers are getting wise to this, and have forged close connections with my . . . for want of a better expression . . . more punctilious colleagues.'

Harry did his best to wade through the man's tangled verbiage. 'And if I were one of those folk,' he said at last, 'could you arrange passage for me?'

The man chuckled, then slipped off his stool and sidled over to the door, where he flipped over the 'Open' sign and nudged down the bolt with one knuckle. Then he turned and regarded Harry, pale eyes gleaming. 'What sort of ship might you be thinking of?'

'One that sails to China.'

'To China!'

'Shanghai, preferably.'

The pawnbroker gave a stage swoon. 'The Whore of Asia.'

Harry made no reply.

'That's more of a Southampton location, sir,' the pawnbroker said with a regretful smile. 'The merchant navy and all that. Tea, silk. Opium . . .'

Harry turned for the door.

'But . . .' the man called after him, and Harry stopped. 'I *have* heard of a certain clipper that has business at the dockyard here. I *believe* she may be headed in the direction of the Far East. I'm acquainted with the captain,' he went on. 'I could petition on your behalf, but . . .' He rubbed the tip of his thumb against one long, waxen forefinger.

'I'll give you the brooch *and* pendant,' Harry said.

The pawnbroker reeled as though Harry had slapped him. 'Passage halfway round the world for eight sovereigns' worth of gems?' he scoffed. 'You'll have to do better than that!'

So, with a reluctant sigh, Harry reached into his shirt and pulled out the locket. The pawnbroker's pale-lashed eyes widened. 'Pass it over.'

Harry took off the necklace and allowed the man to snatch it from his grasp. He examined the hallmark through his glass, then the manufacturer's stamp, clucking with approval as he saw the small dimpled engravings around the rim. 'Very nice,' he said, opening the locket, eyes eating up the likeness within. 'Sweetheart, is she?' he added, shooting Harry a lascivious grin.

A sourness filled Harry's mouth. 'Can you help me or not?'

The pawnbroker put down his magnifying glass, then clasped his hands together and touched the interlaced thumbs against his lips. 'I think we can come to some kind of arrangement, yes.'

No sooner had Harry left the pawnbroker's shop than he began to fear he'd made a poor bargain; promised away his mother's jewels for a fraction of their worth. He dismissed the thought. For what choice did he have – a man on the run!

Favouring caution, Harry chose a different route back to the inn, stopping off at a butcher's to buy some lamb bones for the dog, and a pork pie for himself. On the corner of the next street, he passed a grand Georgian building with bars on the windows and a blue-glass lamp fixed above the door. '*Portsmouth City Police Station*', the sign said. Harry stood there for a moment with one foot on the step, debating whether to walk inside and tell the peelers what had happened to his father. That Frith had murdered him . . . He took a step forward, then stopped, knowing that the deck was stacked against him. For Frith would simply deny the crime – say that it was Harry who was to blame. And what was Harry's word against that of the respected foreman of a profitable Chelsea business? Who would the police believe?

But then an idea occurred to him. Checking the street name, Harry continued down the lane to a stationer's, where he bought a quire of writing paper, a dip pen and some ink.

Back at the inn, Harry laid out the lamb bones before Wilberforce, then sat down and devoured the pork pie. Seeing Wilberforce eye the food but do nothing to eat it, Harry took out his penknife and scraped out the marrow as best he could. Then he set the little dish before Wilberforce, who sniffed it, and took a tentative taste.

Harry smiled. Perhaps things really were looking up. Sinking down on to the bed, he took out the writing paper and readied his pen. '*To the Chief Constable of Portsmouth City Police,*' he wrote. '*Mr Michael Compton of Manor Cottage, Pulborough, was shot to death on Thursday last at half past ten in the morning. His killer was a Mr Decimus Frith of JM Piggott's Plant Emporium, 114–118 King's Road, Chelsea. From: an eye-witness.*'

Then he sealed the letter, addressed it, and set about packing his bag for China.

Next morning, having slipped his anonymous note beneath the door of the police station, Harry waited by the Round Tower, a crumbling stone fort built to protect Portsmouth from raids by French ships. Wilberforce lay at his feet, eyes shut, as Harry glanced around for the pawnbroker, half-suspecting that he would not come, that there must be some kind of trickery at play . . .

'Sir?'

Turning, Harry saw the pawnbroker sidling towards him, with a vast Neanderthal at his side, so large he would have dwarfed even Edwin, the melancholy chucker-outer from the Man in the Moon.

'This is Mr Scragge,' the pawnbroker said, standing back the better to effect the introduction. 'Ship's cook of some distinction.'

Scragge wore a dark-blue jacket and wide-bottomed canvas trousers, with a round sailor's cap wedged upon his boulder-sized head. He glanced from Harry to Wilberforce. 'That dog yours?' he asked gruffly, before dropping to his hunkers. 'Nice little Jack Russell, ain't he?' he said, lifting Wilberforce's upper lip with surprising tenderness and looking at his teeth. 'He ailing?' he asked, glancing up sharply.

'Had a blow to the stomach.'

Scragge's face took on a frightening intensity, and Harry held up his hands. 'It wasn't me,' he protested. 'Not everyone likes dogs, you know.'

'People make me sick,' Scragge said, then looked back at Wilberforce. 'Poor little fella,' he crooned, and the dog fluttered open his eyelids and started to wag his tail. Then Scragge straightened up, rubbing the small of his back, and turned to the pawnbroker. A swift nod was exchanged, and the pawnbroker came over to Harry. 'The items, sir,' he said.

Harry handed over the velvet bag. The pawnbroker's smile died as he shook the gems out into his palm. 'Where's the necklace?' he asked.

'You'll have it when I step aboard that ship,' Harry replied.

The pawnbroker tightened his lips, but then he turned to Scragge, and the two of them moved closer to the curved walls of the fort, out of earshot. Harry saw what looked like a generous number of banknotes switching hands, then Scragge signalled to him with his anvil of a chin, and they made their way down the slope to the harbour, Wilberforce clutched in Harry's arms.

The harbourfront was bustling with people. The horse tram came right down to the water's edge, and was currently decanting a group of Royal Navy sailors, dapper in their blue dresscoats and trousers. But their eyes looked blood-shot and bleary, and Harry suspected that they'd had a final night out on the town, which had probably ended in a knocking shop.

Set into the arches of the harbour wall were ticket offices, chandlers and victualling stores, and a gate giving access to a dry-dock enclosure behind. Beyond that, a small jetty protruded like a stone tongue into the bay. Moored to its end was a rickety skiff . . . 'But that's no clipper!' Harry exclaimed.

Scragge screwed up his face and emitted a bellow of such alarming volume that it took Harry a moment to realise he was laughing. 'Where do you find 'em, Neil?' Scragge sighed, slapping the pawnbroker on the back. 'That's just the tender, boy,' he said, jabbing a thick finger at the har-bour. 'That's where *we're* headed.'

Moored a hundred yards away, Harry saw a magnificent teak-hulled ship, with three square-rigged masts and a pointed, speedy-looking prow. A row of men stood along the deck, watching them with crossed arms.

'That's the *Redemption*,' Scragge said, his voice softer now, almost reverent. 'And she ain't never let me down yet.'

Wilberforce's stumpy tail began to wag again, and Harry became aware of a quiet presence beside him.

'The locket, sir,' the pawnbroker breathed. 'As agreed.'

Harry lifted the chain off his neck and passed it over. The pawnbroker examined it in his palm, tongue clicking as he opened the hasp. Then he looked up with a frown.

'The picture's mine,' Harry said.

For a moment, Harry thought that he'd pushed his luck too far, but then the pawnbroker let slip a smile. 'Why not?' he said. 'You'll need a lucky charm where you're going, I'll wager!'

Scragge was stepping into the tender now, his weight threatening to push it below the waterline. Clasping Wilberforce tight, Harry clambered after him. Once he'd regained his balance, Harry looked up to bid farewell to the pawnbroker, but the man was already gone, lost in the crowds of the harbour.

September 16, 1867

Dear Jack,

Enclosed is repayment for the moneys you so kindly lent me last month — plus a little more. I would be grateful if you would use the surplus to stand the lads a round at the Man in the Moon.

I had planned to say nothing on the matter, but now find myself unable to resist asking if there have been any questions at the nursery regarding my disappearance. Has Decimus Frith questioned you about me? I worry that my name has been tarnished in Chelsea, but if any ill is spoken of me, please know that it is without foundation.

But I shall write no more on the subject, Jack, for the less you know of my predicament, the better. Rest assured that I am alive, though I cannot say well, for I have spent these last few weeks suffering badly from seasickness, which has only now abated. So, alive, then — let us leave it at that.

I think of you often, Jack, and hope someday to return to London to thank you for your kindness in person.

Your old friend,

Harry Compton

PS. If you were minded to reply, our next landing stage is Gibraltar, and I am told that if you address your letter to the poste restante on Main Street there, I shall be sure to receive it.

14 Wellington Lane

Battersea

County Surrey

30 September 1867

Dear Harry,

Moneys received, old stick! I neither expected, nor wanted, them back, but thank you anyway for sending. Writ upon the envelope was 'Porto Delgada', which Banks tells me is capital of the Azores, though he cannot be trusted with his geography — nor, indeed, with anything!

Your name is far from mud here, Harry, despite your fears. True, there has been a bit of puzzlement about your disappearance, with rumours that you stole some of Piggott's best seedstock and plan to set yourself up as a nurseryman at the other end of the country. That muck-spout, Rex Barrington, has even put it about that you pulled a gun on Frith whilst making off with your booty, but no one in Cultivation pays any heed to what that popinjay has to say.

92

As for Old Pie-Gut, he is constantly to be found in the foulest of tempers, which is as much a source of the rumours as anything, and as for our 'Colonel' Frith, well! He glares at all of us slumming it here in Cultivation as though we were part of some conspiracy, but we just smile at him sweetly till he takes his sorry haunches back over the bridge to Chelsea.

Business at the nursery remains brisk as ever, and when I last dragged a barrow over to the stovehouse, Old Pie-Gut had a new salesman slaving away for him — prettier, dare I say, even than you, Harry!

What else can I tell you? The nursery has just secured a sizable contract to smarten up the cemetery at Brompton. Those in Cultivation who wish to undertake the work are few and far between, but such superstitions have never bothered me — not if I can turn a few extra bob, that is!

Anyway, you'll forgive my rabbiting on, for I was never one for writing — not like you, Harry.

I miss you as well, and wish you the very best.

Your pal,

Jack

PS. That outbreak of woolly aphid did jump from the crabapples to the pyracanthas — so we should have moved them like you said.

The Rock of Gibraltar

October 17, 1867

Dear Jack,

I received your letter in Gibraltar this morning! Judging by its contents, it sounds as though things back home are not so different to when I left, so I feel emboldened now to tell you a little more of what I am about, whilst still withholding any information that might land you in trouble should our correspondence be intercepted.

As you will no doubt have guessed, I am on a sea voyage, Jack — the sole commercial passenger on a venerable old 'tea clipper'. The crew are twenty strong, and hail to a man from Southampton. They have made this journey countless times before, and it is a nice little earner for them, as they cram the hold full of hock and gin, which they will sell at their destination, before filling the empty space with tea chests, and bales of cotton & tobacco to sell on their return.

Our captain is a serious-minded fellow named Buchanan — he says very little, so everyone pays rapt attention when he does choose to open his mouth. He has a perfectly round little bald spot on the top of his head, which reminds me of a monk's tonsure — though I doubt he offers many prayers on my behalf, as it was the ship's cook, not he, who secured my passage on his vessel.

He is an interesting chap, this ship's cook. Rejoicing in the name of Cornelius Scragge, he is by some distance the largest human being I have ever seen, and I would fear for my safety had he not declared himself my friend, which assuredly he has, and for reasons that may surprise you. For I have as my travelling companion a little Jack Russell terrier, for whom Scragge has developed an almighty affection, as he has longed to have a pet onboard ever since the ship's cat fell into the sea to be eaten by a shark (I assumed Scragge was joking on this matter, but am assured not). Thanks to his fondness for this little dog, I am permitted to assist Scragge in his galley, which keeps me busy at least, as I have had a number of worries and sorrows crowding around my mind, which, I am ashamed to say, have become oppressive.

Incidentally, you must commend Banks on his geography, for he was correct about the Azores. In fact, we have only lately left the archipelago, though memories of it will remain with me for ever. On Pico Island, where we stopped for a few days to take on food and water, there grow the most extraordinary trees named Dracaena draco, or 'dragon tree'. I will struggle to describe them to you, Jack, as I have encountered nothing like them before, not even in Mr Weeks's stockground. Umbrella-shaped in habit, they have a mass of spiny green branches sprouting upwards from their trunks which form a thick, prickly crown some thirty feet high. According to legend, the trees'

94

existence is down to the first and greatest plant hunter of them all, none other than Hercules, who was tasked with bringing back the golden apples from the Garden of the Hesperides. This garden was guarded by a ferocious 100-headed dragon named 'Landon', and when Hercules finally slew the beast, the dragon trees sprouted from its blood! The specimens we saw were very ancient, though their trunks lack annular rings, so cannot be accurately aged. But as with most myths, there seems to be a grain of truth in the tale, for when cut, the trees bleed a sticky red resin that looks just as one would imagine a dragon's blood might. This gum has long been used by the native Azoreans as a poultice — though whether it would take off on Harley Street, I cannot say!

One tree was in fruit when we passed, so I picked several of the fleshy orange berries, and have now extracted the seeds, which Mr Scragge has allowed me to store in some of his honey. Whether they will survive, I do not know — but I shall keep them regardless, and if I do return to England (of which there is no certainty) they will be with me still.

What else can I tell you? My sleeping arrangements consist of a suffocatingly warm cabin in the aftcastle, shared with six of the ship's boys, all of whom are younger than me — seventeen being the oldest. There is a small skylight set into the poop deck above, with a fixed table below, at which we play a good deal of cards and dice, though my cabin-mates are more skilled at games than me, despite their tender years. My dog, Wilberforce, sleeps on a blanket below my hammock, with a tin bowl of water beside him, which spills most nights in the swell of the sea. Thankfully, my cabin-mates dare not complain about this, as they know I have Scragge in my corner — or Wilberforce does, at any rate!

Now I must close, as I am nearing the end of my page, and we are soon to take the tender out on a visit to one of Gibraltar's many hostelries. It is a very singular place, the Rock, full of more drunken sailors even than Portsmouth, and oddest of all, a troop of wild monkeys that ventures down the mountainside every night and tries to steal your dinner. Thankfully, we all sleep on the boat, as I fear they might carry off Wilberforce as their hostage were we to leave him unattended!

With affection,

Harry

PS. Our next destination shall be Cape Town, where I am told that anything sent to the post office on Adderley Street should reach me in due course.

14 Wellington Lane

Battersea

Co. Surrey

7 November 1867

Dear Harry,

What a time you are having! Your last letter made me green with envy, what with the Battersea mizzle coming down like piss through a sieve, and the reek of the new chemical works burning my eyes. How long Battersea — or Chelsea, for that matter — can remain a centre for exotic plants is beyond me, given how the fumes sicken the air now.

So I won't say I'm jealous, Harry, but . . . know that I am! How can it be that you are out on the high seas, living the life of a Paxton Crosse or Niven McCabe, whilst we're all stuck here? You must have come into money, though I shall ask no more, curiosity having killed the cat and all that.

There have, as it happens, been a few questions about you lately, and they've come from none other than a captain of the Portsmouth City Police! He arrived last week at the growing grounds, accompanied by both Frith and Piggott, keen to know if we'd had word from you, or knew anything of your plans &c. Naturally, none of us breathed a word, but later, Pugh had it from Bill Hartley that the enquiry was connected to your father. For though I am sorry to be the bearer of bad news, Harry, there are rumours that he has disappeared, and that his house has been burglarized, and it seems that the peelers want to ask you what you might know about it. Now, I suspect that neither of these things are true (the burglary nor the disappearance), and it was all just a ruse to scare up information as to where Piggott's No. 1 Salesman has gone, but it was odd for the fellow to travel all the way up from the South Coast to make his enquiries, don't you think?

Anyhow, Harry, I've tried to set out for you here what happened, without making any judgement myself, and I hope that all the wondrous sights you must be seeing on your voyage will help lift your spirits.

Your old friend,

Jack Turner

PS. I am sorry if I have caused you worry about your father but I imagined that you would want to know. I would.

Cape Town

December 12, 1867

Dear Jack,

Many thanks for your letter of November 7. Painful as the news it contained was, I cannot say I was surprised. Please know, Jack, that I bear no blame at all in the distressing matter of which you write. Those at fault will pay for what they have done — and I shall not stop until that objective has been achieved. But no more of that now.

I write to you from Cape Town, where we have been moored some ten days, with the crew busy exchanging their cargo for carcasses of salt beef. The Azores were one thing, Jack, but the Cape boasts a variety of flora that far exceeds it! I had a morning spare last week and used it to climb Table Mountain, where I collected a number of freesias and saxifrages, as well as five different species of protea, all of which I know would fetch an excellent price on the King's Road. Unfortunately, I had with me only my vasculum and a honeypot — neither sufficient for my needs! But be in no doubt that that will be remedied when I reach my final destination.

The province's fauna is every bit the equal of its flora. I have seen ostriches and penguins, and even, near the fish market, a great spotted leopard reclining in a thorn tree, its tail dangling down like that of a contented housecat. There are lions, too, but thank God I have met none! In fact, my principle battle has come with a vicious type of horsefly named 'Tsetse' — which, when swatted, simply dusts itself down and comes at you again, as though armour-plated. Even the tiny beasts of Africa are of a tougher breed than those we find in Europe.

I shall write again, Jack, though I fear it may not be for some time, as we must cross the Indian Ocean next, with no stops for several weeks. But the going promises to be swift and true, for when this clipper fills her sails, there is no stopping her — she cuts at twice the speed of even the most modern steamship.

As you may have gleaned by now, my spirits are much recovered, helped by the fact that Mr Scragge has finally permitted me to take on some duties beyond the galley. Who would have thought that a landlubber like me would have learnt to splice a rope and swab a deck!

I hope that you remain well, Jack. I think of you often, and sometimes even venture to believe that my name will be made by this voyage, and that both our lives may be bettered as a result. No doubt you shall think me mad, but I have a determination in my heart now that will let nothing divert me from my goals.

Ever your friend,
Harry

PS. In the happy event that this reaches you in time — Merry Christmas one and all! In the even happier event that you wish to continue our correspondence, you may try the British Post Office in Shanghai.

The Bay of Chinchew
February 22, 1868

Dear Jack,

What a fool was I to write with such confidence of the future! For just a few weeks later it seemed certain that I would have no future at all, but be reduced to a heap of bones at the bottom of the Strait of Formosa. Let me tell you what happened, Jack, and perhaps my story will provide you with a little entertainment, safe as you are on dry land.

We had just put out from Chimoo Bay, with the clipper cutting her speedy path through the sea, which that morning was a glorious rink of the purest azure. I was alone in the mess with Wilberforce, surprised to find myself with the choicest of pickings, as there was no one else about to eat them. I was aware of a certain amount of activity around me — securing of lading, adjustment of mainsails &c — but nothing so out of the ordinary as to distract me from my boiled salt-pork and pea soup. But then suddenly the cabin door flew open, and in burst Captain Buchanan, his usual calm demeanour a distant memory. 'What the hell are you doing, boy?' he cried. 'Get down below, on the double — there's a storm coming!'

He used a few saltier terms then, to convey the gravity of the situation, which I will not repeat here. Naturally, I did as he asked, though as I passed over deck, his panic did seem to me a little overblown, as truly the sea was still as a millpond, & there was a soft, pinkish hue to the air, as though one were looking through a veil of damask. But, catching sight of some of the crewmen huddled together under the tender that hangs in midships, I was shocked to see their faces drawn and their eyes wide with fear, so I picked up my feet and ran.

And it was just as well I did, for as soon as I reached my cabin, it began. Three of my room-mates were already in their hammocks, arms and ankles twined around the stays. I did the same, with Wilberforce clutched in the crook of one elbow, and my travel bag in the other, and then it was as though we had been sucked into Charybdis's whirlpool, with the wind screaming, and everything not tied down sliding back and forth across the cabin floor.

Soon, there came an ear-splitting crash, as though a bomb had exploded, and I opened my eyes to find a hailstorm of broken glass falling into the cabin, followed by a shower of saltwater that made me certain we were sunk. There were howls then from the midshipmen — these lads who never show fear — so that I found myself intoning a prayer, squeezing Wilberforce so tight I might have choked the life out of him.

When eventually I opened my eyes, I took in a sight that took me some time to comprehend. A fish, at least thirty lbs in weight, snub-nosed & leather-backed, flipping its massive body from side to side on the floor beneath my hammock. And then I realised what must have happened — the sea had tossed up a tunny fish on to the poop deck, and it had smashed through the skylight into our cabin!

Then, as abruptly as it had begun, the swell subsided, and the only sounds I could hear were the jagged breathing of my cabin-mates, and the sad thump-thump of that dying fish.

I remained in my hammock, with Wilberforce trembling on my chest, until one of the midshipmen — a bawdy youth by the name of Stevens — got down and picked up the fish by the gills. 'Well, we'll dine well t'night, anyway!' he said in a voice still hoarse with fear.

From that moment on, nonchalance was the watchword for the crew, and I did my best to mimic them as we patched up the ship. She'd sprung her bowsprit in the gale, and one of her sails had split, with the bulwarks all washed away, but thankfully the hull had held firm, so we were able to continue on our way only a few hours later.

Scragge did indeed cook the tunny fish that night, and everyone was very jolly, save for your ashen-faced friend, who had finally caught a terrifying glimpse of that of which the sea is capable, and will respect and fear her power for evermore.

100

Once the food was finished, Scragge came over to sit with me, though he only had eyes for Wilberforce. 'There's but one true innocent on this ship,' he said, lifting the little dog on to his lap, 'and I'm looking at him now!'

Wilberforce began to wag his tail then, and the crew all gave a cheer, Captain Buchanan included, and everyone drank even more than usual. It was a happy night, I suppose, but a bittersweet one too, reminding me once again how finely balanced our lives are. So do what you can today, Jack, because anything may happen tomorrow!

Anyway, that is enough philosophy from me. When you receive this letter, you shall know that I have made it to my destination, for it will be posted after we arrive.

With much respect and relief,

Harry

PART TWO
March 1868 – Shanghai

Chapter 9

Harry Compton stood on the foredeck of the clipper, watching the small wooden sampan approach over the broad, inky waters of the Whangpu River. Standing beside him was the hulking figure of Cornelius Scragge, whilst at his feet lay Wilberforce, the only creature on the *Redemption* to have gained, rather than lost, weight on the six-month journey from Portsmouth. Little surprise, perhaps, given the quantity of scraps Scragge had been feeding him in the galley.

At the prow of the clipper, awaiting the arrival of the Chinese rowing boat, stood the skipper of the *Redemption*, Captain Edgar Buchanan, tonsured baldspot glinting in the moonlight like a medallion. Buchanan had always been a little wary of him, Harry felt, and the storm they'd recently endured in the Strait of Formosa seemed only to have deepened those suspicions. Sometimes, Harry would catch Captain Buchanan regarding him with uneasy eyes, as though he were some sort of Jonah who had invited disaster upon them. He was tapping his foot now, signalling impatiently to the sampan with one hand, making Harry suspect that he couldn't wait to see the back of him.

At last, the boat drew up by the clipper, and Buchanan climbed down the rope ladder and stepped aboard. Documents were exchanged, along with a loop of 'cash' — the little brass coins used as currency throughout the Far East, with a small square hole punctured in each so that they could be threaded on to a cord to create units of greater value.

Transaction complete, Buchanan called up to Harry, 'Well, come on then, boy!'

Harry turned to his friend. 'Thank you again, Mr Scragge. For everything.'

'Remember what I told you, Harry,' the ship's cook replied. 'In every big city, you'll find those who won't balk at taking advantage of a stranger. Shanghai's no different, so you'll need to watch your step.'

Harry nodded dutifully, fond enough of Scragge not to let on that he'd given him this advice many times before.

'And you,' Scragge went on, bending down to scoop up Wilberforce. 'You'll look after your master, won't you, Wilber?'

The dog made his answer by licking Scragge's massive face all over with his pink tongue. Scragge rubbed his nose against the dog's wet muzzle, then set Wilberforce down and turned away, his eyes damp.

'I said now!' Buchanan snapped, so Harry slung his valise over one shoulder and crossed the deck, nodding farewell to those crew members who'd come up to see him off.

'Go well, Harry,' Buchanan said tersely. Then he shook Harry by the hand, and was gone.

A Chinese boatman awaited Harry at the bottom of the rope ladder, expertly maintaining the position of his sampan with a fixed, punt-like oar at the bow. Only once Harry was seated on the rough plank that ran across the narrow deck, dog in his arms, did the man begin to row away from the clipper, which suddenly seemed huge to Harry, its mighty teak hull gleaming in the moonlight.

Harry turned his gaze towards Shanghai's harbour. It was about half a mile wide, curving gently, with a dozen or so sloping wooden jetties giving access to the anchorage. Behind it, twinkling seductively, ran the Bund, or 'embanked quay'. This was the oldest part of the city, Scragge had told Harry, and home to its grandest colonial buildings: the Shanghai Club, the Customs House, the headquarters of banks, trading houses and shipping companies. 'Too fancy for the likes of you,' had been Scragge's counsel, telling Harry to head for the Bubbling Well Road area instead.

One hand stroking Wilberforce's salt-matted pelt, Harry glanced back at the boatman. He wore a blue tunic and serge trousers, his head clean-shaven save for a long black plait dangling down his back. Fluttering over his shoulder was the green flag of the Chinese Customs Service – an institution with which Captain Buchanan would have to lock horns before the crew of the *Redemption* could begin loading up the cargo they planned to take back to England. Harry wondered if he would see any of the lads again. He doubted it.

They'd almost reached the harbourfront now, and Harry placed a protective boot on top of his valise. Contained in its side pouch – and miraculously unscathed by the storm – lay his letter of introduction to Mr Narcissus Lockhart, his mother's cousin. Numerous times on the voyage, Harry had taken out this letter and contemplated whether to make use of it. But he could guess what would happen if he placed himself in Mr Lockhart's care – the man would want to know why he had travelled to Shanghai, and Harry would have to tell him about the map, and the icicle tree, and whenever that happened, trouble seemed to follow.

Waiting ahead on the jetty was a scrum of eager locals. Once again, Harry found his mind turning back to his letter of introduction — he could hire a hansom cab with the money he'd exchanged with Scragge, ask the driver to take him directly to Narcissus Lockhart's house . . . No, Harry told himself. Stick to the plan.

'Squeeze?' the boatman called out, as he brought the sampan to a halt, broadside-on to the jetty. 'Cash?'

Harry understood that word, at least, and was more than happy to oblige. He handed the man a few coins, then stepped out of the sampan into the crowd. He'd encountered enough greeting parties on his journey here to have learnt the best course of action in these circumstances — keep a smile on your face, and your eyes fixed on some unspecified point in the distance.

'Shanghai Club?' came the first shout, right by his ear.

'Sedan chair?'

'Astor House Hotel?'

'Sedan . . . sedan!'

Harry kept his arms by his sides lest his pockets be exposed to the scrum. He was a deal taller than most of them, at least, and, with his newly grown beard, he hoped that he exuded an air of that experience which had been so sorely lacking in London.

'Bubblin' Well?' he heard, and swivelled towards the man who'd spoken.

'Bubbling Well Road?' Harry echoed, and the tout grinned, then grabbed his sleeve and led him away through the crowd.

The tout wore his hair in the same style as the boatman, Harry saw, but his clothes were far shabbier – raffia sandals, threadbare jacket and ragged trousers tied at the waist with string. Another hawker approached them, but the tout barked something at him with such guttural force that he stopped in his tracks, and watched them depart in a stunned silence.

Hand tight on his sleeve, the tout dragged Harry into a lane between two massive brick warehouses, and there, in the shadows, stood parked one of the oddest contraptions he'd ever seen. Its principal feature was a cartwheel that rose almost as high as a man's neck. Running down either side of it was a wooden plank attached to a set of handles at the back, like those of a wheelbarrow. Seated on the planks, Harry counted eight locals – three women with white tabards over their dresses, one dandling a baby; four men wearing grey tunics and trousers. Harry wondered how long they'd been waiting, and gave them a grateful nod in acknowledgment of their patience.

The tout pointed at the postage stamp of space remaining on one of the benches, and Harry wedged one buttock into the vacant slot, forcing the men to shuffle along. Then he hefted his bag on to his knees, grabbed Wilberforce, and slipped him into the gap between the bag and his chest, the dog snuffling like a piglet as he settled down.

A moment later, Harry felt the bench tip up as the wheelbarrow was raised from its wooden supports. Peering around, he was astonished to see that the tout intended to manoeuvre the contraption all by himself. He was like a circus strongman, Harry thought, as the cartwheel began to turn and the barrow inched forward. All the passengers lifted their feet off the ground, and soon they were rattling down the alley, picking up speed as they burst out on to the broad esplanade of the Bund.

Promenading down the gaslit pavements Harry saw scores of fashionably dressed Westerners — men in frockcoats and top hats; bare-armed women in straw bonnets and showy satin dresses — a few of whom saw Harry travelling with the locals, and made moues of distaste. 'Shanghailanders', Scragge had termed the city's expatriate population, remarking that a more decadent, insular bunch you could not dread to meet.

But the buildings of the Bund were the equal of any Harry had seen along the Thames, he thought, admiring their white marble façades and intricate pilasters. A Union Jack hung from one, the words 'British Post Office' etched in smart black lettering above the door. A few yards on, another Union Jack fluttered from a flagstaff, the sign in the front garden reading, 'British Consulate'.

Harry sensed his fellow passengers anticipating his call to alight, and was sorely tempted, reassured as he was to find this small corner of England some 4,000 leagues from home. But then they turned off the Bund and squeezed into a long, canyon-like alleyway, no more than ten feet across and paved in narrow flagstones.

Flanking the lane on either side were tiny shopfronts that opened directly on to the street, with little masonry counters set at elbow height, from behind which shopkeepers shouted out their wares. The buildings above them all had exquisite gilt signboards running down the timber-framed façades, intricately painted with Chinese characters. And everywhere, strung from the balcony railings, hung oil-paper lanterns, held together by concentric bamboo rings, their lacquered exteriors glowing red.

Seated at one balcony was a beautiful girl with long dark hair, and Harry remembered the excited chatter of his cabin-mates as the *Redemption* had entered the South China Sea, as they'd recalled the courtesans to be had in Shanghai for just a few cash coins. 'There's the flower-girls, and the pheasants, and the saltwater sisters — them's the cheapest,' Stevens had rhapsodised to Harry over a game of whist. 'The madams'll charge you extra for a virgin,' he'd added with a wink. 'But it's only chicken's blood . . .'

Harry was jolted back to the present by the sound of a meat cleaver hitting a butcher's block. Looking up, he saw a sinewy cook standing at his counter, expertly separating the legs and head from an enormous frog. A few yards on, the tout cried *'Nanking!'* and the barrow stopped to allow two passengers to get off, instantly replaced by two more. Then they were off again, passing concessions selling scented tea, and joss-sticks for the Buddha, the rich, sweet smell of soft-shell crabs sizzling in a dozen woks reminding Harry that it had been a long time since he'd last eaten.

On they went, zigzagging through lanes, barging aside sedan chairs, causing bare-chested labourers bearing crates of sandalwood and candied fruit to flatten themselves against sidewalls to allow the barrow passage. At length, they crossed a bridge over a creek, and the labyrinth began to open up, the signage changing from Chinese to French. Harry saw épiceries and patisseries now; trays of golden croissants in the shop windows of a plane-lined boulevard — *'Frenchtown!'*

came the cry, and then on again, and soon they were passing a racecourse, over a mile long, with a gully dividing the track from the street and a grandstand rising on the other side.

Harry sat back, head spinning with the vibrant colours and smells; the bewildering pace of it all. He was just starting to ask himself if it was not too late, after all, to seek out Narcissus Lockhart, when he found that they were stopping by a temple, tall and thin as a watchtower, six tiered wooden roofs stacked one upon the other, each decorated with ornate upturned eaves. '*Pagoda!*' came the cry, and now there were monks aboard, dressed in long brown robes, one of them letting slip a toothy grin as he tickled Wilberforce under the chin.

Then they were off again, hurtling down a country road, with ruts in the mud where carriages must have passed during the day, and a low brick building surrounded by a picket fence set back from the verge. '*Bubblin'!*' came the cry, and Harry climbed carefully down, placing Wilberforce on the ground, before searching through his pockets for coins, which he handed to the tout, who slipped them into a woven pouch around his neck.

Then the wheelbarrow was gone, and Harry stood alone on the moonlit verge, one hand massaging the small of his back. Some sort of orchard extended into the distance, and from deep within it he could hear a faint trickling sound – the eponymous 'bubbling well', perhaps. His wrist felt hot and itchy, and he looked down to see a gangly black-and-white mosquito squatting on the skin. Dropping his bag, he slapped at it, leaving behind a smear of white-banded limbs and crimson blood. Less hardy than the African flies, at least.

As Wilberforce turned his head in the direction of the harbour, a whine issuing from his flabby chops, Harry heard footsteps from behind the picket fence, and looked round to see a stout European woman in a plain day dress and bonnet bustling down the garden path towards him.

'Need a room, lovey?' the woman called out in a singsong Welsh accent. And why not, Harry thought — anything seemed possible in this hotchpotch of a city.

'How much?' Harry asked, as the woman gripped the top of the gate and looked him over with admiring eyes.

'It's one Shanghai dollar a night,' she replied.

'Cash coins?' Harry asked.

'If you must.' The woman peered down at Wilberforce trembling at Harry's feet. 'But it'll cost you eighty with the dog.'

Harry gave the woman the look he'd perfected while haggling in the fish market of Cape Town — a potent blend of outrage and bemusement.

'Sixty, then,' the woman laughed. 'Just for you.'

Harry nodded, and the woman turned back to the house and bellowed: 'Geraint? Shift yourself! We've got guests!'

An hour later, Harry was sitting with Mr and Mrs Geraint Methuen-Campbell in the kitchen of the Bubbling Well Guesthouse, devouring a fried duck egg on a piece of toast that tasted more like sponge cake than bread.

'We've another griffin lodged upstairs,' Mrs Methuen-Campbell was saying, watching Harry eat with uncommon interest. 'Our Mr Dancer. Though he has no employment just at present,' she added pointedly.

'Carys,' her husband chided, busy butchering a duck carcass by the stove.

A 'griffin', Harry had learnt, was a thrusting young Englishman come out East to find work with a European trading house, or *hong*. The Methuen-Campbells had surmised that Harry was one such creature, and he'd been happy to confirm them in their presumption.

'I'm too much in other people's affairs, Geraint tells me,' Carys went on, causing Harry to congratulate himself on his foresight.

'Of course, it's either the flesh trade or the poison trade in Shanghai these days,' Carys continued. 'The flesh trade is for the girls, who are kidnapped from the countryside and sold to the city's brothels, and the poison trade is for opium, which is—'

'Carys!' came Geraint's admonishing voice again. 'I'm quite sure Mr Compton is only too aware of what goes on in Shanghai.'

There was an awkward pause. 'I should turn in, Mrs Methuen-Campbell,' Harry said, pushing back his chair. 'It's been a long journey.'

Recognising the finality in Harry's tone, Wilberforce raised his head.

'Greedy wee tyke, ain't he?' Carys said with an indulgent grin. 'He made short work of that duck neck.'

'I'll show you upstairs,' Geraint said, wiping his hands on his leather apron.

Harry followed his landlord into the hallway, where a Welsh dragon flag, a cross of St George and a saltire had been draped over the walls, presumably to denote equal welcome to all-comers from the British Isles. A sweeping central staircase had evidently been designed to look imposing, but whoever had commissioned it appeared to have run out of funds, as a section of banister was missing, and instead of sconces, little kerosene lanterns burned on every third stair, their feeble flames haloed by insects.

'We don't usually get the mosquitoes 'til later in the spring,' Geraint said, 'but we've had a bit of a warm spell.' He turned his head and, in the light of the lanterns, Harry's heart sank to see his sallow face lumpy with bites.

There were three doors off the main landing, one of which led to the Methuen-Campbells' private quarters, another to a shared bathroom, and the last to Harry's room. There was a second floor as well, Harry could see, and as Geraint opened his door, he wondered if the lodgings up there might not be better furnished. For there was nothing in Harry's room but a low wooden bed, a chamber-pot and an ewer of cloudy water. As if to counter this deficiency, Geraint hurried across the bare floorboards and threw open a louvered door at the other end of the room, revealing a modest balcony furnished with a cane chair and table, and woven bamboo hoardings on either side. 'We wake our guests at eight o'clock,' Geraint said, withdrawing from the room before Harry could respond.

Harry set down his bag with a sigh, considering for a moment the various boarding houses he'd stayed at this past year – Pincham's of Chelsea; the dockside lodgings in Portsmouth – and deciding that this one was by some distance the worst. But at least it was cheap, even allowing for the supplement he'd had to pay for Wilberforce. 'The things I do for you,' he murmured into the dog's wiry fur, then set him down on the floor.

Peeling off his frockcoat, Harry laid it carefully on the bed. Sewn into its silk lining was his precious map, so he liked to keep the garment close. He rolled the stiffness from his shoulders, then stepped out on to the balcony. A thick roof of cloud blotted out the stars, but there were a few Chinese lanterns visible in the distance, suggesting this western end of Shanghai must be populated to some degree. He checked his pocketwatch — it was late, almost eleven o'clock. Time to get some sleep . . .

Just as he turned to go back inside, a creak came from the slatted boards above, and an upper-class English voice called down, 'What-ho?'

Harry stuck his head over the balcony and looked up. A face was peering down at him — a handsome face with black shark's eyes and a thick handlebar moustache. 'Palatial, ain't it?' the man remarked in a droll tone.

'I've seen worse,' Harry said.

'Name's Dancer,' the man said. 'You here for the trade?'

'That's right.'

'Which *hong* you with?'

Harry couldn't think of anything but the name on his letter of introduction. 'Lockhart's,' he said.

Dancer made a face. 'Johnny-come-latelies, that lot. But to each his own.' He gave a contemplative sniff. 'I'm still testing the water meself. Talking to Jardine Matheson, amongst others. Failing that, it'll be Sassoon's or Swire's for me.' There was a slap as Dancer killed a mosquito feeding on his neck. 'Fancy a smoke?' he asked, holding out a black ceramic pipe, the distinctive shape of which Harry recognised.

'Not tonight — I'm all but done in.'

'As you wish,' Dancer said, gazing down at Harry with his mocking black eyes. 'No point in troubling yourself to get that damned balcony door to close, by the way,' he added. 'There's more of them biters inside than out.'

'Thanks,' Harry said. 'Good night.' Then, glad to rid himself of this unsettling new acquaintance, he withdrew to his room and collapsed on to the bed.

A moment later, a sweet, herbal reek began to drift down from above, making Harry think back to that night in Chelsea with Lorcan Darke. It all seemed a very long time ago . . . Wrinkling his nose, Harry stretched out his long legs, and settled down to sleep.

Harry awoke to a high-pitched droning. At first, he thought he was back aboard the *Redemption*, with the wind screaming through the rigging, but then he remembered, and slapped a hand against the mosquito buzzing about his ear. Silence restored, he fumbled an arm across the bed until he found Wilberforce stretched out beside him. Comforted by the warmth of the dog's oily pelt, he felt himself slipping back to sleep.

Seconds later, Harry's eyes flicked open. The floor of his room was bathed in a pewter light now that the moon had escaped cloud cover. The door to his balcony stood open, and . . . Harry sat bolt upright. His valise appeared to be sliding across the floor — of its own accord. He blinked hard, but there was no mistaking it: his bag was creeping towards the open balcony door.

Harry looked over at Wilberforce, sure he must somehow be at fault, but the dog was snoring away, dead to the world. Swinging his legs on to the floor, Harry rubbed his eyes.

His valise had almost reached the balcony now. This must be some kind of witchcraft, some terrible hallucination.

Harry crossed the room, then saw something glinting in the moonlight – a metal hook wedged into the leather seam of his valise, with a glistening line of gut attached to its eye.

Reaching for his bag, Harry yanked it towards him, then heard an aggrieved cry from above. He stepped outside to see Mr Dancer leaning over the edge of his balcony, a split-cane fishing rod held in his hands. 'You almost had me over!' Dancer yelled.

'What the hell do you think you're doing?' Harry cried.

'Just practising my casting, old boy,' Dancer drawled back. 'Did I catch something?'

Dancer's eyes, Harry saw, were glazed, and he was sweating heavily beneath an ill-fitting Chinese dressing gown. Getting hold of the fishing gut, Harry bit it off between his teeth and turned to go back into his room.

'My hook!' Dancer protested, but Harry just slammed the flimsy door behind him, then stamped across the floor with his valise and wedged it as far under the bed as possible.

'I just need a few damn cash to tide me over,' he heard shouted from above. 'You can't begrudge me that, man!'

Wilberforce had one eye open, but was otherwise unmoved. 'Some bloody guard dog,' Harry said, crushing another insect on his arm as he lay back on the bed. Above him, he heard the low creak of floorboards, then the foul reek that told him another pipe had been lit. This would be his first and last night at the Bubbling Well Guesthouse, Harry decided.

The next morning, having settled his bill at the guesthouse – much to Mrs Methuen-Campbell's dismay – Harry made his way back through the streets of Shanghai, Wilberforce at his heel. Though not blessed with a particularly sharp sense of direction, Harry had always had a good recall of place, so was able to navigate by noting the landmarks he'd passed the night before.

Thronging the streets this morning was a multitude of private sedan chairs, upholstered in gilt-trimmed silk, carried on bamboo poles by silent servants wearing long blue robes. The air felt a little fresher — heralding an end to those infernal mosquitoes, Harry hoped — and a few of the chairs had their curtains drawn back, so that he could see the European men sitting inside in their morning-coats, ox-leather document cases resting at their feet.

By the time he reached the British Consulate, Harry was sweating heavily, in spite of the cool breeze that was whipping in off the Bund. Perhaps it was that pot of curd which Carys Methuen-Campbell had forced upon him that morning, before he'd told her he was leaving. It had tasted sharp and alarmingly fizzy, but Harry had grimaced through it anyway. 'Don't get many cows in China,' Carys had said apologetically. 'You grow accustomed to the soy milk in the end . . .'

The policemen guarding the Consulate were Indian Sikhs, bearded and broad-shouldered, with splendid red turbans wrapped around their heads. They nodded at Harry as he climbed the stone steps and walked past them into the lobby, Wilberforce tucked under one arm.

The room was oak-panelled, with potted palms in the corners and spinning fans on the ceiling, one of which was being operated by a young Chinese punkah-wallah, lying flat on his back with the cord tied around his big toe. Harry

119

stared at the youth in amazement, then approached the front desk, where a weak-chinned clerk was filling in an appointments book.

'May I help you?' the clerk asked, without looking up.

'Harry Compton.' Harry cleared his throat and leant forward confidentially: 'I'm interested in making a journey inland.'

The clerk nodded. 'Take a seat and the attaché will be with you shortly.'

Harry made his way over to a pair of rattan chairs by the wall, and sank down into one, eyes drawn again to the supine punkah-wallah, still retracting his leg up and down in a grim silence.

A variety of newspapers and periodicals lay fanned out on a little table. Harry picked up a dog-eared copy of *Punch*, saw last year's date and opted instead for today's edition of the *North China Daily News*. 'JARDINE, MATHESON & CO. TO BAIL OUT SHANGHAI RACE CLUB!' the headline screamed. 'CHAMPIONS STAKES TO GO AHEAD AS PLANNED—'

'Mr Compton?'

Harry looked up to see a young man of about his own age with two islands of mousy hair on either side of his freckled pate. 'Charles Hargreaves,' the man said, seizing Harry's outstretched hand and shaking it warmly. 'Feel free to leave your luggage with Eliott,' he added, and Harry put down his case behind the front desk as the clerk continued with his work.

Charles Hargreaves's office had a writing table at one end, with a single bentwood chair positioned in front of it. Floor-to-ceiling bookcases lined the walls, stuffed with legal tomes and bound copies of what looked like business-registration documents. Behind the desk hung an etching of the Bund, alongside a small English landscape that reminded Harry of Sussex.

'I hope you're not looking for a veterinary practitioner,' Hargreaves said, gesturing towards Wilberforce as Harry sat down. 'If so, you've come to the wrong place!'

Harry glanced at the dog and smiled. 'He travelled with me from England.'

'Dicey time of year to make the crossing,' Hargreaves said.

'It had its moments — we nearly went down in the Strait of Formosa.' Harry felt himself starting to sweat again, and was suddenly glad to be sitting down. He looked up to see Hargreaves's bright, bird-like eyes searching his face.

'Would you care for a glass of water, Mr Compton?' he asked, turning to the drinks cabinet. 'You look a little hot.'

'Thank you.'

Hargreaves poured Harry a glass from a porcelain jug and handed it over. 'It's been unseasonably warm this week.'

Harry gulped down the water, then looked at the glass in his hand.

'Tastes like seltzer, doesn't it?' Hargreaves chuckled. 'Comes up that way from the well. Good for the constitution, I'm told.' He sat down at his desk. 'So, you're after a roll?'

'A roll?'

Hargreaves's lips twitched. 'Travel documents here are so lengthy we have to roll 'em up. Hence the name.' He took in Harry's puzzled expression. 'It's all down to the Treaty of Tientsin. Highly convoluted, or "as confused as tangled silk", as the locals have it. Two thousand years of bureaucracy, and counting. Now' — Hargreaves uncapped a gold-nibbed fountain pen — 'where is it that you would like to travel? Another of our treaty ports? Or Hongkong Island, perhaps?'

Harry took from his pocket the piece of paper on to which he'd copied out a name from Darke's map, and handed it to Hargreaves.

'Hunan province?' Hargreaves said, then looked up in wary surprise. 'But I'm afraid that's quite a different matter.'

'Why?'

'It's a question of distance, Mr Compton. Under Article IX of the Treaty, British subjects can travel a hundred *li*, or thirty miles, from a treaty port. But further than that, and things become more . . . complicated.' Hargreaves's smile was a little cooler now. 'You don't know much about the Middle Kingdom, do you, Mr Compton? Where did you say you were from?'

'I didn't,' Harry replied, feeling a bead of sweat roll down the side of his face and catch in the bristles of his beard. 'I travelled from London.'

'But that's not a London accent, is it?'

Harry swallowed. 'I was born on the South Downs.'

'Lovely part of the world. Bluebell woods. Nightingales . . .' Hargreaves looked nostalgic for a moment. 'Did you school there?'

Harry gave an impatient nod.

'Where was that — Downside?'

'That's right,' Harry lied, eager to move the subject along. 'But surely you're not saying it's impossible to get to Hunan? I've come all this way!'

Hargreaves gave Harry a hard stare, and he could suddenly see how such a young man had advanced so quickly to the

122

position of attaché. 'Not *im*possible, Mr Compton, but extremely problematical. One needs a gunboat escort to travel down the Yangtze these days, what with all the pirates about. Then you'd need written permission from the Taotai of Shanghai to go beyond Hankow, and he's none too keen on countersigning passports at the moment, I can tell you.'

'The Taotai?' Harry echoed.

'The chief mandarin here. Or circuit intendant. Then you'd have at least a week's journey through bandit country, and that's before you've even reached the foothills of the Hunan mountains . . .'

Harry mopped his brow with his handkerchief, feeling Hargreaves's enquiring eyes fixed upon him.

'What exactly is the purpose of your journey?' the attaché asked.

'Exploration.'

'Hunan's *been* explored, Mr Compton,' Hargreaves said. 'By explorers who ended up with their heads stuck on pikes. The local population can be rather, shall we say, hostile to outsiders. Especially Europeans.'

Harry was beginning to feel a little dizzy now. Seeing Hargreaves's face start to swim and multiply before his eyes, he blinked to clear his vision.

'Then there's the matter of legal jurisdiction,' Hargreaves went on. 'Were you to run into trouble here, or in any other of the treaty ports, you would find yourself subject to British law. But deeper in the interior of China . . .' He broke off. 'Do you know anyone in Shanghai?' Harry heard him ask.

'I've a cousin here. Or my mother does. Did . . .'

'And who might that be?'

'Mr Lockhart.'

'*Narcissus* Lockhart?' Hargreaves looked away. 'You'd better wait here, sir,' he said, before disappearing through a door at the back of the office.

Harry rubbed a hand across the back of his slick neck, suddenly afraid that he might be sick. He *was* going to be sick – scrambling to his feet, he scooped up Wilberforce and staggered out of the office, pausing in the lobby only to grab his valise from behind the desk, before careering out on to the Bund.

The sun was blazing now, but Harry's teeth were chattering. He stumbled up the esplanade, finding himself standing next to a redbrick Anglican cathedral, built in the Gothic style by 'Designer: Mr Gilbert Scott' – or so the sign said, its ornate black lettering quivering before his eyes. The tide was in, Harry saw as he turned away, and the waters of the Whangpu were clogged with junks and sampans; with French and British mailboats; with floating market stalls selling starfruit and white cabbage. He searched for the tall masts of the *Redemption*, but saw no sign.

Sucking in the air, Harry felt his nausea slowly start to ease. Should he turn around and go back to the Consulate? But what was the point? Charles Hargreaves had made clear how hopeless his plans were. Harry should have heeded his father's advice. Sought help from his mother's cousin.

A few yards away, beneath a sign urging people to open accounts at the new Hongkong and Shanghai Banking Corporation, Harry sank down on to a bench and reached into his bag for the letter of introduction. '*Mr Narcissus Lockhart,*' he read in his father's crabbed hand. '*Celestial Heights, Thibet Road, Shanghae.*'

Thibet Road . . . Harry was sure he'd seen that earlier – and not too far from here! He looked back down at the letter in his trembling hands. He'd not wanted to use it, but now, it seemed, he had no choice. Gingerly, he got to his feet and set off back through the streets behind the Bund, Wilberforce at his heel.

On the corner of Nanking Road, Harry paused to let a procession go past, a long line of men in tatty robes, each gripping the shoulder of the man in front. Street urchins were shaking copper pots around them, and Harry realised that these men were blind, their eyes cloudy and glazed.

As the procession snaked away, Harry blundered onwards, feeling a headache start up behind his eyes, sharp and percussive. There was the racecourse again, two geldings practising in the gallops, one as pale as the mare he'd ridden to Petworth Station on the day his father had died. Circumventing the grandstand, Harry found himself outside the entrance to Bubbling Well Road, and glanced unreflectingly up at the guesthouse. Reclining on the second-floor balcony sat Mr Dancer, still smoking his pipe. Dancer raised a languid hand and waved, and Harry turned away and walked rapidly on to the next road, the verges of which were newly planted with willow and plane trees.

And then there it was – a fingerpost saying 'Thibet Road'! Harry was going to come through this after all. Surely Narcissus Lockhart would have some fresh water at his house – not that bubbling stuff that Harry could still taste at the back of his throat, bitter as bile.

There were a number of good-sized houses on Thibet road – 'Pagoda View', 'Dragon Villa' – each with a wide expanse of lawn outside. After a hundred yards, Harry still hadn't found his cousin's residence, and was just beginning to lose hope when he saw the largest property so far, surrounded by a high white picket fence.

The fence lowered into a gate, with a sign fixed to the upper bars reading 'Celestial Heights'. Harry peered over the top. The house was faced with yellow-painted, horizontal boards, with curved red tiles covering the roof. Five windows across, three up, a decked verandah on the outside – a graceful villa, modern in style, but elegant.

Harry unlatched the gate and weaved his way up the stone-flagged path, eyes widening as he took in the planting on either side – azaleas, daphnes, clematises. Suddenly, he was back in the stovehouse, with Josiah Piggott bearing down on him. That crook, Old Pie-Gut – that fraudster, that murderous bastard . . . Harry stopped, clutching at his brow. He needed to sit down, he realised, suddenly aware that he was not at all well, but he made himself stagger on, up the steps to the front door, where he raised a heavy arm and banged twice with the pomegranate-shaped knocker.

A few moments later, a tall Chinese man wearing a blue silk robe and black skullcap opened the door.

'I'm here to see Mr Lockhart,' Harry said.

The man glanced at Harry's clammy face, then down at the dog at his heel, and frowned.

'Narcissus Lockhart!' Harry repeated.

'The Mistah is dead,' the man replied, placing one hand on his heart, the nails on each finger two-inches long, shiny and well-buffed.

Harry opened his mouth to speak, but the man merely gave a swift bow, then closed the door in his face.

Harry remained on the verandah, scratching absent-mindedly at the bites on his wrist. Then he turned and made his way down the garden path. At the gate, he looked back and saw a lone figure standing silhouetted at a first-floor window. Harry made out a long black dress, a half-veil covering her eyes and hair. Then, before he could change his mind, he set off back to the house and knocked again on the door. It opened more quickly this time.

'How about a *Mrs* Lockhart?' Harry asked, as the Chinese man glowered at him in irritation. 'May I speak to her?'

The man was about to close the door again, but Harry wedged a muddy brogue into the doorway. 'My name's Harry Compton,' he called over the man's shoulder. 'My mother was Ada Compton, Narcissus Lockhart's cousin . . .'

There were footsteps on the staircase now, quick and light. Harry held out his letter of introduction, and saw it spiral out of his grip. Then the world was spinning like the letter, and Harry felt himself falling, first to his knees, then on to his back, and now he was staring up at the Chinese man with his long fingernails, and the woman in black, and he saw a flash of alabaster skin beneath her crape veil as she leant over him, her breath like honey — like celandines on the coombes of Pulborough, Harry thought, as he closed his eyes and everything dimmed to black.

Chapter 10

Harry was talking to his mother. 'Why d'you have to leave me, Ma?' he was pleading, his Sussex accent thicker than ever.

'Hush,' came her voice. 'The fever will break soon. But you must sleep . . .'

Then his father was in the room. 'I *have* got pluck,' Harry insisted. 'You see? I did what you said, Pa! Came looking for the tree . . .' Harry tried to hold on to the map, but it kept slipping out of his grasp, the names swirling and blurring, changing language as he stared at them. 'Hunan province,' he kept hearing. 'Bandit country . . .'

Now it was Frith standing before him, smiling his self-satisfied grin; then Piggott, marching across the stovehouse floor, gold-knobbed cane in hand — 'Pretty-boy like you, Compton! You're a salesman, not a bloody *plant hunter* . . .'

'Know your station,' Captain Buchanan counselled, before Scragge hoved into view, raising a thick finger to his lips as the shards of glass fell all around him. 'Watch your step in Shanghai, Harry . . .'

'Drink up,' came his mother's voice. 'Oh dear . . . Aki? *Aki!*'

Now he was with Jack Turner at the growing grounds, a skein of geese cutting through the sky, beating their strong wings as they disappeared up the Thames.

'Aki — fetch Dr Rathbone!'

Then darkness again, furry and bilious . . .

'Mr Compton?'

Harry snapped open his eyes. His irises were covered in a sticky film. 'Have I overslept, Mrs Pincham?'

'It's Mrs *Lockhart*,' came the voice. 'Your fever's broken.'

Harry blinked again, and as he glanced about him in confusion, his vision began to clear. He was lying in a high brass-framed bed, the walls around him hung with paper painted a cool, duck-egg blue. Hovering over his bed stood a tall woman with a pale freckled face and wavy auburn hair. The woman smiled down at him, and he gazed up into her piercing green eyes, and felt his chest tighten.

'You look much better, Mr Compton.'

'Where am I?' Harry whispered, and the woman's brow knitted with concern.

'You're at Celestial Heights, Mr Compton. And I'm Mrs Lockhart,' she repeated, resting a hand on the back of his; 'Clarissa Lockhart.'

Her palm felt smooth and dry and warm, and Harry laid his head back down on the soft pillows and closed his eyes. 'Where's Wilberforce? My dog . . .'

'Is that his name?' came her amused voice. 'Oh, he's doing famously. Eating us out of house and home. Now, you must rest, Mr Compton.'

Through heavy lids, Harry saw the woman glide out of the room, her elegant figure sheathed in a long black dress. Black dress, black veil, Harry thought, struggling to remember . . . His mind fumbled for some kind of meaning, but the effort was too great, and soon he was asleep again.

* * *

'I have some breakfast for you, Mr Compton.'

Harry opened his eyes to find the auburn-haired woman standing by his bed again, as a slight Chinese youth lowered a wooden tray on to his sheets.

'Do you think you can manage to sit up?' the woman asked.

Harry found that he could. The bedhead was upholstered with soft quilted cotton, and he rested his aching skull against it.

'Thank you, Aki,' the woman said.

The youth nodded and turned away.

'Will you try and eat something, Mr Compton?' the woman asked.

He looked down at the tray, at a pretty porcelain plate crisscrossed with crisp rashers of bacon.

'It's rather good, in fact. Bacon's one thing Shanghai does very well.'

Shanghai, Harry thought, as he reached for a rasher of bacon and brought it to his mouth. The clipper, the guest-house, that strange interview at the British Consulate . . . The woman was watching him closely now, he saw. She had fine, delicate features, but there were dark circles like bruises beneath her green eyes.

'You're Narcissus Lockhart's wife?'

The woman looked away. 'His widow.'

'How long have I been here?'

'Twelve days. You slept all through the Tomb-Sweeping Festival. Every firecracker, cymbal and tom-tom.'

'Tomb sweeping?' Harry echoed.

'The day the Chinese commemorate their dead. Here.' She speared up one of the rashers and passed him the silver fork.

'That's it,' she said, as he took a first tentative bite, the salty, unctuous taste repelling him at first, before he found his jaws chewing of their own accord, his palate alive with the taste.

'Slowly, Mr Compton,' the woman smiled, as he went back for another rasher.

'It's Harry.'

'Slowly, Mr Harry Compton.'

Harry reached for the cup of water, took a sip then spat the bitter liquid back into the cup in disgust. 'What are you doing – trying to poison me?'

The woman laughed. 'That's Dr Rathbone's special tonic. He calls it his "Fever-tree Wine". The best remedy in the world against malaria.'

'Malaria?' Harry repeated, giving the woman a look of such horror that she rolled her eyes.

'Don't worry, Mr Compton. You're not going to die. Not in my house, anyway. Now get on and finish your breakfast.'

She was wearing the same black bombazine dress, Harry saw as she walked away, but today her auburn hair was tied back into a low chignon, showing off her oval-shaped face. 'I'll send Aki in for the tray,' she called over her shoulder as she pulled the door shut.

Two days later, Dr Rathbone came to consult.

'It is just as I expected, Mrs Lockhart,' the doctor declared in his nasal voice, pinching Harry's wrist as he counted down his pulse. 'Starved of the marshy air of the docklands, the fever has abated.' The doctor raised one forefinger. 'But we must err on the side of caution. The patient is to rest and continue with my tincture for another week.'

'Are you sure that's necessary, Doctor?' Harry asked, looking from the man's stern, bespectacled face to Mrs Lockhart's, suddenly feeling like an interloper.

The physician glared at Harry down his pink-tipped nose. 'Entirely, Mr Compton.' Then he picked up his bag and took Clarissa Lockhart's arm. 'Now, let us return to the matter of your *own* health, my dear Mrs Lockhart . . .'

Widow and doctor repaired to the door, and Harry sat up, feeling well enough this morning to take in his lodgings properly. He saw his old valise in the corner, with Mr Dancer's fishing hook still wedged in the seam. There were his clothes, folded in a pile on the footstool. There was his vasculum, laid out on the dresser, with his honeypot of Cape Province seeds alongside . . . but where was his frockcoat? Harry felt a sudden rush of panic, then saw it neatly draped over the back of the dressing-table chair.

'I rest very well in the afternoon,' Mrs Lockhart was saying as she opened the door. 'It's only at night that sleep eludes me . . .'

Suddenly, from the landing, there came the clumsy clatter of claws, and a blur of white and tan hurled itself on to the bed and began licking Harry's face.

'Get that mangy animal out of here!' the doctor snapped.

'You naughty thing!' Mrs Lockhart scolded. But as she lifted Wilberforce away, the dog began to lick her face too, much to Harry's surprise.

'I'll take my leave, I think, Mrs Lockhart,' the doctor said, florid face bristling with disapproval as he swept out of the room. 'Good day to you!'

'Oh dear,' Mrs Lockhart said, cheeks colouring. 'Aki?'

The servant reappeared and firmly carried Wilberforce away, the dog's docked tail wagging madly.

'We've been keeping him in the scullery,' Mrs Lockhart said, sitting down on the edge of Harry's bed. 'He must have slipped his moorings.'

'He seems remarkably hale.'

'We've put him on reduced rations,' she said with a half-smile, and Harry felt that same, small contraction of his heart. 'So you're Ada Serocold's boy?' Clarissa asked.

'Ada Compton,' Harry corrected, then moderated his tone, 'You read the letter, then?'

Clarissa nodded. 'And Aki found this amongst your things.' She reached over to the bedside table and picked up the tiny daguerreotype that Harry had removed from his mother's locket. 'My husband kept a copy of the image on his desk,' Clarissa said with a sad smile. 'He was very fond of his cousin.'

Mrs Lockhart got up and shook out her skirts. 'You said some rather strange things, you know. At the height of your fever.'

'Did I?' Harry asked, unable to keep the unease from his voice.

'About a map. And something called an "icicle tree" . . .'

'Mere ramblings,' Harry said. 'I'm just here to find work as a trader. Same as every other young Englishman.'

Mrs Lockhart stared at Harry for a moment, then moved towards the door. 'You should rest, Mr Compton.'

'Thank you,' Harry called after her.

She turned, eyebrows raised. 'For what?'

'For helping me.'

'You're part of the family,' Mrs Lockhart said, then closed the door.

As soon as her footsteps had faded, Harry forced himself out of bed and stumbled over to his frockcoat. He felt the crinkle of Lorcan Darke's map safe beneath the silk. Reassured, Harry crawled back into bed, and drifted off to sleep.

Chapter 11

Six days later, and Harry was walking unaided across the morning-room floor.

'Well done!' Clarissa Lockhart exclaimed, as he collapsed into an armchair by the window.

Taking a moment to catch his breath, Harry glanced about the room, thinking that if it weren't for the distant trilling of the crickets, he might almost have been in a Chelsea townhouse. The dark dado panelling on the walls, the throws and silk cushions scattered over the divan, the stuffed barn owl glaring at him resentfully through its glass case – all were in keeping with the latest London fashions. Silhouettes and engravings clustered on the walls, curtains hanging in thick, elegant swags from the brass rails – cloistered in such a room, Harry thought, a man might almost forget he was in China.

Next to the door, Harry saw an easel draped in a dust-sheet, with a block of dry paints on the table beside it. 'Is the easel yours?' he asked, hoping he wouldn't discover that it had belonged to her late husband, and thereby cause her pain. Narcissus Lockhart had died only three months previously, Harry had learnt, leaving behind a childless young widow, and a burgeoning *hong* that he'd built from nothing into a thriving concern. The man had already been ill when

Clarissa had joined him from England four years ago, suffering from some strange, tropical malady that he'd relied on traditional Chinese medicine to cure.

'It is,' Clarissa said.

'Perhaps I might see one of your paintings?'

'They're not much to look at, I'm afraid. It's just a hobby I took up to pass the time.' She bit her lower lip and turned away. 'I found I had rather a lot of it on my hands, you see, with my husband dedicating so much time to his work.'

'I should like to see them nonetheless,' Harry said.

Clarissa stared at Harry for a moment, then turned and lifted the dustsheet from the easel. Her lower arms were bare, and the skin there was as finely speckled as a pheasant's egg.

'See,' Clarissa said testily, as she stepped back to reveal her work. 'I told you.'

The picture was a watercolour, but the colours she'd used were rich and vivid, the paintstrokes confident and bold. Harry had expected the subject to be of some bucolic English scene she'd painted from memory, but found instead an exotic and beautifully rendered Chinese pagoda. He sat up. 'But I've seen that before. It's by the racetrack, isn't it?'

Clarissa nodded, shaking out the dustsheet in order to re-cover the painting.

'Don't!' Harry exclaimed, and she turned in surprise. 'It brightens the room so,' he added, feeling his cheeks start to warm.

'Narcissus didn't approve of my Chinese scenes,' Clarissa said. 'He wished for his house to be an oasis of Englishness.' She snuck a wary look at Harry's face. 'Shanghai can be so frantic, you see. He wanted to escape all that when he came home.'

136

The doorbell rang, and Clarissa glanced at her reflection in the mirror, muttering crossly, 'But who on earth can that be?'

'Is Mrs Lockhart at home?' Harry heard a clipped English voice ask in the hallway. A voice that seemed somehow familiar.

A moment later, Aki appeared to announce the arrival of Mr Charles Hargreaves.

Hargreaves, Harry thought. The attaché from the Consulate.

'I'll receive him in my parlour,' Mrs Lockhart said, then hurried from the room, closing the door so firmly behind her that it made Harry wonder if she was eager to conceal his presence. Not that he could blame her, he supposed. Such a poor relation could hardly be considered a social boon.

Outside, Harry heard Hargreaves's brisk footsteps clicking on the hallway tiles. 'Mrs Lockhart, how are you?' he called out, voice dripping with a solicitude that Harry found strangely vexing. Creeping up to the door, Harry inched it open just in time to see the attaché's prematurely balding pate disappear into the parlour.

All was quiet again, so Harry took the opportunity to examine Clarissa's watercolour more closely, admiring the plump, gilded Buddhas standing guard outside the pagoda; the rows of grimacing, fantastical beasts carved on the roof gables. The woman had talent, Harry decided, his mind wandering back, unbidden, to the delicate, freckled skin of her arms . . . He checked himself. It was high time he left this house. The days were slipping away and he'd achieved nothing!

There was a sudden knock at the morning-room door. 'Mr Compton?'

Harry only just had time to step back from the painting before the door opened.

'Mr Hargreaves is here. From the consular service,' Clarissa said in a low voice. Then she moved aside, and Harry saw Charles Hargreaves standing behind her.

'We've been a little concerned about you, Mr Compton,' Hargreaves said as he strode into the room, tossing his hat on to the chaise longue as if he owned the place. 'I tried to come before, but you were not up to receiving visitors.' He looked Harry up and down. 'You're feeling better now, I understand?'

Harry nodded.

'And how's that pet dog of yours?'

'Thriving.'

'Excellent,' Hargreaves said. 'Well, I just wanted to check that you were all right. We were somewhat alarmed by your sudden departure.'

'I was not myself,' Harry replied bluntly. 'A touch of malaria.'

'It *is* a blight,' the attaché said, gazing at him sympathetically. Then he rallied with a bright smile. 'Still, you must come and see us again when you feel up to it. I do love an Old Gregorian.'

Harry looked at him blankly.

'An old boy from Downside,' Hargreaves said, and Harry suddenly remembered their garbled conversation at the Consulate. Downside probably wasn't on the South Downs at all, he realised, wondering why he'd felt the need to lie.

'Well, I must be off,' Hargreaves said, picking up his hat.

'Charlie's the busiest man in Shanghai,' Clarissa put in. 'He's just joined the Volunteer Fire Service. Whenever there's a conflagration, the church bells ring, and poor Charlie must don his helmet and run off to find the horse truck!'

'It *can* be rather inconvenient,' Hargreaves confided. 'I was at a dance at the Shanghai Club the other night, and was forced to abandon my waltzing partner.'

Clarissa chuckled, then led Hargreaves out into the hallway, where Harry heard them conversing in hushed tones as she showed him to the door.

Harry was resting in the armchair again when Clarissa returned to the morning-room. She looked at him for a moment, her green eyes grave, clouded with something like suspicion. 'I think it's time that you told me the truth, Mr Compton,' she said. 'About why you're really here.'

Harry felt his sense of alarm deepen. 'Why? What did Hargreaves say about me?'

'Just that you'd come to the Consulate hoping to travel inland.' Clarissa narrowed her eyes: 'To find your icicle tree, I suspect.'

Harry swallowed. 'Did you tell him about the tree?'

'Should I have?' Clarissa replied.

Harry looked down at the floor, then made a snap decision. In his delirium, he'd revealed half the truth to Clarissa already, so she might as well have the whole of it. 'May we speak in confidence, Mrs Lockhart?' he asked.

Clarissa opened the door. 'Aki?' she called into the hallway. 'Some tea, if you please.'

An hour later, Harry folded up Lorcan Darke's map, then sat back in his chair. He'd told Clarissa everything, barely pausing for breath, and felt as if a great weight had lifted from his shoulders. A weight which seemed to have fallen upon Mrs Lockhart's slender frame, he realised with a pang of regret, taking in her worried face, the lower lip pinched between her sharp white teeth.

'But leaving England like that,' she said. 'With your father's murderer still at large! It makes it seem like you were running away.'

'Well, I *was!*' Harry shot back. 'Decimus Frith killed my father, and would have killed me too if he'd had his way.' Getting to his feet, Harry began to pace the morning-room. 'I don't think you quite appreciate how valuable the icicle tree is, Mrs Lockhart. My former employer will stop at nothing to get his hands on it.' Harry paused to steady his breathing. Perhaps it had been a mistake to tell Mrs Lockhart, after all. 'Listen,' he said. 'I'm not like you, or my mother for that matter. I have neither money nor rank. If I'd gone to the police and told them what had happened, it would have been my word against Frith's. Who do you think they would have believed?'

Clarissa considered this, and her expression softened.

'I'll make it right in the end,' Harry went on, 'but first I have to find the icicle tree. Then I can return to England a rich man. Someone the police will listen to.' Harry looked away. 'Someone my father could have been proud of.'

Clarissa twisted a hand through a lock of hair that had fallen loose from her chignon. Her fingers were long and elegant, Harry saw, and he liked how she would twine the curls between them as she thought.

'People do take you more seriously if you have money,' she murmured. 'I'm starting to realise that now.'

140

Harry stared at her, wondering what she meant, but she offered no further explanation. 'First things first,' he resumed, 'I have to find a way to get myself to Hunan.'

'Charlie said you would have to petition the Taotai for papers to travel that far inland.'

'I suppose *Charlie* also mentioned that he'd be unlikely to grant them,' Harry replied tartly.

There was a pause, then Clarissa dropped her eyes, plucking at a loose thread in her skirt. 'I could speak to Lam Dookay about it, if you like.'

'Is he the Taotai?'

'The Taotai!' Clarissa repeated. 'Goodness no. Lam Dookay is my comprador.'

Harry stared back at her uncomprehendingly.

'He runs my late husband's business,' Clarissa explained. 'Comprador means "buyer" in Portuguese.'

'The Taotai's from Portugal?' Harry asked irritably, starting to resent always feeling at a disadvantage in this place.

Clarissa laughed. 'The role of comprador originated in Macao, which has been a Portuguese possession for centuries. Nowadays, they're an essential component of every decent trading house in Shanghai. They manage relations with the local Chinese, arrange for export licences, settle bills, pay taxes, change currencies . . .' She canted her head. 'But you've met Lam Dookay before.'

'I have?'

'He was at the house when you first arrived.'

Harry squinted, struggling to remember the events of that strange evening. Of course, the man who'd opened the door to him – then slammed it in his face. 'The man with the talons?' he asked.

Clarissa laughed again. 'The nails are an expression of his status. They show that he's not obliged to do manual work. Lam Dookay knows all the mandarins in Shanghai. I'm sure he could find a way to influence the Taotai.'

'So you'd arrange for me to speak with him? This Lam Dookay?'

'I'll take you to the godown, if you like.'

'The what?'

'Sorry, I keep forgetting how little you know!'

Harry glared at her, and she suppressed a smile.

'The godown is our warehouse, Mr Compton. The word is derived from the old Malay – *gudang*.' She paused. 'It's about time I made an inspection of the place, now I'm sole proprietor of the company.' The thought seemed to cheer her a little, and Harry realised how bored and isolated she must have become during her period of mourning – three months was expected of a woman of her standing.

'Very well,' Clarissa said, rising to her feet. 'I'll have Zhang ready the carriage for tomorrow.'

Chapter 12

The next day, Harry sat next to Clarissa in the back of the brougham as they clopped through the outskirts of Shanghai. She'd instructed her *mafu*, or driver — an ever-smiling youth named Zhang — to avoid the busiest streets, but progress was still slow, delayed as they were by the innumerable water-carriers and donkey carts trundling around them.

Clarissa had been in a buoyant mood when they'd set off, enjoying pointing out to Harry the various landmarks of Shanghai, but as they'd crossed the stone bridge over Soochow Creek, she'd grown more subdued. Perhaps she was remembering her husband Narcissus, Harry thought, and missing him terribly.

At last, they turned on to the service road that ran beside the waterfront, where a row of iron railings delineated each section controlled by a particular *hong*. Harry saw names that he recognised now: Jardine, Matheson & Co.; Butter-field & Swire; David Sassoon & Sons . . . Standing outside the gates were red-coated British soldiers in white helmets, with rifles slung across their backs.

'I thought the Opium Wars were over,' Harry said.

'They are,' Clarissa replied, 'and we won. With a little help from the French, of course. But . . .' She hesitated.

'But what?'

'The Chinese are still forced to pay reparations. They owe four million taels of silver to Britain, and two million to France.'

Quite the deal the British and French had cut, Harry thought. Carving out lucrative concessions for themselves in China – and making the Chinese pay for the 'privilege'.

'But I shouldn't be giving you lessons on Chinese history,' Clarissa went on. 'I know very little.'

'Compared to me, Mrs Lockhart,' Harry said, 'you're a veritable sinologist!'

'Then we both have a great deal to learn, Mr Compton,' Clarissa replied, in a cool voice that told him she wasn't a woman much impressed by flattery.

Lockhart & Co. occupied a smaller section of wharf than its more illustrious rivals, and its fencing was of bamboo instead of iron, the tops whittled into vicious-looking spikes. The guards at the gates were Chinese rather than British, dressed in heavy black coats, with cutlasses at their sides. As soon as they recognised Zhang, they rolled back the fencing so that he could lead the pony by the bridle into the rear courtyard.

Zhang opened the carriage door and offered his hand to help Clarissa descend, which she duly did, hesitating for a moment before placing one neat, laced boot in the mud.

'Sorry, Missy,' Zhang said, but Clarissa waved his apology away and called up to Harry, 'Come on, Mr Compton – we have much to do.'

As Harry jumped down next to her, he saw a tall thin man walking towards them, dressed in blue silk robes decorated with dragons disporting themselves amongst acacia trees. The crown of his head was topped by a black cap, like a hanging judge preparing to pass sentence, whilst his hands were clasped in front of him, ten long nails buffed to a high shine. 'Mrs Lockhart,' the comprador said in a lilting, Shanghainese accent. 'And what a pleasure to see you again, Mr Compton.'

'Likewise,' Harry replied.

The comprador held Harry's gaze for just a moment, then turned to Clarissa. 'You wish to take a tour of the premises, I believe?'

Clarissa nodded. 'And there's also a certain matter I wish to discuss with you, Lam Dookay.'

A shadow of unease flickered down the comprador's long face, but almost immediately his features became placid again. He held out an arm: 'This way.'

The 'godown' turned out to be a huge redbrick barn, with a pitched slate roof and a row of barred windows set just below the guttering. Cut into the rear gates was a smaller door, which Lam Dookay held open as Clarissa and Harry walked inside and looked around.

Piled up inside was tower upon tower of varnished wooden crates. Built against one side were a couple of offices, their walls created from reed matting stretched on to bamboo frames, whilst at the back another set of gates opened on to a pontoon running horizontal to the rear of the building. A wooden pier extended from the pontoon, at the end of which was moored a cargo ship, broad-hulled and sea-worn. A human chain of stevedores were busy unloading chests from its hold, heaping them into piles at the feet of a small group of Chinese officials.

'The new shipment arrived this morning,' Lam Dookay said, as they proceeded through the godown.

'And the quality?' Clarissa asked.

'The situation is even worse than before,' the comprador replied in a low voice, then barked out an order in Chinese. Moments later, a stevedore arrived with one of the shiny mango-wood chests, and began prising off the lid with a crowbar. Stacked inside, Harry saw layers of what looked like miniature black cannonballs, each separated by a sheet of wax paper. He thought back to the wax-paper pouches that had held his herbarium samples, and wondered if the opium and exotic-plant trades might have more in common than he'd imagined.

'Where does the opium come from?' Harry asked.

'Bengal,' Clarissa replied. 'All the best poppies grow there.' She gave a wistful smile. 'That was my husband's piece of good fortune. He had a childhood friend out in India, a Mr Jonathan Maitland, whose family were tea-planters. Narcissus persuaded Jonny to switch to poppy-growing, and the two of them struck an agreement. One would grow and process the opium in India, and the other would import and sell it in China. Look,' she said, and Harry turned to see Lam Dookay using a penknife to gouge lumps out of a number of the little black balls. Then he lit a kerosene burner, placed the pieces of opium into a copper ladle and began to heat them over the flame. As ever, the sweet, heady smoke made Harry's stomach keel.

'My husband loved the smell,' Clarissa said softly. '*Drowsed with the fume of poppies . . .*'

'*While thy hook spares the next swath and all its twinèd flowers*,' Harry completed.

'Yes!' Clarissa exclaimed, unable to mask the surprise in her eyes.

'My mother had a fondness for poetry,' Harry said, a little piqued by the strength of Clarissa's astonishment.

Returning his attention to the comprador, Harry watched as he passed the melted opium through a cone of filter paper into a basin. Once the brown liquid had all run through, Lam Dookay examined the residue of black granules left in the filter paper, then tossed it aside in disgust. 'It is as I thought. This is *man-ling*, not *malwa*,' he said with a grim shake of the head, then marched over to speak to an Indian man sitting on his heels by the open door, chewing betel nuts.

Harry looked back at Clarissa, recognising the same worried look on her face he'd seen the day before. 'What is it?'

'The company's in trouble,' Clarissa replied quietly. 'Since Narcissus passed on, Mr Maitland is no longer inclined to do business with Lockhart's. And our new suppliers,' she added, gesturing disparagingly at the opium, 'offer us inferior merchandise at a superior price . . .' She broke off as Lam Dookay walked back towards them. 'Surely there are other suppliers?' she asked the comprador.

'The best suppliers require a substantial downpayment, Mrs Lockhart,' Lam Dookay replied. 'Capital that we do not have. And given that we are being taxed now at thirty taels per picul, it's scarcely worth going to market with opium of this calibre.' He shook his head. 'We shall struggle to cover our costs.'

'Perhaps we can discuss this further after the tour?' Clarissa said.

Lam Dookay bowed, somewhat chastened, then led them outside on to the pontoon. Harry saw now that there were similar piers lined up all the way down the quayside, with boats loading and unloading everywhere. There must be hundreds of tonnes of opium coming into Shanghai each week, he calculated, finding himself thinking of Lorcan Darke's raddled corpse, and wondering if Clarissa ever felt a twinge of conscience at being involved in such a trade. But the grocers' shops of London were piled high with bottles of laudanum and other opium-enriched potions, he reminded himself, sold as miracle cures against insomnia, dysentery, melancholy – even earache.

Feeling a hand on his sleeve, Harry turned to see Clarissa pointing to a smaller cargo ship moored at the jetty closest to the godown. 'That's the *Kwai-Lun*,' she said. 'Narcissus bought her during the Second Opium War, at a point when no one was sure if the opium trade would ever be made legal in China.' She smiled into the salt-kissed breeze. 'But Narcissus was a gambler! He believed that the Emperor would concede terms eventually, so he begged, borrowed and stole to buy the *Kwai-Lun*. And he was right! In 1860, the French and British invaded Peking and burnt down the Summer Palace. Soon after that, the war ended, and all Narcissus's grand plans fell into place.'

Clarissa's pride in her late husband's achievements was clear, though Harry still found himself questioning the morality of a trade that had required a war to render it legal. But then an intriguing notion struck him. 'Where does the *Kwai-Lun* sail?'

'All down the coast,' Clarissa replied. 'Up the Yangtze . . .'

'Your company owns a boat that sails up the Yangtze?' Harry said, barely managing to suppress the excitement in his voice.

Grasping Harry's meaning, Clarissa turned to Lam Dookay, finding him furiously reprimanding a stevedore. 'When is the *Kwai-Lun*'s next journey inland?' she called out.

'At the end of the month,' the comprador replied. 'She sails first to Chinkiang, then Nanking . . .'

'And Hankow?' Harry asked.

'Naturally,' Lam Dookay said.

'Well, that *is* interesting, isn't it, Mr Compton?' Clarissa said, raising an eyebrow at Harry in a way that made him wonder if she'd known all along that this seemingly fortuitous scenario would present itself. 'Mr Compton is eager to explore the interior of China,' she explained to Lam Dookay. 'He's something of a botanist, you see.'

At these words, the comprador's features softened, and Harry suddenly realised why the man had been treating him with such suspicion. He must have thought that Harry was here to assume control of the *hong*: a male relative of the Mistah's — was that the term Lam Dookay had used? — sent out from England to take the reins, or even to dissolve the company. It all made sense now: Lam Dookay had been in fear for his job.

'Now then, Lam Dookay,' Clarissa resumed. 'We have that little matter to discuss.'

Watching Lam Dookay remove a silver ingot from a safe at the back of his office, then set about determining its weight with a small pair of scales, Harry could see now why such men were known as 'buyers'.

'The same piece of silver is worth more in one part of China than the other,' Clarissa confided to Harry. 'It's very complicated.'

Taking out a handsaw, the comprador began to cut the ingot in two. That done, he weighed the two pieces on his scales, dropped the smaller into a satin bag, then scraped up the silver filings and set them aside. Then, standing up, he opened the door, and the Indian captain of the Bengali ship was ushered in.

Lam Dookay handed the captain the bag of silver, and he peered inside. A heated conversation ensued, which even Harry could tell was conducted in the captain's language. At length, the captain stormed out of the office – still carrying the bag, Harry noted – and the comprador turned to Clarissa with a smile. 'As the Mistah liked to say, "*Money is a good soldier, sir, and will on.*" Now, what was on your mind, Mrs Lockhart?' Lam Dookay asked, casting a glance at Harry. 'We can talk privately, if you wish?'

'No, no,' Clarissa said. 'This matter attaches to Mr Compton too. You may speak freely before him.' She lifted her crape veil over her bonnet, and Harry was struck once again by how lovely she was. 'I was wondering how familiar you were with the Taotai of Shanghai?' she asked.

'I know the Taotai very well,' Lam Dookay replied with an uncertain smile. 'We served together on an advisory board for the Imperial Customs Service.'

'How wonderful,' Clarissa said, throwing Harry a little glance of triumph. 'Well, in that case, I should like you to arrange a meeting between Mr Compton and the Taotai.'

Lam Dookay frowned. 'With what purpose?'

'Mr Compton is in need of travel documents.'

'That is one of the Taotai's responsibilities, I suppose, yes.'

'It is a matter of some urgency, sir,' Harry threw in. 'So when might we meet?'

150

Lam Dookay eyed Harry imperiously, then turned back to Clarissa. 'I believe that His Excellency is soon to host a function at his residence,' he said. 'It would not be impossible to arrange an invitation for the owner of Lockhart & Co., and her . . .' For once, the comprador's excellent English failed him.

'Cousin by marriage,' Clarissa supplied.

The comprador bowed to his mistress's superior grasp of such idiosyncrasies, and Clarissa stood up. 'Thank you, Lam Dookay. I'm much obliged to you for your help.'

The comprador escorted them back to the courtyard, where Zhang was waiting by the brougham, using a fly-whisk to keep the insects away from the pony's flanks.

'Now then, Mr Compton,' Clarissa said, once they were back inside the carriage. 'Perhaps, on our return to the house, we might discuss a little business matter of our own?'

Chapter 13

Clarissa's parlour was adjacent to the morning-room, one of the many airy, well-appointed rooms on the ground floor of Celestial Heights. A walnut ladies' writing desk stood in one corner, next to a set of French windows that gave on to a substantial, if sparsely planted, back garden.

Clarissa sat down at her bureau, then motioned to the carved oak chair next to it, its feet shaped like the paws of a lion. 'So, Mr Compton,' she began, and there was an edge to her voice now that Harry had never heard before. 'This icicle tree of yours – how much is it worth?'

Harry paused, a little taken aback by the young woman's candour. 'It's almost impossible to say, ma'am,' he replied, 'without seeing a live specimen of the plant. There are many factors to consider . . .'

'An educated guess, then,' Clarissa said, challenging him with a smile.

Harry looked at her in exasperation, then ran his hands through his hair. 'Well, I suppose that exclusive stock of such a tree could be worth in the region of . . .' He shook his head. 'A thousand pounds?'

Clarissa drew a sheet of paper towards her, then reached for a pen and dipped it into a porcelain inkpot decorated with pink peonies. *£1,000?*, Harry saw her write in an elegant hand. 'And what percentage would you part with in exchange for the use of my boat?' she asked.

'No more than five.'

Clarissa gave a snort of amusement. 'That's a little mean, isn't it, Mr Compton? Don't forget that even if you *could* find an alternative means of travelling down the Yangtze, you'd still need travel papers. And I wish you well in petitioning the Taotai without my help.'

'Ten per cent, then,' Harry said, unsure whether he liked this more mercenary version of Mrs Narcissus Lockhart.

£100, she wrote, then glanced up again. 'But of course it is I who shall be bearing all the risk, Mr Compton. Putting my vessel, my very livelihood, at your disposal. Surely the price should reflect that?'

Harry tried his best haggler's frown, but she just laughed. 'You may pout all you like, Mr Compton, but we both know there's no guarantee you'll ever find this tree. And if you don't, I shall be out of pocket.'

Harry clenched his fists. 'Your boat is due to travel down the Yangtze in any event! It is already arranged.'

'Ah, but *you* need to go further inland than the Yangtze. And such a journey would require a guide, porters, lodgings . . .' Clarissa put her head to one side and looked at him slyly. 'Have you the means for such an undertaking, Mr Compton?'

'Have you?' Harry fired back. 'I thought Lockhart's was in trouble?'

'Sometimes one has to spend money to make money, Mr Compton.'

Knowing he was beaten, Harry looked away. On the console table opposite sat a framed photograph, showing a tall, well-built man in a shooting jacket, breeches and leather boots, standing before a wall of dead gamebirds. Pheasants, partridge, grouse, quail — hundreds of them, tied together in pairs, hanging from a wooden rack. The man in the photograph had a proud look on his face, his fair hair swept back from his brow, his moustaches twisted into points, in the manner of Decimus Frith. In his left hand he held a bowler hat, and in his right the barrel of a twelve-bore shotgun, stock to the ground. Narcissus Lockhart had been a handsome man, Harry had to admit, though he was at least twenty years older than Clarissa. Yet there was something untrustworthy about his face. Perhaps it was those deep-set eyes, or the sneer on his lips that spoke of a certain amusement at the obscene quantity of game he'd managed to bag — Chinese game, judging by the exotic plumage of the pheasants. Had it been Narcissus Lockhart, Harry wondered, who had taught his young wife how to deal . . .

'Mr Compton?'

Harry looked back into Clarissa's cool eyes.

'I thought that twenty per cent of the thousand might be fair,' she said. 'Plus five per cent of anything you raise above that sum.'

'Two point five,' Harry snarled.

'Four per cent,' Clarissa said, her pink lips turning up at the corners. 'And that's my final offer.'

Harry stuck out a hand, and Clarissa reached out and shook it. She'd taken off her gloves to write; her palm was incredibly soft. Harry turned away before she noticed his cheeks start to colour.

'Narcissus allowed you a bit of China in here, at least,' he said, picking up the porcelain inkwell, keen to distract himself. It was clumsily made, but pleasing to the eye.

'That thing?' Clarissa asked, taking it from him and brushing a thumb across the uneven glaze. She smiled fondly. 'It was made for me by one of my girls.'

'Your girls?'

'I helped to found a reformatory for abandoned girls,' Clarissa said. 'In Zikawei, just outside Shanghai. The children learn dressmaking, weaving, pottery. Some go on to find a husband.' Clarissa shrugged. 'But if they don't, at least they have an honest trade.'

'I like it,' Harry said. 'Its flaws make it unique.'

Their eyes locked for a moment, then Clarissa turned away, putting the little inkwell back in its place. 'So,' she said briskly. 'We have a deal, Mr Compton!'

He grinned. 'We do, Mrs Lockhart.'

Picking up a decanter from its tray, she filled two sherry glasses to the brim, handed him one, then raised hers in a toast. 'To the icicle tree,' she said, green eyes sparkling with triumph.

Clarissa Lockhart drove a hard bargain, Harry thought, as he sipped his sherry. Good thing she didn't know how much their prize was really worth.

The next morning, Harry sat in the armchair of the morning-room, with the two maps of China that he'd found on the bookshelf spread out on the low table before him. He'd spent the last hour checking them against Lorcan Darke's, and was largely reassured by what he'd seen. So absorbed was he in his work that he hardly noticed when the door opened and Clarissa slipped into the room. She came up behind him and laid a hand on the wing of his armchair, startling him.

'Good morning,' Harry said, half-rising to his feet, a little embarrassed.

Clarissa gestured for him to stay seated, then craned over his shoulder at the maps. 'Planning your route?' she asked, so close that he could smell the ambergris in her scent.

Harry swallowed. 'Yes,' he said, tracing a line across one map for her with his finger. 'I'll need to travel down the Yangtze as far as Lake Dongting, then emerge via a different watercourse — the Yuan.'

'Looks like a long voyage. And then?'

'Then, once I've entered Hunan province, I'll continue on foot into the mountains.' He pointed to the cross on Lorcan Darke's map. 'And here, somewhere in the foothills, I hope to find the icicle tree.'

'May I?' Clarissa said, holding out a hand for Lorcan Darke's map.

Harry passed it over, realising that the only other person he'd shown it to was his father. She stared at it for a time, frowning at the word scrawled next to the cross that marked the location of their prize.

'I assumed that was the Chinese for "icicle tree",' Harry said.

Clarissa shook her head. 'I don't think those are Chinese characters.' She glanced up. 'Maybe it's some sort of dialect.'

'Maybe,' Harry said, giving Clarissa a tight, sidelong smile, unnerved to find himself so flustered by her presence.

This is ridiculous, he thought. The sooner he got on that boat the better.

Just then, the doorbell rang, and Clarissa moved away. Moments later, Aki entered. 'It's a local woman, ma'am,' he said quietly. 'It's the second time she's come.'

'Please excuse me, Mr Compton.'

'Of course,' Harry said, rising again as Clarissa hurried from the room.

As he was about to sit back down, Harry heard the sound of a baby crying. Curious to know more about Clarissa's mysterious guest, he went to the door. Opening it an inch, he saw a young Chinese woman in a cotton dress and tabard being ushered through the hallway. Swaddled in a shawl on her back was a squalling baby. Probably one of the girls from Clarissa's reformatory, Harry thought, as he quietly shut the door.

Returning to his maps, Harry found himself marvelling at the sheer scale of China — some three times the size of India. No wonder the Western powers were all so keen to make inroads into the country. The only mystery was why it had taken them so long.

An hour passed; two. Harry heard the front door open and clatter shut, but still Clarissa did not return. Growing a little concerned by her absence, he went to the door to call for Aki, and that was when he heard it — the sound of desperate sobbing. It couldn't be the baby, he thought, as he knew Clarissa's visitors had departed some time ago. It could only be Clarissa.

Harry paced up and down, running his fingers through his beard as he tried to decide what to do. Clarissa would hardly thank him for intruding on her grief, he told himself. They might be near-relations, but they were not so intimate as that! But it pained his heart to hear her cry . . . Then an idea struck him: Wilberforce! Harry would rescue the little dog from the scullery; ask Aki to bring him up to the parlour door. Surely Clarissa couldn't fail to be cheered by such an excitable ball of affection.

Harry was just moving towards the door again when it opened, and there was Clarissa herself, her eyes pink-rimmed, her face so forlorn that Harry was suffused by a sudden, irrational impulse to throw his arms around her. Instantly, he clasped his hands behind his back and bowed his head. 'You were gone so long, Mrs Lockhart, I had begun to worry. Is everything all right?'

'I have had some distressing news, Mr Compton,' she replied. 'But I am quite recovered now. Here,' she said, holding out a stiff rectangular card bordered with red. 'This arrived not long ago.'

Harry took the card from her. One half was marked with Chinese characters in vertical columns, the other had been translated into English.

'*His Excellency the Taotai of Shanghai requests Mrs Narcissus Lockhart and her Cousin to visit his* yamen *on April 2nd at 7 p.m.,*' Harry read aloud. '*Chinese Acrobats and Traditional Delicacies. A Thousand Prayers you do not refuse.*' He looked up into Mrs Lockhart's cloudy green eyes.

'Good old Lam Dookay,' she said, taking the invitation back and frowning at it. 'But that's this Thursday,' she added, looking down at her dress in despair. 'I'll need time to prepare.' Then she glanced up at Harry and narrowed her eyes. 'As will you, Mr Compton. That beard of yours is a disgrace. You look like a hermit!'

Clarissa gave a watery smile, and Harry looked away, a little self-conscious. But at least she wasn't crying, he thought. And they were going to a party.

Chapter 14

On the evening of the Taotai's party, Harry stood before the washstand in the bedroom, using the cut-throat razor that Aki had provided him. It was pleasingly sharp, though Harry was made uneasy by the initials engraved on its handle: N.A.C.L. – Narcissus A.C. Lockhart. He was shaving with a dead man's razor in his widow's house. He could imagine what Jack Turner would have said: 'You'll be in a dead man's shoes next, Harry!'

But he *was* wearing his own shoes, at least. All his clothes had now been cleaned for him by the household staff, but the miracle that Aki had performed with his frockcoat was especially impressive. It hadn't looked this bright since Decimus Frith had picked out the material.

His beard gone, Harry finished dressing, then slipped on his frockcoat, feeling the stitching a little tight around his upper arms. All that heavy work on the boat must have built up some muscle. There was no bear's-grease pomade to hand, so he dipped his fingers into the ewer and ran them through his hair. His reflection in the mirror was pleasing enough to sell a few pot plants, he thought wryly, though his mission this evening was rather different. Tonight, he had to persuade a high-ranking Chinese official to grant him a travel pass to inland China. Harry saw his lips flicker into a smile. It was preposterous how much his life had changed since his encounter with Lorcan Darke. Where it would end he did not know — but he would keep on pressing down this strange path until he found out.

'Mr Compton?' came Clarissa's voice from the hallway. 'Whatever's keeping you?'

Harry wiped a stray floret of lather from one earlobe, then picked up one of Narcissus Lockhart's top hats and headed downstairs. Seeing Clarissa waiting for him on the parquet floor, he stopped dead. She was wearing a black parramatta dress, the ruched collar of her white blouse revealing a tantalising glimpse of her pale, slender neck. Her auburn hair had been gathered at the sides, framing her heart-shaped face, the skin dusted with freckles, those green eyes sparkling in the lamplight.

Clarissa looked as surprised by his appearance as he was by hers. 'But you're so . . . young,' she said.

'I am twenty-two years of age, ma'am,' Harry replied with mock severity.

'But that's just two years younger than me!' she exclaimed.

When Harry said nothing, only continued to stare at her in admiration, Clarissa tossed her head. 'I suppose you think I look older. Well, the sun in Shanghai is hard on the skin.'

Before Harry could protest, Aki had appeared at the front door. 'Your carriage is ready, ma'am.'

'Come on, then,' Clarissa demanded. 'Time to introduce you to Shanghai society!'

The carriage was parked on the near side of Thibet Road. As they walked towards it, Harry became aware of chintz curtains twitching in the houses around them – with whom was the young widow stepping out so soon after her husband's death?

Clarissa followed Harry's gaze, and sniffed. 'If the Queen can go without a veil in mourning, I don't see why I shouldn't do the same.'

Harry gave her a wary glance. There was mischief in her manner tonight, he thought, a devil-may-care attitude. He knew he ought to be pleased that she'd regained her spirits, but there was something about her mood that unnerved him.

The *mafu*, Zhang, was waiting on the road, holding the bridle of the pony. The carriage itself was gleaming – it was clear the prospect of the Taotai's party had spurred everyone into a frenzy of activity.

'Good evening, Missy,' Zhang said, opening the door. 'And Mist–' he began, before checking himself.

Harry had assumed they would be travelling into the centre of Shanghai, but instead they headed west, along Bubbling Well Road. As they passed the guesthouse, he looked up and, sure enough, there on the first-floor balcony sat Mr Dancer – fast asleep. On the balcony below, Harry saw a young man glancing nervously about – no doubt the latest 'griffin' Dancer would be robbing with his fishing rod in due course.

The architecture of the houses changed the further down Bubbling Hill Road they drove. The European guesthouses and bungalows gave way to residences in the Chinese style, low and sprawling, with timber frames and upturned corners on the roofs. Then the carriage slowed to a more sedate pace, and Harry stuck his head through the window to find that they'd joined a long queue of landaus, victorias and dog-carts, all waiting to turn beneath a triumphal arch. Eventually, through a line of banyan trees, he saw the sort of building he'd never expected to find in Shanghai – a Tudor-style mansion complete with gabled roofs, dormer windows and stained black beams set into the white façade.

'The Taotai is an acknowledged Anglophile,' Clarissa said, eyeing the curiosity with rather scornful amusement. 'Perhaps his predilection will play in our favour.'

'Have you met him before?' Harry asked.

'Only once,' Clarissa said. 'At a production of *A Midsummer Night's Dream* in the Yuyuan Gardens. But he was only interested in speaking to Narcissus.'

She murmured something else – far too quietly for Harry to hear – as the carriage passed beneath the arch and trundled down the gravel drive which led to the Taotai's *yamen*. Other carriages, having disposed of their passengers, were parked on the lawn, and Harry caught the reek of fresh manure as their horses took a well-earned rest.

The Taotai's residence had a long porte-cochère extending from the front door, guarded by two snarling Chinese stone tigers, starkly at odds with the prevailing mock-Tudor theme. The carriage in front was releasing its cargo now, a blotchy-faced man in a morning coat and topper, and a woman in a crimson bustle dress, with a flounced lace hat pinned jauntily on to her strawberry-blonde curls. Greeting them was a troupe of men in puffed-sleeved costumes, two of whom were juggling – the promised Chinese acrobats, Harry presumed.

'Shall we?' Clarissa said.

Harry fixed on his hat, then jumped down from the carriage and offered Clarissa his hand, feeling the soft warmth of her breath on his face as he helped her descend. All at once, the acrobats leapt towards them. Their faces had been painted white, Harry saw as they drew closer, with dark rings around the eyes which lent them a faintly sinister air. '*Nong-ho!*' they chorused, twirling around and gesturing to the porte-cochère, at the end of which Harry could see two waiters standing still as caryatids, each bearing a silver tray.

Harry linked arms with Mrs Lockhart, and they advanced inside, each accepting a steaming flannel from one waiter, then a porcelain cup of clear liquor from the other. Rather than the usual entrance hall and suite of rooms, the ground floor of the *yamen* consisted of a single vast open space, with walls of sanded willow and reed mats laid out on the floor. A line of silk screens divided off a smaller section at the back, and Harry made out silhouettes flitting behind them.

There were thirty or so guests already inside, a mix of smartly dressed Shanghailanders and prosperous-looking Chinese merchants, impressive in their long, padded silk gowns. On one side of the room was a cushioned daybed, upon which a lone Chinese man reclined, cooled by a punkah-wallah languidly lowering and raising a peacock-feather fan. The Taotai – for Harry suspected it must be him – was short and fat, with swollen, fieldmouse cheeks and thin black moustaches. Draped around his neck was a necklace of pink coral and beads of polished wood, whilst over his head he wore a headpiece that reminded Harry of nothing so much as a straw lampshade tied with a red ribbon, his ample body wrapped in a shiny costume of green silk and white ermine. There was a long queue of Westerners waiting to petition him, and occasionally the Taotai would lean forward to let one whisper in his ear.

'Mrs Lockhart?' came a voice.

Harry turned to see Lam Dookay standing behind them. 'The Taotai prefers to conclude his business before the entertainment begins,' the comprador informed them quietly.

Clarissa nodded to Harry, and they stepped forward into the queue, which seemed to be composed entirely of brawny-necked gentlemen with bushy sideburns linked into their moustaches. Englishmen, Harry assumed.

'The Taotai is directing the construction of China's first railway line,' the comprador went on. 'From Shanghai to Woosung. He wishes for these men to share their expertise, while they wish to build their railroad without interference.' Lam Dookay smiled: 'A delicate balance to strike.'

Harry drank from his cup, then gave a sharp intake of breath that made Clarissa chuckle.

'It's called *jiu*,' she said, sinking the contents of hers without so much as a shudder. 'Distilled from rice.'

Evidently the temperance movement had gained little ground in Shanghai, Harry thought, wondering if it was wise for Clarissa to be drinking so freely in public. Another waiter swept by with a tray of quails' eggs. Harry took one and found it delicious – poached in sweetened tea, judging by the fragrant taste.

The railwayman in front took his turn with the Taotai. He began with an awkward bow, then launched into his pitch, a few snippets of which Harry caught above the hubbub:

'The Teesdale Railway Company is world-famous, sir, for opening up the most profitable of trade routes . . .'

The Taotai tossed a toasted watermelon seed into his mouth, his face a picture of boredom, and Harry looked away to see a beautiful Chinese girl peering around one of the silk screens, her dark hair secured at the nape of her neck with a pair of long jade pins.

'Concentrate, Harry,' Clarissa hissed, following his gaze, 'it's almost our turn.' Turning back, Harry saw the railwayman bow again and retreat, lantern jaw clenched in defeat, no doubt intending to find solace in the trays of his host's finest *jiu*.

Before Harry and Clarissa could present themselves, Lam Dookay stepped forward. He leant down to the Taotai, whispering into his ear from behind one long-nailed hand. Then the Taotai nodded, and Lam Dookay was gone, lost in the crowd.

'I believe I knew your husband, Mrs Lockhart,' the Taotai began, in an English superior even to Lam Dookay's. 'His death is a great loss to our city.' The Taotai scanned the room with a jaded eye, then added, 'We need more Westerners of his stamp.'

Clarissa made a curtsey, and Harry bowed. For a brief, baffling moment, Harry thought the Taotai was going to cry, but then he saw that his eyes had filled with tears through the effort of suppressing a yawn. 'Apologies for the regalia,' he said, tilting his head so that the punkah could fan the sweaty back of his neck. 'But you Britishers do like a bit of pageantry, don't you? Now,' he added in a perfunctory tone, 'I understand that your nephew seeks travel papers?'

166

Clarissa hesitated, no doubt debating whether or not to correct the Taotai as to Harry's familial status. She decided against it: 'Indeed, Your Excellency.'

'Where does he seek to travel?'

'Hunan province, Your Excellency,' Clarissa replied.

'For what purpose?'

'Exploration,' Harry put in, feeling his cheeks start to burn.

The Taotai had long black eyelashes, like a calf's. He blinked them twice at Harry. 'I do hope you're not going to tell me you're a *plant hunter*, Mr Compton,' he said, dropping his eyes to examine his fingernails. 'I once granted permission to an Irish plant hunter to travel to Hunan, and his conduct so displeased one of my sub-prefects that he has sworn to horse-whip any botanist who enters his purlieus again!'

Harry gave a queasy smile. Suddenly, the ghost of Lorcan Darke was in his ear, sucking on his opium pipe – *You're in trouble now, Harry* . . .

'Dissolute man,' the Taotai went on. 'No respect for Chinese customs. Spent more time trying to dishonour local women than in studying flora.'

Well, that's that, then, Harry thought, feeling his hopes and dreams start to fade away. In the queue behind him, he could sense another group of British engineers shifting impatiently in their boots. He was about to thank the Tao-tai for his time, when he heard Clarissa's voice chime in, 'We come to you under false pretences, Your Excellency. For it is I who wish to travel to Hunan.'

Both the Taotai and Harry turned to her in surprise.

'I have a great passion for painting, you see, and have long been drawn to the beautiful scenery of the region.'

167

Clarissa hung her head: 'I thought it more likely that you would grant passage if you believed a *man* was leading the expedition.'

The Taotai's expression was inscrutable, but then he gave a broad smile which split his chubby face in two. 'But, Mrs Lockhart!' he exclaimed. 'You have entirely the wrong opinion of me. I am all for women leading the way! Is not our young Emperor guided by the wisdom of his mother, the Empress Dowager Cixi? And has not my country lately entered into new treaties with your own Queen Victoria?'

Clarissa's face lit up. 'You're very kind, Your Excellency. Nonetheless, I think it would be wise for my nephew to accompany me. As chaperone, you understand.'

The Taotai reached for Clarissa's silk-gloved hand and touched the very tips of her fingers to his red lips. 'I can deny nothing to the most beautiful woman in Shanghai.'

Her hand released, Clarissa gave another curtsey, and the interview was over. 'Well?' she said to Harry as they walked quickly away. 'We make a good team, don't you think?'

'That's one way of looking at it,' Harry replied, watching as she plucked another cup of *jiu* from a passing tray and gulped it down, cheeks pink with exhilaration. 'You do realise, of course, what this means, Mrs Lockhart . . .'

Before Clarissa could answer, there was a great clanging of gongs, and filing in between a gap in the silk screens came a procession of Chinese girls. Each moved in a series of tiny steps, and when Harry looked down, he saw with a jolt that their feet had been bound. Scragge had forewarned him of the custom, but it was still a shock to see young women hobbling about in tiny dolls' shoes.

The waiters were circulating again, handing out small squares of card and ink-tipped quills, as the Taotai prised himself from his daybed and waddled over to the line of girls.

'Gathered before you now are the finest singers in all the Celestial Empire,' the Taotai announced. 'Each of them is numbered' – he pointed at the girl to his left, and her *amah*, or female attendant, held up a piece of paper – 'from one to twenty. Mark down your favourites, and when we repair to the banquet, they shall visit your tables, and then, if you so desire, journey in sedan chairs to your houses, where they shall sing for you in private.'

Next to him, Harry heard Clarissa let out a snort.

'And now – let the entertainment commence!' the Taotai cried.

A trio of musicians started up, wielding a gong, a tambourine and an oboe-like instrument that Clarissa identified as a lapa. Then the first girl began to sing, a warbling, high-pitched lament that reminded Harry of a glass harmonica. Her lips had been reddened, Harry saw, her eyebrows inked and her slender wrists were adorned with heavy golden bangles. The male guests all nodded approvingly, several of them marking her number on to their cards, then the next singer began, swaying on her mutilated feet, a strand of dark hair falling loose over her rice-powdered brow, eyes lowered.

Clarissa leant over to Harry, a little unsteady now on her feet. 'In Zikawei,' she whispered, lips dangerously close to his ear, 'there is a depository for the bodies of infants who die within their first year. A low stone tower with an iron hatch on either side.'

169

Harry glanced across at her, alarmed to see that reckless look again in her eye.

'One side is for boys,' Clarissa went on, 'and the other for girls. But the odd thing is, Mr Compton,' she said, voice rising now to a pitch that drew disapproving looks from those around her, 'that the girls' side is always full to bursting, swarming with bluebottles, while the boys' side is almost empty.'

Guests were openly staring at them now, Harry was embarrassed to note.

'A girl isn't worth much in this country, you see,' Clarissa concluded bitterly. 'And sometimes I wonder if it's so very different in England.'

'Hush, woman!' came an angry American voice.

'But you've not marked your card, Mr Compton!' Clarissa cried. 'Is there no one to your taste?'

'Perhaps it's time for us to leave, Mrs Lockhart,' Harry said.

Clarissa gave a strange little laugh. 'Leave now? But we should be celebrating! You'll be off on your expedition soon.'

Harry gave an uncertain nod.

'I shan't be coming with you,' Clarissa continued, as the singing finally came to an end, 'if that's what you're worried about.'

Harry was just about to say something he would probably have come to regret when he heard a friendly voice.

'Mrs Lockhart!' Charles Hargreaves beamed at them as he pushed his way through the throng. 'I was unaware you were branching out into railway construction!' Hargreaves took Clarissa's hand, then glanced up at Harry. 'You look a good deal better, I must say, Mr Compton. Much less yellow.'

'We were on our way out, I'm afraid, Mr Hargreaves,' Harry said.

'Really?' Hargreaves replied. 'But the Taotai keeps a splendid table. And the acrobats haven't even begun tumbling yet.'

The waiters were taking away the silk screens now, revealing long trestle tables groaning with dishes. Positioned at each place-setting were miniature wooden lecterns. Already, several of the engineers were bustling towards theirs, eager to place their cards on the frames so that the singers would know on whom to lavish their attentions. At the head of the longest table, Harry saw the Taotai lower his bulk into a throne-like chair.

'He's a vicious sod if you cross him,' Hargreaves said, following Harry's gaze, 'but he has many competing interests to consider. It can't be easy combining a new railway with *feng shui*.'

'*Feng shui*?' Harry repeated.

'Chinese geomancy. An ancient tradition dictating the position of tombs and sacred buildings in relation to the stars and the sea. Build a railway, or lay a telegraph line, and there's a danger you'll disturb the *feng shui*. We've seen riots just at the mention of the idea.'

'He's got a lot on his plate, then,' Clarissa said.

Hargreaves smiled at the joke. 'Had you business to discuss with him, Mr Compton?' he asked, turning back to Harry. 'Concerning your travel plans, perhaps?'

Before Harry could answer, Clarissa leapt in with both feet. 'It is I who am planning a journey, Charles,' she said. 'To paint!'

He stared at her. 'In Hunan?'

'Mm-hmm,' Clarissa said, avoiding meeting her old friend's gaze.

'How fortuitous for you, Mr Compton,' Hargreaves said, eyeing Harry speculatively.

He knows something about me, Harry thought. What had he heard?

'Well! If you really must take your leave, Mrs Lockhart,' Hargreaves said, 'be sure to pay your compliments to the Taotai first.'

'Of course, Charlie,' Clarissa replied, squeezing Hargreaves's hand in hers. Then she swept away, leaving the attaché gazing after her like a lovesick foal.

The platters had been labelled in English as well as Chinese, Harry saw, as he and Clarissa approached the tables. 'Deep fried sheep tails with brown sugar', he read; 'Pig tongues on seaweed'; 'Whole poached duck' . . . The Chinese were already tucking in with ivory chopsticks, whilst the railwaymen made do with silver filigree forks. The prettiest of the singers, meanwhile, was sitting next to the Taotai, slipping sugared grapes into his mouth with fingernails so long that she kept each one protected in a mother-of-pearl sheath.

The Taotai glanced up in surprise to see Clarissa hovering beside him. 'What an honour, Mrs Lockhart,' he said, waving away the singer like a mosquito.

'I'm afraid we must take our leave,' Clarissa said.

'A great shame,' the Taotai replied. 'But I'm honoured that you came at all. Especially whilst in *mourning*.' His wet eyes slid across to Harry's, as he lowered his head to kiss Clarissa's hand. 'I should like to see those paintings of yours, Mrs Lockhart,' he added. 'As soon as you return from Hunan.' He looked at Clarissa closely. 'Perhaps we might make a little arrangement. If you bring them to me, I shall buy the best five — proceeds to go to your girls' reformatory. What do you say?' The Taotai waited for Clarissa's nod before releasing her hand.

'I think we're in a bit of a pickle now,' Clarissa said, as they made their way back towards the carriage.

'Yes, Mrs Lockhart,' Harry replied stiffly. 'I'd say that we are.'

Chapter 15

Whilst waiting for their travel documents to arrive, Harry turned his mind to acquiring his botanical equipment. This business took him to the furthest corners of Shanghai, allowing him to learn a little more of his temporary home.

Situated on the north bank of the Whangpu River was the Chinese City, a tight maze of narrow lanes surrounded by mossy walls, a reminder of the modest fishing settlement Shanghai had been before she'd been targeted by the West for international expansion. All the ancient Chinese guilds were based there – ivory-carvers, instrument-makers, bird-sellers – and a rusty cannon still sat atop its crumbling gates, pointed towards the French Concession, that small slice of Paris which had so bamboozled Harry when he'd first arrived. Then came the English Concession – incorporating the Bund and British Consulate – with the American Concession abutting it on the eastern curve of the river. What would be next? Harry wondered. The Prussian Concession?

The key to successful navigation between the sectors lay in an understanding of the grid system. Running parallel to the Whangpu were streets named after each of China's provinces – Szechuan, Kiangse, even the mysterious Hunan. Perpendicular to the river were streets named after China's main cities – Canton, Nanking, Hongkong and so on. Just by walking around Shanghai, therefore, Harry felt he was increasing his knowledge of the country as a whole.

Wilberforce was his constant companion. The dog had been wary of the streets at first, made uneasy by all the noise. Everyone in Shanghai, it seemed, from the wheel-barrow-runners to the Yankee sailors on shore leave, felt the need to proclaim their presence by yelling and cursing as they went about their business. But once the dog had grown accustomed to the din, he'd become as relaxed in Shanghai as he'd been aboard the *Redemption*, pausing every now and then to sniff at a strange smell, or to eye the canaries and chaffinches that trilled from cages on every balcony.

A trowel, a bowie knife, a tool roll; hessian sacks, a note-book, even a rudimentary flower-press – these items proved easy enough to find in Shanghai. Less easy, though, was the procurement of a Wardian case. Lorcan Darke's case had been built by Dr Nathaniel Ward himself, Harry remembered the Irishman telling him. Well, the great Dr Ward must be tilling the celestial gardens by now, Harry surmised, so he'd just have to improvise.

Eventually, Harry found a carpenter in the Chinese City specialising in display cabinets, and did his best to explain – with the help of a picture culled from *The Gardeners' Chronicle* – exactly what a Wardian case was. The quoted price was 250 cash coins, an extravagant amount that that would all but exhaust Harry's resources, but he knew it had to be done.

As he made his way out of the Chinese City, Harry wondered why he hadn't asked Clarissa to contribute to the cost of the equipment. He told himself it was because he didn't care to trouble her — a widow with financial problems of her own — but deep down, he knew that was a lie. Ever since the Taotai's party, Harry had avoided discussing the expedition with Clarissa, knowing that the conversation was likely to end in anger and recrimination. Surely she must know that the idea of her accompanying him on the expedition was absurd? It would earn her no more money, and the risks were huge. Charles Hargreaves himself had said as much, and anyone who knew anything of plant hunters could tell you that they took their lives into their own hands. On an expedition such as this, Harry thought, it would be all he could do to take care of himself.

He stopped in an alleyway, suddenly realising that he'd lost sight of Wilberforce. To his left was a crumbling stone archway, leading to a small courtyard. Harry peered through it and saw an old woman sitting at a wooden table, one wrinkled hand stroking the little dog's ears.

'Hello?' Harry called out, as he passed through the archway, wishing, not for the first time, that he'd taken the trouble to pick up just a smattering of Chinese.

The woman glanced up with a smile. There was an ornamental plant sitting in a pot on her table. Not just any plant, Harry saw as he came closer, but a tiny gnarled tree, mesmerising in its doll-like proportions.

'*Penjing*,' the old woman said, sensing Harry's interest. Picking up a pair of golden scissors, she began snipping meticulously at one of the little branches.

It was a maidenhair tree, Harry saw; a perfect, miniature maidenhair tree, if such a thing could exist. As he looked more closely, he saw that the stronger shoots had all been pinched out, and the weaker ones left to prosper, made fast to the trunk with cotton thread so that they grew twisted and woody, like mature boughs.

'Remarkable,' Harry said. And as he watched the woman snip away with her scissors, so patient and precise, he was struck by the knowledge that there was magic to be found in this country, if one only kept an eye open for it. '*Penjing?*' he repeated, checking he had the right name.

'*Penjing,*' the woman confirmed with a shy smile, before continuing with her careful cultivation.

Wilberforce had already moved on, so Harry bowed to the old lady, then followed the little dog back on to the street.

Harry's Wardian case arrived a few days later. As soon as he'd paid off the delivery-boy, adding his last few coins as tip – or 'squeeze', as they called it in Shanghai – he retreated to his room to examine his purchase. He was well pleased. Though the base was constructed of bamboo rather than pine, the glass top was nicely fashioned, with a hinged gable that could be tilted back to allow cuttings to be planted inside. The case itself was a little wider than Lorcan Darke's had been, about three feet by two, but that was all to the good. The contraption could hold at least fifty cuttings, Harry calculated, maybe more.

These agreeable imaginings were brought to an abrupt halt by the sound of Lam Dookay's voice downstairs. Moments later, Clarissa summoned Harry to her parlour.

The comprador looked exceptionally pleased with himself, Harry thought as he entered the room, brandishing a roll of documents at Harry as though he were holding Excalibur itself. He stood back and unfurled the thing, revealing long thin pages crammed with columns of Chinese characters, broken by occasional flourishes of red and gold, like in some mediaeval missal.

'Mr Compton must sign here,' Lam Dookay said, pinning down one curling page with a glistening fingernail.

Harry dipped a pen into the inkwell on the desk and scrawled his name.

'And Mrs Lockhart . . . here.'

Clarissa hesitated for a moment, then signed her name below Harry's, and the comprador re-rolled the documents and tied the scroll with a pink ribbon.

'I have good news,' Lam Dookay went on. 'The Taotai has found you a guide. A man who studied with him at the Tongwen Guan – or Interpreters' College – in Peking. He is an expert on Hunan province, and will join you both when you reach Hankow.'

Clarissa glanced across at Harry, but he refused to meet her eye.

Seeing the two pink spots of anger rise on his mistress's cheeks, Lam Dookay's voice faltered. 'This man is highly regarded, Mrs Lockhart. His name is Fang Li-Liang, and he works for the Central Mining Authority in Peking. He shall offer you every assistance.'

Clarissa nodded her assent, and Lam Dookay moved for the door. 'The *Kwai-Lun* departs first thing on Friday,' he continued. 'She sails as part of a convoy of freighters, the cost of the gunboat engaged for your protection to be shared between the fleet. Then, once you and Mr Compton reach Hankow, your onward journey will be arranged by your guide.'

'Thank you, Lam Dookay,' Clarissa said briskly. 'That will be all.'

As soon as the comprador left, Clarissa rounded on Harry. 'You needn't glare at me like that, Mr Compton!' she said. 'You've already made your feelings about the expedition quite clear. It is obvious that you do not wish me to come.'

'Well, I don't see how it can be avoided now!' Harry rejoined. 'You've signed your name to it, after all.'

'Goodness, Mr Compton!' Clarissa said, staring at him in exaggerated astonishment. 'Your tone of voice is quite uncivil.'

'Well, I'm sorry if I've said something to offend you, Mrs Lockhart.'

'I have every right to accompany you on this expedition,' Clarissa went on. 'Tell the truth, Mr Compton. You don't want me with you. Slowing you down.'

'It's not that.'

'Then what is it?'

'Expeditions like this can be dangerous . . .'

'Says he with all his experience!' Clarissa jeered. 'The truth is, you think it too much for a woman.'

'It is a risk neither of us needs to take . . .'

'Well, perhaps *I* want to!' Clarissa said in a shrill voice that startled him. 'All my life, I've done what was expected of me. Married the man my father chose for me, and followed him to some far-off corner of the Empire. And what has it brought me? No children, no husband. No security! And now I have a chance to do something different.' She stood there, staring at Harry, chest heaving. 'I have done so very little with my life, Mr Compton.'

There was a long silence, until finally Harry spoke. 'I, for one, would be intrigued to see how your paintings turn out . . .'

Clarissa looked up in surprise. 'Do you mean it?'

Harry tightened his lips and stared down at his feet. 'It doesn't look like I have much of a choice, does it?'

Clarissa threw her arms around him then, and Harry froze, allowing himself to drink in her scent for just a moment before gently easing her away. 'You're pleased, then,' he said with an embarrassed smile.

Clarissa didn't answer, just pressed her palms together like a child, eyes sparkling. 'I'll need a new wardrobe, of course,' she said. 'Practical clothes, and a sturdy pair of boots . . .' Turning to her desk, she drew a piece of paper towards her and immediately set about making a list.

You fool, Harry said to himself as he headed towards the door. What have you let yourself in for?

Shanghai, China
April 19, 1868

Dear Jack,

I hope that you are very well. I write to you with an unusual proposition. I wondered if you might see your way clear to approaching either Mr Weeks or Mr Wimsett on my behalf. I would like you to enquire of them – very discreetly, mind – how much they would be willing to pay for world exclusive rights to a new exotic tree every bit as spectacular as Pierre

180

Magnol's 'Magnolia grandiflora', or John Tradescant's 'tulip tree'. Please do not mention me yet by name, but if you were able to extract a figure from them, that would be most helpful.

I know that this request comes at you blind, Jack, but I am off next week on a lengthy journey, and if I do not write now, I may not have a chance for several months. Rest assured, though, that exciting things are in motion here — things that could make a man's fortune!

With untold gratitude,

Harry

PS. Please send your reply to the poste restante at the British Post Office in Shanghai as soon as is practicable!

> 14 Wellington Lane
> Battersea
> Co. Surrey
> January 16, 1868

Dear Harry,

Thank you for your letter of 12 December. I was thrilled to read of your adventures in Africa. That leopard in a thorn tree — well, it sounded like something out of a Boy's Own Magazine!

I am sending this by return of post, as I believe it contains news that you should hear as soon as possible.

This very evening, Banks, Pugh and I were taking refreshment at the Man in the Moon, when who should we spot lurking in the snug but Old Pie-Gut! We could scarce believe our eyes, but there was no doubting it — Josiah Piggott, the tightest fist in all the horticultural world, was doing the rounds of the various plant hunters touting their wares!

And he looked like he meant business, too — his interview with Paxton Crosse lasted so long they could only have been discussing terms for a possible expedition.

Now, whether this is connected to your sudden departure for the land of exotic plants, I cannot say, but it wouldn't surprise either of us to see Piggott eager to outdo one of his own.

No doubt this will just be a flirtation for him, and when he learns what plant hunters charge these days, he'll run a mile, but I thought you should know what I'd seen.

Your old friend,

Jack

PS. The messiness of my script is because we went on to the Cremorne after the Man in the Moon, where they were serving a very potent type of punch.

PART THREE
April 1868 – The Yangtze Basin

Chapter 16

That Friday, at three o'clock in the morning, Harry Compton and Clarissa Lockhart stood side by side on the pontoon behind the godown, waiting as Lam Dookay issued his final instructions to the captain of the *Kwai-Lun*.

Harry looked about him nervously, still reeling from the contents of Jack's most recent letter. So Piggott was planning to mount an expedition of his own. Could his chosen plant hunter already be in Shanghai, hot on Harry's heels? Chewing his lip, Harry went through the timings again in his head. Jack's letter had been posted on 16 January. Today was 24 April. Surely Piggott's man wouldn't even be in China yet: the journey had taken Harry some six months! But the *Redemption* had made countless stops along the way, and the conditions of sail had been difficult . . .

Telling himself to keep calm, Harry focused his attention on the humble cargo boat moored at the moonlit jetty straight ahead. She was what Scragge and the boys would have termed a 'tramp' – about fifty foot by fifteen, with a little wheelhouse and steam funnel at the stern, and a railed-off upper deck pierced by a single mast and sail. Her most striking feature was her hold, made of thick curved timbers, which seemed to bulge like an overfull belly. She sat so low in the water that even a modest swell would overturn her, Harry suspected, relieved to recall that they would be travelling exclusively on rivers.

Turning his head, Harry checked their luggage, which – despite his fears – was relatively modest. Clarissa had brought just two trunks – one deep and barrel-staved, containing her clothing and personal effects, and another long and narrow, for her painting easel and canvases. If anything, it was Harry's baggage which was the bulkier: his Wardian case, wrapped in blankets and concealed in a Fortnum & Mason wicker basket that Aki had conjured from God only knew where; his leather valise of clothes; a tea chest containing his vasculum, botanical tools and twelve jam jars filled with honey. And then, of course, there was Wilberforce, who stood trembling in anticipation as he stared out at the *Kwai-Lun*, no doubt hoping that a ship – any ship – must signal a reunion with his beloved Mr Scragge.

At last, Lam Dookay turned to Clarissa. 'Chen Mantze will see to your every need.'

As if in confirmation of this, the captain signalled to two crew members, who ran down the gangplank and carried away their baggage.

'How do you do, Chen Mantze?' Clarissa asked the captain.

The captain looked to the comprador for leave, then seized Clarissa's hand and bowed to it, resting his oil-stained forehead on the back of her wrist.

'Please be careful on the journey, Mrs Lockhart,' the comprador said, as the captain backed away. 'It is not too late to change your mind.'

'Nonsense,' Clarissa replied, reaching down to pick up Wilberforce. 'I shall return invigorated, and together we will rebuild Lockhart's to its former glory!'

'I look forward to it, ma'am,' the comprador said, a faint tremor of emotion entering his voice. 'But in the meantime, you may travel secure in the knowledge that the *hong* is in the most loyal of hands.'

'Of that I have no doubt, Lam Dookay. Now – let us get underway!' Clarissa took a first step on to the gangplank, and both Harry and the captain lurched towards her, vying for her hand. But her arms were firmly closed around the little dog. 'We'll not get far, gentlemen, if we begin in this chary manner!' she said, before marching up alone on to the deck.

Harry turned and met Lam Dookay's eye, and found the comprador staring at him with an intensity that was almost threatening. 'Be sure to look after her, Mr Compton.'

'You may rely upon it, Lam Dookay,' Harry replied, then followed Clarissa aboard.

The upper deck of the *Kwai-Lun* had been subject to a brutal and thorough cleansing, Harry saw, the crates and rope coils that one might have expected of a working cargo vessel all cleared away, and her wooden planks scrubbed clean. Clarissa edged past the wheelhouse to the railings, still clasping Wilberforce, and Harry joined her, aware of the eyes of the ten-strong crew fixed upon them. Out at anchor on the Whangpu, illuminated by the full moon, floated three other freighters, with a British gunboat patrolling behind them, a sleek-looking screw corvette with HMS *Haseley* painted on the hull. Could Piggott's plant hunter be concealed on one of those boats? Harry wondered, then curtailed his line of thought, determined not to let these half-baked worries about his former employer mar his great adventure.

'They were all waiting for us,' Clarissa said, as Harry watched one of the crewmen haul up the anchor. Another let out the sails, and as the wind and tidal currents of the Whangpu took hold, the ship gave a sudden lurch.

'We're off,' Harry said.

'Yes,' Clarissa replied with an excited smile. 'We are.'

'Missy?' came a voice.

It was the captain, Chen Mantze, standing beside the hatchway that led below deck. 'Can walkee just now?' he asked in pidgin – or 'business' – English.

Clarissa set off towards him, Harry following close behind. The companionway led down to two levels, the lower of which held the coalstore and boiler, judging by the acrid smell. But Chen Mantze directed them to the first floor, where they entered a hold area stacked from floor to ceiling with chests of opium, lashed in place with ropes. These chests, Harry had learnt, would be purchased by wholesalers at the various river ports along their journey, before being couriered by donkey cart and canal barge to a number of destinations in mainland China – from Sian in the north to Yunnan-Fu in the east.

A narrow gap had been left between the chests, circum-venting the funnel, which rose from the boiler below. This makeshift passageway was illuminated by candles, the base of each stuck to the floor with a dab of melted tallow. Taking in the naked flames, Harry shuddered to imagine what would happen should one of them topple over unobserved.

At the rear of the hold, two hatchways lay open. Down one, Harry saw a cat's cradle of hammocks crisscrossing the gloomy space, but the captain was signalling to the other, his proud smile revealing two missing front teeth.

Clarissa passed Wilberforce to Harry, then began to climb down, her black dress riding up slightly over one calf. Averting his eyes, Harry set off after her, keeping Wilberforce tucked close to his chest with one arm. As soon as he reached the bottom, he saw to his horror that there was only one bed, a small cot-like berth built against the wall, with two tiny pillows placed upon it.

'Ah,' said Clarissa, throwing him a nervous smile. 'I think there's been some confusion.'

Harry picked up his bag. 'I'll sleep next door.'

Clarissa glanced about the little room, eyes settling on some empty crates piled in the corner. 'Surely we could fashion some kind of partition.'

'I won't hear of it,' Harry said, reassuring her with a grin. 'I spent six months sleeping in a hammock on the way to Shanghai. I should be disappointed to miss a chance to repeat the experience.'

Before Clarissa could protest, Harry was halfway up the wooden stepladder. 'Chen Mantze?' he called out, and the skipper's gap-toothed face reappeared above him like magic. 'I'll bunk with the crew,' Harry said. 'Down there,' he added, pointing into the adjacent hatchway and tucking his hands behind one ear to signify sleep. The captain said something in Chinese, then gave a hearty guffaw. None the wiser, Harry laughed back and followed him down to the adjacent cabin, where a spare hammock was duly located and strung up on ringbolts.

Turning, Harry saw a few of the crewmen gathered together in the gloom on their hunkers. '*Jiu?*' one of them asked, holding up a wineskin.

Harry accepted with a nod of thanks, then took a gulp of the strong, clear liquid. They were on their way now, he thought, feeling the excitement wash through him as fast as the liquor. It was really happening.

Wiping his mouth, Harry passed the wineskin back, then climbed up into his hammock. 'How about this, Pa?' he murmured as he covered himself up with his coat. 'How about this . . .'

Harry awoke to the immense sound of rattling. Feeling the familiar roll of waves, he thought at first he was back aboard the *Redemption*, then took in the layout of the cabin, and remembered.

Light was streaming in from the open hatchway above. Harry checked his pocketwatch: almost eight o'clock. Rolling his legs out of the hammock, he climbed up to the hold to find Clarissa's hatch door open. She must already be at breakfast, he thought, hurrying to catch her up.

The scene he found as he stepped out on to the upper deck astonished him. It was as though they'd sailed out to sea, so wide was the expanse of water. The Yangtze must simply be one of the largest rivers in the world, he decided, as much as two miles from one bank to the other, its waters the rich, rippled brown of Sir Hans Sloane's famous drinking chocolate.

The *Kwai-Lun* was keeping to midstream, close behind the other cargo ships. These were broader and more impressive than the Lockhart's tramp – two funnels on each deck, company names marked in imposing letters on the hulls: *David Sassoon & Sons, Jardine, Matheson & Co., Butterfield & Swire* . . . Harry searched for European faces on board, but saw no one there but Chinese crew.

Alongside the cargo ships sailed the British gunboat, six shiny mortars protruding from her port and starboard flanks. She was twice the length of the largest freighter, and even newer than Harry had thought, built of a composite of iron and wood.

Wondering why such an expensive piece of ordnance might be required for this journey, Harry scanned the scene. The landscape was flat and alluvial, with rows of waterlogged paddy fields running alongside the river, and endless cotton plantations stretching beyond, crammed with white-flecked shrubs. Water buffalos lounged in the shallows, their dark, stocky necks tethered to the stilt legs of the fishermen's huts that rose from the banks. Everything seemed wonderfully peaceful and still.

Edging past the wheelhouse, Harry found a few of the crewmen playing dominoes at a small fixed table. A kerosene stove burnt nearby, with a vat of something fragrant bubbling upon it.

Glancing up, Harry felt his breath catch. Leaning against the railings at the bow stood Clarissa, a silk shawl thrown over her narrow shoulders. At her feet sat Wilberforce, stubby tail sliding back and forth on the polished deck.

'Good morning,' Harry called out, and Clarissa turned and smiled at him. 'It's quite a river, isn't it?' Harry added, as he joined her at the gunwale.

191

'A thousand-mile trading route from west to east,' Clarissa replied. 'They say that the Yangtze is to the Chinese what the Mediterranean is to Europeans.'

Harry tried to think of some equally clever remark, but came up short. 'I hope the engine didn't keep you awake, Mrs Lockhart.'

Clarissa made a rueful face. 'I suppose one grows accustomed to the thumping over time,' she said, then added, 'The *Kwai-Lun* burns only Welsh coal, you know. It reaches an incredible temperature, but emits hardly any smoke.' Turning, she pointed at the ship's funnel. 'See?'

Looking up, Harry nodded. It was true: there was barely a wisp of smoke.

'Narcissus used to say that Welsh coal was evidence of the existence of God,' Clarissa went on. 'Then again, he said a lot of things.'

Harry raised an eyebrow. There was a time when Clarissa had recounted the judgements of her late husband with something akin to reverence. That period appeared to be at an end, Harry thought, wondering what might account for such a change.

'Have you eaten?' Clarissa asked, motioning to the stockpot. 'The broth is quite delicious.'

Harry shook his head.

'Cai caught a fish this morning,' Clarissa went on. 'Some sort of barbel, I think. *Shey-shey*, Cai,' she said, as a young boy handed Harry a bowl, then retreated with a blush, clearly in Mrs Lockhart's thrall already.

'*Shey-shey*,' Harry repeated to Cai, then turned to Clarissa and lowered his voice: 'That does mean "thank you", doesn't it?'

Clarissa blinked. 'I hope that you have more of a flair for botany than for languages, Mr Compton.'

The soup was indeed delicious, and Harry drained the liquid straight from the bowl, then scooped up the white flesh of the fish with the porcelain spoon, a few flakes of which he fed to Wilberforce, who was watching intently from his feet.

There were more vessels on the river now — flat-bottomed sampans, with their fixed oars at the sterns; Chinese junks with their rigid, bamboo-battened sails; slipper boats with narrow bows and rounded roofs. Inside them, Harry saw fishermen and rice traders; fan- and lantern-makers; children weaving garlands of jasmine blossoms; old women selling lychees and shiny orange persimmons.

Standing in one boat was a toddler with a lightweight piece of wood tied to his back, a buoyancy aid should he topple into the water, Harry suspected. The boy stared in wonder at the convoy as it swept past. 'We must be going at least nine knots,' Harry said, hoping to impress Clarissa with his nautical knowledge.

'Really? It feels to me like we're slowing down.' She drew a chatelaine keychain from the pocket of her skirts and checked the time. 'We must be nearing our first stop. Is that Chinkiang over there?' she called to a passing crewman.

The man grinned. '*Chin*kiang,' he said, putting the stress on the first syllable.

'*Chin*kiang,' Clarissa repeated, trying to perfect her pronunciation.

A few moments later, the freighter at the front of the convoy banked to the right. Then the two ships behind did the same, and the *Kwai-Lun* followed suit. All the while, the

British gunboat kept close by, moving up and down the line, waiting and watching.

As they neared the harbour, an armada of smaller boats began to approach — monks beating tom-toms to collect alms for their pagoda; craftsmen selling effigies of gods and warriors, beautifully carved from camphor wood; quack doctors hawking pots of what Chen Mantze claimed were dragon saliva and monkey glands. White ducks bobbed on the water, setting off on sudden bursts of low flight whenever a boat drew too near.

Woodsmoke scented the air as the port town of Chinkiang opened up before them, revealing a fort on a low hill sur-rounded by bamboo stockades; a dirty canal snaking away into the distance. It looked like a very poor and desolate place to Harry — one of the warehouses lacked a roof, the walls of another were cratered with holes, the bricks stolen by looters.

'This part of China was badly damaged during the Taiping Rebellion,' Clarissa said.

'The what?'

She looked at him in surprise. 'You've never heard of Taiping? The rebel uprising against the Qing Dynasty?'

Harry shook his head.

'It all began when a provincial schoolteacher named Hong Xiuquan failed the Chinese Civil Service examinations for the fourth time. He was so upset that he declared himself to be the Son of God, and mustered an army of followers to avenge himself upon the Emperor.'

Harry wasn't sure if she was joking.

'It was one of the bloodiest wars in history,' Clarissa went on, in a tone that told him she was not. 'Lasting from 1850 'til only a few years ago. Tens of millions dead, all over the country. It was what made the Emperor blink when the British were pushing for trade concessions.'

Harry was just considering the morality of pressing home that particular advantage when something broke the surface below the boat, pumping out a burst of air and water.

'Look!' Clarissa exclaimed in delight. 'A dolphin!'

The beast revealed itself again, its skin a ghostly white, before disappearing back beneath the water. 'Maybe it's a sign of good fortune,' Clarissa said.

'Let's hope so,' Harry replied.

The engines slowed as the convoy began its approach. Four separate groups of men waited on the wharf, one for each vessel – evidently each *hong* employed its own band of wholesalers. From inside the wheelhouse, Chen Mantze began shouting instructions, and his crew sprang to life, throwing hawsers from the deck, each rope weighted by a little stone ball fixed to the end. A few minutes later, the *Kwai-Lun* sat broadside-on to the wharf, her propeller stilled, her sail down.

'Fascinating to see the process in action,' Clarissa said, as they watched the men unload the first chests of opium. 'Everyone seems to know exactly what they're doing.'

Two gangways had been extended from the *Kwai-Lun*, though only one was in use at present, the crewmen carrying a chest apiece as they made their way down to the wharf, where their greeting party was ready to receive them, one official already seated at a little table, a paintbrush in one hand and an abacus in the other. The man glanced up at Chen Mantze as he approached, and some sort of negotiation began – Harry wondered if the declining quality of the Lockhart's opium was the matter under discussion.

195

Wilberforce was staring at the shore now, panting heavily. 'I should probably take him for a walk,' Harry said.

'Yes,' Clarissa replied with a bright smile. 'Let's.'

Harry offered her his arm, but she must not have seen it, as she headed unaccompanied down the empty gangway. But there was such a lot of activity on the wharf now that no one paid much attention to a tall Englishwoman dressed in half-mourning making her way on to dry land.

Harry followed her, Wilberforce trotting at his heel. 'Don't you think we should tell someone we've got off the boat?' he called out, a little breathlessly.

'You worry too much, Mr Compton,' Clarissa laughed. 'Just like Narcissus.'

She set off across the quayside, and Harry suddenly realised how little he knew her – should he trust her judgement, or persuade her to listen to him? Because every instinct was telling him it was unwise to wander off in a strange Chinese port . . .

Thankfully, Clarissa had stopped now on a little piece of scrubland to the side of the harbour, nose crinkling as Wilberforce answered a call of nature. The dog kicked up some dust, then moved over to sniff at a muddy puddle.

'He must be thirsty,' Clarissa said. 'Probably that fish you gave him. Come on!' she urged, pointing to a little teahouse further up the slope. 'Perhaps we can all have a drink up there.'

Irked to be lectured on how to treat his own dog, Harry followed Clarissa up the hill, to where Wilberforce had already found a stream-fed fishpond, stippled with orange carp. As the dog began to lap happily at the water, Clarissa lowered herself into a chair at one of the rickety tables that had been set up on the terrace outside the teahouse.

Harry threw an anxious glance at the *Kwai-Lun*. When he looked back, Clarissa was chuckling. 'We're in clear sight of the boat, Mr Compton. Don't be such a worry-wort!'

Biting his tongue, Harry sat down next to her, groaning as he saw a small boy with jug-ears running over to them, arms outstretched.

'Have you any coins?' Clarissa asked Harry, smiling as the urchin grabbed at the skirts of her black satin dress, fascinated by the material, so different to the mean rags he wore.

Harry reached into his pocket and took out a few cash. Moments later, another boy appeared. But then a wizened old woman emerged from the teahouse, clapped her hands smartly, and the urchins vanished. Catching sight of Clarissa, the woman stared at her in frank amazement – this red-haired European in the middle of rural China – then smiled to reveal two rows of yellowing stumps for teeth.

'*Chá?*' Clarissa asked.

The old woman held out a hand.

'Money up front, it seems,' Harry muttered, pulling out a few more cash.

The woman took the coins from his palm, then returned inside.

'I've ordered us some tea, in case you were wondering,' Clarissa said, and Harry gave her a flat smile.

The aroma wafting over from the teahouse was tainted by the rancid reek of sewage, and Harry found it hard to believe that anything potable could come from within. But then he saw something quite wonderful. For, growing on the other side of the pond, dangling over the water, was a shrub with glorious, bell-shaped yellow flowers.

'What is it?' Clarissa asked, seeing his face brighten.

'I think it's a weigela,' Harry replied. 'Though the flowers are unusually large.' He got to his feet. 'Do you think they'll mind if I gather a few seeds?'

'I'm sure nothing could bother them less.'

Harry looked again at the ship: Chen Mantze was down on the quay now, collecting payment. 'Back in a moment,' Harry said as he climbed over the fence.

He'd seen nothing quite like this shrub before, Harry realised, as he hurried towards it. The leaves of a dipelta, but with the flowers of a weigela. And the fragrance! Specimens like these would fly off the shelves in Chelsea. Harry felt a first tickle of excitement at the pit of his stomach as a series of tantalising possibilities flitted through his mind – fame, financial independence, the satisfaction at seeing Piggott and Frith arrested, tried, then strung up from the scaffold . . . Swiftly, Harry's hands began to work though the shrub's foliage. A few of the blooms were overblown, seeds already formed in their swollen carpals. One by one Harry picked them, slipping them carefully into his pockets.

Wilberforce had lost interest in the fish now, and was busy decorating some reeds with a spray of his seemingly inexhaustible urine. 'Hold on, boy,' Harry said as the dog began to wander off. 'I'm coming with you.'

But the table on the terrace was empty now. Where was Clarissa? Harry wondered, feeling his excitement fizzle away. He spun around in panic, but the *Kwai-Lun* was still

198

moored at the wharf, the British gunboat prowling in the background.

Turning, Harry ran to the open door of the teahouse, catching a new aroma now, one that took him straight back to Lorcan Darke's dingy room at the Man in the Moon. Clarissa was standing just inside, wearing an expression of shock and revulsion. Fearfully, Harry followed her gaze. The room was devoid of furniture, in the Chinese style, and the floor lined with reed mats. Sprawled on one was a Chinese youth with a pale, haggard face. His eyes were open, though glazed like a dead man's, the only sign of life the rise of his chest, lifting and lowering the clenched fist which lay upon it, in the grasp of which was an opium pipe.

Pinned to the back wall, Harry saw a cord strung with an assortment of pipes. Squatting below it, another man sat cross-legged, his eyelids flickering as he inhaled deeply from a water-pipe. Slumped in one corner, meanwhile, lay a local woman of no more than twenty, with a baby in her bulging belly and one breast hanging loose from her dress. She was snoring loudly, propped up against a cushion, a small pot resting between her thighs, its lid ajar to reveal the treacly black poison within.

Harry and Clarissa turned as one of the street urchins ran in, laughing and pointing at the woman. The boy grinned at Harry and Clarissa, then stepped forward to the man with the water-pipe, who was mumbling some kind of imprecation, lips stretched into a smile. The man was completely unaware, or unable to act, as the urchin snatched the pipe from his hand, and drew in some fumes from the still-smouldering bowl.

Then, from behind a drape at the back of the room, came the old proprietress, holding up a tray containing a lamp, some needles and another pot of opium. Seeing the child, the woman kicked out at him with a moccasined foot, but he dodged out of her reach, laughing as he skipped out of the teahouse.

'I'd like to go now,' Clarissa said in a strange, tight voice. 'At once.'

Harry gave her his arm, and she let him lead her out of the teahouse.

'*Aya!*' the proprietress called after them, but they ignored her, heading instead for the *Kwai-Lun*, Wilberforce capering at their heels, stomach full of fresh water and Lord only knew what else.

The last of the coal was being loaded now, and most of the crew were back aboard, readying for departure. As the Butterfield & Swire vessel began to pull away from the harbour, Clarissa returned to her position at the bow of the boat.

Harry joined her, still amazed by the stunned look on her face. 'But surely you must have known about opium dens, Mrs Lockhart?' he said gently. 'Shanghai's full of them!'

'I'm not some ingénue!' Clarissa shot back. Then she covered her eyes with both hands and shook her head. 'That poor woman. And her unborn child . . .' Opening her eyes, she stared out at the river, rigid as a figurehead. 'Narcissus always said it was harmless. A form of recreation.'

'Oh, come now!' Harry said, feeling his temper rise. 'Even I know that was the main reason for the Opium Wars. The British didn't want the narcotic infecting their work-force in India, so they inflicted it on the Chinese instead.'

Stubbornly, Clarissa shook her head. 'It was to plug a trade deficit. We imported tea from China, so we needed to sell them something in return.' Her face hardened: 'Besides, we pay duty on all our merchandise. And there was plenty of opium in China *before* the British came . . .'

Not on this scale, Harry was tempted to reply, but the unease in Clarissa's voice had been clear, and to say more would have been boorish. Besides, was it not opium that was funding this expedition? Who was Harry to judge? Reaching a hand into his pocket, he felt the reassuring swell of the flowerheads tucked inside.

Then the gangplanks were coming up again, and they were casting off, making their steady way upriver towards the next port.

Clarissa retreated to her cabin after lunch, so Harry did the same, pleased to find it empty as the crew busied themselves about the ship, readying the next consignment of opium. At first, Harry found the rattle of the engine irritating, but gradually it became something of a comfort, blocking out extraneous thoughts and sounds, allowing him to focus fully on his work.

Having unpacked one of the honeypots from his luggage, Harry set about laying out his first set of specimens. Twelve flowerheads he'd acquired from the teahouse garden. He placed them all on the floor beneath his hammock, watching them vibrate with the force of the engine. Three had been damaged in his pocket – he must remember to bring the vasculum ashore in future.

Slowly, he began to dig the seedpods out of the throats of the flowers, then slice them open with his thumbnail. He had an old linen handkerchief in his valise, and he flattened it out and placed the seeds upon it, each no bigger than a pinhead. As he worked, he thought back to the happy days he'd spent at the growing grounds of Piggott's, before he'd been transferred into Sales. There'd been a rickety lean-to behind the hotbeds, where Harry had worked for over a month on nothing but seed extraction. The thought that each little pip had contained the possibility of a bloom – one that might end up in the orangery of some magnificent stately home, or in the conservatory of a Westminster town-house – had always given Harry a strange, indefinable charge of excitement. And now, to be collecting the seeds in their natural habitat, thousands of miles beyond the poky confines of a Chelsea potting shed . . . it exceeded even his most extravagant daydreams.

'Mr Compton?' came a voice.

Harry looked up to see Clarissa standing at the hatchway, a book held in one hand. 'I've been watching you for a good ten minutes,' she called down. 'But you were completely lost in your work.'

'You should have alerted me to your presence,' Harry replied, getting to his feet. 'I would not have had you wait!'

Clarissa smoothed down her skirts, then climbed down to join him. 'It is I who should apologise,' she said. 'I'm sorry about earlier. I shouldn't be bothering you with my moral quandaries.'

'Bother me all you like, Mrs Lockhart,' Harry replied with a grin.

They said nothing for a moment, just sat there in a companionable silence, until Clarissa reached over and picked up one of the spent flowers, turning it in her hand. 'What is it you like so much about your work, Mr Compton?'

'I suppose it's . . .' Harry paused. 'It's a question of nurture.'

'Nurture?' Clarissa repeated, her gaze falling upon the neat line of seeds laid out on the handkerchief. 'Is it not about imposing your will on Nature? Trying to master her?'

'I suppose there's an element of that,' Harry replied a little defensively, remembering how helpless his mother's seizures had made him feel; how he'd longed to be able to control them. 'One has to manage the conditions of growth. But really . . . it's about allowing a plant to flourish.'

'I see,' Clarissa said, meeting his eye with a smile.

Feeling his spirits lift, Harry checked himself, wondering why it should matter so much what Clarissa Lockhart thought. It shouldn't, he told himself.

She was looking again at the broken remnant of the weigela flower. 'But is it really worth collecting plants such as these? Shouldn't we save our resources for the icicle tree?'

Harry touched a fingertip to his tongue, then dabbed up one of the tiny black seeds and held it up for Clarissa to see. 'This seed alone could be worth a sovereign in Chelsea.'

'Come, Mr Compton,' Clarissa scoffed. 'Surely you can't be serious.'

Harry smiled. 'I'm deadly serious, Mrs Lockhart. It would need to be germinated, of course, and grown on. But then – dazzling new Yangtze weigela!' Harry bellowed like a costermonger. 'Get 'em quick before they all sell out!'

'If only I'd known,' Clarissa said, looking at Harry shrewdly. 'I should have modified our arrangement. Asked for a percentage of *all* our bounty from the expedition – not just the icicle tree.'

Reluctant to reopen that discussion, Harry reached for one of the glass jars. Clarissa watched as he flicked the seed into it, waiting for it to be claimed by the golden honey.

'So that's how you store the seeds,' she said. 'In honey!'

'It's a technique I read about on the voyage from England. Honey is one of the few things in nature that doesn't decay. It contains almost no water, and it's too acidic for mould to survive – they've found honey in pharaohs' tombs that's still good to eat.' Reaching into his valise, Harry rummaged about until he found what he was looking for – his old issue of *The Gardeners' Chronicle*. He had marked the relevant article with a feather, but when he handed Clarissa the periodical, she barely glanced at it, her eye caught by a wonderfully detailed sketch of a *Magnolia grandiflora*.

'That's just an advertisement,' Harry said. 'A botanical illustrator touting his wares. Any good plant catalogue needs illustrations – people have to see what they're buying.'

But Clarissa was still examining the drawing, seeming to gauge the skill with which the artist had depicted the leaf, seed cone and rich, creamy flower. 'Might not we need illustrations, Mr Compton?' she asked. 'To help sell the icicle tree – and the other exotic plants?'

'That's why I bought the flower-press,' Harry said. 'To record what I collect.'

'But pressed flowers lose their colour, do they not?'

Harry nodded, wondering where this was going. With a woman like Clarissa, one never knew.

'So an illustration would be better?' she went on.

'If the illustration is accurate, then yes, absolutely. It would be better even than a daguerreotype.'

Clarissa glanced up at Harry, eyes dancing with excitement. 'I could do this, Mr Compton. I'm sure of it!'

'Aren't you meant to be painting pictures for the Taotai?'

'Might I not do both?'

Harry took in her flushed cheeks and trembling mouth, and couldn't help but smile. 'Yes,' he said. 'I expect you could.'

'Then you will bring me specimens to paint?' she demanded, clutching her hands together.

'Yes!' he laughed.

'I'm very glad,' she said, then turned to go, picking up her book as she went — *The Travels of Marco Polo*, Harry saw.

'Have you found a reference to the icicle tree yet?' he asked.

'Marco's still in Greater Armenia. But as soon as he reaches China, I'll be sure to—' There was a sudden boom from outside, and Clarissa broke off, startled. 'What was that?'

The ship was slowing down, Harry realised, though it seemed too early for their next stop. Unthinkingly, he placed a hand on Clarissa's shoulder. 'Wait here.'

'I'd rather not, if it's all the same to you,' she replied, so he let her climb up first, then hurried after her.

Up on deck, the crew were lined up on the starboard side, their weight causing it to list slightly. Out on the water, no more than fifty yards away, Harry saw a large Chinese junk sailing in the opposite direction, with the British gunboat tight behind it, her deck busy now with red-coated soldiers. A posse of men stood on the junk, thick-necked and shaven-headed, their canvas tunics fastened with ropes around their waists.

'Who are they?' Clarissa asked, and Chen Mantze turned to her with a concerned look on his face.

'*Jan-dous*,' he replied. 'Pirates.'

'They want to steal the opium?' Clarissa asked.

Chen Mantze nodded. 'Then maybe ransom boat. And people on boat.'

Harry felt his stomach give a slide of fear. What if the pirates sneaked aboard at night, he wondered, when the gunboat soldiers were asleep? They had no armaments on the *Kwai-Lun*, nothing with which to defend themselves . . . He looked again at the pirate junk, eyes drawn to a bizarre, spherical object which had been wedged on to a spike at its bow. As the vessel passed closer, he was appalled to see it was a severed human head.

'Don't look,' Harry hissed to Clarissa, but it was too late: she was staring at the thing, her lips parted in shock. He took her hand in his, and she let out a sharp little cry and buried her face in his shoulder.

Harry stood there like a statue, heart beating fast. But then the pirate junk moved away, banking towards the shore, and as the gunboat fired off another warning shot to speed it on its way, Clarissa stepped back, eyes averted in embarrassment. 'Please excuse me, Mr Compton. I was . . .' She swallowed. 'I was not myself.'

'There is no need to explain, Mrs Lockhart.'

At length, the crew dispersed, and the convoy picked up speed again. 'I suppose that's what we're paying for,' Clarissa said in as airy a voice as she could muster. 'Gunboat diplomacy.'

Harry nodded, looking back out at the chocolate-brown waters of the river, searching for more boats that might belong to Yangtze pirates. 'Worth every cash,' he replied.

That evening, they reached Nanking. Harry had assumed that cover of darkness would preclude the offloading of chests, but no, the procedure took place in much the same way as in daylight, though this time Harry and Clarissa remained aboard, much to Wilberforce's displeasure.

A new vat of soup had been prepared, and as the crew went about their business, Harry and Clarissa sat opposite one another on the upper deck. There were river prawns in the broth tonight, Harry had found to his delight. He tried to peel one, but it disintegrated in his hands, so he stuffed what was left of it into his mouth.

'Hungry, Mr Compton?' Clarissa asked, chuckling as she saw the juices cascade down his chin.

Harry wiped them away with a self-conscious frown.

'No need to be embarrassed. Shock affects people in different ways. Some people can't eat a bite, whilst others . . .' Clarissa popped a whole prawn into her own mouth, puffing out the steam. 'Whilst others find themselves quite ravenous.'

Harry looked away, knowing it would take more than a square meal for him to forget the horrifying sight of that severed head. He shook himself. He would need to toughen up if he wanted to forge a career as a plant hunter — or at least learn to put on a brave face, like Clarissa.

'Nanking looks a little larger than Chinkiang, don't you think?' Harry said, gesturing towards the port, where a tall pagoda rose above the tumbledown city walls, silhouetted against the starlit sky.

'During the Ming Dynasty, it was the capital of China,' Clarissa replied. 'But I don't think there's much left of the old city.' She reached down to stroke Wilberforce's back, staring out at the glowing lanterns of Nanking, listening to the shouts and cries of the dockers. Then she turned to Harry and steepled her fingers. 'I have a proposition for you, Mr Compton.'

'Oh yes?' he said doubtfully. This didn't sound good.

'I propose that each night we reveal three things about ourselves to each other.' Seeing the wariness in Harry's eyes, she gave him her most persuasive smile. 'We may be in one another's company for some time, Mr Compton. We might as well learn something of one another, don't you agree?'

'I should be honoured,' Harry muttered, but then he smiled. It would be intriguing to find out a little more about his travelling companion . . . 'Shall I go first, then?' he asked, swatting away a moth that had been drawn in by the kerosene stove. He paused for a moment, trying to think of something suitable. 'I once trod on Charles Dickens's foot.'

Clarissa leant forward, mouth agape. 'You did not.'

'I most certainly did,' Harry said. 'The great Charles Dickens was strolling down the King's Road one Saturday morning, and there was a crowd all about him. I was in a dreadful rush, and tried to squeeze past and . . . whoops!'

'Are you sure it was him?'

'I swear on my life. He gave an almighty howl.'

'I'll bet he did,' Clarissa said, with a knowing roll of the eyes. 'Men have such little tolerance for pain!'

Harry sat back and crossed his arms. 'Well, what have you for me then, Mrs Lockhart?'

She bit her lower lip, then looked up at him. 'I never learnt my twelve times table.'

'How can that be?'

'I had the ague, and missed the lesson. Then a new tutor started, and I never caught up.'

'What's twelve times twelve?' Harry asked.

'I have absolutely no idea.'

Harry laughed. 'Want me to teach you?'

'No thanks.' Clarissa was smiling now too, and Harry suddenly found himself wishing that there was a flagon of *jiu* to hand, so that they could forget all about opium dens and decapitated bodies.

'Your turn,' Clarissa said.

Harry thought again. 'When I was ten years old . . .' he began, but then there were footsteps on deck as Chen Mantze hurried over, snapping out instructions to a subordinate.

'What is it?' Clarissa said, eyes round with alarm.

'Upriver,' Chen Mantze replied, then broke off at the sound of an explosion. '*Jan-dous*,' he added. 'Have godown there, you savvy?'

Harry clambered to his feet just in time to see the HMS *Haseley* fire again. She was holding stationary in the current, her guns pointing at a thatched bamboo shack that rose on stilts beside the riverbank.

'What are they firing at?' Clarissa asked, coming to stand by Harry.

'Some kind of warehouse, I think. Perhaps where the pirates keep their weapons.' Harry shrugged. 'The gunboat commander must have received some local intelligence.'

Detritus was beginning to appear on the water now. Harry looked down and saw bamboo poles drifting past them, then a broken boathook, then . . . He gave a sudden intake of breath. That was a corpse! A corpse, floating face-down in the river, just the shoulders and back of the head visible, a long plait of black hair waving like seaweed in the current.

'Come, Missy,' Chen Mantze said, seeing Clarissa staring down at the body, her face pale.

For once Clarissa did not contradict him, just reached down to pick up Wilberforce, then followed Harry as they made their way down to the hold.

'Would you like me to stand guard outside your cabin?' Harry asked.

'This could be a nightly occurrence, Mr Compton,' Clarissa replied. 'You'd be dead on your feet. And besides,' she added, caressing the shaking terrier in her arms, 'I have my trusty protector.'

Harry plucked up a burning candle and passed it to her. She smiled back, her green eyes glistening in the flame. 'But I enjoyed our little game, Mr Compton. Perhaps we might continue it tomorrow?'

'I hope so,' Harry said, stooping down to pick up a candle for himself. 'Good night, Mrs Lockhart,' he added, before turning to his hatchway, a mad voice playing in his head, wondering if Clarissa might possibly have wanted him to kiss her. But then he heard the firm scrape of her bolt, and dismissed the idea for the absurdity it was.

Topside on the 'Kwai-Lun'
200 nautical miles from S'hai
May 3, 1868

Dear Jack,

This letter will be mailed from a river port named Ma-an-shan, though whether it will ever reach you I cannot say. The settlement, like many we have visited on our journey up the Yangtze, has been rendered desolate by a recent civil war in China, so I find it hard to believe that the postal service can operate with any kind of efficiency.

Yet the people of this country show astonishing fortitude, and seem determined to carry on whatever the circumstances, so I shall bury my concerns as well, and have faith that this will somehow make its way by packet boat to Shanghai and thence . . . to Battersea!

You may wonder at my haste to board another boat after so nearly drowning on the last, but I can assure you we are in little danger of going down in a storm here. Though the Yangtze may be huge — three times the width of the Thames at Chelsea, and at least twenty times her length — her waves in springtime are insufficient to unbalance our little steam freighter. The principal danger we face is from pirates — 'Wasps of the River', as they are known here — but we travel as part of a cargo convoy, and are well protected from such irritants by a hardy British gunboat.

Cargo convoy, I hear you say, perhaps wondering if your old friend has abandoned his botany? Not a bit of it, Jack — in fact, I have already collected many fabulous plants along the way. A maidenhair tree (which the Chinese are very fond of dwarfing), a Forsythia viridissima, a luscious, cream-coloured gardenia, and several cultivars of chrysanthemum — most of them found growing in the ruined kitchen gardens of houses laid waste by the war. Does such plundering make me a battlefield looter, like our 'Colonel' Frith? Maybe, but I have taken only seeds & root cuttings, so that the parent plants may continue to flourish just as I found them — in overgrown tangles.

211

Accompanying me on these sorties is an artist-friend who has succeeded in capturing the charms of these exotics quite perfectly on her sketchpad. As well as being a talented painter, she owns the boat on which we travel, and lest that 'she' give you pause, I should mention that she is 1. A widow, and 2. A distant relative. I know how your mind works, Jack!

The natural curiosity of this artist is all-consuming, and on our last stop, she dragged me by the arm through the open door of what turned out to be a silk workshop. There was a battalion of weavers inside (all women), the first row of which were busy soaking silkworm cocoons in basins of warm water. As soon as the threads had come free from each cocoon, they were worked through a slit in a wooden board. The women in the row behind then twisted these threads into a single strand, which was wrapped around a loom, to be woven into sheets of the softest silk. Think on that the next time you spy a gentleman in a top hat sauntering down the King's Road!

What other curiosities can I describe for you? Well, the banks of the Yangtze are all heaped with tombs — stone coffins thatched with straw mats to shield them from the weather, or large conical mounds, overgrown with grass. It is forbidden for anyone to interfere with these tombs, so that the fields where they lie are lost to agriculture, and even railway lines cannot be laid for fear of disturbing the dead. And those who come to mourn there are all dressed in white, rather than black, so that it seems to me that everything in China is topsy-turvy!

Another tradition which has surprised me is the coiffure of the menfolk. The style is really quite peculiar, and I am told dates from more than two hundred and fifty years ago, when the current rulers of China — the Qing — first rode down from Manchuria to conquer the Celestial Empire. Having overthrown the Ming, the victors then demanded that the locals mimic their Tartar hairstyles — a close-shaven head with a long black pigtail dangling down the back. The fashion persists to this day, though you will be relieved to know I have not yet given into it!

More shocking is a tradition forced upon some of the girls here, who have their feet broken in infancy, then bound in cloth so that they can neither heal

212

nor grow properly. The result is that they must totter about on little more than stumps, for which special silk shoes are made in doll-like sizes. In certain ports, we have seen women being carried on the shoulders of men merely to get about from one place to another. This tradition may predate the Tartar invasion, but it is still abominable, as my companion has volubly pointed out to me on numerous occasions.

Just prior to my departure for the Yangtze, I received a letter from you, Jack, that spoke of your belief that my erstwhile employer might be considering mounting an expedition of his own. Have you, by any chance, heard more on this matter? Or has he — as you suspected — been put off by the crippling fees that experienced plant hunters demand?

As it happens, a few days before your letter arrived, I sent one to you, requesting that you make enquiries with certain nurserymen on the King's Road. Have you had any success yet in this affair? Though I know you would never expect anything in reward for your kindnesses to me, I should nonetheless have added that it will be worth your while to accede to my proposal. 'If you want happiness for a lifetime, help someone else,' as they say in China (there are many such proverbs here, which my companion, who falsely claims to know little of the country, regularly brings to my attention).

Anyway, Jack, the crew have just finished unloading the day's cargo, and the ship's cook (different to the last, but equally kind) has offered to post my letter, so I must seal it now.

Your old friend,

Harry

PS. Two days ago we saw a meteor shower, which was quite something, I can tell you!

Chapter 17

Wuhu, Anqing, Kiu-Kiang . . . The days slid by as the convoy made its steady way up the Yangtze. Soon, Harry and Clarissa found themselves falling into a languid routine. She spent the days reading in her cabin, avoiding the heat and the sun, whilst Harry whiled away the time filling in his notebook with details of the plants he'd seen or collected, and making copies of Lorcan Darke's map — leaving out the name of the icicle tree. Lunch and dinner were taken on deck, playing their information game, discovering more about each other.

Clarissa, Harry had learnt, had met her husband at a county hunt-ball at the age of fifteen — she'd grown up in the south of Suffolk, in Constable country, and it had been a pair of the illustrious painter's landscapes hanging in her parents' dining-room that had provided early artistic inspiration. Harry, in turn, had revealed that he'd been named after *Childe Harold*, as his mother had been a devotee of Lord Byron's poetry. Clarissa had countered with tales of a black sheep of a great uncle, who'd been transported to Australia, much to the family's disgrace.

Thus far, there'd been no further threat from pirates, thanks to HMS *Haseley*'s unfailing attentions, though one dispute had arisen on a smaller scale, when they'd been moored up near a market town, watching the sun go down over the flat, grassy floodplains of the Yangtze. Instead of going on to shore to walk Wilberforce, Harry and Clarissa had taken to dropping the little dog overboard, then letting him paddle about for a while, before lowering a gaff into the water, which he would grip with his jaws until he could be pulled out. Whilst enjoying his bath that evening, Wilberforce had seen a turtle swimming close by, and had taken hold of the thing in his jaws, trying to get at the soft, succulent body within the shell. An old man watching from the bank had flown into a paroxysm of rage, so that Cai, the ship's cook, had been forced to dive off the boat to retrieve the dog, and free the terrified turtle.

After a deal of pidgin English on both sides, Chen Mantze had conveyed to Harry and Clarissa that the aggrieved man had purchased the turtle that day from the local market. He had then freed it into the river, in accordance with the ancient Buddhist custom whereby a life – any life – spared constituted a sacred action. Wilberforce's clumsy attempt to eat the turtle had therefore represented a grave violation of the poor man's religious beliefs.

The evening after this incident, having just finished supper, Harry watched Clarissa pick up a squirming Wilberforce. 'I can't imagine he's likely to run into two sacred turtles in as many days,' Harry said.

'No,' Clarissa agreed, 'that would be improbable.' Gently, she set the terrier down on the deck, and he trotted back over to the rail, gazing out longingly at the darkening water.

Clarissa seemed a little pensive tonight, Harry thought. Perhaps it was because tomorrow they would reach Hankow, where they would find their guide waiting for them. Harry was about to suggest that they resume their information game when she rose to her feet, eye caught by something on the river.

Harry joined her at the gunwale. Twenty yards away, a sampan had appeared on the water, her pilot holding her steady while her little group of passengers lit strips of paper – some covered in Chinese characters, others decorated with animals – and dropped them overboard.

'Whatever can they be doing?' Harry asked.

'They're making burnt offerings,' Clarissa replied. 'A dragon lives beneath the waters of the Yangtze, or so Cai says. These gifts are to propitiate its wrath.'

More sampans began to arrive, and for a time everyone on the *Kwai-Lun* was silent, watching spellbound as the pilgrims dropped their burning strips of paper on to the black surface of the river – thinking, perhaps, of the many aspects of existence which lay hidden just out of sight.

As the final offering flickered and died away, and the bullfrogs resumed their steady dirge in the reedbanks, Clarissa gave a shiver.

'Would you like me to fetch your shawl?' Harry asked. 'Or your book, perhaps?'

Clarissa shook her head. 'I finished Marco Polo's travels this afternoon.'

'And?'

'Well, there were some pretty fanciful trees described. Box trees with timber as fragrant as perfume. Even trees that generated kings from their sap, would you believe? But no mention of any icicle tree.'

Harry stretched, stifling a yawn. 'That doesn't mean Marco Polo didn't search for it.' Seeing Clarissa twine a curl of hair between her fingers, Harry tilted his head. 'You have something on your mind, I think, Mrs Lockhart?'

'Not really,' Clarissa said. But then she swallowed. 'Only – this Irishman, Lorcan Darke. Are you sure he was trustworthy?'

Harry looked at her, then said, half in jest, 'You choose this moment to start questioning the existence of the icicle tree? *Now?* Halfway up the Yangtze, having committed God knows how much money to the enterprise?' Harry paused, gathering himself. 'Lorcan Darke was entirely trustworthy,' he resumed. 'I saw his dried specimens of the icicle tree with my own eyes. Next thing you'll be saying you don't trust me!'

They both fell silent for a moment, suddenly conscious of the crew watching them from across the deck.

'It's late,' Clarissa said, 'I should get to bed. *Wanan,* Chen Mantze,' she called out, and Harry followed her down to the hold, still feeling the weight of the men's gaze fixed upon their backs.

Nothing more was said until they reached Clarissa's cabin. 'Good night,' she murmured, refusing to meet his eye.

'Please, Clarissa,' Harry said. 'Let's not quarrel.' It was the first time he'd used her Christian name.

She turned, and he opened his palms to her. 'I held blossoms from the icicle tree in these very hands,' he went on. 'My employer, Josiah Piggott, was only too aware of their value – as my father found out to his cost.'

That shadow of doubt flickered across Clarissa's face again. 'What?' Harry said. 'What is it now?'

She looked away. 'It was something that Charlie Hargreaves said to me.'

'*Hargreaves*?'

Clarissa turned back to him, cheeks burning. 'There are rumours in London.'

'What rumours?'

'They say that you robbed your father and killed him. That the only reason the police haven't issued a warrant for your arrest is because they cannot find the body.'

Harry stood there, stunned, not just by the false allegation, but by the fact that Hargreaves knew anything of his past life at all. Surely Harry hadn't been in Shanghai long enough for Hargreaves to make enquiries about him in London; certainly not to receive a reply. *So how?* An alarming thought insinuated its way into Harry's mind. Might not the Portsmouth Police have written to the British Consulate, informing them of their suspicions about him? It would not have been especially difficult for them to ascertain that his destination was Shanghai, he realised, thinking back to the loquacious pawnbroker who'd procured him his passage. But then an even more insidious notion occurred. If the police *had* found out where Harry was going, might not they have mentioned it to Piggott when they'd come to question him in Chelsea? If so, it was entirely possible that Piggott could have sent someone after Harry to China within weeks of his own departure.

Fear sharpening his resentment, Harry rounded on Clarissa. 'I told you what happened on the day my father died,' he hissed, feeling his mouth stiff with anger. 'I trusted you, and you alone, with my secret. Yet you take the word

218

of Hargreaves over me?' He looked Clarissa up and down, feeling his admiration for her sour. 'What are you doing here, Mrs Lockhart, if you think me a criminal? Has Hargreaves sent you here to spy?' He gave a cruel smile. 'I knew you to be mercenary and avaricious, but I put that down to the difficulty of your personal circumstances. But a common spy?'

Clarissa recoiled as though he'd struck her. 'I am sorry that you think so little of me, Mr Compton,' she said, barely controlling the contempt in her voice.

'And you of me!' Harry shot back.

They stood there for a moment, glowering at one another. Then she turned her back on him, and walked away.

Chapter 18

The next morning, still troubled by his argument with Clarissa, Harry threw himself into helping the crew shift the opium chests to the upper deck, in advance of their arrival in Hankow. It was hard, hot work, but it felt good to be using his muscles again, and by the time he'd finished, he was feeling a little brighter.

Joining the crew on deck for a cup of green tea, Harry leant back against the rail, enjoying the warmth of the late May sunshine on his skin, watching as Chen Mantze skilfully steered the boat towards Hankow harbour. Then he heard the clatter of claws on wood, and turned to see Wilberforce hurtling towards him.

Crouching down to give the dog a stroke, Harry looked up to see Clarissa emerge on to the deck, wearing her usual black dress and wide-brimmed hat. Seeing her hesitate as she took in the group of bare-chested men ranged on the deck before her, Harry felt a little of his rancour dissipate. It couldn't be easy being the only woman aboard.

Evidently, Clarissa had not noticed Harry among the throng, as when she recognised him, she gave a sudden start, and turned bright red.

Harry pulled his shirt back over his head in embarrassed haste, ignoring the guffaws of the crew. 'Good morning, Mrs Lockhart,' he said.

'Good morning,' she replied in a tart tone that told him she was still angry with him.

'I'm extremely sorry,' Harry said, and suddenly found that he meant it. 'I behaved abominably.'

She cast him a quick glance, and he saw there was genuine pain in her eyes. He had hurt her, he realised. What a cad . . .

'Yes,' she said. 'You did.'

'My temper got the better of me.'

'We have a business arrangement, Mr Compton,' Clarissa said, straightening her gloves. 'A partnership for the duration of the expedition. Once that is complete, you may be assured that I shall impose on you no further.'

'Please, Clarissa,' Harry said softly, and she looked up again at the sound of her Christian name. 'What I said to you, I said in anger. And I did not mean it.' He looked into her cloudy green eyes. 'I do not think you mercenary or ruthless at all.' He swallowed. 'To tell the truth, I think you quite remarkable. The way you treat the most junior crewman in the same manner you would the grandest member of Shanghai society. The way you refuse to be cowed by your recent bereavement, and launch yourself into life with unflinching courage and curiosity.'

Clarissa stared at Harry for a moment, then turned away, lips twitching. 'Your apology is accepted, Mr Compton. Now let us say no more on the matter!' She joined him at the gunwale, a few tendrils of her auburn hair catching in the breeze as she gazed out at the harbour. 'So, this is Hankow.'

Harry nodded, relieved that the moment of tension had passed. 'It reminds me a bit of the Bund,' he said, seeing the quayside up ahead, which resembled a miniature version of Shanghai's famous embankment – a curving stretch of shore, jetties running off it, impressive classical-style buildings set along the embankment, British flags flying from the facades.

'It's called the Bund here too,' Clarissa said. 'Hankow's the last treaty port on the Yangtze, and it has a good-sized English concession. Beyond this point, all European influence ends.'

They both fell silent as they considered the implications of her words. For, once they left Hankow, there would be no more gunboat, no more convoy. They would be entirely alone, unprotected against whatever dangers lay on the waters ahead. Might there be river pirates watching them from afar, Harry wondered, awaiting their moment to kidnap them and ransom them off to the British authorities? Or could Mr Piggott's plant hunter be lurking out of sight, ready to swoop when the time was right to steal Lorcan Darke's map – or even the icicle tree itself?

Shaking these dark misgivings from his mind, Harry looked back up at the harbour. 'Does Lockhart's have an office here as well?' he asked, seeing the names of other *hongs* daubed on the brickwork of two of the buildings.

Clarissa shook her head. 'We're a long way behind the older companies – they've been selling opium in China since the start of the 1830s.'

'Before the Opium Wars, then?' Harry said.

Clarissa glanced at him sideways, then nodded.

'So before that, they were smuggling the drug illegally?'

She gave a shrug. 'They ran guns as well. That's what kept the Taiping Rebellion going for so long.'

These *hongs*! Harry thought. Using superior weaponry and swifter boats, they'd built up a market in China for strong, Indian-grown opium. Then, once the locals had developed a taste for the stuff, they'd persuaded the British government to wage a brutal war to force its legalization.

Amongst the usual scrum of tidewaiters and stevedores crowding the quayside, Harry saw one man who stood out. His face was clean-shaven, and he wore a long robe of immaculate green silk, gathered at the waist by a tasselled belt. On his head he wore a round, flat-topped black cap, and on his feet a pair of brown boots, with a thick layer of solid white felt at the heel, lending him a good two inches of extra height on most of his compatriots. He kept glancing from one cargo boat to the other, his stern, almost aristo-cratic face, with its hawk-like nose, seeming to radiate dis-approval.

'I think we've found our guide,' Harry said, motioning to the man.

Clarissa nodded. 'Fang Li-Liang.'

'How do we address him, do you suppose?' Harry asked. 'Mr Li-Liang?'

'The surname comes first in China,' Clarissa reminded him.

'Mr Fang, then,' Harry said. 'Sounds ominous.'

'Hush,' Clarissa scolded, biting back a smile.

The guide had seen them now, taking off his silk cap and waving it at them in greeting. Rather than a shaven head and queue, he wore a short neat haircut, with a sprinkling of grey about the temples.

As Clarissa moved towards the nearest gangplank, Harry tugged at her sleeve. 'Remember,' he warned. 'Fang is close to the Taotai. We must be careful what we say.'

'Have faith in your elders, Mr Compton,' Clarissa teased. 'I shan't say a word about the true purpose of our expedition.' Then she picked up her skirts and swept away, Wilberforce at her heel.

The guide was talking to Chen Mantze now, the captain listening nervously, both hands clasped together like a supplicant. As Clarissa approached them, Fang Li-Liang turned and looked at her appraisingly, then lowered his head into a gracious bow. 'Mrs Lockhart,' he said in a deep, commanding voice. 'You have kept to your itinerary precisely.'

'We have Chen Mantze to thank for that,' Clarissa replied, with a quick smile at the captain.

The guide turned to Harry. 'And you must be Mr Harry Compton.'

'How do you do, Mr Fang?' Harry asked, sticking out a hand.

The older man took it with a smile that opened up his noble face. 'Please – call me Li-Liang.' He released Harry's hand and turned to the Bund. 'Come now. Let us take a little refreshment while we wait for your luggage to be transhipped.' Then he swivelled on one felt-heeled boot, and plunged into the crowd.

Exchanging an amused glance with Clarissa, Harry followed as Li-Liang weaved his way through the busy port, replete with strange smells and sounds. Eventually, they came to a large square building set back from the harbour road, fronted by a Palladian-style colonnade.

'The Hankow Club,' Li-Liang announced, ushering them into its cool, marble-floored entrance hall.

As Harry gazed up in admiration at the vaulted ceiling, Li-Liang barked something at a waiter, who showed them to a round table at the back.

At the next table sat a pair of English griffins, one half-heartedly flipping through the *Hankow Times* as the other sat back in his chair, watching Clarissa through a pair of insolent, hooded eyes. Harry glared at the man, until he picked up his sherry glass and looked away.

Li-Liang reached down to stroke Wilberforce, who'd found a warm place to curl up at Harry's feet. 'A handsome creature.'

'And a faithful friend,' Clarissa said.

The waiter appeared with a bowl of fried beancakes, and Harry fell upon it, suddenly ravenous. Clarissa suppressed a smile, then turned her attention to Li-Liang. 'What an agreeable place.'

'I suppose so,' Li-Liang said. He raised his thoughtful eyes and looked about him, taking in the airy atrium at the back, with a sign directing members to the Billiards Room, Library and Reading Room upstairs. 'I do not come here often, I must admit.'

'Because of the clientele?' Harry asked, throwing a disapproving glance over to the griffins at the next table.

'Partly,' Li-Liang replied. 'But also because, until 1861, my mother's house stood upon this site.'

Clarissa canted her head. 'Your mother?'

Li-Liang nodded. 'The house had been in her family for over sixty years until the British came. They forcibly purchased the entire river frontage for their new settlement.'

'But surely they paid for it?' Harry asked indignantly.

'Naturally,' Li-Liang said. 'But only a fraction of its worth. The dispute went all the way to Peking. In the end, the British won.' He smiled. 'As you so often do.'

'I'm sorry to hear that,' Clarissa said, her brow furrowed.

Li-Liang dismissed her concern with a graceful wave of the arm. 'Why be sorry? It's hardly your fault, Mrs Lockhart. What's done is done – we must look to the future now.'

The drinks arrived, three whisky sodas in heavy cut-glass tumblers, tinkling with cubes of ice.

'Bottoms up,' Li-Liang said, raising his glass.

Clarissa caught Harry's eye. 'Bottoms up,' she echoed, and they all drank.

'So,' Li-Liang said, setting down his glass with a sigh of satisfaction. 'You are an artist, I understand, Mrs Lockhart?'

'I wouldn't say that . . .' Clarissa began.

'Yes,' interjected Harry. 'A very fine landscapist and illustrator.'

For once lost for words, Clarissa's cheeks went pink.

'I see,' Li-Liang said, taking it all in. 'And what of your plans in Hunan? I thought perhaps a leisurely excursion up the River Yuan, stopping off at the most attractive places along the way?' He looked from Clarissa to Harry, eyebrows arched enquiringly. 'Is there any particular area you wish to visit?'

Harry reached into a pocket and took out the best copy he'd made of Lorcan Darke's map – with all mention of the icicle tree omitted. 'Here,' he said, tapping a finger on the place where 'X' had marked the spot.

'The most beautiful painting spot imaginable,' Clarissa threw in. 'Or so I've been led to believe.'

226

Li-Liang stretched his fingers apart, calculating distances. 'You must mean the Mian Jian Guang pagoda.' He gave Clarissa a shrewd look. 'It means the "Vestibule of the Sojourn of Death".'

'Sounds cheerful,' Harry muttered.

'But it's in Guizhou, Mrs Lockhart,' Li-Liang went on. 'Not Hunan.'

'Does that matter?' Clarissa asked.

Li-Liang paused. 'May I see your travel papers?'

Clarissa handed them over and watched, the side of one thumb pressed to her lower lip, as Li-Liang unfurled the roll and examined it. 'Oh, but this is good news,' the guide said, laying the paper out on the glass-topped table. 'This is the stamp of the Zongli Yamen, do you see? The Foreign Ministry in Peking. It gives you permission to travel throughout the interior of China, as long as you are accompanied by me. So, extending the journey to Guizhou should be no trouble at all. Although it *will* increase the price . . .'

'By how much?' Clarissa asked.

'Fifty taels, perhaps?'

Clarissa looked at him sceptically.

'But you may rely on me to secure the best possible price from the steam-launch captain,' Li-Liang added hurriedly, then looked back down at the map. 'For my part, I shall be very pleased to visit Guizhou.' He gave a modest smile. 'I am something of an engineer, you see, and hope to collect mineral samples as we progress, on behalf of the Central Mining Authority in Peking. Guizhou has rich potential for mining – copper, mercury, saltpetre. And in China, the Qing government owns everything that is under the ground.'

Grasping Li-Liang's meaning, Harry balked. 'So that means, what — that the government can mine any land without seeking the owner's permission?'

'Exactly!' Li-Liang said.

Harry was about to express his astonishment at this state of affairs, until he remembered how the British had behaved towards Li-Liang's mother, and held his tongue.

'Given that you intend to carry out a little work on behalf of the Central Mining Authority during our journey,' Clarissa said, 'I wonder if they would be prepared to make some contribution to the cost. We might deduct it from your fee, perhaps?' she added, giving Li-Liang a look of unalloyed sweetness.

Li-Liang glanced up at her sharply. But then he laughed. 'The Taotai was right, Mrs Lockhart, you are indeed a formidable woman. We shall come to some little arrangement, you will see! But now,' he added, finishing his drink, 'let us return to the harbour, so that I may introduce you to your new captain.'

When they reached the quayside, the other freighters had left, and only the *Kwai-Lun* remained, the crew busy heaving massive bales of hemp and cotton into the hold to take back to Shanghai. As Clarissa and Harry approached, Chen Mantze ran down the gangway towards them.

'*Ni tai hao la*, Chen Mantze,' Clarissa said earnestly, taking both his hands in hers.

Chen Mantze gave a deep bow, then reached down and stroked Wilberforce's hairy cheek with the tip of one finger.

'Goodbye!' came a cheerful cry from the upper deck, and Harry looked up to see Cai and the rest of the crew waving to them. 'Goodbye, goodbye, goodbye,' Cai continued to shout, beaming with pleasure to have an opportunity to use one of the English words that Clarissa had taught him.

Clarissa and Harry waved fondly, then — once she'd handed Chen Mantze a bag of coins as 'squeeze' — they followed Li-Liang along the harbourfront. Moored to the next jetty was a rather different collection of boats to those they were used to. At the far end bobbed a small Chinese junk, but with its mast replaced by a rickety stovepipe funnel. Tied to its stern were two wide-beamed, roofed wooden boats, bound together by ropes, whilst at the rear floated a larger junk with its sail down.

'This is our flotilla,' Li-Liang explained. 'Steam launch at the front. Two *chuans*, or houseboats, behind. And the armed junk at the back.'

Harry looked for mortars, cannons or even carronades protruding from the sides of this 'armed junk', but it appeared to be nothing more than a traditional Chinese sailing ship. But Clarissa's concerns lay elsewhere. '*Two* houseboats?' she was saying, no doubt thinking of her purse. 'Is that not rather excessive?'

'Each *chuan* is fitted with only two cabins, Mrs Lockhart,' Li-Liang replied coolly. 'I shall require one of my own — for the storage of my mineral samples — so unless you and Mr Compton intend to share . . .?'

Exchanging a rapid look of embarrassment, Clarissa and Harry shook their heads.

'Well, that's settled then,' Li-Liang said.

There was a group of burly men sitting on a bench in the armed junk, joshing and laughing. Harry motioned towards them. 'They seem a lively bunch.'

229

Li-Liang smiled. 'They're our mercenaries, Mr Compton.'

'I beg your pardon?' Clarissa said.

'They have been retained for your protection, Mrs Lockhart. As you must know by now, the river can be a dangerous place. There is a reason why travel into the interior is rare.'

Harry nodded, remembering the corpse they'd seen floating in the water . . .

'But mercenaries,' Clarissa said.

Li-Liang shrugged. 'They fought for the Emperor during the Taiping Rebellion. For which they were richly rewarded. Bo Lungsin!' the guide called out, and a grizzled, swarthy man strolled towards them. 'This is Bo Lungsin,' Li-Liang said. 'Captain of the *Jinji*, or *Golden Pheasant*.'

The steam-launch captain must have been nearing middle age, but he looked as fit as a much younger man. He refused to meet either of the Westerners' eyes, preferring to gaze aloofly into the middle distance as he puffed on a black ceramic pipe.

Wilberforce – so often an astute judge of character – began to growl. 'Shh,' Clarissa chided, nudging the dog with her foot. 'How do you do, Bo Lungsin?' she asked, bowing her head. '*Ni hao ma?*'

But the captain made no reply, just picked a sprig of tobacco off his tongue and flicked it into the river.

'Bo Lungsin is a man of few words, I'm afraid, Mrs Lockhart,' Li-Laing said.

Clarissa shook the dust off her skirts, then looked round at the guide and smiled. 'He has not been employed for his conversation!'

'Indeed,' Li-Liang said. 'And in regard to his professional abilities, please be assured that I have not a single reservation.

Bo Lungsin is perfectly equal to the task at hand.' Turning, Li-Liang spoke to the captain for a time, doubtless bringing him up to date on their adjusted travel plans, and he gave a curt nod and sauntered back towards the jetty.

'The *Golden Pheasant* will tow the flotilla until we reach the River Yuan,' Li-Liang resumed. 'We shall then pick her up again on our way back.'

'But why can't Bo Lungsin take us all the way to Guizhou?' Clarissa asked.

'The Yuan is too shallow for a propeller. The armed junk will take over then as the tug.' Li-Liang sucked his teeth. 'It will be a lengthy journey, I'm afraid. Eight days to reach Lake Dongting. Two more to cross it. And three weeks to sail up the Yuan.'

'Three weeks!' Clarissa exclaimed.

'There are a number of awkward rapids on the Yuan. In some parts, we will need the mercenaries to drag the flotilla by hand.' Li-Liang smiled. 'You'll see.'

Harry looked again at the men. Most were smoking little black pipes, just like their captain. Was that the familiar aroma of opium Harry detected on the breeze? 'Do the mercenaries carry guns?' he asked.

Li-Liang shook his head. 'Only cutlasses.'

'What if the pirates have guns?' Harry pressed.

'That is extremely unlikely,' Li-Liang replied. 'Most of the guns in this part of China were confiscated by the army after the Taiping Rebellion.'

'*Most* of them?' Harry echoed.

But Li-Liang wasn't listening now, busy removing a gold pocketwatch from his silk robes and scowling as he read the time.

I should have bought a gun in Shanghai, Harry thought. They'd known that the gunboat would be leaving them after Hankow. Securing a firearm would have mitigated the dangers for the second half of the journey.

'Bo Lungsin!' Li-Liang hollered, then set off quickly towards the flotilla, barking out a commandment in rapid Chinese. A moment later, Harry saw thick black smoke start to billow from the rusty funnel of the steam launch.

'Looks like we're off,' Clarissa said.

'So it would seem,' Harry replied, watching uneasily as the entire hull of the steam launch began to rattle – it would be a miracle if they made it out of the harbour, he thought, let alone to the River Yuan.

And so, one by one, they stepped on to the jetty, Wilberforce leading the pack, hackles raised.

Chapter 19

But any worries Harry had regarding their new mode of transport were soon dispelled when the speed of the steam launch became apparent. Somehow, for a vessel with so small an engine, the *Golden Pheasant* moved up the Yangtze at a tremendous lick, dragging the houseboats and armed junk so fast behind it that when Harry dipped a hand over the edge, the side of his palm cut a sleek 'V' through the water. Even if they were being pursued, he thought — by pirates, or, Heaven forefend, by some rival expedition mounted by Mr Piggott — it was hard to imagine they would be caught at the rate they were travelling.

Dashazhen, Tengjiakao, Paizhou, Yongjixiang. . . The settlements they passed now were little more than fishing villages, their inhabitants more rustically dressed than those upriver — shirtless men in calf-length trousers; women in plain woven dresses, their hair in braids — and their houses mere straw huts, covered in clay and white-washed with lime.

Every evening, the flotilla would moor up whenever they found a suitable location, and if any villagers approached on foot, they would back away as soon as they saw the Imperial

233

Government ensign fluttering from the steam-launch stern — a yellow triangular flag decorated with a flying dragon, which had been given to Li-Liang by the Mining Authority.

This flag proved an efficient passport wherever they went — even when crossing the border between Hubei province and Hunan, the customs sampan patrolling the river merely waved them through. And had the flag not worked its magic, there was always the armed junk. The mercenaries that crewed it wore their machetes fixed to their waistbands, and they would stare out at the passing water traffic with an unflinching hostility. Sometimes, when the wind changed direction, Harry would catch the sweet smell of opium and wonder how many of their protectors were under its malign influence. But then he would remind himself that these were battle-hardened soldiers — if Li-Liang was satisfied with the level of security they provided, then he should be as well.

What was beyond doubt was that one of their number was a skilled cook, preparing a multitude of steamed dumplings in the galley of the junk each mealtime. No bigger than a tangerine, these were fashioned from some kind of sticky, translucent dough, each crammed full of fish, goat or vegetables purchased from the floating markets. At first, Harry found the dumplings a little bland, until Li-Liang encouraged him to dip them into the salty black sauce that accompanied them, and he soon found himself growing quite fond of the dish.

As for their living quarters, Harry deemed those onboard the *chuans* more comfortable than any he'd experienced so far. Just as Li-Liang had promised, the houseboat which

234

he shared with Clarissa boasted two separate cabins at the bow, each about ten feet by five, with a good-sized living area adjacent, a hold beneath for storing luggage, and a 'head' at the front of the boat that served as a primitive water closet. The interior was all made of a fine spruce wood, richly lacquered in varnish, which only added to the sense of luxury.

Li-Liang was less enamoured with his lodgings, however, having discovered that much of his living area was crammed with sacks of coal. So he seemed pleased when Clarissa suggested that they take their meals together, even if Harry thought such an arrangement unwise, concerned that their guide might stumble across his botanical equipment.

'You see dangers around every corner, Mr Compton,' Clarissa chided as she came upon Harry draping a blanket over his honeypots and vasculum. 'Must you think the worst of everyone?'

I didn't used to, Harry reflected, a little glumly. But he was right to be cautious, he reminded himself. They were moving further and further away from British officialdom. If Li-Liang reported them for breaking the Taotai's edicts, then there was no telling what the local authorities might do.

'I've asked Bo Lungsin to unload the trunk containing my easel when we moor up this evening,' Clarissa went on. 'So I shall be painting tonight, and allaying any suspicions that Li-Liang may' — she smirked — 'or may *not* have!'

Clarissa was as good as her word, and every evening henceforth would take out her watercolours and begin work. It was wonderful to watch, and even Bo Lungsin and the mercenaries would look on mesmerised as she painted a pagoda rising from a hilltop, or a fisherman emptying the bill of a cormorant that he'd trained to catch perch. The Taotai would have a wealth of paintings from which to choose when they got back to Shanghai, Harry adjudged.

Li-Liang, meanwhile, made use of these precious pockets of calm to scour the riverbanks for minerals. It was evidently a passion for him, and he would return each night exhilarated, brandishing little vials of unusually coloured mud or silt – pink for iron, green for potassium, black for coal – then retreat to his *chuan* to note down his observations and the precise provenance of each sample.

These absences gave Harry a chance for some discreet botanising. Keeping to the woods, and eschewing the company of a guard – unlike Li-Liang – Harry stumbled upon copious treasures, and soon had root cuttings from a viburnum, from some anemones in a sesame field, from two unusual species of jasmine, and from a white abelia he'd found growing behind an oxen paddock. Twenty-five years ago, he knew, the famous Scottish plant hunter, Robert Fortune, had disguised himself as a Chinese merchant to travel this way, and Harry was impressed at how much of the local flora the great man had managed to collect on behalf of his sponsor, the Horticultural Society of Chiswick. Harry's latest findings might not be new to science, but he was in no doubt they would fetch a pretty penny on the King's Road.

Back on the *chuan*, Harry elected to soak his specimens in jars of river water – when the roots began to sprout, he would transfer them to his Wardian case, but he did not want to start filling up the contraption until absolutely necessary.

Sleeping on the houseboats was a particular joy, not least because the berths were all fitted with muslin mosquito nets. The bulkhead between Harry's and Clarissa's cabins was rather thin, though, so that he would often hear her moving about at night – talking to herself, or humming – and felt sure that she could hear him, too. Sometimes, Harry would dream of her, then jolt awake, embarrassed to find himself undone, and would be struck by the absurd notion that Clarissa was awake too, and knew all about his mortifying predicament. This sensation of unease would then persist all through the next morning, when he would find himself abashed in her presence, and struggle to meet her eye – until the day wore on, and he would forget all about it – until the next time.

A week into this second leg of their journey, shortly after they'd passed the village of Yueyang, Bo Lungsin became preoccupied with the depth of the river, constantly slowing the launch in order to lower a notched bamboo pole into the water. Only when satisfied that the river was sufficiently deep would the captain push the crankshaft forward, so that they could continue further up the Yangtze. As they progressed, Harry became aware of the landscape altering around them – the floodplains receding; hills rising in the distance, densely planted with terraces of black tea and sugar beet.

Then, one afternoon, just as they were making their approach to Lake Dongting, something happened to disturb their peaceful routine. Clarissa was down in the living area of the *chuan*, completing a painting she'd made of the mercenaries laying bets on a fight between two of the huge male crickets they kept for sport. Harry was in his cabin, carefully making notes on the plants he'd collected so far, when suddenly there was an enormous bang, and the entire flotilla shook.

Harry rushed outside to find Clarissa waiting for him in the living area. 'What on earth was that?' she asked.

'I don't know,' Harry replied, brows furrowed, 'but . . .'

'But what?' Clarissa demanded impatiently.

'Li-Liang says there are dangerous sandbanks near the mouth of the lake.'

Clarissa groaned. 'Come on.'

They made their way up on to deck, where it was immediately apparent what had happened. The steam launch had run aground on a sandbank, and the houseboats and junk had smashed into her bow, wedging her stern deep into the mud.

'How can we free it?' Clarissa called to Li-Liang, who was standing on the deck of his *chuan*, engaged in a heated discussion with Bo Lungsin. But the guide just raised a forefinger, telling her to wait.

'Oh, for Heaven's sake,' was Clarissa's irritated response.

Feeling the houseboats judder beneath his feet, Harry looked around to see the mercenaries making their way across the flotilla. They gathered on Li-Liang's boat, causing it to list so heavily that he climbed hurriedly over on to Harry's and Clarissa's *chuan*, grumbling at the inconvenience.

A few of the men were in the water now, Harry saw, trying to shake the steam launch free, but the currents funnelling around the sandbank were too strong, and it soon became clear it was hopeless.

Bo Lungsin seemed remarkably sanguine about their predicament, Harry thought, watching as the captain leisurely took a seat in his wheelhouse and lit up his pipe. By contrast, Li-Liang was scanning the river with a concentration that Harry found unsettling.

'There's something else, isn't there?' Harry said in a low voice.

Li-Liang nodded. 'We're like sitting ducks here, Mr Compton.'

Harry stared at him. 'Pirates?'

The guide was about to respond when Clarissa came into earshot. 'There's a village close by,' she said, pointing to the near bank. 'Couldn't they scare us up some help?'

Harry glanced round and saw a row of shaven-headed men watching them from the waterfront. They didn't look especially friendly, he thought.

'A capital idea, Mrs Lockhart,' Li-Liang replied. 'I shall put it to the captain at once.'

The two men conversed for several minutes, then Li-Liang turned to Clarissa. 'Bo Lungsin tells me that there are two possibilities. The first is that we wait for rain.'

They all looked up at the perfect blue sky, and Clarissa let out a sigh. 'And the second?' she asked hopefully.

'There's a man in the village with a steam launch. Bo Lungsin thinks he can be persuaded to tow us out.' The guide gave a delicate cough: 'For the right price.'

Clarissa put her hands on her hips. 'And how much is the "right price"?'

'A hundred taels.'

'But that's daylight robbery!'

'How much is a tael worth?' Harry asked.

'A thousand cash!' Clarissa replied.

Li-Liang clasped his hands before him and said plaintively, 'But what choice do we have, Mrs Lockhart?'

They were all silent for a time, then Harry spoke. 'Why doesn't Bo Lungsin simply reverse the steam launch?'

'There is no reverse mechanism on the *Golden Pheasant*,' Li-Liang replied. 'That is what the boathooks are for.'

'Well,' Clarissa said, casting another glum look up at the sky. 'I suppose we must wait 'til the weather breaks.'

'It seems a bit of a coincidence, doesn't it?' Harry said. 'For us to find ourselves high and dry, directly opposite the village where Bo Lungsin's friend lives? And for Bo Lungsin to know exactly how much this man would charge us for the use of his boat?'

Clarissa weighed Harry's words, then gave a rueful smile. 'You have a very jaundiced view of human nature, Mr Compton.' She paused. 'Which is not to say that you are wrong.'

Harry turned and gazed at the steam launch. 'What's the Chinese word for "reverse"?' he asked Li-Liang, who was slowly making his way back on to his own houseboat.

'*Fǎn xiàng*,' Li-Liang called back. 'Why?'

Harry answered by pulling off his jacket, then stripping down to his underclothes.

'Mr Compton!' Clarissa exclaimed, averting her eyes. 'What *do* you think you're doing?'

'Taking the initiative, Mrs Lockhart,' Harry replied, as he leapt off the edge of the *chuan*.

For a river that originated in the snowy peaks of the Himalayas, the water was warmer than Harry might have imagined, but the temperature was still invigorating, and he enjoyed the sensation of it washing over his skin. He surfaced, beaming, then looked round to find Clarissa glowering down at him, clutching Wilberforce in her arms. 'I can't imagine what you hope to achieve!' she called out.

'Nothing ventured,' Harry rejoined with a grin. Then he kicked around and began to swim towards the steam launch, using the clumsy front crawl he'd taught himself in the Arun as a boy. Grasping the knotted-rope fender that dangled over one side, he hauled himself aboard, and found himself standing face to face with Bo Lungsin, who looked none too pleased by this invasion of his fiefdom.

'I wondered if we might have a try at reversing the boat,' Harry announced cheerfully.

The captain scowled at him, then muttered something darkly under his breath.

'Mr Compton!' Harry heard Clarissa call out, and turned to see her gesturing towards the armed junk, where three of the mercenaries were up on their feet, paying close attention to what was going on between their captain and this upstart Westerner.

Harry looked back at Bo Lungsin. '*Fǎn xiàng*?' he tried.

Perhaps it was Harry's poor pronunciation, but these words seemed to enrage the captain. Leaning in close to Harry, he started yelling at him, shooting flecks of spittle into his face. Suddenly, unexpectedly, Harry was transported back to the stifling heat of the stovehouse, with Josiah Piggott bellowing at him for some trifling misdemeanour. Before he knew it, Harry had his hands on Bo Lungsin's shoulders and was shoving him back against the wheelhouse, a little shocked by the power in his muscles and the fury in his heart.

241

'Stop that!' Clarissa shouted across the water. 'Stop that immediately!'

Harry ignored her. 'I know you can reverse this boat, Bo Lungsin,' he said quietly, staring into the captain's opium-dulled eyes. 'I've seen a thousand steamers do it on the Thames.'

Bo Lungsin tried to push Harry away, and this time Harry slammed him back against the wall, so hard that the man's head smacked against the wood. Almost immediately, Harry heard a series of heavy splashes from the far end of the flotilla, as three of the mercenaries leapt into the water, cutlasses still fixed to their waistbands.

'You're going to get yourself killed, Mr Compton!' cried Li-Liang.

Harry looked back at Bo Lungsin and saw a hint of triumph in his eyes. *Just wait until my men get here*, they seemed to say.

'*Fǎn xiàng?*' Harry tried again, a little less confidence in his voice this time.

Just then, an urgent cry drifted across the water, and Harry saw Bo Lungsin's expression change. There was fear in his eyes now – panic, even. Then the cry came again, louder now, and when Harry turned his head, he saw several of the mercenaries gesticulating frantically from the armed junk. '*Jan-dous!*' they were yelling. *Pirates*.

Thirty yards away, a sailing ship was approaching from downstream. Its deck was busy with men, and as it drew closer, Harry recognised at the prow the hideous shape of a severed head jammed on to a spike. The mercenaries in the water must have seen it too, as they were already swimming back the way they had come, shouting urgently to one another.

242

Harry swung back round to Bo Lungsin. '*Fǎn xiàng!*' he cried.

This time, the captain nodded. 'Yes, Mr Compton,' he said in English. 'Time for reverse boat.'

Shaking himself free, Bo Lungsin barked something at the mercenaries, then hurried down the hatchway that led to the boiler room. A moment later, Harry heard the clank of the boiler doors, then smelt the sharp stink of kerosene as a handful of oil-soaked rags was ignited and thrown into the furnace.

'Please, Mrs Lockhart,' Harry heard Li-Liang beseech Clarissa, 'you must go below deck – it is not safe here.'

'He's right,' Harry called out. 'Get down to your cabin now, and bolt the door!'

A moment later, there was a horrible, shrieking cacophony, and Harry turned to see the pirate ship pulling up close to the armed junk. The mercenaries had brought up wicker baskets of sharp rocks from the hold, he saw, and were hurling them at the pirates, drawing blood and screams of fury. But they wouldn't be able to hold off their attackers for long, Harry thought – there must be fifty *jan-dous* on that ship . . .

'Harry!' he heard Clarissa shout, and snapped back to attention. 'Behind you!'

He spun around, and there, at the stern of the steam launch, he saw a tall, thickset man hauling himself aboard. The pirate was bare-chested, his torso roped with sinewy muscle and dripping with water, and in his right hand he held a massive machete.

Harry's knees almost buckled with fear. He glanced about for Bo Lungsin, but the captain was still down in the engine

243

room, busy firing up the boiler. Switching his attention back to his adversary, Harry saw the man grinning at him, his bare feet planted wide on the deck in a solid, balanced stance, flitting his machete from one hand to the other with a practised dexterity. Seeing Harry take a step back, the man peeled back his lips into a snarl, then produced a soft, high-pitched whistle between his teeth, and advanced.

Harry felt a bolus of vomit creep up his gorge. The man was only ten yards away now, his eyes fixed on Harry's face, utterly focused on what he planned to do. He's going to kill me, Harry realised. And then everything he'd gone through — his father's death, his flight to Shanghai, the adventure that he and Clarissa had embarked upon together — it would all have been for nothing.

Harry's eyes flicked desperately around the deck, searching for something — anything — he might use as a weapon. Finally, they fell upon a boathook lying flat against the gunwale, a thick bamboo pole with a curved metal claw on the end. Making a lunge for it, Harry raised it above his shoulder like a broadsword, conscious of a rapid pulsing in his temples as his heart began to accelerate.

Harry met the pirate's eye, then made a first, false strike, and the man skipped back a yard, murmuring to himself as he regained his balance. Harry lashed out again, but the pirate was surprisingly agile for a man of his size, and he neatly dodged the blow, weaving to one side as the boathook smashed uselessly on to the deck. As Harry caught his breath, he saw the pirate charging him, and swiped the boathook across the wooden planks, forcing the man either to leap over it and make a stab at him, or to retreat. Thankfully, the pirate chose the latter course, and Harry had time to raise his weapon once more, though his arms were tiring now and shaking badly.

Seeing the boathook waver in Harry's hands like a sapling in a gale, the pirate gave a small, triumphant smile. If I don't strike soon, Harry thought, I'm done for. So, with a great roar of fury, he raised the boathook high above his head, and was about to swing it down when he heard an explosion behind him: the sharp crack of a gun. The boathook flew out of his hands, as though someone had struck it with a cricket bat. As it clattered down on to the decking, the knifeman scrambled away from it and made for the edge of the boat, his eyes wide with fear.

The shot must have come from downstream, Harry reasoned, and glanced back over his shoulder. He expected to find that it was an armed mercenary who had saved him, but, to his astonishment, he saw Clarissa Lockhart standing on the deck of her houseboat, her red hair blowing in the wind like Boadicea, a shiny black shotgun pressed to one shoulder.

'What in God's name are you doing?' Harry demanded.

'Taking the initiative, Mr Compton,' Clarissa called back, then turned the shotgun towards the pirate, who gave a yell of terror and leapt into the water. Then she swung the gun back to Harry, who instinctively ducked. 'Not at me! Over there!'

'Sorry,' Clarissa mouthed, swivelling the gun around, the arc of its aim passing over Li-Liang's head, until it was pointing squarely at the pirate ship.

The pirates stared at her, seemingly unsure what to make of this deranged Western woman with the shotgun and the flaming red hair. 'Go!' Clarissa cried. 'Leave us in peace! Or I'll . . .' She hesitated. 'I'll shoot.'

But the men must have sensed the uncertainty in her voice, as they began to nudge one another, jeering and pointing. Oh Lord, Harry said to himself. He was just wondering whether to swim over to Clarissa's *chuan* when he was thrown violently off his feet, landing painfully on one elbow as the steam launch gave a sudden judder. Looking up, he saw the reason why he'd just been upended. For the propeller was spinning backwards now, as Bo Lungsin finally switched the engine to reverse.

The effect on the boats behind took a little longer to manifest. The rope attaching the steam launch to the *chuans* slackened, causing them to lurch backwards in the current. Though the jolt was less severe than Harry had experienced, it was still sufficient to unbalance Clarissa. As she stumbled backwards, she raised her shotgun into the air, and the gun went off, blasting out a cloud of lead pellets at the pirate ship, punching a massive hole in its stiff, bamboo-lined sail, just inches from the ear of a stunned pirate.

Clarissa fell back on to the deck with a little scream, watching in horror as the shotgun slipped from her grasp and rolled under the railing into the water. No one said anything for a moment, but then a shout went up, and Harry was amazed to see the pirate ship tacking away as fast as its damaged sail would allow. A couple of the bolder pirates dived off its deck – perhaps minded to retrieve the sunken shotgun – but then the flotilla was on the move again, speeding away from the scene, as Bo Lungsin switched the direction of the propeller once more and steered them onwards up the river.

Harry looked round and saw Clarissa sitting on the deck of her *chuan*, mute with shock. Glancing down, he saw the

246

boathook lying at his feet, its shaft splintered by her shot. Having returned it to its place by the gunwale, Harry straightened up to find Bo Lungsin standing in his customary position in the wheelhouse, humming under his breath as though nothing untoward had happened.

That evening, after the flotilla had moored up for the night, the three travellers took their supper as usual in the lower deck of Harry and Clarissa's *chuan*. Li-Liang had produced a wineskin of *jiu* from somewhere, and was chattering away as he filled their cups, still in a state of exultant animation.

'I suspect Bo Lungsin has performed this swindle many times before,' he was saying, 'on passengers who do not realise — as you did, Mr Compton — that a steamboat such as this is capable of reverse. But for the pirates to have attacked us at that very moment . . .' The guide gave a merry chuckle. 'Well, at least it will deter Bo Lungsin from practising the ruse on anybody else. He will have realised now how dangerous it is to strand oneself deliberately on the Yangtze!'

'It was Mrs Lockhart who saved the day,' Harry said.

Li-Liang nodded vigorously. 'Mrs Lockhart was indeed magnificent.' He turned to her. 'All this time you had your late husband's shotgun in your possession, and never said!'

'It seemed a sensible precaution,' Clarissa replied. 'Especially for our foray overland.' She dropped her eyes. 'We must do without it now.'

'But what work it did for us!' Li-Liang exclaimed. 'We shan't have any more trouble from Bo Lungsin, you may depend on that. For he cannot know what terrible weapon Mrs Lockhart will produce next!'

'Where was it?' Harry asked, unable to shake the small sense of pique he felt at having been excluded from Clarissa's secret.

'I kept it hidden with my easel,' she replied. 'In the long narrow trunk.'

'A formidable woman indeed,' Li-Liang laughed, 'just as the Taotai said!' He took an enormous slug of *jiu*, then wiped his sweaty brow. 'Of course, I can only apologise for the conduct of my countrymen, but you must know by now that there are some who regard you British with suspicion, and even contempt.'

'So it would seem,' Clarissa said – a little sadly, Harry thought, wondering why she was so subdued on tonight of all nights, when surely they should be celebrating a narrow escape from disaster.

'You see, for some Chinese, you Britishers are little more than animals,' Li-Liang went on. He adjusted his position on the bench, and his green silk robes fell open, revealing a pair of turquoise stockings beneath. He looked like a grand Shakespearean actor, Harry thought, celebrating the opening night of a successful West End play.

'Animals?' Clarissa repeated.

'I'm afraid so,' Li-Liang said, then lowered his voice dramatically: 'The British can be unnatural, almost ridiculous – such pale skin, such an unmusical tongue! When they first appeared in China, they seemed almost animal-like – the redhead with his bushy whiskers like a fox, brush hidden within his breeches; the fair-haired man like a weasel, and so forth. Crafty but inhuman, and to be used roughly, as such beasts deserve.' Li-Liang reached again for the wineskin of *jiu*. 'Of course, what we ought to do is keep the cunning

248

fox close,' he said, as he topped up their cups. 'Not too close, though, for there is no denying that the British have caused us much harm. The treaties that your country has forced upon us are unequal, and have allowed China to be flooded with Indian opium.'

Seeing Clarissa lower her eyes, her face wretched, Li-Liang softened his tone. 'But there is much that the British can teach us,' he resumed brightly. 'You will have heard of the Self-Strengthening Movement, of course?'

Harry glanced at Clarissa, and they both shook their heads.

'But how can this be so?' Li-Liang exclaimed. 'The Self-Strengthening Movement is a progressive philosophy that the more enlightened members of the Qing government have embraced. It teaches us not to ignore Western techno-logy, but to learn from it. To study your weaponry and industry – even your mining techniques.' Abruptly, Li-Liang leant over and squeezed Harry's bearded face between his hands, peering up at him with unfocused grey eyes, his breath scented with rice liquor and salty bean sauce. 'You see, we shall take your technology, Mr Compton,' he said, 'and we shall make it *better!*'

Clarissa cleared her throat, and the guide sat back, as though suddenly aware of where he was and to whom he was speaking. 'My apologies,' he said. 'I have allowed my tongue to run wild.' Setting down his cup with a deliberate hand, he rose slowly to his feet. 'And now I must take myself to bed. Today's events have unsteadied me.'

'You're not the only one,' Clarissa said graciously. 'Good night, Li-Liang.'

Harry offered the guide his arm, but he waved it away, ascending alone the little wooden staircase that led to the

249

upper deck, silk robes sagging. Then they heard his heavy steps as he made his way over on to his *chuan*.

'He certainly likes a drink,' Harry chuckled, but when he looked over at Clarissa, she wasn't smiling. 'You are tired, Mrs Lockhart.'

'It is not fatigue that troubles me, Mr Compton,' Clarissa said in a tight voice. 'But what happened earlier . . .'

Beneath the table, Wilberforce cocked an ear, instantly registering the change in mood.

'Earlier?' Harry echoed. 'When I risked my life to get us out of a very tricky predicament?'

'When you picked up Bo Lungsin by the scruff of his neck and threatened him!' Clarissa returned.

'The man was trying to steal from you, Mrs Lockhart,' Harry said, shaking his head in bafflement. 'You heard Li-Liang — it's a fiddle he's performed before. And on this occasion, it could have got us all killed!'

Clarissa responded with a snort of derision.

'And you almost shot me, you realise,' Harry went on. 'Six inches lower, and I'd be dead.'

'I did the best I could,' Clarissa said.

'As did I!' Harry retorted.

Clarissa glared at him, her jaw tense with anger. 'What you did to Bo Lungsin was unspeakable, Mr Compton. I know the man is a crook, but that's still no excuse for treating him so roughly.' She looked away. 'Such behaviour makes me wonder if I know you at all.'

'What the blazes does that mean?'

Clarissa kept her eyes averted, cheeks burning. 'It doesn't matter.'

'Well, it does to me!' Harry retorted. 'So what happened this afternoon — my *behaviour*,' he repeated in an icy tone. 'It's made you conclude that I'm a violent man? That what Charles Hargreaves told you about me might be true?' Seeing Clarissa struggle to know how to respond, Harry raised his eyebrows. 'You said you trusted me, Mrs Lockhart. What sort of woman changes her view of a man so easily? Do you not know your own mind?'

Clarissa gave a flinch, then closed her eyes. A moment later, Harry was horrified to see tears spilling from them, rolling down her cheeks. She slapped them away. 'You are quite right, Mr Compton,' she said, refusing to meet his gaze. 'These days I do not know my own mind at all.'

'What do you mean, Clarissa?' Harry asked, wondering if he would ever understand this exasperating woman and her bewildering moods. Reaching over, he took her hand. 'What is it?' he added, more gently now. 'You must tell me so that I can try to help.'

She sat there for a moment, staring at the floor, then took out a small silk handkerchief and dried her eyes. 'Do you remember the day you first told me about the icicle tree?' she asked.

'Of course.'

'A woman came to the house. A young Chinese woman.'

'With a baby?'

'You saw,' Clarissa murmured, then shook her head. 'Of course you saw.'

'I thought it must be connected to your charitable work,' Harry said. 'A girl from your reformatory, perhaps, fallen on hard times.'

Clarissa let out a mirthless laugh. 'I wish it had been so. No, that young woman was Narcissus's concubine. And that baby was his son.'

Harry stared at her. How unbelievably awful, he thought. To have one's grief tainted with anger. To have been so betrayed. He refilled Clarissa's cup with *jiu* and handed it to her. 'Are you quite sure?'

'At first, I didn't want to believe it,' Clarissa said, taking a sip. 'Though perhaps I was a fool not to have suspected something of the kind. Most of the griffins take concubines, only to abandon them as soon as they've found a suitable English wife. I thought Narcissus was above all that, but now, as I look back . . .'

That must be one of the worst aspects of such a betrayal, Harry thought. Forcing one to look back at a shared life with new eyes — eyes that saw treachery and deceit everywhere.

'The woman has two more children by him,' Clarissa continued. 'Daughters. But the son was a more recent addition.' She paused. 'As you will no doubt have ascertained by his tender age.'

'She may have been lying,' Harry ventured. 'Trying to extort money.'

Clarissa shook her head. 'Her son had his father's eyes.' She said nothing for a moment, just sat there staring out of the *chuan's* little square window, twisting the handkerchief in her hands. Then she looked up at Harry with a sigh. 'Do you know what the worst thing is? I sent her away without a penny. Sent her children away to starve. What kind of a person does that?'

Harry imagined that there must be many aggrieved wives who would do the same. And husbands. 'It must have been a fearful shock,' he said. 'Only . . .'

'What?' Clarissa asked.

'I just wanted to say that if ever you decide that you would like to assist this young woman, then you might rely on me for my help – with money, or anything else.'

'Thank you. It's a very kind offer, and I promise that I will think on it further. But perhaps not quite yet.' Clarissa gave a sad smile. 'I'm not always in thrall to my better angel, Mr Compton, as you will no doubt have perceived. Now I must go to bed,' she said, getting to her feet. 'Let us hope for a less eventful day tomorrow.'

After she'd left, Harry remained for a time below deck, finishing the dregs of the *jiu*. Catching the low chatter of the mercenaries on the junk behind, and the whiff of their opium-laced tobacco, Harry wondered what they might be talking about. Mrs Lockhart's heroics, probably, he thought, his mind drifting to what might have happened if she hadn't appeared when she had with her shotgun.

Reaching a hand beneath his shirt, Harry felt for the small, raised scar on his upper arm where Frith's bullet had nicked him, and realised once again how close he had come to dying for the sake of the icicle tree.

Chapter 20

The next morning, Harry found Clarissa sitting with Li-Liang on the upper deck of the *chuan*, sipping a cup of chamomile tea. The mercenaries occupied their usual places on the junk behind, cutlasses at the ready, whilst Bo Lungsin was back in his wheelhouse, smoking his pipe. It seemed as if everyone had decided to erase all memories of yesterday's adventure.

'Good morning,' Harry called out.

The guide stood up and shook Harry by the hand, but Clarissa merely offered him a vague smile before looking away. So this was how it was going to be, Harry thought. Last night, upset and overwrought after the pirate attack, Clarissa had taken Harry into her confidence – trusted him with her darkest secret, an intimacy which this morning could only embarrass her. Well, two can play at that game, Harry decided, sinking down on to a stool and crossing his boots at the ankle, making sure not to look at her.

But there was soon plenty else to distract them, as the flotilla had finally entered Lake Dongting. Though the scale of the water was significant – some 90 miles by 60, or 300 *li* by 200, to use the Chinese measurements – its currents were gentle, and the flotilla made swift progress, passing the occasional fishing boat trailing nets, one of which Harry saw being pulled from the water, flapping with enormous, grey-skinned sturgeon.

'China was a great maritime nation once, you know,' Li-Liang declared, gazing out at the limpid green waters of the lake. 'Empress of the Indian Ocean! But we relinquished our dominion when the Manchus took over. Turned in on ourselves.'

By and by, the flotilla drew closer to the bank, and Harry perceived a pinkish hue to the land.

'Perhaps there is bauxite in the soil!' Li-Liang exclaimed, hurrying down to his cabin to fetch a telescope. But he was to be disappointed: 'Oh,' he said, as he lowered it from his eye. 'It's only flowers.'

'May I?' Harry asked, holding out a hand. He peered through the telescope, and gasped to see thousands upon thousands of lilies covering the bank. 'Looks like some sort of tiger lily,' he murmured. 'But the sheer *number* . . .'

Turning, Harry found Clarissa standing beside him, one hand shading her eyes as she stared at the shore. Picking up on the excitement in his tone, she asked to look as well. Harry wasn't sure if she could have had time to focus the telescope properly, because she took just the briefest of glances, then said, 'How marvellous! I think I should paint them, don't you, Li-Liang?'

'A capital idea, Mrs Lockhart,' Li-Liang replied, then relayed her request to Bo Lungsin, who steered the flotilla towards the shore.

'Thank you,' Harry mouthed to Clarissa, feeling his spirits lift as she flashed him a smile.

As they approached the bank, Harry saw that the lilies stretched for almost as far as the eye could see, and shook his head in disbelief, knowing that each one of those bulbs would fetch at least a half-sovereign in Chelsea.

Bo Lungsin dropped anchor some twenty yards from shore. As Clarissa set up her easel, Harry unlaced his boots. 'I thought I might stretch my legs.'

'Then I shall join you,' Li-Liang said. 'I know very little of the soils in this area. If you'll give me a moment, I'll just fetch my tools . . .'

Seeing Harry frown, Clarissa laid a hand upon Li-Liang's arm. 'But then I'll have no company!' She pursed her lips: 'And after yesterday, I'm not sure I wish to be on my own.'

Li-Liang glanced at Harry and shrugged. 'Well, it seems I have no choice, Mr Compton. For I can deny nothing to such a charming lady!'

'Well, that's settled then,' Harry said gruffly. 'Perhaps I might trouble you to hand me that bag once I'm in the water, Mrs Lockhart,' he asked, pointing to the hessian sack containing his boots, trowel and bowie knife — never again did he want to find himself unarmed as he had against the pirate.

'Of course,' Clarissa replied.

Harry turned and leapt off the boat. The water of the lake was warmer than the river had been, but shallower too, he realised just as his feet hit the bottom, sending up billowing clouds of sludge. Clarissa passed him down the sack, and he started to wade to shore, holding the bag above his head.

Finally, Harry reached the shallows and hauled himself up on to the bank. Stepping away from the water's edge, he feasted his eyes upon the lilies. They were exquisite: adorned with gorgeous, trumpet-shaped flowers, a touch smaller than the tiger lilies he knew from Piggott's, and with rich reddish bands on the petals. Most were in full bloom, which was a boon for his senses (their perfume was extravagant) but made them less appropriate for collection, as it was risky to lift a bulb at this stage of its cycle. But then he saw one with its flower fading, and crouched down with his trowel to prise it from the soil. Into the sack it went; then another, and another . . .

Before Harry knew it, his sack was full. Time seemed to have sped up, and he wasn't sure how long he had been on land. His orientation also seemed to have gone awry, as it took more than a moment for his sun-blinded eyes to find the flotilla, and it was only then that he realised he'd wandered much further than he'd intended.

He set off back towards the lake, noting that a few of the mercenaries were in the water now — bathing, he assumed, until he saw one man making his way towards him. As the mercenary climbed ashore, Harry saw a machete in his hand, and felt a sudden, primitive rush of fear. Was this to do with his altercation with Bo Lungsin? Some sort of revenge?

Harry watched, heart thumping, as the man walked towards him, wondering if he should draw his bowie knife — or simply turn and run. The man was older and heavier than him, so Harry reckoned he could probably outpace him, but like all the mercenaries, he was strong, his upper back and shoulders heavily muscled and burnished by the sun.

Harry was just about to sprint away when the older man let out an enormous yawn, then flopped down on a rock just a few yards from him. As Harry watched, he unfastened a leather canister tied to his waist and took a leisurely gulp, then let out a soft burp.

Feeling Harry's thirsty eyes upon him, the mercenary offered him the canister, before using his machete to attack nothing more dangerous than the orange he'd had hidden in his pocket. What a fool I am, Harry thought, as he greedily gulped down the sweetened tea. Perhaps Clarissa was right, and he really was destined to see danger and treachery everywhere.

Signalling his thanks to the mercenary, Harry set off back through the water. When he reached the *chuan*, Li-Liang leant down to take the sack from his hands.

'But what is this, Mr Compton?' the guide said, his face falling as he saw the sharp-tipped leaves protruding from the mouth of the sack. 'The Taotai gave *specific* instructions . . .'

'The lilies are for me, Li-Liang,' Clarissa said, leaning in to daub at her canvas with her paintbrush.

Harry turned to look at her.

'The flowers are just so gorgeous, don't you think? I thought I'd make a close study.'

'I see,' Li-Liang said — somewhat suspiciously, Harry felt.

'Just give me a moment to dry off, Mrs Lockhart,' Harry put in. 'Then I'll select the best bloom for you to sketch.'

So, still dripping with muddy water, Harry carried his hoard below deck. A moment later, he heard a soft knock at his cabin door. He flung it open and was surprised to see Clarissa standing there, looking a little awkward. 'May I come in?' she asked.

'Of course,' Harry said, remembering himself. 'It's a bit . . .' He glanced about in embarrassment, then stooped down to snatch a pair of breeches off the floor. 'I wasn't expecting company.'

'So I can see, Mr Compton,' Clarissa said with an amused smile.

'About last night, Mrs Lockhart,' Harry blurted out. 'I want you to know that your secret is safe with me. I shall never mention it to another living soul.'

Clarissa looked away. 'Thank you. It means a great deal to me to know there's someone I can trust.' Picking up one of his honeypots, she turned it to the light, marvelling at the little seeds suspended in the golden liquid. 'But I've not come about that,' she said, setting the pot down and turning to face him. 'I think we should tell Li-Liang.'

'About the icicle tree?' Harry exclaimed.

'No, but we should tell him that you're a plant hunter, making a collection of local exotics.'

'But why?'

'He's a highly intelligent man, Mr Compton – I imagine he's guessed the truth already. And after what we went through yesterday, I don't want you sneaking about on your own any more. I can't always be there to save you.'

Harry raised a sceptical eyebrow, then finally conceded a nod. 'Very well, Mrs Lockhart. We'll tell him tonight.' He expected Clarissa to leave then, but she just smoothed down her skirts and sat down on his berth, saying, 'You don't mind if I watch you work, do you? Just pretend I'm not here.'

'If you must,' Harry replied. Shivering slightly, he took out a fresh sack and laid the bulbs he'd collected upon it, counting some fifty-five. Then he started to trim off the greenery and roots with a pruning knife, throwing them

259

into a pile that he would discard later. The bulbs would need a few days to dry out, then he would clean them and store them in a tea chest between sheets of newspaper, and pray that neither the rats nor the mould got them . . .

'May I help?' Clarissa asked.

Harry glanced up.

'You're soaking wet, Mr Compton. I could finish the job whilst you change into dry clothes.'

'I'm not sure . . .'

'Come now, Mr Compton. We're in this together, aren't we?'

Harry hesitated, then laid the knife on top of the remaining bulbs, watching as Clarissa folded the sack in two and carried it out into the living area.

Ten minutes later, when Harry emerged dressed from his cabin, Clarissa was gone, and the remaining bulbs had been perfectly trimmed, the pile of roots and greenery put neatly to one side. Sitting in a vase on the table was a solitary tiger-lily bloom – a specimen for her to paint later, he presumed.

Smiling to himself, Harry took out a tea chest and started laying down the bulbs for storage.

That evening, after supper, Harry, Clarissa and Li-Liang sat together below deck, enjoying another wineskin of *jiu*.

Clarissa cleared her throat. 'Mr Compton and I have a small confession, Li-Liang.'

The guide put up an eyebrow.

'We are not just here to paint,' Clarissa said slowly. 'We also hope to collect a little of the local flora.'

'I see,' Li-Liang replied, looking down as he swirled the *jiu* around his glass. The liquid left a sticky residue on the sides. 'And you're concerned that I will report you to the Taotai?' He looked up, black brows beetled. 'Because you know that such plant-stealing – for that is what it is – has been outlawed in these parts.'

Clarissa and Harry exchanged a glance. This was not going well . . .

'So you place me in an awkward position, Mrs Lockhart,' Li-Liang went on. He fell silent for a moment as he finished his *jiu*, then looked up. 'These plants that you are collecting. Are they for your own pleasure, or for sale?'

Harry sensed Clarissa carefully weighing her answer. 'For sale,' she replied.

Li-Liang nodded. 'And the people who will purchase them. They will know of their provenance?'

'They would know that they came from China,' Harry put in. 'But they wouldn't necessarily connect them to this specific expedition.'

Li-Liang gave a faint smile, his dark, velvet eyes drawn towards the window that gave on to the still waters of the lake. 'I should like to think of our treasures being admired by your countrymen,' he said.

'Maybe even by the greatest one of them all,' Clarissa suggested slyly.

Li-Liang pressed a hand to his chest, eyes wide. 'Her Majesty?'

'Why not?' Clarissa said, lips twitching as her eyes met Harry's. When he said nothing, she gave him a sharp kick under the table. 'Don't you agree, Mr Compton?'

Harry glared at her, one hand reaching down to rub his bruised shin. 'I don't see why not. My former, er . . .

patron, Josiah Piggott, has recently been endowed with the Royal Warrant.' It was almost true, Harry thought.

'I see,' Li-Liang said. Steepling his elegant hands, he pointed them at Harry. 'Well, perhaps we might compromise on the matter, yes?'

Clarissa gave him a charming smile.

'If the Taotai questions me directly on your activities, then naturally I shall not lie. But I will not volunteer the information. I shall — how do you say — turn a blind eye. Does that seem reasonable to you both?'

'Quite reasonable,' Clarissa said. 'We are in your debt, Li-Liang.' She picked up the wineskin and began to replenish their glasses, but the guide was already on his feet.

'I'm too old for another night of celebrations, I'm afraid, Mrs Lockhart. So I bid you good night.'

Harry stood up as well as Li-Liang made his way out of the lower deck, then turned to Clarissa with a wry grin. 'Do you always get your own way, Mrs Lockhart?'

'With Narcissus, very rarely,' she said, in a tone that made Harry regret his flippant remark. But then her face brightened. 'Though I must say I'm developing rather a taste for it!'

She had such a mischievous look on her face that Harry couldn't help but laugh, and soon she was laughing too. But then she leant forward and gasped, her finger pointing directly at Harry's neck. 'What on earth is *that*?'

Reaching up above his collarbone, Harry was repulsed to find attached to the skin something warm and slimy to the touch, about two inches long. He tried to flick it off, but to his alarm it would not budge. 'Get it off me!' he said in panic, leaping to his feet. 'Quick!'

'Stand still!' Clarissa ordered, but Harry found to his shame he could not.

Pulling off his shirt and undershirt in one go, he gasped to see three more creatures attached to his skin.

'Is that a leech?' Clarissa said. 'Oh my Lord . . .' She laughed, one hand covering her mouth. 'And another one!' Picking up the candle, she drew closer.

Harry peered down and saw, just to the right of his navel, what looked like a large black slug. Grabbing it between thumb and forefinger, he yanked it loose, feeling a sharp sting as he did so.

'Don't!' Clarissa cried, and they both saw the trickle of blood oozing down his belly. 'Can't you see? You're damaging the skin!'

Moving closer to him, so close that Harry could see the copper glints in her hair, Clarissa felt delicately for a leech that had fixed itself to the right side of his chest. 'Some people talk of naked flames,' she said, 'or salt, but I find . . .' Sliding a fingernail under the mouthpiece, Clarissa eased the leech away, and it fell to the ground. 'There,' she said, with a small triumphant smile. 'Now, that wasn't too bad, was it?'

'Where did you learn such a thing?' Harry asked, as he watched her apply herself to the next leech.

'My father,' she replied. 'He would get them out stalking.' She glanced up with a wicked smile. 'Under his garters.'

She was so close to Harry now, her scent intoxicating. Too close, he realised, feeling his loins stir. Hurriedly, he took a step back, then turned away and reached for his shirt. 'Thank you,' he heard himself mutter in a deep voice. 'I think I can manage now.'

'Well,' Clarissa said, 'if you're sure. Good night then, Mr Compton.'

'Good night,' he replied.

Harry waited to hear her cabin door close, then let out a long, shuddering sigh, leaning his hot forehead against the wooden wall. They still had weeks left together, he realised. This was not going to be easy.

Chapter 21

The following afternoon, they made it across the lake to the village of Jiejiang, at the mouth of the River Yuan. As they tied up at the stilted wooden pier, a small crowd of villagers gathered, greeting the mercenaries with obvious warmth and affection.

'Our crew seems well-known in these parts,' Clarissa observed.

'As well they should be,' Li-Liang replied. 'Most of them were born here. Ah,' the guide said, seeing an unsmiling official walking towards them.

'He looks a little less friendly,' Harry said.

Li-Liang threw Harry a sharp look. 'He'll be expecting us to pay *likin* – the local customs fee.' But then he winked: 'Though he has not yet seen the stamp of the Zongli Yamen on your passports!'

The effect of the government pass was indeed powerful, and the official's glacial demeanour thawed before their eyes. He and Li-Liang spoke for a time, then the latter turned to Clarissa. 'Forgive me, Mrs Lockhart, but I must leave you for an hour. There is a letter I need to compose for the Sub-Prefect of East Guizhou, forewarning him of our arrival. Now, he will be less likely to let us pass without paying a fee, I'm afraid — but more of that later. In the meantime, I shall ask Tan Lin to look after you in my absence.'

'Who?' Clarissa said.

Li-Liang pointed to a short, squat man standing a few yards away, and Harry recognised him as the mercenary who'd given him the sweet tea on the shore of the lake. 'Tan Lin is to be our new captain for this stretch of the journey,' Li-Liang explained.

'Bo Lungsin is leaving?' Harry asked, rather too eagerly perhaps.

'Of course,' Li-Liang said. 'Do you not remember? The Yuan is too shallow to allow a steam launch to pass. Bo Lungsin will rejoin us for the return journey to Hankow.'

Looking over his shoulder, Harry saw that the steam launch had already been uncoupled from the houseboats, and was chugging back into the lake. The armed junk, meanwhile, had hoisted its sail and was tacking around to replace it at the front of the flotilla, the Imperial Ensign now fluttering from its mast.

'Tan Lin?' Li-Liang called out.

The big man came over, smiling shyly. He exchanged a few words with Li-Liang, then they all stood back and watched as the guide disappeared into a bamboo shack to write his letter.

'*Guolai*,' Tan Lin said, taking hold of Clarissa and Harry by their wrists.

Clarissa let out a little gasp, but the smile Tan Lin gave her was so good-natured that she consented to allow him

266

to lead her up the slope that rose behind the pier. 'Where's he taking us, do you think?' Clarissa asked Harry.

'Into the village, I suppose,' Harry replied, pointing to the cluster of clay huts that flanked the mud track ahead. A pack of children fell into step with them, fascinated by their appearance and charmed by the Jack Russell trailing them. Then a pig appeared, snuffling at the hem of Clarissa's skirts. She let out a shriek, sending it squealing away.

'They must roam free here,' Harry said, watching another dark-skinned, bristly pig pause to sniff at Wilberforce. The dog bared its teeth, and the pig lurched away, much to the children's delight.

Tan Lin stopped in front of one house, and gave a bow. Pinned above the doorway were three squares of red paper painted with black Chinese characters. Seeing Clarissa staring at them, Tan Lin pointed up at the first square. '*Cái*,' he said.

'Wealth,' Clarissa translated, then tapped the pocket of her skirts, so that a few loose coins jangled within.

Tan Lin smiled and pointed up at the next character. '*Fú*.'

'Good fortune,' Clarissa said. 'And the third . . .'

'*Xǐ*,' Tan Lin added, pointing to the last character.

'The third means happiness,' Clarissa said with a smile.

'Bravo!' Harry exclaimed, genuinely impressed.

'Jiao!' Tan Lin called out, raising his hand to wave at a young woman who was coming down the slope towards them. Her black hair was twisted into a knot, and she wore a long grey skirt and short-sleeved tunic. She bowed politely to Harry and Clarissa, then led them inside the hut. In her arms, she held a cloth bundle, and cocooned in a sling on her back was a tiny baby.

Harry glanced over at Clarissa, reminded of the last time he'd seen a baby carried that way. Their eyes met just long enough for him to see the hurt in them, then she looked away.

The interior of the hut was smoky, and what light there was came from two small rice-paper windows set high into the walls. A low table stood opposite the fireplace, and Jiao put down her bundle there, then released the baby from her back. She was about to place the child on the floor when Clarissa held out her arms. 'May I?' she said timidly.

Jiao hesitated, then handed the child over.

'Aren't you a lovely thing?' Clarissa whispered, stroking the baby's soft black hair with a gentleness that, for some reason, brought a lump to Harry's throat. Averting his eyes in embarrassment, he watched as Jiao untied her bundle, revealing a bunch of green fronds, furled and twisted at the ends.

'But I know these!' Harry said, letting out a laugh of delight as he looked around at Clarissa. 'They're royal-fern fiddleheads – three crowns a piece at Piggott's!'

'Fiddleheads?' Clarissa repeated.

'The end is curled like the scroll of a violin,' Harry said, picking one up and holding it out for Clarissa to see.

'*Chi*,' Jiao urged, raising her fingers to her mouth.

'I think she's encouraging you to eat it,' Clarissa said.

Mouth contorted into a grimace, Harry bit off the curly end of one frond, then chewed and swallowed. 'It's delicious!' he said. 'Just like asparagus.' He shook his head in smiling disbelief. 'All that time selling them, and I never knew.'

Tan Lin turned back from the fireplace, carrying three steaming cups of chrysanthemum tea. '*Ganbei*,' he said, raising his own cup.

268

'*Ganbei*,' they all repeated, then took sips of the clear golden liquid.

As Tan Lin began gathering clothes and provisions for the next leg of the journey, and Jiao knelt at the table to prepare the ferns for cooking, Harry sank into a chair by the fire next to Clarissa, watching as she rocked the baby, humming a lullaby. Perhaps it was the warmth of the fire, or the peaceful sound of Wilberforce sighing and snoring at his feet, but soon he found his eyes closing.

Harry wasn't sure how long he slept, but it felt like moments later when he heard Li-Liang's stentorian voice outside – 'Mrs Lockhart? Mr Compton?' – and the baby started to cry. So, yawning, Harry got to his feet and joined Clarissa as they followed Tan Lin back down the hill to the harbour.

As they approached the pier, Harry saw that the deck tables of both houseboats had been removed, with masts erected in their place, their dirty canvas sails filling with breeze. 'I hadn't realised the *chuans* were equipped to sail,' he said.

'It is not easily achieved, Mr Compton,' Li-Liang replied, holding out a hand to help Clarissa aboard. 'There is a great deal of skill involved in navigating the Yuan – as you will soon see.'

Harry climbed up to join them, finding a mercenary manning the sail of each *chuan*, and five more, including Tan Lin, gathered ahead on the junk. They seemed in excellent humour, he thought, happier than he'd seen them in days. Perhaps it was because Bo Lungsin was gone. Harry certainly wouldn't miss the man.

The villagers untied their moorings, and then they were off, the junk's stiff, bamboo-fretted sail dragging the flotilla upstream, the smaller canvas sails of the *chuans* billowing in the breeze behind it, urging them on.

'It's almost as fast as the steam launch!' Clarissa enthused.

As soon as they were free of the lake, the topography began to change. There were green ridge-backed mountains on both sides now, hemming them in, and the riverbed was lined with gravel rather than mud. Soon, as the banks became more thickly wooded, the temperature grew muggier, and the spirits of the mercenaries began to ebb.

'We are coming into the territory of the Miao,' Li-Liang said quietly, as he joined Harry and Clarissa at the rail.

'The Miao?' Clarissa echoed.

'The indigenous people of this region,' Li-Liang said, motioning with his chin towards the bank, where Harry saw a number of tall bamboo houses on stilts, almost hidden amongst the trees. A few of their inhabitants were standing on the upper platforms, strong arms folded across their chests, watching the passing flotilla with suspicion in their dark eyes.

'Is Tan Lin of the Miao people?' Harry asked, glancing at their new captain as he worked the tiller of the junk.

Li-Liang nodded. 'They are fierce warriors, who have not taken too kindly to Chinese rule. There have been many Miao rebellions over the years.'

Harry had never thought of China as being composed of different peoples and languages. The imperial forces who governed the country were colonisers, in a sense. Harry found his mind drifting back to history lessons at his little school in Pulborough, and felt an unexpected pang of nostalgia as he recalled how he'd learnt of the woad-painted

Picts, and the Iceni of Boadicea. How far away such things seemed now . . .

Something hard hit Harry on the shoulder. 'Ouch!' he complained, rubbing his arm. Looking up, he saw a group of pot-bellied children huddled in the lee of the next hut, giggling into their hands, and realised that the flotilla was being pelted with pebbles.

Tan Lin barked out a threat to the children, who quickly scattered.

'It is best if you keep your head down, Mrs Lockhart,' Li-Liang warned. 'The Miao remain extremely hostile to Europeans. They are hated here almost as much as the Han.'

'The Han?' Harry asked.

Li-Liang gave a tight little smile. 'My people.'

Harry looked back at the woods. There was unfamiliar birdcall in the trees now, and he caught a flash of something bright orange flitting past the *chuan*. The flora was changing, too — he'd seen tropical orchids earlier, growing on a spit by the river, and longed to start botanising. But the sails were coming down now, the masts and stays being removed and laid upon the decks.

'Watch this, Mrs Lockhart,' Li-Liang said with a grin, as the mercenaries began leaping overboard and swimming to shore, each with a rope gripped in one fist. 'I think you will find it interesting.'

Clarissa leant forward to get a better look, one arm restraining Wilberforce, who looked as though he was itching to join the men.

'They're going to tow us,' Harry said, seeing the men lining up along the bank, two to a rope. 'Like shire horses pulling a barge!'

271

'It must be very heavy,' Clarissa said, as the flotilla began to move, Tan Lin still steering from the junk, one large powerful hand making tiny adjustments to the rudder.

'The men are well used to it,' Li-Liang replied. 'This is how they've traded in these parts for centuries. Wait 'til we come to the rapids.'

'Are they close?' Clarissa asked, glancing at Harry in some alarm.

Before Li-Liang could answer, they heard a low rumble up ahead, and Harry saw tell-tale clumps of dirty froth floating on the surface of the water. The men heaved the ropes forward, Tan Lin directing them in their labour with shouts and whistles. Then, as they rounded the meander, a twenty-foot stretch of white water appeared, churning over sharp boulders cutting the surface. High above, on a rocky bluff, stood a small triangular wooden hut with red wax candles and fragrant joss-sticks burning in its black-and-gilt frame.

'Every set of rapids has its own shrine,' Li-Liang said, following Clarissa's gaze. 'To appease the genies of the rapids.'

'I should like to paint it,' Clarissa said.

'You'll see plenty more on the river ahead, Mrs Lockhart, I assure you.'

Two merchants carrying opium chests on their backs were passing on the far bank. To Harry's surprise, they gave the flotilla not so much as a second glance, evidently accustomed to seeing a team of men dragging roped boats up the rapids.

A narrow channel ran down the nearside of the river. Though the water sluiced hard through it, there were no rocks there to snag the base of the boats, and the men began steering the flotilla along its course, yelling instructions to one another as they worked.

Midway down the tow-channel, the men held the boats still for a moment, groaning and sweating with the effort. They could use some help, Harry thought, eyeing the distance from the *chuan* to the bank. Surely he could jump it . . .

Leaping off the boat on to dry land, Harry ran over to the nearest pair of men and seized hold of a section of their rope, helping to drag the flotilla onwards. Before long, his chest was heaving like a bellows, and there were blisters burning on the palms of his hands. But they were making better progress now, there was no denying it, and little by little, the flotilla crept up the last few yards of the rapids before crashing down into the slack water on the other side.

'Feeling a little tired, are we, Mr Compton?' Harry heard Clarissa call down from the deck, as he collapsed on to the bank, shoulders aching.

'Just resting my eyes,' Harry replied.

Seeing him lying there, spread-eagled on the grass, a few of the mercenaries started to laugh. Harry laughed too, staring up at the cloudless sky, until one of the men came over and extended a hand. Harry reached up, feeling himself pulled to his feet with incredible ease. '*Shey-shey*,' he said, and the mercenary clapped him on the back, so hard that he almost fell into the river. Harry might have been making strides as a plant hunter, he thought, but he was still some way from going toe to toe with the mercenaries.

'We shall take our luncheon here, I think,' Li-Liang said, then threw Harry a meaningful glance. 'It may take a while to prepare, so please feel free to "stretch your legs" in the meantime.'

Harry and Clarissa spent almost an hour in the woods, barely exchanging a word, so intent was their focus on the work in hand. But their diligence paid off, and they returned to the flotilla having added a golden clematis, a purple acer and two unusual species of camellia to their collection. A pretty decent haul, all told, Harry thought, giving his vasculum a small tap of triumph as he stepped aboard the *chuan*, catching a mouth-watering aroma of dumplings and soy sauce drifting over from the junk.

Li-Liang paid them little heed, engrossed in a booklet of Chinese poetry, so Harry headed below deck with their spoils. But then he saw the state of his cabin, and his face fell. At first he thought it had been ransacked by some intruder, until he realised it must have been the turbulence caused by the rapids that had upended all his equipment. His precious cuttings were strewn all over the floor, and there were bulbs everywhere. He was going to have to secure his possessions more carefully in future . . . Quickly, he checked the Wardian case, remembering the fateful crossing of the Irish Sea that Lorcan Darke had spoken of, but thankfully the wicker basket had protected it from any damage.

The crew chose to eat on the riverbank, so Harry, Clarissa and Li-Liang lunched together on the upper deck of the *chuan*.

'Tell us more about the Miao people, Li-Liang,' Clarissa said, as she pushed away her bowl and sat back. 'I can't eat another bite!'

'I have few anecdotes about the Miao fit for female ears, I'm afraid, Mrs Lockhart,' Li-Liang replied. 'So I shall tell you a traditional story, if I may?'

'Excellent!' said Clarissa, clapping her hands. 'I love fairytales.'

'Thousands of years ago,' Li-Liang began, scooping Wilberforce up on to his lap, 'in the time of the Five Emperors, there was a handsome prince named Prince Gaoxing. Now, the prince had a terrible enemy called General Wu – a fearsome warrior, whom he found it impossible to defeat. One day, at his wits' end, the prince offered his daughter's hand in marriage to whomever would bring him the head of General Wu.'

'I'm sure the princess was delighted,' Clarissa remarked drily.

'Some time later,' Li-Liang went on, 'Prince Gaoxing's hunting dog, a massive beast named Panhu, appeared at the palace gates carrying something in his mouth. When the Prince went out to greet his faithful hound, he was amazed to find neither a bird nor a dead hare in Panhu's mouth, but General Wu's severed head.'

'Oh dear,' Clarissa said, with a roll of her eyes. 'I think I can see where this is going.'

'Prince Gaoxing was thrilled, of course,' Li-Liang continued. 'He built Panhu a splendid kennel, and promised him all the sweetmeats and delicacies he could eat. But Panhu was not to be so easily satisfied. He refused to eat a morsel, barking and howling all through the night, so that no one in the palace could sleep a wink.' Li-Liang stroked his fingers through Wilberforce's coarse pelt, removing a burr that was caught in his fur. 'Eventually, the prince's counsellors advised him to be true to his word, so reluctantly, having shed many tears, he entrusted his daughter to Panhu, and the dog led the princess away to his lair in the mountains, where they made a life together – not far from here, it is said.' Li-Liang gestured towards the dark woodland rising above the river. 'And from their union, the Miao people were born. A warrior race,' he went on, glancing at the crew as they took hold of their ropes again, and began dragging the flotilla upriver once again, 'imbued with Panhu's strength and the princess's beauty, even now.'

That night, after Li-Liang had retired, Harry remained below deck with Clarissa as she worked on her latest botanical illustration. At her urging, Harry had finally agreed to read *The Travels of Marco Polo*, and found that he was rather enjoying the journey of the famous Italian explorer, though he was disappointed to have come across no mention of the icicle tree.

Finishing another chapter, Harry stretched his shoulders and clambered to his feet, his legs stiff. 'May I?'

Clarissa hesitated, then turned her sketchpad around for him to see.

'The golden clematis!' Harry said in unforced admiration.

Clarissa nodded self-consciously, twiddling her squirrel-hair paintbrush in one hand, a smudge of yellow paint on her chin. She'd caught the lantern-shaped flower perfectly, Harry saw. He could almost sense it bobbing its head in the warm, humid breeze. She'd painted the foliage too – those dark-green, heavily toothed leaves – and was just beginning on one of the wispy seedheads.

'This is your best work yet!'

'Really?' she asked, eager as a little girl.

'Really. I've seen a lot of botanical plates in my time, and this is every bit their equal.'

Clarissa let out a giggle of pleasure, and without thinking, Harry reached across the table and placed his hand on hers. She looked down at it, and a blush of embarrassment crept up her neck.

'Clarissa . . .' Harry began, feeling his heart beat fast.

She scrambled to her feet. 'It's getting late. I should go to bed.'

'Of course,' he said, watching helplessly as she bustled away. 'Good night!'

'Good night, Harry,' Clarissa replied, and then she was gone.

He stood there for a moment, one hand pressed against his brow, wondering how he could be such a clumsy oaf. But then he realised something. She called me Harry, he said to himself, a smile creeping over his face.

Sitting back down to read, Harry found himself unable to concentrate on a word. So he retired instead to his cabin, and did his best to sleep.

Chapter 22

As the flotilla made its steady progress up the Yuan, a new routine began to assert itself. Harry had made a rod for his own back, it seemed, and henceforth was called upon to assist the crew every time the flotilla reached a new stretch of rapids. But he enjoyed the physical challenge, and the camaraderie, and after the job was done, he and Clarissa would slip away into the woods to hunt for plants as the men rested. There were many treasures to be had, they soon discovered, as they added such exotics as a meconopsis, a campanula and a gorgeous ivory-bloomed dogwood to their collection. Clarissa made close studies of them all, pausing work only to paint the occasional larger canvas – some scenic shrine they passed, or a waterfall cascading down the mountainside – that would satisfy the Taotai on their return to Shanghai.

Li-Liang, for his part, spent his leisure time exploring the many caves that flanked the river – he'd found porphyry in certain of the outcrops, and had chipped off a number of samples that he hoped to present to the Central Mining Authority in Peking. He had taken to making these excursions alone, reassured, he said, that no pirates or bandits would dare to operate in territory dominated by the Miao.

278

'What about the Miao themselves?' Harry asked, as Li-Liang returned one afternoon to the flotilla with his rock-pick and samples.

'Tan Lin says they are watching us all the time,' the guide replied. 'But so long as he is leading our group, they will leave us in peace.'

And thus far, Tan Lin's assessment had proved correct. In fact, the Miao seemed more interested in fishing than in fighting, and Harry had been fascinated to see how they would beat cylinders of bamboo above the water in order to drive shoals of mandarin fish into their nets. Some of their catch was then purchased by the expedition cook, and its sweet flesh found its way into their nightly dumplings.

The landscape was changing again. 'Quite Alpine now, don't you think?' Clarissa said to Harry – though how or when she'd ever visited the Alps, he was yet to establish. But there was certainly much to admire: steep grassy meadows rising above the riverbanks, familiar birdlife in the trees – flycatchers, magpies, wagtails. Only the occasional thicket of bamboo reminded Harry that they were in China rather than Europe. Indeed, Li-Liang had tantalised them with tales of the 'bear-cat' which might be found in the region – a large black-and-white beast idolised by the mercenaries, many of whom carried drawings of it on their person, like an Orthodox icon.

One evening, midway through their second week on the Yuan, the three travellers were dining below deck when Li-Liang brought out an object that looked to Harry very much like a compass – a circular face set into a square of cherrywood, with a needle pointing to a series of Chinese characters.

Clarissa peered over. 'Is that a barometer?'

'Made by the finest horologist in Peking,' Li-Liang replied. 'And look.' He held it out.

'Ah,' Harry and Clarissa chorused, though in reality neither of them was able to decipher its meaning.

'The dial has moved from "Fair" to "Tempestuous",' Li-Liang explained.

'A storm's coming?' Clarissa asked, a look of anxiety clouding her face. 'Is it accurate?'

Li-Liang nodded. 'And Tan Lin agrees. The weather is changing.'

'Should we remain below deck?' Clarissa asked.

'I can't imagine that will be necessary, Mrs Lockhart. It's the river I'm worried about.' He paused. 'May I see your map, Mr Compton?'

Harry hurried to his cabin, returning with Lorcan Darke's original map. He flattened it out on the table before Li-Liang, who peered down at it, huffing and tutting. 'The storm may render the river unnavigable,' he said, rubbing his brow. 'In order to reach the Mian Jian Guang pagoda, we would need to continue on foot.' He looked up at Clarissa with something approaching irritation. 'There are plenty of other exquisite pagodas closer to our current position. Will they not suffice for your purposes?'

'I'm quite resolved on the matter, I'm afraid,' Clarissa replied.

'There's a particular plant growing close to the pagoda that we are keen to collect,' Harry added, knowing that he was taking a risk. 'It's marked here.'

280

'I see,' Li-Liang said, giving Harry a shrewd look before peering back down at the map. '*Xiuxiu*,' he read aloud. 'I can't say I'm familiar with the word. It's not Mandarin or Shanghainese, at any rate.' He looked back up. 'I don't understand why this plant should matter more than any other, but if you're insistent on making the journey then I must advise you in the strongest terms to leave the boats here and continue on land.'

'Because of a cloudburst?' Harry said.

'It will be more than a cloudburst, Mr Compton,' Li-Liang replied sharply. 'You may depend upon that!'

But the rainstorm, when it came, was less severe than Li-Liang's barometer had warned. It had been a still, humid day, drifting on a stretch of slow open water, and Harry enjoyed the refreshing sensation of the first warm, fat drops upon his face.

Almost instantaneously, a hatch of what looked like mayflies rose from the river. Clarissa began swatting at them furiously, before Li-Liang reassured her that they were harmless. The fish were a good deal happier at the flies' arrival, however, and the pools of the Yuan were soon thrashing with rises and leaps, attracting a crowd of Miao men, who thronged to the banks with their cylinders and nets.

Then there was a clap of thunder, and Tan Lin steered them into a backwater, where they quickly moored up. The men in the junk all moved below deck, whilst Li-Liang retreated to his cabin, declaring that the high pressure was giving him a headache.

Clarissa met Harry's eye, and they headed down to the living area of their *chuan*, and there, with the thunder booming overhead, and the rain drumming on the roof, they continued with their work.

'Mr Compton?' Clarissa asked, looking up from the water-colour she was making of an aspidistra. 'Have you given any thought to what you will do when we find the icicle tree?'

'A little,' Harry said, though in reality he'd been grappling constantly with the matter, not least because he was sure that Jack Turner would have received the letter he'd sent from Shanghai by now. How would the likes of Weeks and Wimsett have responded to his overtures? 'In fact, I've already begun to make some discreet enquiries about potential buyers,' he added.

Feeling Clarissa's eyes searching his face, Harry looked away. 'But it's a delicate matter. One doesn't wish to reveal too much at such an early stage.'

'Of course,' Clarissa said, cleaning her paintbrush in a jar of linseed oil. 'But these potential buyers,' she resumed. 'Are they based in England?'

Harry nodded.

'Not your former employer?' Clarissa asked.

'Certainly not!' Harry replied. He wondered if now was the time to voice his suspicions that Piggott had mounted a planthunting expedition of his own. But there seemed little point: the only people who'd been following them up the Yangtze were pirates . . . 'My enquiries have been directed towards other nurserymen on the King's Road,' Harry said.

'A wise decision, I think,' Clarissa replied, testing out a new mix of green on her palette.

There was a long pause. 'And your share', Harry asked, 'will be invested in Lockhart's, I presume?'

Clarissa nodded. 'If the company is to survive, I will need capital. A very great sum, I fear.' She threw Harry a sidelong glance. 'Perhaps I might persuade the bank to provide a line of credit, but . . .' She sighed.

'They will want collateral?'

'Exactly.' Clarissa set down her paintbrush and looked at him. 'And whether my future earnings from the icicle tree will suffice is anyone's guess!'

That night, after they'd retired to their respective cabins, Harry found his mind returning to the more worrying – and very real – possibility that they would fail to find the tree at all. He could imagine what would happen then: the long, depressing journey back to Shanghai, the bitter taste of failure in their mouths; Clarissa forced to seek alternative financial assistance for Lockhart's, turning to her friends perhaps, or to Charlie Hargreaves. Would the specimens they'd collected so far provide a lifeline for them both? Harry knew in his heart they would not. They were small fry compared to the real prize – a spectacular new tree that every gardener in the Western world would want for their garden.

Fail to find the tree, and Harry would soon find himself quietly discarded. What other use could someone like Clarissa Lockhart have for an impecunious mountebank with a bad temper and a dubious past? Suddenly, it seemed more important than ever to find the icicle tree – not just for his own prosperity, but because it was the only way he could be sure of staying close to Clarissa.

Harry awoke the next morning to find sunlight streaming in through his cabin window. The flotilla was on the move again, and as he emerged blinking from his cabin, he saw that the storm had passed, and that the river – though higher – remained navigable.

'So much for Li-Liang's barometer,' Clarissa called across the upper deck. She was sipping a cup of hibiscus tea, her hair loose and flowing about her shoulders. 'I'm glad we had a chance to talk last night,' she added quietly as Harry came closer. 'It helped to clarify some things in my mind.' She smiled. 'Made everything seem more . . . possible.'

'I agree,' Harry said, though all he seemed to have clarified was how much there was at stake.

The flotilla was passing a clearing now, where a pair of Chinese pheasants was courting, the male exquisitely plumed in blue, red and yellow, the female dull and speckled. Odd, Harry thought, admiring Clarissa's auburn curls, how the opposite was true of human beings . . .

Then the flotilla slowed, and Harry saw the masts coming down, and realised they must be approaching more rapids. Winking at Clarissa, he leapt out on to the towpath, where he joined his usual companions at the rope, and began dragging the flotilla along. Soon, they rounded a corner and the rapids revealed themselves. These made an especially alarming sight, Harry thought, the water seething viciously over sawtooth rocks, and the tow-channel at the near bank a foaming torrent. But the crew steeled themselves for the task, and began to drive forward, hoping to hit the rapids at a run. Their momentum was soon lost, though, when the sheer force of the water made itself felt. Harry could sense Li-Liang's eyes fixed upon them now, and knew what the guide would be thinking — that they should have followed his counsel, and pursued their journey on land.

As they continued dragging the flotilla onwards, the pressure of the water seemed to double, then triple, and Harry felt the sinews of his arms start to burn. Then, just when he thought he could bear it no longer, he found himself flying backwards through the air, landing in a heap beside a crewman named Ren Hao. For the rope must have snagged on a boulder, Harry quickly realised, and snapped.

Harry clambered back to his feet, heart pounding. The crew were just managing to hold the flotilla steady in the current, but Li-Liang's *chuan* was yawing badly to the right, the water driving hard against its exposed hull. On board, Li-Liang had been thrown on to his back, and was lying on the deck, upturned like a beetle, whilst Clarissa leant over the edge of her *chuan*, reaching out a hand to him . . .

'Clarissa!' Harry cried. 'Be careful!'

Li-Liang's *chuan* lurched again — it was almost at a right angle to the current now, the pressure on the ropes increasing by the second — and Tan Lin made a sudden decision. Abandoning the tiller, he leapt overboard into the river, then dragged himself through the frothing water, and climbed aboard Clarissa's *chuan*.

'Come on, come on . . .' Harry hissed to himself, as he took hold of a rope beside Ren Hao, feeling the weight of the flotilla almost unbearable.

Li-Liang had regained his feet now. Reaching out, he clasped Clarissa's outstretched hand, letting out a small groan of pain as he stepped across on to her houseboat. Then, as Clarissa dropped to her knees to tend to the guide, Tan Lin lifted his cutlass and cut through the ropes binding the *chuans* together, and Harry watched in amazement as Li-Liang's houseboat shot away down the rapids, almost capsizing as it crashed into the slacker water below.

285

'My samples!' he heard Li-Liang cry.

But the weight of the flotilla was immediately lighter, and though the task of heaving the other two boats up the rest of the rapids remained an arduous one, it was just possible.

As soon as they were past the rapids, Tan Lin leapt down on to the towpath and went haring after Li-Liang's stricken boat, while Harry climbed on to the *chuan* beside Clarissa. 'Are you hurt?' he asked, eyes flickering over her person, searching for signs of injury.

'Don't worry about me,' Clarissa replied in a low voice. 'Look to Li-Liang.'

The guide was sitting on the gunwale of the *chuan*, teeth chattering despite the warmth of the day. 'It is nothing,' he said, clutching his left arm to his chest. 'I merely knocked my shoulder when I fell.' Grimacing in pain, Li-Liang turned his head and looked downriver. Tan Lin had retrieved the loose rope of his boat now, and was dragging it in to shore, where several of the mercenaries were awaiting him.

'Your samples will be fine,' Harry said, standing back as Clarissa crouched down in front of Li-Liang and gently took hold of his arm. He tried to straighten it, then let out another yelp of pain.

'But I fear you may have fractured your clavicle,' Clarissa said, peering up at Li-Liang with concern.

The guide shook his head. 'It's just a . . .' The English word must have been lost in his shock and distress, as he gave up the search for it and sighed. '*Niǔshāng*, we call it.'

'A sprain?'

Li-Liang gave a weak nod.

'In any case,' Clarissa said, 'you must have a sling.' She looked up at Harry. 'Can you bring me up a clean pillow-case, please? And that sharp knife you have?'

Harry hurried below deck, returning to find Clarissa holding a flask of something warm to Li-Liang's pale lips. Then she took the pillowcase from Harry and cut it into a square of material, which she deftly folded into a triangle, then slipped under Li-Liang's left arm.

'There,' she said, tying the sling in place, careful not to hurt him. 'You should be a little more comfortable now.'

'You are a very able nurse, Mrs Lockhart,' Li-Liang said with a brave smile.

'My mother helped to found a nursing school in London,' Clarissa replied. 'She was a great admirer of Miss Nightingale's work.'

'I shall be for ever in your debt, Mrs Lockhart.'

'Then I shall collect on it now, Li-Liang, and insist that you call me Clarissa!'

Harry found himself gazing at Clarissa then, this woman who constantly surprised him, wondering what on earth she might do next. She glanced round with a hint of admonishment. 'Now then, Mr Compton, I wonder if you would go and find Tan Lin, and tell him of our intention to continue our journey on land.' She turned and looked back into Li-Liang's soft black eyes. 'If you're up to it, that is?'

'I feel better already,' the guide replied.

Though his colour was starting to improve, Clarissa still looked concerned. 'We should have taken your advice, Li-Liang, shouldn't we?' she said.

The guide patted her hand. 'We have a proverb, Clarissa, that sometimes gives me comfort. *Do not anxiously hope for that which is not yet come, and do not vainly regret what is already past.*'

'I shall try to remember that,' Clarissa said with a smile.

Easier said than done, Harry thought, as he watched Li-Liang close his eyes, and fall into a restive sleep.

PART FOUR

July 1868 – The Miao Mountains

Chapter 23

The party travelled in close formation – Tan Lin up front, machete held before him, leading them up the paved track that ran through the mountains, which Li-Liang had told them was called the Imperial Highway. Next came the guide himself, walking stick in his good hand, eyes fixed upon his felt-heeled boots, lest he misstep and jar his shoulder. Following behind was Clarissa, flanked by a mercenary on either side, her full mourning dress lending their little group the look of a Western funeral cortège, an impression which had the fortunate effect of discouraging the attentions of the various merchants and goatherds they passed on the track. Bringing up the rear was Harry, with two porters behind him, bulging packs hoisted high above their heads, yet their moccasined feet moving so swiftly that it was as though they carried no weight at all.

The landscape was even more spectacular than at river level, and when they rested every few *li*, Harry was able to drink it in at his leisure. The River Yuan snaked below them, weaving between the interlocking spurs of the verdant Miao Mountains. Harry's pockets were already stuffed with allium bulbs, and his vasculum was rattling with rhododendron seeds. There were great clumps of the woody shrubs growing wild on the mountainsides here, and Harry used his bowie knife to cut the seed pods free from their luscious purple flowers, keeping the blade close at hand in his vasculum, just in case he should need it for less decorative purposes.

Built along the Imperial Highway were a series of lodges known as '*Bin Guans*', or 'Mandarin Inns'. Only members of the Chinese Civil Service were permitted to stay there, but thanks to the official stamp on their passport, an exception was made for the three travellers. Each inn was constructed on a similar design, comprising a guardhouse, an inner courtyard with lodgings around it, and an outer gate decorated with the genie and dragon carvings that Harry had seen everywhere on their journey. Servants had to sleep in the stableblock, but Tan Lin and his second-in-command, Ren Hao, were permitted to curl up on mats outside the bedrooms of their charges, the better to protect them from sneak thieves.

It wasn't until the third day of their journey that they had their first unsettling encounter. The cortège had just paused for its mid-morning refreshment of ham, enlivened with slices of raw onions and mushrooms. Li-Liang and Tan Lin were busy poring over a compass, trying to establish the precise location of the Sub-Prefect's *yamen*, when, quite suddenly, children began to appear on the path ahead. Their clothes were caked in grime and filth, and they kept their eyes on their bare feet, so that even the sight of Wilberforce wagging his tail failed to excite their interest.

Clarissa stared at them in horror. 'What are those marks on their heads?' she asked.

Harry looked more closely at one girl as she sidled past. Decorating her forehead was a red weal, about the size of a sixpence. Glancing back, Harry saw that the other children wore the same marks.

'The children work at the mercury mines,' Li-Liang replied. 'The men scrape holes in the mountainside, then fill them with saltpetre. Then, after the rocks have exploded, it is the children who must collect the cinnabar crystals. It is hot, dangerous work, and many of them suffer with dreadful headaches. So the women burn pieces of paper in cups, and apply them to the children's heads. The fire in the cup makes a . . .' Li-Liang broke off, having come across another rare lacuna in his English.

'A vacuum?' Clarissa said.

Li-Liang nodded. 'It alleviates the pain.'

Clarissa watched, face etched with pity, as another child shuffled by, the red mark on her forehead bright and raw. 'Even at the reformatory where I assist in Shanghai,' she said in a faltering voice, 'I have never seen anything like this.' She turned back to Li-Liang. 'Where are these mines?'

'All over Guizhou,' he replied. 'Each Miao family must provide a certain weight of mercury ore every month for the Sub-Prefect.' The guide glanced furtively over one shoulder, then lowered his voice, though Harry suspected there was no one within a hundred miles who spoke English. 'With respect, we do not need reformatories and orphanages set up by well-meaning foreigners,' Li-Liang said. 'For this is *precisely* the sort of situation that the Self-Strengthening Movement seeks to remedy. *We* would bring modern mining techniques to Guizhou, and extract the mercury properly. No more hand-chisels and steel awes. And no more child workers!' He twisted his mouth into a bitter smile. 'But of course, that would require change, and there is nothing that terrifies the Qing Dynasty more . . .'

The guide broke off as they watched the last of the children trudge past, heads lowered.

'But can't we do something to help them now?' Clarissa said in frustration. 'At least give them some of our provisions?'

Li-Liang put her question to Tan Lin, who shook his head. The guide turned back to Clarissa, his face strained. 'These children are Hei Miao. Or "Black Miao".'

'And?' Clarissa demanded. 'What of it?'

'The Black Miao are the fiercest and proudest of all their people – even Tan Lin is afraid of them. The children would be severely punished for accepting our gifts.'

They all fell silent.

'Shall we?' Li-Liang said, and they set off again, Clarissa still gazing after the children as they plodded away, no doubt chastising herself for having done nothing to help.

Later that afternoon, they were forced to stop again, when a party of men approached them on the highway. Harry and Clarissa stood aside, watching in silence as Tan Lin spoke to the strangers. They were Hei Miao too, Harry could tell, dressed all in black, their calves and feet bare. The men up front carried wooden crossbows on their backs, their sun-weathered faces hard and implacable.

A rapid conversation ensued, but then some accord was reached, and as the Hei Miao drew closer, Harry saw that the men at the rear were balancing bamboo poles on their shoulders, with a deer strung between them by the hooves.

'It's just a hunting party,' Li-Liang said, the relief clear in his voice.

294

Covertly, Harry resheathed his knife and slipped it back into his vasculum. False alarm, he thought. Thank God.

As the hunting party passed by, Wilberforce began to growl, and Clarissa reached down and clasped the scruff of his neck. But it wasn't the men that were attracting the little dog's attention, Harry realised, but the deer. For the animal was still alive, its forelegs broken, its beautiful chestnut eyes wide with panic.

'Muntjac,' Li-Liang said. 'Delicious roasted.'

'Why not kill the poor creature, for pity's sake?' Clarissa asked. 'Put it out of its misery?'

Li-Liang shrugged. 'It fetches more money alive.'

'*Fan kwei*,' the last man hissed as he passed, flashing Harry a look of such raw contempt that he felt a shiver crawl across his skin.

'What does it mean, *fan kwei*?' Harry asked, having fallen into step with Li-Liang.

The guide looked ahead, checking Clarissa was out of earshot. 'It means "foreign devils", Mr Compton.'

'I see,' Harry said, remembering what Li-Liang had told them about the British, and how they were viewed by some of his countrymen. And perhaps they had a point, Harry reasoned, considering the way the British were ruthlessly squeezing China for profit. Harry clutched the vasculum to his chest, struck by the unwelcome notion that he might somehow be contributing to this unjust state of affairs. But surely plants and flowers were just part of the bounty of nature, he told himself — God-given gifts for anyone to enjoy and benefit from? Suddenly, he wasn't so sure.

The group pressed on until they came to a ridge. A charred stone building lay on the slope below, with an acre or so of treeline cleared around it. 'Is that a mercury mine?' Clarissa asked.

'Goodness no,' Li-Liang replied with a chuckle. 'That's the old Jesuit mission. The Black Miao burnt it down last year.'

'Why don't they rebuild it?' Clarissa asked.

'Both missionaries were killed in the raid — Belgians, I think.'

They walked on in silence, Harry wondering how a pair of Belgians had come to live — and die — in such a wild and solitary place.

'How long 'til we reach the Sub-Prefect's house?' Clarissa asked, her voice a little anxious now.

'Tomorrow afternoon,' Li-Liang replied. 'All being well.'

Perhaps it was the knowledge that they were drawing close to their destination, but that night at the Mandarin Inn, Harry, Clarissa and Li-Liang decided to stay up a little later than usual, remaining in the smoke-filled dining-room with Tan Lin and his men long after they'd all finished eating.

Dinner had comprised a dish of live freshwater shrimps, squirming in a black-bean sauce, but to Harry's amazement, Clarissa had partaken liberally of it. Much laughter had ensued, and the mercenaries were now smoking their pipes by the fire, which was built of smouldering rhododendron logs.

Their meal over, and a few glasses of *jiu* having dulled the pain in his arm, Li-Liang was sitting back in his chair, telling them more about the Sub-Prefect of East Guizhou, and his notoriously avaricious nature. 'The man's residence is quite magnificent, but do not be fooled by the sense of opulence.' Li-Liang leant forward and waggled a finger at them, his face gleaming in the heat of the fire. 'No, my friends! The Sub-Prefect is many things, but generous is not one of them. He will expect a sizable cash gift in exchange for opening his house to us.'

Letting slip a grimace of pain, Li-Liang reached for his pipe, a sleek white device with a neat little bowl at the end. 'It is made of asbestos,' he said proudly. 'A lightweight mineral resistant to heat. Quite miraculous.'

'I did not know you smoked, Li-Liang,' Clarissa said.

'Very rarely, Clarissa, in normal times. But I find that it eases my shoulder.' Getting to his feet, Li-Liang walked to the end of the dining-room, where Harry watched him hand a few coins to the innkeeper, who took his pipe from him and filled it.

'Is it . . . pleasant?' Clarissa asked, watching closely as Li-Liang lit up.

'You've never tried it?' Li-Liang said, inhaling the pale vapours.

Clarissa shook her head. 'My husband used to say that opium was . . .' She hesitated.

'What?' Harry asked.

'That it was for the peasants.'

'We are all of us peasants,' Li-Liang replied firmly. He held out his pipe to Clarissa; she hesitated, then took it.

'Clarissa!' Harry said, unable to hide his disapproval.

'I'm not a child, Harry,' Clarissa replied, drawing on the pipe, much to the amusement of Tan Lin and his men. She passed the pipe back to Li-Liang, and when she looked up, Harry detected a languor in her cat-like eyes, her pink, freckle-lined lips curving as she gazed at him through the fragrant air.

Li-Liang offered Harry the pipe next. He was about to decline, remembering Lorcan Darke's warning, but then he thought, If Clarissa can do it, why not I! Taking the pipe from Li-Liang's hand, he slipped the stem between his lips and inhaled, feeling the sweet-smelling smoke fill his lungs, the taste surprisingly bitter.

'A relaxant, if taken in small doses,' he heard Li-Liang say. 'Not unlike *jiu*.'

Harry canted his head to one side, hearing noises everywhere that he'd not previously cared to notice. The soft snufflings of Wilberforce at his feet; the clatter of the innkeeper's crockery; the murmurings of the mercenaries, who kept glancing at him from the fireplace, cunning and mischief dancing in their eyes . . . Looking up at Clarissa, he found her seemingly transfixed by some grains of rice spilt on the table during supper, busy arranging them into little piles with the tips of her long pale fingers. 'I think perhaps we ought to retire,' she said breathlessly.

'Very wise, Mrs Lockhart,' Li-Liang replied, motioning to Tan Lin.

Moments later, they all were being escorted upstairs to their sleeping quarters, Harry feeling strangely discombobulated, as though he were back in the stockground at Piggott's, walking through drifts of spring blossom.

Tonight's inn was a particularly humble affair, and the three of them found themselves sharing a room, part-divided by a rattan screen. 'I feel quite peculiar,' Clarissa said, as she sat down heavily on her divan. She breathed deeply for a time, then peered around the partition to Li-Liang. 'How is your shoulder?'

'It still throbs a little,' the guide replied. 'But the opium gives some relief.'

'May I examine it?' Clarissa asked.

Li-Liang nodded, and she made her way over to his bed, a little unsteady on her feet, Harry noted, as she knelt down to untie his sling, the linen grimy from their long journey.

'Harry?' Clarissa called over. 'Could you bring me the candle, please?'

He carried it over, watching Clarissa's face as she examined Li-Liang's shoulder. 'It looks a little inflamed,' she said, her voice faltering as she gently pressed a thumb against the red skin. 'Does this hurt?'

Li-Liang bit his lip. 'A little,' he replied, then gave a tight smile. 'But I'm sure it will improve over the coming days.'

'I commend you for your optimistic disposition, Li-Liang,' Clarissa said, as she retied his sling. 'It can aid recovery.'

'Optimism is indeed a powerful tool,' Li-Liang said, easing himself back against his pillows. 'And it is the natural optimism of my countrymen that will ensure a glorious future for China. In the West, you are brought up to believe in original sin. But in China, we follow Confucius, who teaches that man is essentially good. This makes it easier for us to work together, and believe in each other. And it is that which will lead to our inevitable success.' Li-Liang's eyes were half-closed now; a moment later, he was snoring.

'Time we got some sleep too, I think,' Harry said.

They both lay down on their beds, and Harry extinguished the candle. Seconds later, he heard a faint rustling behind the partition, and knew that Clarissa was turning to face him, her lips only inches away from his own. 'Harry?' he heard her whisper.

'Yes.'

'I think Li-Liang should see a doctor.'

That much had been clear even to Harry's uneducated eye. 'Perhaps the Sub-Prefect can recommend someone local,' he suggested.

'I hope so.'

Harry lay awake for a time, head still reeling from the opium. But then he heard Clarissa's breathing fall into a rhythm, and closed his eyes, determined to follow her into sleep.

They set off again at first light, and any grogginess the opium might have caused was soon dissipated by the fresh, invigorating mountain air. The Imperial Highway curved ahead of them in the distance, rising like the ladder in Jacob's dream, and they followed its paving stones at a decent speed, Harry marvelling at the banks of blue and yellow wildflowers that carpeted the hillsides.

Reaching the crest of the valley, they saw something that stopped them in their tracks. For the mountain range on the other side was on a completely different scale to anything they'd encountered so far. Its peaks were frosted with snow, the highest disappearing into haloes of grey cloud that hung above them, like smoke issuing from a volcano.

'Have you ever seen a mountain so beautiful?' Clarissa said.

'I've rarely seen a mountain so high,' Harry countered, reaching down to massage his aching calf muscles. 'We don't have to climb it, do we?'

Li-Liang conferred for a moment with Tan Lin, then said, 'We need only skirt the side.'

They pressed on, no one talking now, but Wilberforce more alert than Harry had seen him in weeks, feeling some atavistic compulsion to cock his leg against almost every boulder. Did he sense wolves in the vicinity, perhaps? Or tigers – Harry had heard there were tigers in central China . . .

Emerging from the cover of some camphor trees, Harry saw the route ahead, and cursed. A huge outcrop of bare limestone rose above them, protruding outwards from the mountain. Rather than go around it, the builders of the Imperial Highway had continued the path diagonally up its side.

'I hope you have a head for heights, Mrs Lockhart,' Harry said, eyeing the iron chain fixed to the sheer wall of rock, the path below it no more than three feet wide.

Clarissa tossed her chin at him. 'It's no worse than the Cairngorms, Mr Compton,' she replied, striding ahead in her wolfskin ankleboots. 'Come on!'

As the porters adjusted their packs, Harry caught a glimpse of his precious Wardian case in its wicker basket, and prayed that there would be no mishaps along the way. At times like this, it was hard not to remember Lorcan Darke; to picture the hollowed-out look in his eyes when he'd shown Harry the missing frame at the back of his Wardian case. To have travelled that far only to lose everything at the last moment – it didn't bear thinking about.

Tan Lin went first, gripping the iron chain with one strong hand, and Li-Liang followed, walking stick tucked under his arm, moving cautiously. Then came Clarissa, with Harry close behind.

The chain felt cold and rusty to the touch, each ring over an inch thick, fixed to the cliff-face by U-shaped iron bolts driven deep into the limestone. The party moved slowly along it, concentrating on every step, doing their best to ignore Wilberforce, who kept scurrying up and down the line, seemingly oblivious to the dangers below.

Midway up the path, Harry dared a glance down. Rows of tiny paddy fields were visible in the foothills, the water carried up to them by various pipes and irrigation wheels, a clever feat of engineering which— Harry felt his boot slip on some scree, and clutched more tightly to the chain. He needed to keep focus, he told himself. Even the small amount of opium he'd smoked last night was having an effect on his brain.

At last, they rounded a corner, and the path widened out a little. Tan Lin deemed this a good place to stop, and they settled themselves down on some tufts of grass, while Ren Hao began to heat some water on his kerosene burner.

As Li-Liang and Clarissa debated whether or not an indentation on the next mountainside evidenced the presence of a mercury mine, Harry's eye was caught by a bank of foliage on the escarpment below the path. Succulents, he thought, and small enough to be lifted from the soil by hand, and slipped into a vasculum . . . He stood up and wandered down the path, Wilberforce at his heel.

The succulents were sprouting from a rough patch of earth some ten yards down the slope. The gradient wasn't too steep, just a few pebbles coming loose as Harry edged downwards, keeping his hobnailed boots side-on to the incline.

Wilberforce joined him for a few paces, then stopped, whining. 'Hush, boy!' Harry said as he inched further down the slope, realising that there were miniature plants here that would dazzle any rockery-fancier in Chelsea. Just as he stretched out an arm to grasp them, the shingle beneath his feet gave way. He slithered down a few yards, clutching at the plants to steady himself, his panic rising as he saw them come away in clumps in his fists. And then he was really sliding, and it might have been comical, except that when he looked down he saw a precipice below, some five or six hundred feet of empty air above a canyon of jagged boulders . . .

'Help!' Harry cried. '*Help!*'

He was flat on his arse now, palms cut to ribbons as he skidded, his speed only increasing. Eye falling on a small, gnarled tree, Harry reached for it in desperation. His elbow was nearly yanked from its socket, but somehow he got a hold of the trunk with one hand, then the other, until finally the scree around him had stopped moving.

Then, as the dust cloud settled, he looked up to see Tan Lin, Clarissa and Li-Liang standing thirty yards above, staring down at him, open-mouthed. 'What on earth are you *doing*!' Clarissa cried.

'I slipped,' Harry called back. 'I'll just try and—'

'*Tíngzhǐ!*' Tan Lin bellowed in Chinese. *Stop there!*

Another shoal of pebbles came away, and Harry gripped more tightly to his tree. Several of the roots were exposed now, grains of earth and sand trickling down into the abyss. Above him, he heard Tan Lin issuing urgent instructions.

'In a moment, Tan Lin is going to roll my walking stick down to you,' Li-Liang called down. 'Grab hold of it if you can, and push it into the earth above your head.'

The men began to form a human chain, lowering Tan Lin down a few feet at a time. A cascade of friable scree came tumbling down after him, but once it had cleared,

Harry saw Tan Lin just fifteen yards above him, Li-Liang's walking stick held in his hand.

Their eyes met, and the tree to which Harry was hanging gave a sudden lurch, as yet another root sprang free from the earth. Harry was sure he was lost then, but somehow the little tree clung on. My life, dependent on a tree, Harry thought, suppressing a hysterical urge to laugh. When he looked back up, Tan Lin had lain the walking stick vertically against the slope. His eyes widened, charged with meaning, and Harry took a breath and nodded.

Tan Lin let go of the stick, and it began to roll down the escarpment, loosening pebbles as it fell. Just as it was almost within Harry's reach, it clipped a larger rock and changed direction. Harry flailed out an arm, and his fingertips got a hold of the end. Digging his nails into the wood, he drew in his arm, and finally he had it in his grasp.

'That's it, Harry!' Clarissa cried.

Harry could feel the tree roots growing looser now, and knew that he could have only moments before the last one was ripped from the ground. Using all the strength he could muster, he plunged the pointed end of the walking stick into the soft earth above him. It sank in, and he just had time to transfer both hands to the shaft before the tree tore away and tumbled into the void.

'Well done!' Li-Liang called down. 'Now you must make a foothold. Use the caps of your boots.'

Harry nodded, kicking repeatedly into the earth beneath him. Once he'd created a deep enough hole, he moved both feet into it, then pulled out the walking stick and plunged it into the earth above him. Then he repeated the process, and slowly but surely made progress up the escarpment, hearing Wilberforce's whimpers punctuated by shouts of encouragement from his audience.

After twenty long minutes, Harry finally reached Tan Lin's outstretched hand, and felt himself hauled up on to safe ground, as the walking stick came loose from his grasp and rattled down the escarpment to join the uprooted tree at the foot of the mountain.

Collapsing, Harry closed his eyes. As he drifted off, he tucked his hands between the buttons of his shirt, in part because it gave comfort to his raw, torn palms, but mainly because he wanted to check that the four little euphorbia succulents he'd managed to stash inside were still in place.

'You're an utter fool, Harry,' were the first words he heard when he opened his eyes. Clarissa was standing over him, green eyes flashing. 'No more botanising until we reach our destination. And no more opium!'

'Aye-aye, Captain,' Harry said, thinking how very beautiful she looked as she glowered down at him, before she tutted in exasperation and stalked away.

He must have been out for a while, he realised, as the sky had clouded over. A few yards away, the porters were waiting impatiently to leave, packs ready on their backs, while Li-Liang stood massaging his shoulder, looking bereft without his walking stick. 'That was a little close for comfort, Mr Compton,' he said.

Harry sat up and began transferring the succulents from his shirt to his vasculum, feeling suddenly ashamed of himself. 'It was stupid of me.'

Li-Liang looked at him shrewdly. 'Perhaps we should all stick to the path from now on.'

A moment later, Ren Hao handed Li-Liang a new stick, hewn by hand, and they all set off again, keeping their feet firmly on the paved highway.

'Don't you think it's odd?' Harry called to Clarissa, who was walking a few yards ahead of him. 'One worries about bandits, or wolves – or even tigers. But then something you don't expect, something that seems entirely harmless, like a pile of pebbles, nearly does for you.'

'The trick, Mr Compton,' Clarissa replied crisply, 'is not to go looking for danger. That's my motto!'

She was still angry with him, he could tell from the set of her jaw. Surely that *must* mean she felt something for him, he thought with a grin.

Then, from up ahead, there came a sudden shout, and Li-Liang turned. 'Your papers,' he called to Harry, motioning for him to follow. 'As quick as you can.'

Harry hurried up the line after Li-Liang, one arm clutching his vasculum. And then he saw why such urgency was required, for standing on the path ahead were three Chinese soldiers with their swords drawn.

Harry handed Li-Liang the roll of documents, who held it out. The chief soldier unfurled it, then his eye fell upon the magical stamp of the Zongli Yamen, and he looked up at Li-Liang and nodded.

Straight away, the swords returned to their sheaths, and Li-Liang called back to Clarissa with a triumphant smile, 'Come, Mrs Lockhart! These men will take us where we want to go.'

Chapter 24

It took them another twenty minutes to reach the Sub-Prefect's *yamen*. The last section of path wound through a grove of citrus trees, their branches filled with clouds of fragrant blossom, and then they saw the triumphal arch that marked the entrance to the grounds.

A guardhouse had been built on one side of the arch, and on the other rose a series of what looked like decorative wooden arbours. Each was formed of five thick pinewood poles, tapering up in a tepee shape towards what appeared to be . . . Harry felt Clarissa clutch at his arm, and knew that she'd seen it too. Poking out of the tops of the arbours were human heads.

The macabre sight caused even Tan Lin to gape in horror. Made impatient by the delay, the chief soldier muttered something tersely in Chinese.

'These men were criminals,' Li-Liang translated. 'They were of the Hei Miao people.'

The dead men looked like they were treading water, their chins tilted up as though gasping for air. Wrapped around their necks were circular pieces of wood, like ruffs, with their bodies dangling beneath. The man in the nearest cage might almost have been asleep, but for the raven jabbing away at his eyelid with its heavy black bill. Clarissa, her face filled with disgust, averted her gaze, and not a moment too soon, Harry thought, as seconds later the raven twisted its neck and flew off, an eyeball clutched in its curved beak, trailing a line of pinkish sinew.

'Their crimes must have been terrible indeed,' Clarissa said.

Strangely stung by the disdainful expression on her face, the chief soldier spoke again.

'These men failed in their duty,' Li-Liang translated. 'They are the enemies of China.'

'It must be a vital duty indeed,' Clarissa rejoined, 'the disregard of which would merit such a punishment!'

Li-Liang dropped his eyes. 'He says that they failed to meet their quota of cinnabar crystals for the Sub-Prefect.'

Clarissa glanced at Harry, wordless with outrage, then turned and marched onwards.

As they neared the arch, Harry said quietly into Li-Liang's ear, 'But aren't these soldiers from the Hei Miao tribe? How can they stand for their own people being treated like this?'

Li-Liang shook his head. 'The soldiers are Tartars — Manchus. From Manchuria, in the north. You can tell by the way they wear their moustaches. Most members of the Imperial Court are of Manchurian extraction, so it is Manchus who are often sent to govern the most unruly provinces.'

They passed beneath the execution cages, and the foetid smell of decomposing flesh became almost unbearable. 'Try not to look,' Li-Liang said to Clarissa, as he pressed a silk handkerchief to his own nose.

The triumphal arch was made of pinewood, Harry saw, with an inscription written in red lacquer above the gilded doorway.

'What does it say?' Clarissa asked, as they emerged into the inner courtyard of the *yamen*.

'That the Sub-Prefect is the Living Buddha of Guizhou,' Li-Liang replied in a flat voice.

The household had evidently been expecting their arrival. The Sub-Prefect was seated on a wooden throne in a shady colonnade at the end of the courtyard, with two women occupying smaller chairs on either side of him. Midway across the courtyard, the soldiers all fell to their knees to kowtow, foreheads pressed to the dusty ground, palms splayed. Li-Liang performed a more modest bow, Harry was relieved to see, and he followed the guide's example as Clarissa sank into a deep curtsey.

The Sub-Prefect made neither sound nor movement as they approached. The sun, which had been blotted out before by the lintels of the colonnade, shone unchecked now, and Harry could see the man's face more clearly. He looked to be about fifty years old, and wore the same thin black moustaches as his guard – originating in the corners of his mouth, then drooping down past clean-shaven lips in two long dark tendrils. Fitted on his head was a bowl-shaped hat of red rattan, with a coral button on the top, whilst over his embroidered robes hung a weighty tunic of brocaded blue silk. He looked hot, and not a little bored.

They drew closer. The woman on the Sub-Prefect's left was elderly, the skin of her face pulled back tight under a blue silk headpiece. Her cheeks were powdered, and she wore an elaborate robe of red and green made of heavy shot silk. In the other chair sat a much younger woman, more plainly attired in a pleated yellow gown. Her face was finely featured, and around her neck she wore a stiff necklace of silver wire. Harry stared at the necklace, wondering where he'd seen something like it before.

Li-Liang bowed again to the Sub-Prefect, and the chief soldier handed their roll of papers to his master. As the Sub-Prefect gave the documents a perfunctory glance, without seeming to move his head, Harry's eyes slid across to the Sub-Prefect's daughter, and widened. Now he knew where he'd seen that necklace before! The girl who wore it was the same woman whose likeness Harry had seen captured in one of Lorcan Darke's daguerreotypes. Entirely naked, with her head angled back to the camera . . .

'Harry?' Clarissa said sharply.

Harry turned to see that the chief soldier was holding out the roll of documents to him. As he took it, his vasculum swung off his shoulder and hung before him. Suddenly, the Sub-Prefect snapped out an order, and the soldier stepped forward and seized hold of the vasculum strap.

'Hey!' Harry said, tugging back. 'What d'you think you're doing?'

But the Manchu soldier was strong, and despite all his efforts, Harry felt himself being dragged towards the Sub-Prefect. What if the Sub-Prefect opened the vasculum and saw the plant specimens inside? And the knife? Or if he read the plaque that was still on the lid, engraved with the name 'L.R.C. Darke'?

Glancing up, Harry saw the Sub-Prefect's daughter frowning at him. Did she recognise the vasculum? What had she been to Lorcan Darke, he wondered? Merely his muse? Or something more . . .

As if aware of some impending diplomatic incident, Li-Liang began talking rapidly in Chinese, desperately trying to placate the Sub-Prefect. Next to the guide, Harry could hear Clarissa's skirts rustling. What was she *doing*, he asked himself irritably, as he saw her reach into her pockets – did she not realise what was at stake?

'Your Excellency!' Clarissa cried out.

Everyone turned to see Clarissa holding out a small satin bag. 'A token of our respect,' she said, lowering her eyes deferentially.

The Sub-Prefect made a gesture with two closed fingers, and the soldier released Harry's vasculum. Taking the bag from Clarissa's outstretched hands, the soldier carried it over to his master, who untied the silken strings and peered inside. When he looked up, Harry was relieved to see the faintest of smiles on his face. He uttered a few words in a hoarse whisper, and the atmosphere immediately lightened.

'His Excellency is most pleased,' Li-Liang translated. 'He asks you to join him in his salon at sundown.'

The elder woman hissed something at Li-Liang from behind a cupped hand. 'And His Excellency's mother wishes you every blessing,' he added.

So the elder woman was the Sub-Prefect's mother, Harry realised. That must mean the younger girl was his wife! He dared another glance at her, and found her laughing, entirely besotted, it seemed, with Wilberforce, who had rolled over on to his back, hoping to have his tummy stroked.

'I think he likes you, Your Highness,' Harry chanced.

311

The young woman looked up. She had the dark, delicate features of the Miao, Harry saw now, and as she surveyed him coolly with her jet eyes, he was left in no doubt that she'd understood exactly what he'd said to her in English.

Then the Sub-Prefect dismissed them with another languid wave of his hand, and the armed guard was leading them off to their quarters.

'What was in that little bag of yours?' Harry asked.

'Half an ingot of silver from Lam Dookay's safe,' Clarissa replied. 'It felt like the right moment to pull out all the stops.'

'You're a wonder,' Harry said.

Clarissa snorted. 'I'm surprised you noticed, Mr Compton! Your attentions seemed concentrated in an entirely different direction.' Then she strode away, leaving Harry staring after her, shaking his head in righteous disbelief.

'I can't think what she means,' Harry said to Li-Liang.

'Can't you, Mr Compton?' the guide replied, a knowing smile playing upon his pale lips. 'Ah well – perhaps it will come to you after you've had some time to rest. This way, Mr Compton. Our rooms are through here, I believe.'

Harry must have been more exhausted than he'd realised, as he slept from the moment he sat down on his low bed until Clarissa woke him with a sharp rap at the door, informing him that they were expected in the salon imminently.

Seeing Harry appear a few minutes later, still buttoning up his frockcoat, hair wet and slicked back from his sun-browned face, Clarissa dropped her eyes.

'What?' Harry demanded.

'Nothing! It's just . . .' Her cheeks coloured, just a little. 'I'd forgotten that you scrub up rather well, Mr Compton.

312

That is all!' Then she turned and walked ahead, while Harry sauntered after her, feeling oddly elated — he who'd always detested any personal remarks about his looks.

The Sub-Prefect's 'salon' turned out to be a draughty pavilion set behind the main courtyard. Nailed to its wooden walls were three tiger skins, their eyes replaced by green jade balls that lent them a ghoulish, rather than ferocious, air.

'Ping Ru shot each of the tigers himself, you know,' Li-Liang called to Harry and Clarissa as they came in. 'He owns two of only three rifled muskets in all of Guizhou!'

Thank God there weren't more guns than that, Harry thought, recalling the executed prisoners decomposing outside the walls of the *yamen*.

Li-Liang was attempting to engage Ping Ru in conversation, but whatever subject he had chosen — and Harry sincerely hoped it wasn't the Self-Strengthening Movement — proved a failure, as the Sub-Prefect's eyes began to glaze over much like those of his slaughtered tigers.

The ladies of the household, meanwhile, focused their attentions on Clarissa's dress, so drab and worn compared to theirs. Tonight, the elder woman wore a long red robe, bedecked with purple ribbons, each with a little silver bell attached to the end that tinkled whenever she moved, whilst the Sub-Prefect's wife was resplendent in an indigo smock and flower-embroidered trousers, that gleaming filigree necklace still clasped around her throat. The girl really was very beautiful, Harry thought, as she caught his eye and smiled. Sensing Clarissa watching him, he took a sip from his thimble-sized cup of black tea, and looked away. No sign of any *jiu* here, more was the pity.

313

'Ping Ru has been telling me that there are gold deposits in the River Yuan,' Li-Liang said. 'He has already deployed some of his Miao labourers to pan for it.' Li-Liang leant forward and whispered confidentially: 'I have suggested that he might study what the Americans did in California, with the extraordinary development of hydraulic mining. Imagine how the Chinese could improve such a technique, given the vast abundance of—'

The Sub-Prefect cut in, the sharpness of his tone sending a shudder through the room.

'What did he say?' Harry asked.

'That he does not want foreign barbarians coming to Guizhou to exploit its resources,' Li-Liang replied. 'And that Prince Chun, of the Royal Manchu Court, is in complete agreement with him.'

'Well, this is going famously,' Clarissa said through clenched teeth, letting out a sigh of relief as she saw the Sub-Prefect rise to his feet. 'At last! Shall we go through?'

Dinner was served in the courtyard, with the servants positioned in lines on either side of the entrance, like a guard of honour. One half of the courtyard was covered by a bamboo canopy, with a large square table laid up beneath it. A silk-gowned major-domo was waiting next to it, ready to show them to their places, whilst in the corner a tiny Miao man sat cross-legged, tapping at a tom-tom.

The diners sat down, Harry positioned between Clarissa and the Sub-Prefect's wife. Presently, the first dishes arrived: poached river turtle; boiled ducks' feet with bamboo shoots; chicken livers fried with lotus seeds. No one spoke much, and as night closed in and the air began to cool, Ping Ru slipped a sumptuous robe over his tunic, a heavy fur made of hundreds of foxes' ears.

'He looks like Henry VIII,' Clarissa hissed into Harry's ear, mischievous eyes glinting. 'As captured by Holbein.'

Before Harry could answer, he felt a tap on his arm and turned to see the Sub-Prefect's wife smiling at him, holding out a dish of hardboiled green eggs. At first, Harry declined, but the girl looked so crestfallen that he soon capitulated, cutting an egg in two with the side of one chopstick. He was taken aback to find the insides – both white and yolk – as green as grass. Seeing his alarmed expression, the Miao girl gave a silvery chime of laughter, silenced by the thunderous look Ping Ru shot them both across the table.

'It's rather good,' Harry said to Clarissa between mouthfuls. 'Preserved in lime juice and brine, I think,' he added, but she seemed not to hear, turning instead to Ping Ru.

'We hoped we might visit one of your pagodas tomorrow, Your Excellency,' Clarissa said, maintaining her smile. 'The Mian Jian Guang?'

Li-Liang quickly translated, and Harry waited, holding his breath, as the Sub-Prefect considered Clarissa's request. Finally, he nodded, as though granting royal assent.

Sitting back in relief, Harry caught sight of Li-Liang's face in the candlelight, and was struck by the marked deterioration in his appearance. Their guide had lost weight, he realised, the skin hanging sallow and loose around his jaw, and his eyes, normally so alert, looked dull and sunken.

'You must ask the Sub-Prefect about seeing a doctor, Li-Liang,' Harry said, leaning across the table. 'You do not look well.'

'Nonsense!' Li-Liang replied. '*Vis medicatrix naturae*, as the Romans used to say. Give the body sufficient time, and it will heal itself.' He glanced round. 'Ah! The speciality of the region.'

The largest platter yet was being carried to the table, a whole suckling pig, a tangerine clenched in its snout, legs folded back on themselves, ears erect, tiny tail crisp and curly. The servants looked on hungrily, yet beneath the delicious aroma of roasted pork, Harry caught a hint of something putrid on the breeze – the stink of open drains, and the high reek of decomposing flesh, which made his appetite vanish.

The tom-tom beat on as Li-Liang made another attempt to engage Ping Ru in conversation, but this time he barely replied, just kept glaring across the table at Harry and at his wife, who appeared to take amusement from her husband's displeasure.

The meal seemed interminable, so Harry was relieved when the sweet dishes began to arrive: melon segments, sugared medlars, quarters of pears floating in their fermented juices. Then, mercifully, it was over, and they all left the table and returned to the salon. Pipes were readied, but Clarissa had already dropped into a curtsey, her auburn head lowered, revealing to Harry, standing behind her, a tantalising glimpse of the nape of her neck. 'We have travelled a great distance, Your Excellency,' she was saying, 'and must bid you good night . . .'

Then Harry was bowing too, and increasing his stride to match Clarissa's. He could sense Li-Liang longing to follow, but he was too polite to abandon his host, and turning,

Harry saw him accept a pipe from the major-domo just as they left the room.

'I don't think I've ever wanted to leave a place so badly in my life,' Clarissa said as Harry walked her to her chamber. 'Though you seem to have enjoyed yourself!' At her bedroom door, she turned. 'We're almost there now, Harry. Don't let anything ruin our chances, will you?' And then she was gone.

Retreating to his own room, Harry performed his ablutions, then lifted the wicker basket down from the cupboard where he'd stowed it, and carefully slid out the Wardian case. The clasp that fixed the hinged gable to the crate had come a little loose, so he screwed it back in place with the tip of his bowie knife. The contraption was even roomier than he remembered – he could fit scores of cuttings from the icicle tree inside, and still have space for his other plants. We've come all this way, he said to himself, feeling the hairs on his neck start to tingle with excitement. We're so close now . . .

Another waft from the latrines drifted in as Harry settled down on the low wooden bed, its frame pitted with wormholes. Small green lizards clung to the lime-washed walls, motionless every time he looked at them, as though somehow sensing his gaze. He was just entering the borders of sleep when he heard a gentle knocking at his door. He sat up, unsure whether to ask who was there, or to ignore it. Then the knock came again. Could it be Clarissa?

Harry was about to answer the door when he recognised the silvery laugh of the Sub-Prefect's wife. He froze, but then the knocking resumed, louder now. For a brief, mad moment, Harry allowed himself to imagine ushering the beautiful Miao girl inside — slipping the indigo smock from her bronze shoulders, unclasping that silver necklace. But then he remembered Clarissa's wise words; such behaviour would be absurdly reckless. If Ping Ru was minded to horse-whip any botanist who entered his domain, how much more violently would he treat an adulterer? And besides, Harry had more pressing matters on his mind. The icicle tree . . . and Clarissa.

Eventually, Harry heard the woman's small feet tiptoeing away, and lay back in his bed, waiting for sleep to come, and for the day he'd anticipated for so long to arrive.

Chapter 25

Breakfast the next day was taken in the salon. Harry found himself placed next to the Sub-Prefect's mother, and served a dazzling array of *dim sum*, as he'd learnt that the dumplings were called. They were sensationally good — much smaller than those they'd eaten on the *chuan*, and each with a different pattern imprinted on the dough, and containing a variety of fillings, each more delicious than the last.

Breakfast was almost over by the time Clarissa arrived at the table. 'Pity you overslept, Mrs Lockhart,' Harry said, sitting back in his chair with a contented sigh. 'You missed an excellent spread.'

Clarissa's lips tightened. 'I did not oversleep, Mr Compton. I was with Li-Liang.'

The Sub-Prefect's mother glanced up, perhaps alerted by the tension in Clarissa's voice.

'He is not well,' Clarissa went on. 'He insists he merely smoked one pipe too many last night, but it's his shoulder — I'm convinced of it. I fear that the bone is broken, and has done some terrible damage to the muscle.' She chewed on her cheek. 'I think it may be infected.'

Harry thought for a moment. If Clarissa was right, then there was no way Li-Liang should come with them today. 'He must stay here and rest,' Harry said. 'Then perhaps we can make some arrangement for our return journey.'

Clarissa nodded. 'I thought a sedan chair. I've already spoken to Tan Lin about it, in fact.'

'Thank you,' Harry said, and Clarissa looked up at him and smiled.

The Sub-Prefect's wife entered the salon, scowled at the pair of them, then left the way she'd come in.

'That was odd,' Clarissa said.

'Perhaps she hoped to see Wilberforce,' Harry improvised. 'Here,' he said, pouring Clarissa a cup of sweet tea and handing it to her. 'Drink this. We've an arduous journey ahead.'

An hour later, the party set off – Harry, Clarissa and Wilberforce, along with Tan Lin and Ren Hao to carry the luggage. Ping Ru, who was yet to make an appearance today, had provided them with two Manchu soldiers, one as guide and the other as guard, the latter with one of the Sub-Prefect's precious 'rifled muskets' slung across his back.

'For tigers?' Harry asked, gesturing at the firearm. The guard looked blank, so Harry did his best impersonation of a tiger, and the man laughed so heartily that his thin black moustaches quivered like slowworms. But once his composure was recovered, he shook his head.

'Hei Miao,' he said, putting the stock to his shoulder and mimicking letting off a round.

Harry raised an eyebrow. So the Black Miao were considered more dangerous even than tigers . . . Doing his best to ignore a mounting sense of trepidation, Harry reached into his jacket and pulled out a copy of Lorcan Darke's map. 'Mian Jian Guang?' he asked, showing it to the Manchu guide.

'Mian Jian Guang,' the man answered, pointing with such certainty into the distance that Harry felt his heart swell.

They descended the valley through a thick conifer forest, the ground soft with fallen needles, the air redolent of pine resin and crumbling bark. Many of the trees were China-firs, or *Cunninghamia* as they were known in Chelsea – introduced to Britain by Dr James Cunningham in the early 1700s. Perhaps the good doctor had been to this very wood, Harry thought, struck by the enchanting realisation that he was now one in a long line of plant hunters, striking out in the name of progress and glory.

At the bottom of the valley, there flowed a clear mountain stream. There was no bridge, so the Manchus began to wade across. 'Here,' Harry said, holding out both hands to Clarissa.

She looked at him and laughed. 'What are you proposing, Mr Compton? To carry me?'

Before Harry could respond, Clarissa had stepped into the stream, her black dress floating up around her waist, so that Harry had no choice but to follow, shivering as the icy water spilled into his hobnailed boots.

Having clambered out on to the other bank, they set off up the other side of the valley. The air was cooler here, with patches of mist just visible at the tops of the scaly pine trunks. At one point, the guard held up a hand, telling them to stop, and they all watched apprehensively as he swivelled his head, scanning the trees.

'What is it?' Clarissa whispered to Harry.

'I think he's worried about the Black Miao,' Harry said. 'An expedition originating from the Sub-Prefect's *yamen* is unlikely to be popular.'

Clarissa shuddered, perhaps recalling the executed men in their cages. But then Tan Lin appeared with a canteen of water that he'd filled from the stream, and offered it to Clarissa. 'Perfectly chilled,' she said, with a smile of thanks that made their captain's chubby face beam.

Soon, they emerged from the woodland on to a rocky ridge, and Clarissa gave a gasp. Harry turned to follow her gaze. The panorama was indeed breathtaking. Rising in the misty distance was a row of massive limestone pillars, their crowns garlanded with trees, their walls festooned with creepers and ferns, like the ruined house of some ancient giant. Beyond that, to the left of the line of pillars, came the mercury glint of a river.

'Is that the River Yuan?' Clarissa asked the Manchu guide.

'It can't be,' Harry said, but the guide cut him off.

'Yuan,' he repeated with a nod. 'Yuan, Yuan . . .'

Harry and Clarissa both turned to Tan Lin, who was suddenly looking rather sheepish. If that was indeed the Yuan, then they could have reached this point without taking the Imperial Highway at all. They could have saved *days* of travel!

But the guide was nodding at them now, and then they were off again, descending through another valley, the trees different here — hollies, crabapples, mountain ashes. The rock formations had changed too, Harry noted, seeing granite rather than limestone, which would have altered the tilt of the soil. No doubt that was why the icicle tree could be found only in this tiny corner of the world. The region comprised a plethora of different soil types — seeds that dispersed from one habitat would fail to geminate in another. Someday, there would be scientific papers written about this place, Harry thought, suddenly picturing himself addressing the Linnean Society in Piccadilly, gazing out at a sea of rapt faces as he described their perilous journey . . . He checked himself. First find the damned thing!

As they continued up the path, Wilberforce let out a sudden volley of barks, ears pricked. A moment later, Harry heard a rumble of water ahead. The noise grew louder as they came to a clearing and banked left. Trees became grasses, and Harry felt a chill breeze on his face, seeing the silvery River Yuan visible once again in the distance, gleaming in the sunlight. Then they rounded a crag of rock, and drew to a halt.

'Mian Jian Guang,' the guide said proudly.

Harry and Clarissa exchanged a thrilled glance, then stepped forward. The pagoda rose on the near side of a deep ravine. The structure itself was a modest affair, only two storeys high, but the beauty of its setting was incomparable.

Looking round, Harry gave a start as he saw a solitary monk standing on the grassy clifftop, holding a heavy log in his hands. The man wore long grey robes with a hood at the back, lowered to reveal a shaven head and wind-beaten face. He seemed to be building a shrine of sorts, using rocks and wood to create a kind of enclosure. Pausing to wipe his brow, he caught sight of the Manchu guards, and his forehead furrowed in concern. But then his eye fell on Clarissa, and he seemed to relax a little.

'*Ni hao!*' she called out.

As the monk edged towards them, the soldier slipped his gun from his shoulder and laid it down on the grass. The monk made a bow, then began a hesitant conversation with the Sub-Prefect's Manchu men. Before long, they were laughing, the monk gesticulating so enthusiastically that Harry wondered how long it had been since he'd seen another human being.

Eventually, the monk turned to Harry and Clarissa, and ushered them towards his pagoda, leaving the Manchus to join Tan Lin and Ren Hao in resting on their hunkers, pipes gripped between their teeth.

The structure the monk had been building was not a shrine, but a privy, Harry saw as they passed – there was a drop-hole already dug in the ground, its stink suggesting that the monk had been using it for some time.

'I think I shall omit that particular feature from my painting,' Clarissa said to Harry, nose wrinkling.

The monk threw open the door to his pagoda, then beckoned them inside. There was an unglazed aperture opposite, leading on to a wooden platform that extended into the void. The monk hopped up on to it, surefooted as a mountain goat, eyes glistening as he drank in the majesty of the view, and gave thanks for it to whichever Creator he believed in. Then he turned and urged Harry and Clarissa to join him.

'I won't, thank you all the same!' Clarissa said briskly, but Harry climbed carefully up on to the platform, hearing Wilberforce's whimpers of unease behind him. Looking to the right, he made out a small rope bridge crossing the ravine, leading to a kind of ruined watchtower. He took out

Lorcan Darke's original map and showed it to the monk. The monk stared at it, then pointed at the strange word which Harry had been unable to decipher.

'Xiuxiu,' the monk said, looking up at him with a Delphic smile playing on his lips. Then he pointed at the stone tower on the other side of the ravine and repeated, 'Xiuxiu.'

Finally, Harry said to himself. We've found it . . . Eager to share the news with Clarissa, he hurried over to where she stood, face tilted upwards, examining the bas-relief carved high on the back wall of the pagoda. It was a grim piece of work, Harry saw – ghastly figures in animal masks overseeing the torture of sinners, one being sawn in half, another stretched on a rack. The sculpted wood was shiny with age – probably centuries old.

'It's like something from Dante's Inferno,' Clarissa said, her voice full of awe. 'No wonder this place is known as the Vestibule of the Sojourn of Death.'

Before Harry could respond, the monk had appeared beside him, shaking a small brass bowl filled with coins. 'Xiuxiu?' he said.

Dipping a hand into his pocket, Harry took out the few coins that remained and dropped them into the pot. The monk bowed his head in thanks, then signalled to the door.

'He's going to take me to the icicle tree,' Harry said to Clarissa. 'The guards will be expecting you to begin work on your painting. I'll be back as soon as I can.'

'Of course,' she replied, though Harry could see she was disappointed.

At the door of the pagoda, Clarissa laid a hand on his arm. 'Good luck, Harry,' she said, her freckled cheeks flushed with excitement.

Their eyes met, and Harry could see Clarissa's chest rising and falling, her lips soft and inviting. He had never wanted to kiss her more. Perhaps . . . They sprang apart as they heard the monk approach.

Harry squeezed Clarissa's hand, then jogged over to retrieve his kit from their luggage. None of the men seemed in the least bit interested in what he was doing, their dark eyes all drawn to Clarissa, who was opening up her easel now, and positioning a blank canvas upon it.

Then the monk reappeared at Harry's side, and the two of them slipped away from the main party, Wilberforce following close behind.

The suspension bridge was formed of thick bamboo ropes, stretching from one side of the ravine to the other, secured by iron ringbolts driven into the rock. The walkway of the bridge was laid with fat wooden planks, its hand ropes positioned at waist height. It was no more than thirty feet from one end to the other, but the drop was sheer, and Harry could see puffs of white cloud floating in the empty chasm below.

The monk was utterly fearless, of course, whistling tunelessly to himself as he marched across the bridge without breaking stride, confirming Harry in his suspicions that the man might not be in full possession of his faculties. Harry sneaked a last glance back at Clarissa, who was about a hundred yards away on the clifftop, busy at her easel. Though she wasn't looking in his direction, Harry knew she would be following his every step, taking care not to alert the others.

Suddenly, Wilberforce dashed past Harry, and he gave a start, cursing the little dog as he saw him dart between the monk's legs and scurry on to the far bank. Harry waited for the monk to reach the end of the bridge, then stuffed his tool roll into his waistband, and picked up his vasculum and the wicker basket containing his Wardian case. He yearned to grip the rope with both hands, but only one was available, so he kept it tightly curled around the rope as he walked, no matter how the friction burned his blistered and cut palm. At least the pain was a distraction – it kept him from looking down, the perils of which he remembered from the rockslide he'd barely survived.

Step by step, Harry advanced across the bridge, feeling the structure wobble alarmingly as he approached the centre, then grow more secure as he made his way up the slope. Finally, he hopped off the far end on to solid ground, Wilberforce leaping up at his shins in celebration.

The monk was eager to get moving, it seemed, as he was already some way down the overgrown deer path that led to the ruined watchtower. It must originally have been part of some defensive rampart, Harry decided, as he stepped inside its shell – there was even the remnant of an arrow slit in the surviving wall. The other walls had long since collapsed, their crumbling stones covered in moss, reminding Harry of the ruined manor house in Pulborough.

There was a pile of fresh-cut logs stacked against the rear wall, and the monk began gathering the wood in his arms. Just beyond, Harry saw the stump of the tree that had been felled. He was just about to look away when he caught sight of something lying on the forest floor – something that made his throat tighten. Stepping out of the ruined tower, as if in a dream, he dropped to his hunkers next to what remained of the tree. Picking up a slim branch with shaking hands, he saw eight crisp pinnate leaves hanging from its stem . . .

'The bastard cut it down,' Harry murmured, as he turned to look at the monk, whistling happily to himself as he went on with his work. 'He cut down the icicle tree!'

Leaning back against a rock, Harry heard his breathing coming fast and hoarse, and tried to regain control of himself. He had other specimens, he told himself – the lily bulbs, the clematises, the weigela. But then he thought of the cost of the expedition, the bag of silver Clarissa had given away only yesterday. It would not be enough, he knew. He was ruined, and he had ruined Clarissa too.

Closing his eyes, Harry felt his mouth twist in self-disgust. All his hopes of wealth and glory were childish fantasies. The icicle tree had eluded him, just as it had Lorcan Darke. He would be returning home empty-handed.

But then Harry blinked, seeing something pale, deep within the vegetation. Rubbing his face with both hands, he straightened up. Could it be . . .

Stumbling out of the ruins and into the forest, Wilberforce capering at his ankles, Harry found himself standing before a small tree. It was barely taller than he was, just a sapling really, but . . . He reached out a hand. Three blooms hung from the sapling's upper branches. Three blooms of the most exquisite ice-white colour, long and intricate, with a scent as fragrant as orange blossom.

Harry fell to his knees, and the monk ran over, eyes full of concern, but then Wilberforce began licking Harry's face, and suddenly Harry was laughing, and the monk was laughing too, and Harry was embracing him, as they shared this wondrous moment together, this handsome young Englishman and this tiny, leather-skinned monk, and Harry wondered if he'd ever felt so happy in all his days.

Gradually, Harry came back to his senses. There was work to be done. Drawing the Wardian case out of its basket, he set it down next to the sapling. Then, using a trowel from his tool roll, he began scraping free the loose soil from around the icicle tree's thin trunk. Pausing to touch a fingertip to his tongue, he was relieved to find it tasted tart. The soil was acidic, just as he'd suspected! The icicle tree was ericaceous.

Working quickly now, Harry packed the Wardian case with soil, then picked up a pruning knife and began to take his first cuttings. Meticulously, lovingly, he nicked off the branches at a 45-degree angle, stripping back the bark at the base, isolating the leaf buds at the top just as he'd been taught to do at Mr Piggott's nursery. Soon, his Wardian case was three-quarters full, and Harry stood back to examine the rest of the sapling. The flowers on the lower part of the tree had been and gone, and in their place hung clusters of small black fruits, like elderberries. Too early to hope for seeds, but one never knew, so Harry picked as many of the clusters as he could find, and stashed them safely inside his vasculum. Then he cut off the three young icicle tree flowers and placed them beside the berries. Clarissa would need those for her illustrations.

A good deal of time had passed, Harry suddenly realised, glancing about half-dazed. The monk was gone, and the sun was high in the sky. He looked back at his Wardian case, smiling to see it finally verdant with life. The cuttings would be happy in there, he sensed, as he closed the glass roof and fixed the little hasp around the catch.

Stooping down, Harry tested the weight of the Wardian case by raising the leather handle. Though it was much heavier now, the structure held firm. There was no putting the case back into the Fortnum & Mason basket now, so he cut a hole in the middle of the blanket in which it had been wrapped, then worked the handle through, so that the blanket hung down over the sides of the case, concealing it like a shroud.

Slowly, carefully then, Harry began to make his way back to the rope bridge. When he reached its foot, he saw a sight that filled him with admiration. For on the other side of the bridge, still busy at her easel, stood Clarissa, with the entire party, including the monk, sitting cross-legged around her. She had provided the perfect diversion.

Eager to catch her eye, knowing that he would be able to communicate his success to her with a single look, Harry stepped up on to the bridge. It bellied under his weight, but there was no stopping him now, and he made his way across quickly, knowing that every step was bringing him closer to Clarissa. Smiling, he ran up the last few rungs of the bridge, and jumped back down on to solid land.

Clarissa glanced up, and Harry raised an arm in triumph. He could see her ecstatic smile even from where he stood, but then he heard something that made his heart sink.

Wilberforce! He'd forgotten Wilberforce. The little dog was whining from somewhere out of sight – no, worse than whining, howling in pain, a leg broken perhaps, or a paw pierced by a thorn.

Harry looked again at Clarissa, who was frowning at him now in consternation. He turned back to the bridge. 'Wilberforce?' he called out.

That dreadful howl came again, so Harry put down the Wardian case and vasculum and hurried back on to the bridge. It was good to have both hands free to grip the ropes, and this time he made rapid progress. But when he reached the other side, he found no sign of the dog. 'Wilberforce?' he called again. Where could he be?

The whine sounded again, further away now, so Harry headed into the trees that lined the cliff. And that was when he saw the men. Three Hei Miao, all dressed in black, rope belts around their waists, rice-straw sandals on their feet. The tallest was holding Wilberforce by the hind leg, dangling him in the air like a rabbit.

'Put him down!' Harry shouted.

The man holding Wilberforce turned to stare at him, his expression charged with a look of pure loathing. Hearing Harry's voice, Wilberforce began to struggle, scratching at his captor's wrist with his claws. The man glanced down at the dog as though he were nothing more than an insect, then swung him through the air, smashing his head smartly against the bough of the nearest tree.

Harry let out a low, guttural moan, seeing the dog's skull dashed open, his muzzle dripping with blood. Then, with a roar, he charged at the man, and they tumbled together on to the forest floor. Harry was vaguely aware of the other men kicking at his head and back, but he fought like a wild beast, determined to punish the man who'd killed his father's dog.

Suddenly, there was an almighty clap – an explosion – that brought Harry back to his senses. Coming to, he found himself lying on the ground, hands still clamped around the man's throat. But the man was already dead, he saw, black blood spilling from a massive crater where the top of his head had been.

Rolling the man's corpse away from him in disgust, Harry scrambled to his feet to see the two Miao men crouching side by side at the foot of the bridge, knives raised. On the other side of the ravine stood the Manchu soldier, readying his rifle to fire again. Next to him stood Clarissa, watching the scene with eyes filled with horror. She took a step towards the bridge, but the Manchu guide held her back. And a good thing too, as it was just at that moment that one of the Miao men cut the suspension ropes, and the bridge swung free, hanging limply into the void.

Harry clutched at his brow. What was he to do now? Marooned with two Miao cutthroats; the woman he loved stranded on the other side of the ravine with his Wardian case . . .

'Harry!' came Clarissa's distressed voice.

'Go!' Harry called back. 'I'll meet you at the boats — take the cuttings with you!' His words echoed across the ravine, fading until there was nothing left but the distant roar of the rapids. Then he turned and sprinted away down the slope, running in what he hoped was the direction of the River Yuan.

Chapter 26

It wasn't until Harry had reached the bottom of the next valley that he knew beyond doubt that the Miao men were following him. He'd run all the way through the woods without stopping, hearing nothing but the pounding of his boots and the thumping of his heart. He must have been going for at least an hour before he allowed himself to pause at a stream, kneeling down on the rocks like an animal and sucking the water into his mouth, gulp after gulp until . . .

A sharp snap came from behind, and Harry wheeled around to see two figures standing at the edge of the wood, watching him. He reached at once for his vasculum, but he'd left it on the other side of the ravine, with his bowie knife stored inside! His tool roll, he thought, trying to steady his breathing — there were weapons in his tool roll. With a shaking hand, he drew the canvas sleeve out of his waistband, and pulled out his pruning knife. Then he let out a furious bellow and charged at the two men, certain that he must be running to his death.

But to his astonishment, his pursuers turned and fled, perhaps believing that it was a revolver Harry held in his hand. Standing at the edge of the wood, chest heaving,

Harry scoured the trees for movement, then slipped the knife back into his tool roll, slid the sleeve into his waistband and began to run.

He'd escaped for now, but the two men were back on his trail, he could tell. Each time he stopped to rest, he could sense them nearby; hear the crackling of twigs, the whispering of voices. They were tracking him, he realised, determined to avenge the death of their companion. It would take Harry approximately two days to reach the Yuan, he had calculated. At some point, he would need to sleep, and that was when they would close in and kill him.

The next valley led down to a larger stream than any he'd encountered so far, a small footbridge erected across its narrowest part. Harry started to cross it, then stopped. A plan had just occurred to him. Glancing over his shoulder, he leapt off the far end of the bridge into the shallows of the stream, gasping at the chill of the water through his boots.

Knowing that the Miao men could not be far behind, Harry splashed his way quickly up the stream. Suddenly, the water became deep, and he plunged down to his waist, feeling his feet sink into the silty floor. Turning, he waded through the deep pool and pulled himself up the bank. It was only after he'd collapsed on to the muddy ground that he realised his tool roll was gone, lost in the water. It was all the more vital now that his plan worked.

Hearing a rustle in the undergrowth, Harry rolled on to his front and carefully raised his head. There, on the other side of the stream, were his two pursuers. They glanced left and right, then stepped up on to the foot of the bridge.

Lying flat in the undergrowth, Harry watched their every move, seeing the two men advance across the bridge, then stop at the far end, foreheads furrowed. Finding no foot-prints in the mud on the other side, they paused, unsure which way to go. They spoke for a moment, then turned to their right, heading in the opposite direction to where their quarry lay.

Harry's heart gave a bound. He'd done it! He'd shaken them off. He waited until the men were out of sight, then clambered back to his feet and hurried away, entering a thick forest of bamboo. Crunching dry leaves underfoot, swiping the pale woody stems out of his face, he made a steady pace, somewhere between a run and a jog. But he was extremely hungry, he found, glancing up at the sky and realising the sun had started to dip. He checked his watch, but it had stopped some time ago. From the position of the sun, he guessed that it must be late afternoon: he had been going for over four hours.

At last, the bamboo forest began to thin out, and Harry reached a clearing. Taking a few moments to rest, his eyes fell upon a pink azalea that under other circumstances he would have collected in an instant. Growing around it were clumps of bracken, thin curly fronds sprouting from their base. Harry sat up. Not bracken at all, but royal-fern fiddle-heads! Swatting a cloud of gnats away from his face, Harry broke off a frond and crammed it into his mouth, rejoicing to find it as sweet and crunchy as he remembered. Picking several more, he devoured them, feeling the strength return to his limbs. He could do this, he told himself. He must.

Then he froze. Someone was watching him. Not someone, something — a black-and-white bear, plump and dozy, sit-ting in a glade not twenty yards away, its chubby, piebald legs stuck out before it like an infant upon a parlour floor.

The creature was gorging itself on foliage too, Harry saw, chewing on it as greedily as he had.

The bear-cat, Harry realised, as he watched it roll on to all fours and bound away into the forest. How he wished Clarissa could have seen it too . . . 'Clarissa,' he said aloud, wondering where she was at this very moment. She must have left the *yamen* by now – hopefully with Li-Liang safely installed in a sedan chair. If they travelled by the most direct route, they would reach the Yuan not long after him. What a reunion that would be!

There were some cultivated fields on the other side of the bamboo forest, fields of tall, white-cupped poppies. *Papaver somniferum*, Harry saw – the sleep-bringing poppy. So the locals were starting to grow opium for themselves. He would have to tell Clarissa – the monopoly of the Shanghai *hongs* would soon be broken.

Fields must mean farmers, Harry thought, and sure enough, he saw footprints on the muddy paths, and picked up his pace. But the terrain was gentler now, up one rolling valley, then down to another streamlet. He looked again at the sky. The light had almost faded, and his legs were aching with fatigue, the soles of his feet burning. It was time to rest.

Looking about for a suitable place to lay himself down, Harry found a fallen ash tree a few yards up the slope. Settling down next to it, he pushed himself back against its soft, rotten wood, and closed his eyes.

Harry was back at Mrs Pincham's, his mind waking him just in advance of her usual sharp knock. But then his eyes opened and found moist earth, moss and fungi, and he remembered where he was.

336

The sky was bright again. He must have slept right the way through to morning. Time to get moving . . . Harry was just starting to sit up, when he froze. For there, amongst the trees at the base of the slope, not more than forty yards away, stood the two Miao men. They were studying the forest floor, lost in concentration; then one of them pointed upwards, and they moved forward again, concealed from his view by the trees.

Harry felt a tide of hopelessness rise. He was done for. He would never escape them. But then his eye fell on the muddy slope on which the men would surely soon appear. Even from here, Harry could see the tracks that he'd made, his bootprints obvious. His hobnailed boots were giving him away, he realised. None of the farmers or labourers in this part of China wore boots like his. Find the bootprints and you would find the Englishman!

One eye still scanning the trees for signs of movement, Harry reached down and started to undo his shoelaces. His fingers were shaking so much it was hard to get them to do his bidding, but then, slowly, the knots came apart. Hearing voices, he glanced up and saw the men no more than twenty yards away. There were more than two of them now, he thought, feeling fear sharpen his mind.

Rising noiselessly to his feet, boots in hand, Harry turned and ran at a crouch into the woodland. The dampness of the forest floor soaked through his stockings, chilling his feet, but he knew that every step he took was a step further away from his pursuers – and closer to Clarissa.

Reaching another field filled with dazzling white poppies, Harry bore left down a little path, then right, twisting his way between the plantations until he reached another wood.

Plunging into the trees, he ran and ran until he thought his lungs might burst. Only when he could go no further did he dare to stop and listen for his pursuers, but to his relief he heard nothing but the breeze whipping through the branches. Time to put his boots back on.

On he went, pausing only to drink from streams and check the position of the sun, reaching occasionally into his pocket to munch on another fernhead. Hours passed, and the roll of the hills and valleys began to level off, and he knew he must be nearing the floodplains of the Yuan. Eventually, he heard swifter water running in the distance, and pushed through a tangle of bushes to reach the river-bank. It was the Yuan – it had to be – but how far along he couldn't be sure.

Sleep, Harry thought. A few more hours' sleep, and then he would work out which way to go next.

Chapter 27

Harry awoke to find a circle of children's faces peering down at him. Shiny-eyed and plump-cheeked, each with a string of tiny cowry shells slung around their neck. The sky above them was tinted with the orange glow of sunrise. He must have slept right the way through another night, he realised, his body utterly exhausted by his flight from the ravine.

Harry pushed himself up into a sitting position, causing the children to scatter like fish, before they closed in again, watching in fascinated silence as he clambered painfully to his swollen feet.

'Yuan?' Harry called out, seeing the children back away from the strange, adenoidal timbre of his voice. He tried again, pointing at the river this time, 'Yuan?'

A brave little girl stepped forward, her ears pierced with silver filigree wire, and whispered, 'Yuan.'

Harry could have kissed her. 'Thank you!' he exclaimed, but as he lurched forward, arms outstretched, the children scattered again, giggling at this strange, limping Westerner with his filthy clothes and matted hair.

Which way now? Harry asked himself. He was sure that the flotilla must be moored not far from where he stood, but had no way of knowing whether it was up- or down-stream. Turning towards the river, he searched for something familiar – anything that might show him which way to go.

Just as he was starting to lose hope, he saw a fine *Salix babylonica* growing on the far bank, its graceful fronds over-hanging the slack water. He *knew* he couldn't have seen that weeping willow before – he wouldn't have forgotten such a magnificent specimen – which must mean that the flotilla was moored downstream.

Boom, boom, boom, he heard, and swivelled his head to look. He recognised that sound – the thump of the fishermen's drums as they scared the catch into their nets. It was com-ing from upstream, on the other side of the meander. Time to go, Harry thought – before the fishermen returned to the village. Miao fishermen who might know the man he'd attacked.

So he turned and ran along the path, scaring up a mangy flock of hens as he approached a crude piggery, a fat sow wallowing in the mud. There was a narrow ditch surrounding it, either to keep the animals in, or . . .

Harry let out a roar of pain. Teeth clenched, he looked down and was appalled to see a three-inch bamboo spike protruding from the top of his left boot, its tip whittled down to a sharp, fire-hardened point. Wanting the thing out of himself at any cost, he put both hands under his knee, closed his eyes and yanked his leg upwards, letting out a howl of agony.

Toppling back upon the grass, Harry saw the pig watching him inquisitively from between her large, cupped ears. There was blood dripping out of the sole of his boot now; letting out little gasps of pain, Harry drew his knee into his groin

340

and took off first his boot, then his sock, shrieking in fresh agony as the filthy woollen fibres were ripped from the open wound. Then, once his dizziness had calmed, he started to twist the blood-soaked stocking around his foot, knotting it so tightly that he thought he might faint.

Looking up, Harry saw the Miao children watching him again, joined now by two women. One of them called out an order, and the children vanished. Had she sent them to fetch their fathers from the boats? His heart start to thud again as he realised that, injured as he was, he could not hope to flee.

Forcing himself on to his feet, Harry found stars bursting behind his eyes. When his vision cleared, he saw one of the women standing next to him. He shrank back, anticipating a blow, but instead she offered him a gentle smile, and held out an arm. Tentatively, he took it, then hazarded a step forward. His stomach keeled as he leant his weight upon the injured foot.

An older woman approached, holding out a stick. Harry accepted it, then bowed his head respectfully to them both. 'Shey-shey,' he said, meaning it with all his heart, before hobbling away.

His foot was horribly painful, and it took him some time to make his way back on to the path by the river. As the water rushed and gurgled beside him, strange images began to skitter before his eyes like a kaleidoscope. Wilberforce's bludgeoned skull; his father lying dead in the cottage courtyard. What had Frith done with the body, he wondered? Thrown it into the River Arun? The river . . . Would he find Clarissa waiting by the river? Or would she give him up for dead. Dead . . . dead as the man he'd throttled . . .

Suddenly jarring his injured foot on a sharp stone, Harry let out a cry of agony. But it was the stone that told him the grassy bank had given way to rocky terrain, and soon he could hear the surge of rapids from up ahead. Wiping the tears of pain from his eyes, he hobbled on until he saw a jagged boulder protruding from the near channel, the very boulder which had snapped the tow-rope of Li-Liang's houseboat what felt like a lifetime ago.

Spirits lifting, Harry drove himself onwards up the path. A few yards on, he saw a flotilla of boats moored to a flat section of bank, with a rudimentary camp laid out on the grass beside it. A fire, some wooden stools, a makeshift sedan chair . . . 'Clarissa?' he called out, hearing his voice rasping and weak.

Looking up, Harry saw a woman in black running towards him. It was probably just a hallucination, he thought, but he hardly cared now, for he could go on no further, and to have seen Clarissa's face again, imagined or otherwise, was surely enough.

But then Harry felt her hands cupping his head, her lips kissing his brow as he fell on to his knees before her. 'I found you,' he whispered.

'I knew you would,' Clarissa said, gazing down at him with tears streaming down her face.

Harry smiled, and allowed his eyes to close, vaguely aware of being lifted into strong arms, then laid down gently on to a soft bed.

'Hush now,' came Clarissa's sweet voice from somewhere in the distance, and for a moment it was as though he'd never left her house in Shanghai at all.

Chapter 28

Harry awoke in his berth on the *chuan*, and the first thing he saw was his Wardian case. He sat up and slid his legs off the bed, gasping at the pain in his foot. It was thickly bandaged, he saw now, remembering how he'd almost fainted when Tan Lin had doused the wound in *jiu*; the care with which Clarissa had dressed it. He would just have to hope that their efforts had staved off infection. He didn't *feel* feverous, he thought, as he limped across the cabin, just horribly weak.

Twenty icicle tree cuttings, Harry counted inside the case. There was mist on the glass, so the leaves must be breathing – an encouraging sign. Putting an eye to the glass, he took in the beautiful, pale-green oval leaflets that hung from each stem, like sequins trimming the most delicate piece of lace.

Looking up, Harry saw the icicle tree berries he'd picked, laid out on the cabin table. Beside them, in a cup of water, were its flowers – a little withered now, but still magnificent. And propped against the wall was a painting of the icicle tree in all its glory. After studying the flowers, foliage and berries, Clarissa had used her imagination to create an image of a fully grown tree that would surely be irresistible to any buyer. And all that while Harry had recuperated in bed.

A moment later, there was a knock at his door, and Clarissa bustled in with a cup of tea. 'It's dreadfully stuffy in here, Mr Compton,' she grumbled. 'Though you look much better,' she added, handing him the cup. 'I wish I could say the same for Li-Liang.' She shook her head. 'He has a fever, Harry. And his arm is badly swollen.'

'Did he manage to see a doctor at the Sub-Prefect's?'

'There was no time! We left the *yamen* in a tearing hurry.' She shook her head. 'He'll have to wait until Hankow – I've asked Tan Lin to cast off as soon as possible.' Clarissa turned and followed Harry's gaze towards her painting of the icicle tree. 'Do you like it?'

'I'm speechless.'

'Speechless indeed! That's not like you,' she said tartly, though he could see from her face that she was pleased. 'It's a fair likeness, then? I had to speculate a little, not having had the chance to see the tree for myself.'

'You did a sensational job.'

'Let's hope so,' Clarissa said briskly. 'For I shall look forward to seeing a return on my investment!'

Eyes settling on the Wardian case, Clarissa pursed her lips. 'You'd better tie that thing down before we hit the rapids. It's going to be a rough ride.'

Harry nodded, frowning as he imagined how awful it would be to lose their precious bounty just when they were so close to success. It would have been that, he knew, which had finally broken Lorcan Darke . . . When he looked back up, he saw Clarissa watching him closely, a tender look on her face. 'What is it?' he asked.

344

'Nothing.' She turned to go, but he laid a hand on her arm and waited until she lifted her eyes to meet his.

'It's just . . .' she began, then hesitated. 'I thought I'd lost you.'

Harry scoured his mind for the right thing to say — something that would tell her how much she meant to him. But, as always, the words came to him too late, and before he knew it Clarissa had pulled away, and was busying herself with his berth, smoothing the rumpled blankets into place. 'You should get some rest, Mr Compton,' she said without looking up. 'I shall come and check on you later.'

Then she was gone, leaving Harry to kick himself for not daring to open his heart to her when he'd had the chance.

It was not until later that afternoon that Clarissa deemed Harry sufficiently fit to leave his cabin. He wore new shoes for the occasion, a pair of soft leather moccasins, kindly donated by Ren Hao, the left one of which Clarissa had cut open at the top in order to accommodate his bandage.

Leaning heavily on his stick, Harry followed Clarissa to the upper deck of the *chuan*, then carefully made his way across on to Li-Liang's boat, which had been fully repaired now by the mercenaries.

If Clarissa had found Harry's cabin stuffy, then Lord only knew what she made of Li-Liang's. A muslin cloth had been fixed across the window, and the sultry air carried with it the sweet reek of decay. But Harry could see the care with which Clarissa had arranged all of Li-Liang's treasures — his little ceramic pots of mud and rock placed neatly in a box next to his collections of Chinese poetry.

'Mr Compton,' Li-Liang said, reaching out a limp hand. 'I cannot tell you how glad I am to see you.'

His colour was very bad, Harry saw, the pallor of his skin broken only by an angry rash dappling his cheeks. 'And I you, Li-Liang.'

'You've been in the wars as well, I understand?' Li-Liang said, eyes bright with fever. 'I should never have let you go to the pagoda alone. It was my *duty* to . . .'

'Shh,' Clarissa chided, taking his hand in hers.

'I could have accompanied you in a sedan chair, just as I did on the journey here,' Li-Liang went on, clicking his tongue. 'Confrontations happen so easily where there is a deficiency of language. Had I been there, I am convinced the situation could have been avoided entirely.'

'Without doubt, Li-Liang,' Clarissa said, soothing him. 'But you were unwell, and you still are. You must focus all your energy on getting better.'

Li-Liang laid his head back on the pillow. 'I wonder, Mr Compton,' he asked. 'Did you see any minerals of interest on your wanderings? A seam of anthracite, perhaps? Or some antimony?'

'Just opium fields, I'm afraid.'

Li-Liang gave a faint smile. 'You see how the Chinese start to take control of their destiny . . .' His words faded as he drifted back to sleep. Clarissa covered him with a blanket, then they both left the room, pulling the door shut behind them.

They didn't have long to wait before they reached the first set of rapids, and then Harry could see why Clarissa had warned of a 'rough ride'. The two houseboats, tightly

346

bound again behind the junk, surged together in the powerful downstream current, then hit the rapids and flew through the air before crashing down into the water on the other side.

Miraculously, the mercenaries remained on their feet throughout, each armed with a gaff, which they used to protect the flotilla from the rocks, banks and other vessels. They had evidently performed this function many times before, some of them even managing to smoke their pipes as they worked.

After a few brief forays above deck, Harry kept to his cabin. He'd tied down his crates of seeds and bulbs as best he could, but had decided to keep the Wardian case close to him at all times, cradled in his arms like a child. So far, the jolts and juddering did not seem to have caused any serious damage, though he could see that some of the cuttings had begun to work their way loose from the soil.

'More rapids coming,' he heard Clarissa shout down from the upper deck. As the only able-bodied passenger amongst them, she'd elected to stay topside, and seemed to be thoroughly enjoying the ride.

Harry held on tight, feeling the *chuans* surge into the air, then plummet down, hitting the water with a resounding smack. He wondered how Li-Liang was faring next door, and imagined how painful he must be finding every sharp movement.

'And again!' came Clarissa's voice, and Harry adjusted his grip on the Wardian case, steeling himself for the next bump or crash.

Presently, Harry heard the ominous crunch of splintering wood, and Clarissa climbed down below deck. 'They've lost two of the boathooks,' she called breathlessly into his cabin. 'But we're almost there . . .'

She looked magnificent, Harry thought, green eyes flashing, soft hair pulled loose by the wind. An energy seemed to be coursing through her, perhaps fed by the relief she felt at disaster averted, or the excitement of their imminent return home. 'Brace yourself,' she cried as she clambered back up to the upper deck. 'I think there's a big one coming . . .'

At length, the rapids abated, and Harry was able to sleep for a time. When he awoke, daylight was fading. Hobbling tentatively out of his cabin, he knocked on Clarissa's door, which opened to the touch. 'Clarissa?' he called inside, but there was no one there. Turning to leave, Harry's eye was caught by a pile of canvases bound together with string. On the very top was a watercolour he'd not yet seen – Clarissa's depiction of the Mian Jian Guang pagoda. The scene had been rendered in a style that differed from Clarissa's usual work. She must be experimenting, Harry realised with a grin, and it was an enterprise which had paid off. It was as though she'd found a way to infuse the careful precision of her botanical art with a wild and imaginative energy. The landscape seemed alive: the rock formations coiled and savage, like beasts poised to pounce; the ravine serpentine as it twisted into the distance, radiant and sinuous. Harry didn't know much about fine art, but he had a feeling this work could grace any gallery in London.

Suddenly concerned Clarissa might come upon him and feel he was snooping, Harry left her cabin and limped up on to deck. What he found there raised his spirits still further. For ahead of them, no more than a mile away, lay the glistening expanse of Lake Dongting.

'Can you believe it?' Clarissa said, pushing a hank of copper hair behind one ear, freckled face glowing. 'We'll be back in Jiejiang before sundown!'

Harry grinned at her. 'I think I prefer travelling downstream, Mrs Lockhart.'

'As do I, Mr Compton,' Clarissa replied. 'As do I.'

They found the *Golden Pheasant* waiting for them in Jiejiang, Bo Lungsin standing on the upper deck, watching the flotilla approach with crossed arms, pipe clenched between his teeth. Harry hadn't been looking forward to seeing the steam-launch captain again, but the man acted as though he were meeting Harry for the first time, so Harry followed his lead. That aside, it was a relief to be towed once more by an engine, and across a smooth flat lake at that. At this rate, they'd be disembarking in Hankow ahead of schedule!

They ate below deck, then – while Clarissa went to check on Li-Liang – Harry returned to his cabin to examine his specimens. Two of his honeypots had cracked on the descent down the Yuan, meaning that the seeds had to be decanted into new jars. It was messy work, but Clarissa had left a fresh ewer of water in his cabin, and as soon as he'd completed his task, he set about cleaning the stickiness off his hands, using the soapberry paste that was provided as carbolic – a brown mush obtained from the fruit of *Sapindus mukorossi*, a species of local tree that Harry wished he'd had time to collect. Then he heard a gentle knock on his cabin door, and looked up. 'Yes?'

'It's me,' came Clarissa's voice.

Harry shot to his feet, winced in pain, then hobbled over to the door and threw it open. 'How's Li-Liang?' he asked, knowing just from the look on her face that the answer would not please him.

'Not good. I tried to make him comfortable, but he's very hot.' She cast him a guilty look. 'I filled a pipe for him, Harry. I didn't know how else to salve his pain.'

Harry put a hand on her shoulder. 'You did the right thing. No one could have done more.'

'A doctor could!' Clarissa retorted. A tear slid down her cheek, and she looked up at him in a way that made his heart cramp. 'I think he may die, Harry.'

Harry pulled her into his arms. 'Don't cry,' he whispered, as he felt her body shudder in his embrace. 'The doctors in Hankow will see him right, I promise.'

'You promise?' she echoed, like a child.

Harry nodded, and then suddenly, before he realised what was happening, she was kissing him. He stepped back, his head swimming with the delicate perfume of her skin, knowing that what they were doing must be wrong. 'Clarissa . . .' he began, but she just kissed him again, and soon he was kissing her back, cupping her head in his hands, running the auburn curls between his fingers, her hair even softer than he'd imagined.

As Clarissa began to undo the buttons of her dress, Harry pulled away again, his heart thumping like a piston. 'We shouldn't,' he whispered, though there was no one there to hear them. 'Should we?'

'When you were lost,' Clarissa breathed into his ear. 'I knew then how I felt about you.'

350

Then, keeping her eyes fixed on his, she let her dress slip from her shoulders, and led him by the hand to the bed. Seeing her lying there amongst the pillows, clothed only in a white chemise, her pale throat luminous in the candlelight, Harry was overwhelmed for a moment, but then he pulled off his shirt, and soon he was lying next to her, chest heaving.

She took his hand and guided it to the hooks of her chemise, and then he was kissing the soft skin of her breasts as she tipped her head back, breathing deeply. Slowly, he moved his lips down to her stomach, seeing the dusting of freckles even there, and feeling himself almost undone. But now her hands were moving beneath his undershirt, nails digging into his flesh, then creeping down further and gripping him, until he knew he could hold on no longer.

'Wait,' he said, pulling away from her. 'We shouldn't go on. Not unless you're sure.' He pushed himself up on to one elbow and looked at her, seeing her green eyes gleaming in the flickering light. 'I am utterly, hopelessly in love with you,' Harry said, 'but you . . . you have so much to lose.'

'I've never felt more certain about anything, Mr Compton,' Clarissa replied. Then she kissed him again, and soon she was his, as he was hers, and he had never known anything like it in all his life.

Four blissful days and nights passed before the flotilla began its approach to Hankow. Harry was a little sorry to see this part of their journey come to a close, but Clarissa could barely contain her excitement.

'We're nearing the end of our adventure, Harry,' she said, taking his hand in hers. 'Come, let us bring the news to

Li-Liang! Perhaps he'll be well enough to join us on deck as we reach the harbour.'

But as soon as they entered their guide's cabin, Harry knew that this was unlikely. For the man was clearly very ill.

'What will you do next, Li-Liang?' Harry asked, trying to ignore the sickly yellow hue of the older man's skin, which had seeped even into the whites of his eyes.

'Why, I shall gather my samples together, and write up my report for the Mining Authority,' Li-Liang replied valiantly.

'I've told him to take a month's bed-rest,' Clarissa said. 'But the man's as stubborn as a mule!'

'Oh, don't you worry about me, Mrs Lockhart,' Li-Liang replied, gazing up at her with burning eyes. 'Like you, I have much to do. The sooner China has modern mining systems, the sooner she shall break free of her chains!'

'And the sooner *you* see a doctor,' Clarissa rejoined, 'the sooner you can help her.'

Before long, the *Golden Pheasant* had docked in Hankow, and Harry was pleased to see the Messageries mailboat that was to take them on the final leg of their journey already in harbour, with a French gunboat waiting behind her, ready to provide escort.

Carefully, Harry helped Li-Liang to disembark, then set about arranging for their baggage to be moved on to their new transportation, though he kept his Wardian case with him still, hidden under its blanket.

'You look the very picture of an eccentric Englishman, Mr Compton,' Li-Liang said, as they reconvened on the quayside. 'Carrying his pet bird in a cage!'

Harry smiled, though the remark had made him think of Wilberforce, and how much he was missing the little dog.

But then they were taking their leave of Tan Lin and the crew, and Clarissa was slipping Li-Liang a loop of cash coins for him to distribute amongst them as 'squeeze'. No sign of Bo Lungsin, Harry noted, which was all to the good.

'You *will* see a doctor this afternoon?' Clarissa said to Li-Liang for perhaps the hundredth time.

'Yes, yes,' he replied, smiling back at her.

Harry shook Li-Liang's good hand, and they exchanged a few fond words. But the guide's greatest affection, as Harry had always known, was for Clarissa, and when it was time to bid her farewell, Harry saw that his eyes were wet with tears.

'Goodbye, Li-Liang,' Clarissa said. 'You'll come and visit me soon in Shanghai?'

'I should be honoured,' Li-Liang replied, taking hold of both her hands, careless of the pain it caused him.

'Thank you for showing me China,' Clarissa whispered. 'For opening my eyes.'

Li-Liang bowed grandly, and they watched as he made his slow, painful way down the quayside, the usual scrum of Hankow harbour bustling around him — cargo ships arriving and leaving, white egrets wading in the filthy water, rats scuttling across jetties. Suddenly, Harry felt an overwhelming desire to be free of these river ports, to be somewhere far away, up near the coast, smelling the fresh, ozone breath of the sea.

'I wish we didn't have to leave him,' Clarissa said, anxious eyes still trained on their guide as he turned and threw his young friends a warm smile. Then, lifting his good arm, he waved them on towards the mailboat.

'He'd never forgive us if we missed our transit,' Harry ventured.

'That's true, I suppose,' Clarissa said.

So, letting out a sigh, Clarissa took Harry's arm, and let him lead her up the gangway, and into the waiting boat.

PART FIVE
September 1868 – Shanghai

Chapter 29

The weather, when they re-entered the Whangpu River, was horrendous. Typhoon season was underway, and pulses of freezing rain kept spurting from the dark sky, driven into the passengers' faces by a vicious northerly wind.

There was barely any life in Shanghai Harbour, Harry saw, just a few freighters at anchor, their decks deserted. As they drew closer to the Bund, he made out the tall masts of a clipper creaking in the wind, and squinted through the rain to read the word '*Redemption*' stencilled on her hull. So Scragge, Buchanan and the boys were back in town, he realised with a grin, though there was no sign of anyone aboard.

At length, the mailboat moored, and Clarissa took Harry's arm as they hastened down the gangway towards the shelter of the customs waiting room. A few plucky touts were lurking outside, and Clarissa tipped a boy a few coins to run down to the Lockhart's godown and notify Lam Dookay of their arrival.

They repaired to one of the wooden benches inside, where they sat, wet and shivering, as their luggage was unloaded. Harry still had his Wardian case with him, but there was value enough in the other specimens, so he carefully checked off each item until he was sure that everything was accounted for.

A cart selling green tea appeared, the hawker shaking the rain from his pigtail as he stirred his vat with a wooden ladle. Harry paid for two cups, and as he headed back to Clarissa, he glanced unthinkingly at his heel, feeling that familiar jolt of sadness as he remembered that Wilberforce was no longer there.

'Bit of a damp squib of a return,' Clarissa said, as Harry sat down next to her.

He took her hand in his and pressed it to his lips. 'In some ways.'

She looked at him then, and it was as though she were lit somehow from within. But then the door flew open, and in came Lam Dookay, and immediately Clarissa let go of Harry's hand and jumped to her feet.

'Mrs Lockhart!' the comprador exclaimed, gliding towards them across the damp floor. 'Welcome home!'

The man had gained a few pounds while they'd been gone, Harry thought, seeing his neck straining at the collar of his embroidered gown.

'And Mr Compton too – why, I'd hardly recognise you!'

Harry glanced down at his dirty breeches, ripped and frayed by thorns and sharp rocks; at his stained moccasins, one slipper hacked open to reveal the dirty bandage on his left foot. And his hands . . . Were they thinner now than when he'd left? Certainly they looked different – burnt the colour of amber honey, and lightly freckled, as his face must be, he supposed, though it had been many weeks since he'd looked in a mirror.

'Shall we?' Lam Dookay said, turning for the door. 'Zhang is waiting for us.' He barked out an order to a porter, who leapt from his hunkers and started gathering up their luggage.

'I trust your tour was a success?' Lam Dookay asked, watching with interest as Harry refused to surrender his Wardian case to the porter.

'A tremendous success, Lam Dookay,' Clarissa replied. 'But now let us hurry home so that we may get the warmth back into our feet! Then we can talk.'

Outside, the rain was still sheeting down. Squelching through the mud, Harry, Clarissa and Lam Dookay hurried towards the carriage. Zhang was standing next to it, busy negotiating with the miserable-looking wheelbarrow-runner who would transport their luggage separately to the house. Seeing them approach, the driver grabbed an oilcloth umbrella and splashed towards them. 'Welcome, Missy,' he said with an infectious smile as he held out the umbrella.

'Alas, I think it is too late for that!' Clarissa laughed, looking down at her black dress, so wet that the bodice was clinging to her stays.

Inside the brougham, the leather seats were beaded with moisture. 'Well,' Clarissa said, wiping the rain from her eyes as the thunder rumbled above the city. 'Home at last!'

Celestial Heights was unchanged, impeccably maintained by Aki in Clarissa's absence. As Harry was shown up to his old bedroom, Lam Dookay hovered in the hallway to speak to Clarissa. Snippets of their conversation drifted up to him from downstairs – 'Any word from Calcutta?'; 'Have the orders been steady?' – but then the front door closed, and Harry knew that Lam Dookay was gone.

Aware that Clarissa would be busy overseeing the unloading of their luggage, Harry left her to it, content to check on his cuttings. There were new leafbuds growing on several of them, he noted with excitement, and, keen to share the news with Clarissa, ran down the stairs to tell her. She was at her desk in the parlour, working methodically through her correspondence. 'Anything interesting?' Harry asked.

'I've barely begun,' Clarissa replied without looking up, busy with her ivory letter-opener. 'I've asked Aki to prepare a cold collation for seven o'clock. I hope that suits.'

Harry was being dismissed, he realised. 'Is everything all right, Clarissa?' he asked. 'You seem a little . . .' She glanced up, and he smiled. 'Distracted.'

'Sorry. It's just . . .' She blew a strand of hair out of her eyes. 'Coming home, one discovers that all the problems one left behind are still here. Some have even multiplied!' She peered down at her papers in despair. 'The most recent run of the *Kwai-Lun* yielded the lowest returns yet. The business is teetering on the brink!'

'All problems that we shall solve together,' Harry said calmly, stepping towards her. 'Trust me.' He bent down and kissed the side of her neck. She leaned back against him for a moment, then pulled away.

'The servants, Harry . . .' She glanced up – a little sheepishly, he felt. 'We must be careful. Shanghai is a very small place.' Then she gave him a quick smile, and returned to her work.

She was drifting away from him, Harry thought, as he headed back upstairs. It was as though those nights they'd spent together on the boat had never happened. He remembered a favourite phrase of Mr Lazenby, the yew-nursery owner who'd given

Harry his first job — *If the roots go deep enough, the frost can't touch them.* Well, the roots of this relationship obviously needed a bit more time to grow.

Conversation over dinner was even more stilted. They sat at opposite ends of the long mahogany table, Harry finding reminders of Narcissus Lockhart everywhere he looked — the man's Teutonic good looks captured in an oil painting above the mantelpiece; the initials N.A.C.L. engraved on his silver napkin ring. Lockhart was omnipresent in this house. Perhaps that was the problem.

'Did you tell Lam Dookay of your plans for Lockhart's?' Harry asked, forking up a slice of roast quail. 'Of the money you hope to raise?'

'It's too soon for that,' Clarissa replied, pushing away her untouched plate with a frown. 'Forgive me, Harry,' she said, two fingers massaging her temple. 'I'm not myself tonight. I think I need some rest. I'm sure you do too.'

Harry nodded. He was exhausted, he suddenly realised, wondering if it was due to a change in atmospheric pressure brought on by the typhoon.

Clarissa reached over and rang the handbell. 'How is your foot?' she asked.

He shrugged. 'It aches if I walk too far. But it's getting better.'

'Sleep,' Clarissa said, as she rose from the table. 'That's what we both need.'

And how they slept — for a week, practically, in their separate bedrooms — turning in early, not rising until ten or eleven o'clock each morning. Little by little, Harry felt his strength returning, nourished by the delicious meals so solicitously prepared by Aki and his staff.

It was the following Tuesday before Harry decided to venture into town, eager to know if a letter from Jack Turner might be waiting for him at the poste restante. Clarissa had offered him the use of the carriage, but Harry declined, heading out instead on foot, armed only with a stout walking stick and an umbrella.

It was a curious sensation, passing along Thibet Road alone. Harry remembered the journey he'd made six months ago – stumbling down these same streets, half mad with malaria, before he'd met Clarissa. Before he'd found the icicle tree . . .

The outer roads of Shanghai were quiet, the shutters of the Bubbling Well Guesthouse closed, no sign of Mr Dancer prowling on his upper balcony. Even the stables of the race-course had the louvres down on the doors, the horses no doubt cloistered inside, munching on their oats as the incessant rain hammered on the roof.

But it would take more than a typhoon to subdue the bustle of the Nanking Road. The woks sizzled more loudly than ever in the rain, and the wheelbarrow-runners splashed mud over Harry's trouser cuffs as they rattled past.

Turning on to the Bund, Harry followed the esplanade towards the British Post Office, and as he neared the front gate, he heard a voice call out his name. A voice he recognised . . .

Impossible, Harry thought. But then it came again, clear as day – 'Harry? Don't you know your old pal?'

Harry whipped around, and there, standing before him in the rain, was Jack Turner. 'I don't believe it!' Harry exclaimed, throwing open his arms. The two men embraced, and Harry stepped back, still struggling to comprehend what he saw. But it *was* Jack — carrot-coloured curls just visible under a sopping wet bowler hat, round open face beaming, snub nose peeling.

'Why, I'd barely know you, Harry,' Jack said. 'With that walking stick and beard . . . you look ten years older!'

'It's been an interesting couple of months,' Harry replied, trying not to let his wounded vanity show. 'But what in God's name are *you* doing here?'

Leaning in, Jack lowered his voice conspiratorially, 'Well, it's been an interesting couple of months for me too.'

Their eyes met, and for the first time in his life, Harry saw something shifty in Jack's. 'When did you get here?' he asked.

Jack puffed out his pink cheeks. 'Came in last week on the P&O packet from Singapore.'

'And you've been here ever since?' Harry asked. 'Waiting for me?'

Jack nodded. 'I've been sitting in that coffee house from dusk 'til dawn, hoping to catch sight of you.' He glanced behind him, as though worried that someone might be watching. 'I thought you'd be looking for me too, Harry.'

Frowning, Harry took his friend's arm and led him off the main thoroughfare into a quiet corner. 'Whatever do you mean, "looking for you"?'

Jack stared at him. 'But I wrote it all down in the letter I sent you. Didn't you get it?'

'I'm just back from Guizhou, Jack! Why do you think I've come here?' He jabbed a finger in the direction of the British Post Office.

'Right,' Jack said, shifting on his feet as he scratched his ear. 'Tell you what, Harry, why don't you read the letter first, then we'll have a natter?'

'Just tell me now, Jack!' Harry said, starting to lose patience with his old friend.

Jack pulled a dubious face. 'You know me, Harry. I can't talk well – not like you. You mightn't understand if I tried to explain it all standing here, face to face. But in the letter, it's all set out. Clear, like.' Wiping a hand on his trousers, Jack fumbled about in his fob pocket. He was wearing a tailcoat, Harry suddenly realised – not an especially smart one, but a tailcoat nonetheless. A printed card was soon produced, which he passed to Harry.

'The Garden of Perfumed Flowers,' Harry read aloud, then looked up in perplexed irritation. 'A sing-song house, Jack?'

'Meet me there on Friday night, Harry. Whatever you make of the letter.' He gnawed on his lower lip. 'Whatever you think of me. Promise?'

'Very well, but I still don't . . .'

Jack held up a hand to cut him off. 'I know a bit more now than I did when I wrote that letter, that's all I'll say. So I'll meet you there on Friday, when you've had some time to think. Nine p.m.?'

'As you wish.'

Jack squeezed Harry on the shoulder, then disappeared into an alleyway, head lowered against the rain.

Turning, Harry ran across the road and walked into the British Post Office. It made no sense. Had Piggott chosen Jack Turner as his plant hunter? Surely not – the man didn't trust Jack as far as he could throw him. And besides, Jack was meant to be on Harry's side, helping him to sell the icicle tree. Wasn't he?

And there, at the poste restante counter, just as Jack had promised, Harry found a letter addressed to him in his friend's untidy scrawl. There was a row of chairs at the back of the room, so rather than read the letter in the rain, Harry took a seat, and tore open the envelope.

Port Saïd, Egypt
4 August 1868

Dear Harry,

Well, old stick? Where to begin? At the beginning, I hear you say. So I shall.

As soon as I received your letter telling me to look for buyers, I acted on it. That very evening, I went to the Man in the Moon, and there was old Wim-sett, so I stood him a drink, and asked him straight up how much he'd be willing to pay if I could get him exclusive rights to a spectacular new tree &c. He was pretty offhand, to be fair — and I wasn't sure if he believed me — but the next day, a note was left at my lodgings summoning me to see Josiah Piggott, and at his house, no less!

I thought I was for the chop that night, Harry, make no mistake. And I was right to be worried, because Piggott had had word of my conversation with Wimsett, and what's more, he knew that I was good pals with you. But then things took a surprising turn — rather a promising turn, as I hope you'll see.

You and he, said Piggott, having set me down in a big chair by the fire and handed me a glass of his finest sherry, you and he had had a falling-out. Wrong had been done on both sides, but Piggott was all for forgiving and forgetting — so long as you sold him your tree, that is. And he was willing to pay handsomely for it, enough to make a rich man of you! But, knowing that you might be unwilling to do business with him, he wanted me, Jack Turner, to put the idea to you in person, me being someone that you trust.

In Shanghai, says I? almost toppling off my chair.

In Shanghai, says Old Pie-Gut.

Naturally, I respond that I will do no such thing — that your interest in the matter lies with other nurserymen, and that these other nurserymen would be willing to put up a very high price &c.

But then Piggott rounds on me. Old Wimsett won't lift a finger without my say-so, he hollers. Didn't he come to me and tell me all your secret plans? And you'll find the same with Weeks and Veitch, and with every other nurseryman on the King's Road. He'd spoken to them all, it seemed, and warned them that you, Harry Compton, were his man. You see, that was what Piggott was up to that night I saw him at the Man in the Moon. He wasn't making plans for any planthunting expedition. He was making sure you couldn't sell the tree to any of his rivals!

So I realise then that if you want your payday, Harry, it must be on Piggott's terms. And it's my payday too, because he's already paid me a good deal to make this trip, and he'll pay a good deal more if I come back with this tree of yours.

The big advantage for you, it seems to me, is 1. you will be very rich, and 2. you won't have to take the risk of keeping the tree safe as you travel back to London (that falls to me, and I'm bringing along plenty of equipment to make sure I do the job right!).

So that's the situation we find ourselves in, Harry. I'm not sure if you'll be displeased with me, and the decision is, of course, yours alone. But all being well, I should be with you in Shanghai by late September. Unless I melt in the sun first, which is probably the likelier, as it's near burnt me to a cinder already!

Perhaps you'll tell me to sling my hook, Harry, and if so, I'll understand. But I'm pleased to be out of London anyways, and seeking my fortune (like we always talked of at the Man in the Moon), so I'll try to make a go of things regardless. Whatever happens, I never want to return to Port Saïd, as it is truly a flea-ridden sinkhole that makes Battersea look like the Earthly Paradise.

Your old friend,

Jack Turner Esq.

366

That stupid, stupid dim-witted fool! Harry said to himself as he crumpled the letter in his hand. Why had he involved Jack Turner in the first place? The man hadn't the wit he was born with! The moment Harry had been given the map, he'd known not to tell Jack about it. So why write to him about the tree after he'd got to China? In his deepest heart, Harry knew why — he'd been proud of himself; he'd been lonely, and he'd been greedy too, wanting his 'payday', as Jack had put it, as soon as possible. Well, he'd got what he deserved.

Stuffing the letter into his coat pocket, Harry picked up his umbrella and walking stick, and marched out of the post office. The Bund was crowded, full of Shanghailanders eager to get out of the pouring rain. Harry scanned every face, half expecting to catch sight of Frith, or Piggott, or Banks — anyone from his old life who might have found their way to Shanghai, grubbing for their cut of the icicle tree. But he recognised no one but the usual touts and hawkers.

Turning off the Bund, Harry hurried through the English Concession. He understood now why Jack had skulked away so fast, and had left him to read all about it in his letter — he'd known that Harry would be angry. Was it also possible that Jack knew Piggott had been responsible for killing his father? Harry couldn't believe that of him. No, Piggott had approached Jack with care, telling him there was blame on both sides. The man would have kept it deliberately vague, spun Jack a yarn that made it seem like he was doing his old friend Harry a favour — an old friend who'd had a captain of the Portsmouth Police looking for him only a few months previously . . .

By the time Harry got back to Celestial Heights, his boots were soaked through and his foot was aching terribly. Clarissa was still sequestered in her office, so he proceeded up to his room, where he changed into dry clothes, then cast an eye over his cuttings. One had failed, he saw, but the remaining nineteen still looked vigorous. How he longed to dig down and check their fragile root systems, but he knew that would risk disturbing their growth. So instead he took out Jack's grubby little card, and looked at it again. 'The Garden of Perfumed Flowers,' he read. Just Jack's sort of joint . . . Tucking the card into his pocket, Harry lay down on his bed and closed his eyes. Time for some more sleep.

'Mr Compton?'

Harry flicked open his eyes, shaking himself from a dream in which he'd found himself naked in the nursery stock-ground, before an audience of laughing, pointing under-gardeners. 'Yes?' he called back.

'Mrs Lockhart would like to see you,' Aki called through the door. 'She's in her parlour.'

So now Clarissa was sending her houseboy to summon him, Harry thought dourly, as he pulled on his clothes. He must have been asleep for several hours he realised, as he hobbled down the stairs, catching sight of the dusk-dimmed sky through the landing window. On the ground floor, he found the door to the little parlour open, and Clarissa sitting at her desk, finishing another of her infernal letters.

'You rang, m'lady?' Harry said, flopping down in the chair opposite her desk.

Clarissa took the time to complete her sentence before looking up.

'I can come back later, if you like,' Harry said pointedly. 'When you're less busy.'

'No, no,' she said, putting down her pen. 'Now's as good a time as any, I suppose.'

Charming! Harry thought. Was it not she who'd summoned him?

'Did you hear the doorbell earlier?' Clarissa asked.

'I was asleep.'

'At this hour?' Seeing Harry's face darken, she swiftly moved on. 'We've had an invitation,' she said, picking up a stiff card and holding it out to him.

Harry looked up in surprise. 'The Taotai?' he said, recognising the red edging around the card, though he could decipher none of the Chinese characters.

'He's invited us to a party on Friday.'

'This Friday?'

'Why,' Clarissa said, 'are you busy?'

'I am, as it happens,' Harry replied. 'I have a meeting with a plant collector.'

Clarissa fiddled with a lock of her hair in a way that Harry found almost infuriating.

'I'm not just sitting on my hands, you know,' Harry went on. 'I've been following up on enquiries. Trying to find us a buyer!'

'I'm sure you have, Harry.'

He frowned at her. 'I thought that was what you wanted, Clarissa. But now I'm not sure what you want at all!'

She said nothing, eyes lowered under her dark lashes, examining the elegant hands which lay folded in her lap.

'What *do* you want?' Harry blurted out, suppressing the urge to shake her. 'One moment you say you have

369

feelings for me – allow me to hope we might share a future together – and then . . .' He flung out a hand in disgust. 'Nothing! Since we've returned to Shanghai, we've barely spoken. It's as though our time together was just a figment of my imagination!' He fell to his knees before her chair. 'Are you ashamed of me, is that it? Has coming back here – to your old life – reminded you of the disparity in our positions?' He grasped her hand, looking up into her eyes. 'If so, you need only say the word, and I'll go.' Then he dropped his gaze and added tersely, 'Our financial arrangement would remain intact, of course, if that's what you were worried about.'

'Are you quite finished?' Clarissa asked, arching one eyebrow.

'Yes.'

'Then get up off your knees, please, Harry, for I have something to say to you.'

Harry did as he was told, and Clarissa sat back in her chair and took a steadying breath. 'I've come to a decision,' she said. 'I'm not going to go through with it.'

Harry looked at her in confusion. 'Go through with what?'

'Everything that we planned. It was all done to save Lockhart's. But I've realised now that I'm not interested in saving the company. Not after all that we saw.'

'The opium den . . .' Harry said, suddenly understanding.

Clarissa nodded. 'I've seen first-hand the damage that opium causes, and I want no part in it.'

'So what will you do?' Harry asked. 'You can't just let the company fail.'

'Lam Dookay has expressed an interest in purchasing it.'

Harry thought for a moment. 'So Lockhart's would come under Chinese ownership . . . Li-Liang would be proud of you!'

'Though I'm not sure I'll get much for the business, given the state of our finances.' Catching something in Harry's expression, Clarissa tilted her head. 'What is it?'

'I have a confession of my own to make,' Harry said.

Now it was Clarissa's turn to look anxious.

'The icicle tree is worth a good deal more than I let on.'

'How much more?' Clarissa asked.

'Perhaps . . . twice as much?'

Her eyes widened. 'So you lied to me!'

'I barely knew you then,' Harry protested. 'The man I met today,' he went on, hoping to distract Clarissa from his earlier dishonesty, 'Jack Turner. He's come all the way from London on behalf of a potential buyer.' Harry paused. 'He's promised to make me a very rich man. Which would make *you* a very rich woman – someone who wouldn't have to worry if Lockhart's went for a song.'

Clarissa's anger seemed to mollify a little. 'So would you sell the tree to him,' she asked, 'this Jack Turner?'

Harry hesitated. A moment ago Harry would have scoffed at the idea, but now, suddenly, he was not so sure. 'I'll hear him out,' was all he said. 'As you should Lam Dookay,' he added. 'At least get a price from him.'

Clarissa nodded, but then another thought seemed to strike her, and she bit her lip. 'I've been thinking a lot about Narcissus's mistress. And his children,' she added slowly. 'I should like to do right by them. So if I did sell Lockhart's, I should want to settle the proceeds on them.'

'All of it?' Harry asked.

'Why not?' Clarissa lifted her chin defiantly. 'After all, your icicle tree is going to make us a fortune, isn't it? So I shall have riches to spare!'

Harry chuckled. 'Let's hope so.' Then he stood up and kissed her on the cheek. 'You're wonderful, Mrs Lockhart, and I hope you know it.'

'And you make me very happy,' she said, face glowing. 'Now,' she added, turning back to her bureau and picking up the invitation. 'What shall I say to the Taotai? We're expected at seven p.m.'

'Then I shall attend both engagements,' Harry said, leaning down to kiss her behind the ear. 'Accompany the most beautiful woman in Shanghai to a party, then go on to meet Jack Turner afterwards.'

There was a moment of silence.

'I don't suppose,' Harry said, grazing one fingertip down the side of Clarissa's neck, 'that you'd care to see the cuttings, Mrs Lockhart?' He leant in and kissed her on the collarbone. 'They're doing extremely well, you know.'

'I should like that very much, Mr Compton,' Clarissa replied, turning her head to kiss him on the lips.

So, taking her by the hand, Harry led Clarissa upstairs.

Chapter 30

For the next few days, Harry dedicated himself to his specimens. He raided the scullery and requisitioned a wooden tray, into which he bored a number of tiny holes with the surprisingly efficient hand-drill that Aki kept in his workroom. Then — braving the sheeting rain, which seemed never to stop — Harry dashed outside to the garden, where he collected enough soil to fill the tray.

Tasting a pinch of the soil, Harry grimaced. It was bland and alkaline, not at all like the acidic soil he'd sampled near the pagoda. So he borrowed a jar of rice vinegar from Aki's stores and diluted it with a gallon of water. This admixture he dribbled on to the soil, crumbling the loam apart as he did so, tasting it again and again on the tip of his tongue until it seemed a fair approximation of the icicle tree's native soil.

Only then did Harry address himself to the seeds. The berries had dried hard and black on their journey, but there was no sign of decay, thank God. He soaked them in water, then broke down the berries with a pestle and mortar, straining the mulch through a sieve until he was left with a score of viable-looking seeds. These he sowed in his newly acidified soil, before placing the seedtray on his windowsill.

Then he turned his attention to the bulbs. Several had grown soft, so he discarded them, smearing the surviving bulbs in clay-rich soil, just as he'd learnt in his time at Piggott's.

These tasks complete, Harry ran downstairs and knocked on the parlour door, eager to go through Clarissa's botanical studies with her.

'I wondered if I was ever to see you again!' Clarissa teased. 'You've been up there for hours with your plants and seeds.'

'Sorry,' Harry said distractedly, eyes scanning the piles of canvases and sketches leaning against the wall. 'May I?'

Clarissa nodded, and Harry dropped to his knees and started sifting through her work.

'I've just been looking through them myself, as it happens,' she said. 'For tomorrow.'

Harry looked at her blankly.

'The Taotai wants the best five paintings,' she reminded him.

Harry shook his head. It all seemed such a long time ago now. 'May I take these ones?' he said, reaching for a pile of sketches he'd set aside.

'Of course.'

He paused at the door, admiring Clarissa's illustration of the golden clematis at the top of the pile. 'These open up such possibilities for us, Clarissa,' he said. 'If ever we want to sell some of the collection at auction, they could go into a catalogue. Christie's, Bonhams . . .'

'Sotheby's,' Clarissa said with a smile.

Back in his bedroom, Harry tucked Clarissa's botanical illustrations into the relevant pages of his notebook, skimming through all the information he'd collated on the journey – the provenance of each specimen; the nature of the soil and climate; other flora growing nearby. Then he sat back and read through the inventory: *Bulbs preserved in clay – 27 x tiger lily, 5 x allium, 4 x Freesia refracta. Seeds preserved in honey – 7 x clematis, 1 x dragon tree, 5 x Cape protea, 3 x dogwood, 2 campanula, 1 x weigela, 5 x species rhododendron, 8 x meconopsis. Succulents: 4 x euphorbia pekinensis. Pinecones: 6 x umbrella pine, 3 x China-fir. Seeds planted in soil – 20 x icicle tree. Cuttings planted in Wardian case – 19 x icicle tree, 3 x viburnum, 2 x jasmine, 4 x anemone, 3 x abelia, 5 x forsythia . . .*

The list went on. Even without the icicle tree, they'd managed to amass a very valuable collection, one of which any plant hunter could be proud. But it was the icicle tree that would make his name, he knew. And his fortune . . . Harry lay back on the bed, folding his arms across his chest. For the first time in his life, it felt as though he might have the whip hand of what happened to him next, rather than just twisting in the wind, buffeted by stronger forces and by richer, more powerful men.

The following evening, Harry prepared himself with more care than he had in months – shaving his neck with Narcissus Lockhart's razor; tidying up his beard; dressing in the smartest clothes he could find. He descended the stairs to find Clarissa smiling up at him from the hallway, a small stack of canvases lying at her feet.

'You look beautiful,' Harry said, pressing the tips of her gloved fingers to his lips.

'I look like a woman in mourning,' Clarissa replied, with a doleful glance down at her old black bombazine.

'Come on,' Harry urged, stooping to pick up the paintings.

Outside, the rain was lashing down, the skies low and brooding.

'You're too good to us, Aki,' Clarissa said to the ever attentive head servant, as he appeared with an umbrella, holding it over their heads as they hurried down the garden path to the brougham.

Zhang was waiting on the verge, the pony's bridle in his hand. He helped them into the carriage, and then they were off down the puddle-strewn road, the rain drumming on the leather roof, the wind howling around them.

'*After the typhoon, there are pears to gather,*' Clarissa said, gazing out of the window into the grey deluge. 'Li-Liang taught me that.'

'Bring me the pears, I say!' Harry replied. It felt like it had been raining for ever. 'How long does the season last?'

'Sometimes up to three months. But it's usually over by this time of year.'

They passed another carriage, and Harry heard laughter from within: evidently the terrible weather was not enough to prevent the Shanghailanders from pursuing their lively social life.

'Did you speak to Lam Dookay?' Harry asked.

Clarissa nodded.

'And?'

'He offered me 2,400 taels for the business, warts and all.'

That sounded a most fabulous sum to Harry, until Clarissa added, 'That's only 800 pounds in English money, Harry. When Narcissus started as a junior clerk at Jardine's, he was on 175 pounds a year!'

Harry gave a tight smile, suddenly remembering how different their positions really were. 'I shan't tell you how much I was paid at Piggott's,' he said shortly, 'but 175 pounds a year seems like a king's ransom to me!'

Clarissa's face fell, and Harry suddenly regretted making the distance between them felt. 'I interrupted you,' he said in a softer voice. 'How did you respond to Lam Dookay's offer?'

'I told him I'd think about it.'

They were approaching the outer arch of the Taotai's *yamen* now. No queue of carriages this evening — perhaps the weather had put people off after all.

'Are you sure the Taotai's expecting us tonight?' Harry asked.

'I had Aki check the invitation twice.'

The brougham pulled up at the end of the porte-cochère, and an underling emerged, splashing through the puddles in his haste to open the carriage door. He helped Clarissa down, and urged Harry to hand over the canvases. Then he ran ahead, carefully shielding the paintings from the rain as he led the guests inside.

Upon entering the *yamen*, it was immediately apparent that whatever was going on this evening, it was not a party. The silk screens had been brought forward towards the door, leaving just a portion of the state room exposed. In the corner, Harry saw the Taotai reclining on his daybed, his swollen frame encased in a shiny black robe, looking for all the world like one of the leeches that had attacked him on Lake Dongting. And sitting in a rattan chair, talking intently to His Excellency from behind his fingernails, was none other than Lam Dookay.

Both men turned sharply as Clarissa and Harry entered. Lam Dookay scrambled to his feet and made a low bow, but the Taotai remained as he was, looking his guests up and down with placid, knowing eyes.

'I do hope we've not mistaken the night, Your Excellency,' Clarissa said anxiously.

'Not at all, Mrs Lockhart,' the Taotai replied. 'Please – accept a drink.'

A servant bearing a silver tray had silently appeared at Harry's shoulder. Harry handed a glass of *jiu* to Clarissa, then took one for himself and sat down.

'I sent notice of cancellation to the other guests,' the Taotai explained.

Harry felt a tremor of alarm. Was this to do with the icicle tree? Were they to be arrested for illicit botanising – explicitly against the Taotai's edicts?

'You're not unwell, I trust, Your Excellency?' Clarissa said, exchanging an uncertain glance with Harry.

'I am in perfect health, Mrs Lockhart,' the Taotai replied. 'But there is something that I must say to you.'

From the corner of his eye, Harry saw Clarissa twisting her peacock-feather fan between her hands. She was just as worried as he was, he could tell.

'I'm afraid that I have distressing news,' the Taotai said. 'I received a letter this week from Hankow. My dear friend, Fang Li-Liang, is gravely ill.'

Clarissa gasped.

'The letter came from his mother,' the Taotai went on, 'explaining how Li-Liang had sustained a serious injury in the course of your travels, which worsened when the rains came.'

378

'But he promised me he would consult a doctor!' Clarissa protested. She swung round to face Harry, fan held taut between her hands. 'We should have *made* him go . . .'

The Taotai gave a sad smile. 'No one can make Fang Li-Liang do something he does not want to do, Mrs Lockhart. He can be infuriatingly obstinate.' The Taotai blinked his long black lashes. 'One of the finest physicians in Shanghai has been despatched to Hankow to attend to him, but . . .' The Taotai paused, his face darkening. 'I think we must all prepare ourselves.'

There was a long silence, then Clarissa rose and walked over to her canvases. Harry shifted in his chair. 'I'm not sure if now is the right moment, Mrs Lockhart . . .'

But it seemed that Clarissa didn't hear him, for she stooped down and untied the pile of paintings, searching through until she found the one she wanted. 'Here,' she said, holding up a large canvas. 'Now is as good a time as any to put this one on display.'

It was a painting Harry hadn't seen before, and one that made him smile. A portrait of Li-Liang, sitting on the deck of his *chuan*, imperious in his magnificent green silk robes. He was smiling slightly, his velvet eyes turned towards the riverbank, no doubt searching for a particular shade of sediment that might denote the presence of some precious mineral or ore.

Clarissa propped the canvas up on a chair, so that they could all admire it, then raised her glass. 'To Fang Li-Liang,' she called out, 'and the Self-Strengthening Movement!'

The Taotai flinched just a little at the latter half of her toast. But then he looked over at Li-Liang's clever, patrician face, and lifted his glass. 'To Fang Li-Liang!' he repeated.

They all drank deeply, Harry feeling the *jiu* scald the back of his throat as always.

'You will let us know, Your Excellency,' Clarissa said quietly, 'if there is any change in his condition?'

'Of course,' the Taotai replied.

'That's very good of you,' Clarissa said, lowering her head.

The Taotai bowed his own in response. 'Li-Liang was extremely taken with you both.'

'And we with him,' Harry interpolated.

The Taotai cast his eyes upon Harry, left them there for a moment, then pulled them away in such a withering fashion that Harry found himself wondering once again how much the man really knew about their expedition. Best leave the talking to Clarissa, he thought, resolving to say nothing further for the remainder of the interview.

'I made some other studies on our journey, Your Excellency,' Clarissa was saying, 'but there is no need to examine them now. Your thoughts will be elsewhere, I know.'

'But you must be recompensed for your efforts, Mrs Lockhart,' the Taotai insisted. He clicked his fingers and, almost instantaneously, a servant appeared with a silk purse. The Taotai pulled open the drawstring and dipped his soft, chubby fingers inside. 'How much did we agree?'

Clarissa held up both palms in protestation. 'Please accept them as a gift — for Li-Liang's sake.'

The Taotai smiled. 'But I promised to purchase them in aid of your girls' reformatory, and I am a man of my word.'

'I am in no need of money, I assure you!' But then Clarissa paused and lifted her chin, giving Harry another glimpse of that enterprising spirit which he had once feared, but had learnt now to admire. 'I do have one request, Your Excellency.'

The Taotai inclined his head indulgently. 'Yes, Mrs Lockhart?'

'All I ask is that, were I ever to leave Shanghai, you would offer the reformatory your gracious patronage, and your protection.'

'It would be my honour,' the Taotai replied.

'Thank you, Your Excellency,' Clarissa said, dropping into a deep curtsey. 'Now, I'm sure that you would like some time alone to reflect upon your friendship with Li-Liang, and the happy times you spent together.'

'The delicacy of your feelings does you credit, Mrs Lockhart,' the Taotai said, as Clarissa gave him her hand. Then she turned to her comprador. 'Perhaps you would care to share our carriage, Lam Dookay?'

'You are most considerate,' the comprador replied.

And then they were on their way to the door, Harry casting a final glance back at Li-Liang's portrait, fixing him in his memory just as Clarissa had fixed him in her painting.

'Worrying news indeed,' the comprador intoned, as the carriage clopped through the rain. 'We must pray for a miracle.'

Wedged in between his two companions, Harry gave a solemn nod. No one spoke for a time, but Harry knew from the look on Clarissa's face that she was thinking of Li-Liang, and the strange, dreamlike time they'd spent together in central China. Eventually, she cleared her throat and turned to the comprador. 'Lam Dookay,' she began, and on his other side, Harry felt the older man brace. 'I have considered your offer for Lockhart's. And I accept.'

In the damp darkness of the carriage, Harry heard Lam Dookay let out a long, slow exhalation. 'Very good, Mrs Lockhart.'

They turned down Thibet Road. 'I have one or two stipulations, however,' Clarissa added. 'Perhaps we might discuss them over a cup of tea?'

'With pleasure, Mrs Lockhart,' the comprador replied.

The carriage stopped, and Zhang leapt to the ground with a splash and opened the door. The comprador descended, then helped Clarissa down.

'Mr Compton has a business meeting in town,' Clarissa said to Zhang. 'Will you drive him there, please, then return immediately for Lam Dookay? I shall not detain him long.'

The *mafu* bowed, then climbed back into his sodden box-seat. Clarissa just had time to meet Harry's eye, before Aki came hurtling out of the house with an umbrella.

Leaning his head back against the leather bench, Harry sighed. He felt suddenly very weary – and the real work of the evening had not yet begun.

Zhang slid open the little hatch behind the driver's station. 'Where to, Mr Compton?' he asked.

Harry passed him the trade card Jack Turner had given him. 'Do you know this place, Zhang?'

Zhang handed back the card, then gave a curt nod. 'The Mistah, he liked it – very much.' Then he snapped closed the slat, and whipped on his wet, reluctant pony.

Chapter 31

It was still raining heavily as they approached 'The Garden of Perfumed Flowers'. Harry would have liked the carriage to pull up right outside their destination, but the Foochow Road was too narrow to permit vehicles wider than a wheelbarrow, so Zhang dropped him on the corner, and he set off down the alley on foot.

Every third door seemed to lead to a sing-song house, the upper floors crammed with rooms where the 'flower-girls' would entertain their clients. The reek of opium seeped from the open windows, whilst crowds of drunk British and French sailors careened up and down the road, singing at the tops of their voices.

Harry kept his head down, checking the name outside each establishment. Midway down the alley, he dodged aside as a customer burst out of one door and fell to his knees, vomiting copiously into the gutter. He was a massive man, Harry saw, almost as colossal as . . . 'Mr Scragge?' Harry exclaimed, as the man wiped his mouth on his sleeve.

Cornelius Scragge angled his enormous head up at Harry, his small eyes unfocused. Then he reached up and laid a huge hand on Harry's shoulder, almost grinding him into the dirt as he levered himself to his feet.

'Harry, m'lad!' Scragge said, firing a fleck of regurgitated rice on to Harry's frockcoat. 'You've done well for yourself, I see.' He lowered his gaze to Harry's heel, then peered about anxiously. 'But where's my little Wilber?'

Harry swallowed. 'I'm very sorry to tell you, Mr Scragge,' he began, 'but Wilberforce is dead.'

'Dead?' Scragge repeated, his face like that of a small boy overwhelmed by grief. 'But how?' he said, reaching out and grabbing Harry by the lapels. 'How did such a thing happen?'

Worried Scragge would blame him for putting Wilberforce at risk, Harry decided the best course would be to lie. 'It was the blow to the stomach he took in England, sir,' he said quickly. 'It did for him in the end.'

It was hard to tell if those were rain- or teardrops streaming down the sides of Scragge's face. 'I knew he weren't right,' he murmured, shaking his head. 'That's why I tried to keep him well-fed. Give the little fella a bit of joy.' Scragge wiped his nose on a dirty yellow handkerchief, then looked up at Harry with a sigh. 'Will you come inside, Harry? The boys'll be glad to see you.'

'Actually, I have to—'

But Scragge was already hauling Harry into his sing-song house of choice — 'The Temple of Supreme Happiness'. And there, gathered around a large table on the ground floor, sat Captain Buchanan, Stevens and the rest of the crew of the *Redemption*.

'Look who I found strolling the streets of Shanghai!' Scragge called out. 'Harry Compton!'

A few of the midshipmen glanced up and nodded, but in truth they were more interested in their game of whist.

'We're stuck in Shanghai 'til the typhoon breaks,' Scragge said to Harry. 'Still,' he added with a wink, 'there's worse places to sit out a storm!'

'Listen, Mr Scragge, I've got an appointment to meet someone. But maybe I'll pop back later.'

'You do that, Harry,' Scragge said. 'We can raise a glass to Wilberforce. Life can be so damned . . .' He paused, searching for the right word. 'Disappointing.'

'It can indeed, Mr Scragge.'

Putting on his hat, Harry headed back out to the Foochow Road and continued his search for The Garden of Perfumed Flowers. Twenty yards on, he found it. A dark-red velvet curtain hung across the entrance; just as Harry started to move it aside, a claw-like hand appeared, finishing the job with a practised flick. The hand belonged to a shrew of a madam, her long, greying hair twisted into a bun on the top of her head, secured with a jade comb. She peered suspiciously at Harry, a French cigarette clamped between her lips, her disapproval diminishing just a little as she appraised the weave and cut of his Jermyn Street coat; the silk of his top hat, faithfully brushed by Aki to a warm sheen.

'I'm here to meet a friend,' Harry said, but the old woman was already gesturing up at the balcony which circumscribed the main room. Standing around its edge were at least twenty girls, pale hands grasping the wooden railings for balance. Their faces had been whitened with the same rice powder as the singers Harry had seen at the Taotai's party, but their outfits were considerably more revealing.

'Harry! You came!'

385

Harry spun around and saw Jack Turner sitting at a table next to a flower-girl. She was caressing the back of his hand as her *amah* crouched beside him, offering him a black pipe packed with what Harry knew could only be opium.

'I knew you wouldn't let me down!' Jack went on, distractedly waving the *amah* away with one hand. Muttering under her breath, the old woman helped her charge to her tiny feet and led her, tottering, away.

'Sit down, Harry,' Jack said, 'and make yourself at home. Wong?' he called to the bar. 'Two more gin *pahits*, if you would. And this time, stick some booze in them.'

Harry sat down opposite Jack, eyes nervously scanning the room. There were a couple of Westerners at the other tables, but none he recognised.

'What a *city*,' Jack sighed, sitting back in his chair as a waiter brought over the cocktails. 'Turns out they love a carrot-top out here,' he said, waving at his flower-girl. 'Can't get enough of us.'

'I expect they'd like you if you had no hair at all, Jack,' Harry retorted. 'If you paid them enough.'

Jack had clearly been in the sing-song house for some time, judging by the flush of his cheeks and the liquor on his breath. Bags hung beneath his eyes, pale as curls of melted candlewax. 'So you read my letter, then, Harry?' he asked.

'I did.'

'And?'

A musician started up in the corner — the sad, slow strains of the lapa.

'I've no wish to do business with the likes of Piggott,' Harry said. 'So if he wants to deal with me, he'll have to pay a premium for the privilege. It'll cost him nine thousand taels. Or three thousand pounds in English money.'

Jack pushed out his lips and nodded. 'Sounds doable.'

Harry felt a brief surge of joy, tempered by an almost immediate jolt of suspicion. 'Piggott let you travel with that kind of money?' he asked.

Jack said nothing, just sat back in his chair and smiled in a way that made Harry suspect his old friend might be better at this sort of thing than he let on.

'But I'd need proof, of course, Harry,' he said. 'That what you've found really is the icicle tree.'

'I've a Wardian case full of cuttings back at my lodgings. Will that do you?' Harry asked curtly. 'And they're thriving,' he couldn't help but add.

'I'll bet they are,' Jack said. 'No one tends a plant like Harry Compton.'

The compliment, Harry knew, was genuine. But something Jack had said earlier still niggled. Harry leant forward in his chair. 'You're seriously telling me Piggott let you travel to China with a chestful of gold sovereigns?'

Jack's lips stretched into one of his old, roguish grins. 'Diamonds.'

'*Diamonds?*'

'Each stone alone worth two hundred pounds!'

Harry took a moment to absorb this. 'So Josiah Piggott,' he resumed, 'the man who wouldn't trust you with a barrow of daffodil bulbs, gave you care of a sack of diamonds?'

For the first time that evening, Jack looked a little unsure of himself. 'You're right, Harry,' he said, squirming in his seat. 'As it happens, I didn't travel alone. I had someone else with me.' He raised one arm, and before Harry had even looked around, he knew who it would be.

Seeing Decimus Frith come down the staircase from the balcony, a smile of triumph etched upon his face, Harry almost vomited. The bastard looked just the same, Harry thought, blond moustaches waxed to two perfect points, ulster coat swinging. Was there a revolver hidden beneath it, he wondered? He moved with confidence, nodding graciously at the madam as though he knew her well, and perhaps he did. Frith was a man of the world, after all, an English officer who'd travelled all over with the army – he'd probably been to Shanghai many times before, using and exploiting people wherever he went.

Still smiling, Frith snatched up a chair from the adjacent table and sat down opposite Harry.

'The deal's off,' Harry said at once. But as he got to his feet, Frith reached out and grabbed him by the wrist. Harry tried to pull away, but it was as though his arm was pinned to the tabletop.

'Get your fucking hands off me,' Harry said, feeling the drumbeat of blood in his ears.

'Hear him out, Harry,' Jack pleaded. 'For my sake.'

Harry glared into Jack Turner's desperate, mud-brown eyes, then lowered himself back down into his chair.

'That's better,' Frith said, releasing Harry's wrist and sitting back. 'Now, I do understand that you're upset, Harry. But if you'll just let me explain, I'm sure we can come to some arrangement.'

'Hell will freeze over first,' Harry said through gritted teeth.

Frith responded with a condescending grin. 'The night that you first told us about the icicle tree,' he began in his upper-class drawl. 'You came to *us*, remember? Whetted poor Mr Piggott's appetite with your fantastic tales, then ran away!' Frith shot Jack a meaningful look. 'I'd only stepped out for a few minutes. Gone to fetch the notary, so as to make everything legal and above-board – just as our friend Harry wanted – but when I came back, he'd vanished!'

'Liar,' Harry said. 'You didn't go to the notary at all.'

Another round of drinks arrived, but Harry waved his away.

'So Mr Piggott sent me after him,' Frith resumed. 'Then, when I turned up at Mrs Pincham's, the silly boy assaulted me, and disappeared.' Frith took a sip of his cocktail, leering at Harry over the rim of his glass. 'But it didn't take me long to find you, did it?' He looked over at Jack Turner and winked. 'He'd run home to his daddy, would you believe?'

'You murdered him,' Harry spat.

'What's this?' Jack said, glancing uneasily from Harry to Frith.

'Shut your mouth, Turner,' Frith snapped, then turned back to Harry. 'It was self-defence,' Frith said, with an airy, cheerful tone that made Harry want to kill him. 'The old man came at me with a coal shovel! What could I do?'

'What did you do with my father's body?' Harry asked, feeling his throat tighten.

There was a moment of silence, and Harry saw Jack twisting his lower lip between his fingers, staring anxiously at the floor.

'Come now, Harry,' Frith resumed. 'Let us leave this distressing matter behind us. We may never be friends, but even enemies can find a way to do business together?' He tilted his head and smiled again. 'You have something to

389

sell — something special, I grant you that — but it's a buyer's market, Harry. And the only buyer is Josiah Piggott.' He turned back to Jack. 'Has Mr Compton named his price?'

'Three thousand quid,' Jack said.

'Well, that's realistic, I suppose. At least he's not asking for guineas this time.'

Harry suddenly realised that this was the moment. The moment that could change the course of his and Clarissa's lives for ever. He was tempted simply to give in — to say yes; shake Frith's hand and be done with it — but then he remembered his father's face as he'd drawn his final breath. 'I'll need a couple of minutes to think it over,' he said, getting to his feet. 'I'll be over the road at the Temple of Supreme Happiness.'

'An enlightened choice, I'm sure,' Frith said, snickering at his own joke. 'Just don't take too long, eh?'

Stumbling out on to the street, Harry leant back against the rain-slicked wall and shut his eyes, breathing steadily through his nose and mouth to calm himself, until, slowly, a plan began to formulate in his head. Maybe, just maybe, it might work, Harry thought, as he ran across the road to the Temple of Supreme Happiness.

Inside, he found Scragge and the rest of the crew still playing whist in the taproom, with Captain Buchanan keeping score.

'Any chance I could have a piece of that paper, Captain?' Harry asked.

Head half-befuddled with drink, Buchanan just stared at him, so it was Scragge who handed Harry the scrap of paper. 'Won't you join us, Harry?' the big man asked.

390

'Later,' Harry promised, looking about anxiously for a table, but they were all taken, so he headed instead up the cramped wooden staircase to the balcony.

Positioned all along the walkway was a series of tiny tables, several of them occupied by flower-girls. They smiled at Harry as he approached, but he hurried past until he found an empty table and sat down. Then, laying his piece of paper out in front of him, he pulled a fountain pen from his pocket and began to write. '*I, Decimus Frith . . .*'

Ten minutes later, Harry set down his pen and stood up, finding the balcony completely deserted now, the girls all summoned to their work. Harry looked over the balustrade just in time to see Frith walk into the taproom, with Jack Turner following behind, shame-faced and sweaty.

'Frith!' Harry called out.

The two men looked up, then made their way through the crowded bar to the staircase. An *amah* materialised at the top to greet them, but Frith pushed past her and strode over to Harry's table. 'Well, Compton?' he said. 'What's it to be?'

'I have two conditions,' Harry replied. 'The first is that the icicle tree be named after my mother. *Adacomptonia sinensis.*'

'Bit of a mouthful,' Frith said. 'But I'll let you shanghai me into it.' That smile again . . .

'The other is that you sign this document,' Harry said, handing it over, 'and take it to Mr Charles Hargreaves at the British Consulate.'

Frith's smile died as he looked down at the opening para-graph. '*I, Decimus Frith,*' he read aloud, then looked up with a scowl. 'What the fuck is this?'

'Keep going,' Harry urged, turning to look at Jack, who refused to meet his eye.

'*I, Decimus Frith, do solemnly swear that I murdered Mr Michael Compton in cold blood on the morning of August 29, 1867, at Manor Cottage, Pulborough, whilst attempting to steal property from his house. Mr Davy Grigson of the Oddfellows Arms, Pulborough, will vouch that he saw me that morning, and rented me a horse. Signed in Shanghai,* blah, blah, blah . . .'

'Sign it,' Harry said, gesturing at the paper. 'Or the deal's off.'

'I'll do no such thing, you jumped-up little prick.'

'Then I'll introduce you to someone who might help change your mind.' Turning to the balustrade, Harry called down, 'Mr Scragge? Come up here for a moment, will you?'

'What are you playing at, Harry?' Jack hissed.

They all heard a heavy tread on the stairs, then looked round to see Cornelius Scragge emerge on to the balcony.

'Mr Scragge?' Harry said. 'I'd like you to meet Decimus Frith.'

'Who?' Scragge asked.

'The man who hurt Wilberforce,' Harry said, then stepped smartly aside. 'Who nearly kicked him to death.'

With a roar of outrage, Scragge lunged forward. 'You disgusting piece of . . .'

Seeing Frith pull out his revolver, Harry struck out with an arm, knocking the weapon out of his grip. Then Scragge charged at Frith, head lowered like a bull, and Frith flew backwards, slamming into the balustrade. There was a terrible moment as Frith stared at Harry in shock, before he lost his balance entirely and tipped backwards over the rail, and then they all heard the nauseating thud as his body hit the floor of the taproom some twenty feet below.

Harry peered down. Frith must have clipped the back of his head on the corner of a table, as his neck was twisted at a strange angle, blood pumping from the crown. Somewhere, a woman screamed, and Scragge made the sign of the cross with one thumb. 'Jumped, didn't he?' Scragge yelled down into the taproom.

No one spoke.

'Didn't he?' Scragge pressed.

'He did indeed,' came a hesitant voice. It was Stevens.

'I saw him too,' came another, more certain this time – Captain Buchanan.

Scragge turned to Harry and shrugged. 'Guilty conscience, probably. You get a lot of that in Shanghai. The women, the poppy pipes – spices and vices, I call it.' He broke off, shaking his head at the city's baleful effect upon the weak of mind.

'Thank you, Mr Scragge,' Harry said.

'Pleasure's all mine,' Scragge replied, then turned and lumbered back down the stairs.

Jack rounded on Harry. 'What the *hell* . . .'

'I'll explain later,' Harry said. 'Now quickly, sign Frith's name.'

'Are you mad?'

'Just do it!'

So, shaking his head, Jack scrawled the words 'Decimus Frith' on to the affidavit.

'Now, first thing tomorrow,' Harry went on, folding up the sheet and slipping it into Jack's inside pocket, 'you're to take it to Charles Hargreaves at the British Consulate. Hargreaves — you got that?'

Jack nodded.

'Tell him you found it in the lodgings you've been sharing with Frith. That Frith wrote it, then killed himself.'

As Jack stared at him in bafflement, Harry continued, 'But whatever you do, don't tell Hargreaves you know me. You understand?'

Jack nodded again.

'I'll be outside the British Consulate at midday tomorrow,' Harry said, picking up Frith's revolver and slipping it into his coat pocket. 'Don't be late.' Then he ran back down the stairs, and out on to the Foochow Road.

Chapter 32

Harry had barely slept the previous night, not just because he was still so shaken up, but because it had taken him so long to fill Clarissa in on everything that had happened. She knew it all now – how Frith had died; the fact that it was Piggott who was trying to buy the icicle tree, with Jack Turner as his agent.

Following Clarissa's advice, Harry concealed himself opposite the British Consulate well before midday – early enough to see Jack walk up to the front gate, where he glanced warily at the Sikh policemen, who waved him in through the door.

Jack was inside the Consulate for nearly an hour. As soon as he emerged, Harry stepped out of the shadows and called his name.

Greeting him with one of his old grins, Jack jogged over the road, narrowly avoiding being knocked down by a wheel-barrow-runner.

'Well?' Harry said, ushering Jack down the Bund.

'I spoke to your man,' Jack replied. 'Hargrove.'

'Hargreaves.'

'That's the one. He already knew all about Frith's death. Apparently, the peelers turned up just after we left.'

'And?'

'They found a lot of witnesses lining up to swear that Frith jumped.'

Harry exhaled in relief. 'And you gave Hargreaves the note?'

'He read it through,' Jack replied with a nonchalant sniff. 'Said I'd done the right thing to bring it to his attention.'

Harry grinned. 'You did brilliantly, Jack.'

'Oh well,' Jack said, a little tartly, 'that's a relief then!' He swung round to face Harry. 'Don't you think it's about time you told me what the fuck's going on?'

'We can talk at my lodgings,' Harry replied.

'No,' Jack said firmly. 'We'll go to my lodgings first. And we can talk on the way.'

So they set off together, and Harry told him about how he'd met Lorcan Darke at the Man in the Moon on the night they'd all gone out together, then how the Irishman had died and left him the map. About what had really happened when Frith had chased him down and shot his father. About his escape to Shanghai, and Clarissa Lockhart, and the difficulties they'd endured on their expedition to find the icicle tree. The one part of the story he didn't reveal was the plan he'd concocted with Clarissa the night before. That bit could wait.

Jack took it all in, then stopped outside an ornate marble-fronted building. 'Well,' he said. 'This is me.'

'Piggott put you up at the Shanghai Club?' Harry said, unable to conceal his surprise.

'Frith's club in London has some kind of arrangement with it,' Jack replied with a shrug. 'He got us connecting rooms on the fourth floor.'

Harry took a step towards the colonnaded entrance, but Jack held up a hand. 'Probably best if I go up alone, Harry. The concierge can get a bit funny.'

Harry wondered who else Jack might have tried to smuggle into his room over the last few days.

'I won't be long,' Jack added.

So Harry retreated to the other side of the Bund and watched as Jack passed through the grand revolving doors, catching an alluring gleam of the black marble within. Leaning against the wall of the Oriental Bank, Harry blew out a sigh, wondering once again if he could trust Jack. His eye was caught by a peculiar sight a few yards away, where a young Chinese man was crouching beneath a gingko tree, dipping a bamboo stick into a pot of glue. Having coated the tip, the youth slotted the stick into a series of others, like a chimney sweep assembling his broom. Then he raised it up into the canopy of the tree, held it there for a few moments, and brought it abruptly down. And there, affixed to the sticky end of his rod, flapping desperately with one wing, was a house sparrow. Sensing Harry's appalled interest, the youth grinned at him, before ripping the poor creature away from the stick, slipping it into his shoulder bag and beginning the whole macabre dance again.

Harry looked up to see Jack crossing the road towards him. 'All well?' Harry asked.

'Frith had the diamonds hidden in his sponge-bag,' Jack replied with a wink. 'I saw how jealously he guarded it when we landed at Marseilles. So,' he said, tapping his trouser pocket, 'where to next?'

*   *   *

'You must be Mr Turner,' Clarissa said, as Jack walked into the morning-room.

'And *you* must be Mrs Lockhart,' Jack replied, the admiration obvious in his eye. He wiped his palms on the sides of his trousers, then decided against a handshake and settled on an awkward bow.

'Will you take some tea, Mr Turner?' Clarissa asked.

'I wouldn't say no,' Jack replied.

Aki was despatched, and Jack sat down in an armchair and placed his hands on his knees, looking about him eagerly. Suddenly, his eyes found the Wardian case in the corner of the room, and lit up. 'Is that it over there?' he said. 'The icicle tree?'

Harry nodded.

'Well, give us a look, then!'

Harry stepped aside, and Jack hurried over, dropping to his knees to peer through the misty glass. 'The leaves are gorgeous. How many cuttings have you got in there? Twenty?'

'Nineteen.'

'And they're the only ones?' Jack asked, turning to give Harry a shrewd look.

Harry nodded, and Jack moved his attention to the illustration propped against the wall. 'How the hell'd you get this done?' he asked, eyes eating up the painting of the long ice-white flowers dripping from the tree.

'It's mine, Mr Turner,' Clarissa said. 'I am an artist, and Mr Compton is a plant hunter.'

'Not going to argue with that,' Jack muttered. '*Adacomptonia sinensis*,' he read at the bottom of the painting. 'Quite right too.'

Just then, the tea tray arrived. 'I'll serve, thank you, Aki,' Clarissa said, and the head servant retreated with a bow.

'On second thought, I'll pass,' Jack said, as Clarissa began to pour the tea. 'It's just not the same without a drop of milk!'

'I quite agree, Mr Turner,' Clarissa replied, with that generosity of spirit which Harry so admired.

There was a moment of silence. 'I can speak openly before you, can I, Mrs Lockhart?' Jack asked.

'Of course!' Clarissa replied. 'Mr Compton and I are as one in this matter.' She turned to Harry and smiled, and he felt a little flare of joy explode in his chest.

Jack cleared his throat. 'Yesterday, a figure of three thousand pounds was discussed.'

Harry glanced at Clarissa, who nodded. Noting the gesture, Jack reached into his waistcoat and took out a small but heavy-looking velvet bag. 'That comes to fifteen of these little gleamers,' he said, as he untied the drawstring and tipped a sparkling cascade on to the table, each diamond striking the glass top with a brisk ping.

Each stone was about the size of a hazelnut, Harry saw, and even in the dull light of the morning-room, their glitter was mesmerising.

'May I?' Clarissa said, picking one up and tapping it twice against her front tooth. 'Seems real enough to me,' she added, her voice shaking just a little.

'I've the jeweller's certificate to prove it,' Jack said, taking out a folded square of paper and handing it to Clarissa, who scrutinised it for a time, then nodded.

'I suppose that's it then,' Jack said, taking hold of the Wardian case by its handle. 'I trust the illustration's included in the price.'

Clarissa slid the painting into a carpet bag and handed it to him.

'Well, it's been a pleasure doing business with you both!' Jack said, hooking the bag over one shoulder.

'And you, Mr Turner,' Clarissa replied, shaking him by the hand. 'I'll have Aki ready the carriage. Then our driver will take you wherever you would like to go.'

'That's most obliging of you, I must say, Mrs Lockhart,' Jack said, blushing to the tips of his ears.

As Clarissa disappeared to find Aki, Jack turned to Harry and grinned. 'Remember that day I found you hiding at the growing grounds, Harry? Shivering like a kicked dog and covered in mud?'

'A fair bit's changed since then,' Harry said.

'It most certainly has,' Jack replied. 'It most certainly has.'

The two men shook hands again. 'I'll be in touch, old friend,' Harry said.

Jack winked back. 'And I shall await your correspondence with interest.'

Two hours later, Clarissa and Harry were lying in each other's arms when the doorbell rang. Leaping out of bed, Harry bolted for his own room, where he was surprised a few moments later by a discreet knock at the door. 'Mr Compton?' came Aki's soft voice. 'A visitor.'

'For *me*?' Harry said, frantically throwing on some clothes. He knew no one in Shanghai who would come to Celestial Heights looking for him. What could this mean?

Reaching into his trouser pocket, Harry pulled out the black velvet bag that Jack had given him, wondering if it could be the diamonds that had brought a stranger to their door. He tossed the bag into the bureau drawer, then saw

Frith's revolver lying inside, and considered it for a moment, chewing on his lip. Having first made sure that the gun wasn't cocked, he pushed it into his waistband, glancing in the mirror to check it was well-hidden by his coat. Then, heart thumping, he ran down the stairs and paused outside the morning-room door, telling himself that whatever awaited him, he and Clarissa would face it together.

Taking a deep breath, Harry pushed open the door and, to his relief, found no one more threatening than Charles Hargreaves waiting for him.

'Mr Hargreaves!' Harry exclaimed. 'What a surprise! Have you been offered some refreshment? Tea, perhaps, or some coffee?'

The attaché set down the Sprimont vase he'd been examining and beamed at Harry, as affable and unruffled as ever. 'Aki has made a valiant attempt to force any number of sweetmeats upon me, but I have rebuffed his every effort,' he announced, casting a sorrowful glance down at his expanding paunch. 'Alas, one cannot eat like a school-boy for ever!'

'Indeed,' Harry said, a little suspiciously, wondering, as he always did with Hargreaves, when he would discover what the man really wanted under those layers of charm and attentiveness. 'Mrs Lockhart is resting, I believe,' Harry went on, 'but she should be down in a matter of moments.'

Hargreaves examined his fingernails. 'It is actually you whom I have come to see, Mr Compton. For I had a curious visit this morning.' He looked back up at Harry, hoisting one eyebrow towards his shiny pate. 'A young man bringing me a suicide note, would you believe?'

401

'Not his own, I trust?' Harry remarked drolly.

'No,' Hargreaves said, eyeing Harry's shirt, the top button of which was still undone, Harry was embarrassed to note. 'In fact, it pertained to a matter particular to you, Mr Compton.'

'To me?' Harry asked, simulating astonishment.

'Yes,' Hargreaves said, watching him closely. 'Perhaps you ought to sit down while I tell you about it.'

And so, perching on a side chair, careful not to dislodge the revolver that was wedged into his breeches, Harry listened patiently to the strange tale of Mr Frith's confession, widening his eyes in all the right places.

'But how extraordinary!' Harry exclaimed, as soon as Hargreaves had finished.

'Isn't it?' Hargreaves said. 'I find it particularly odd that Mr Frith should choose to end his life in the very city where you, the son of his victim, had taken up residence. But there you have it! Such things happen, I suppose,' he said, though he didn't look especially convinced by his own words.

'Perhaps he was trying to find me,' Harry offered. 'To make amends.'

'Perhaps,' Hargreaves said, then was silent for a moment. 'It must be a terrible shock for you, of course. To hear of your father's violent death?'

'I am beyond shock these days, Mr Hargreaves,' Harry replied truthfully. 'But I'd be most obliged if you would contact the relevant authorities in England, and inform them that the man who murdered my father has confessed to his crime.'

Hargreaves gave Harry another of his piercing stares, but then his face softened. 'I shall ask my clerk to produce a facsimile of the note, then have the original despatched to London by Queen's Messenger.'

Harry stood up to shake Hargreaves's hand. 'Thank you for your help, Mr Hargreaves.'

The attaché made a vague gesture with one arm, as if to suggest that it was the least he could do. Then, picking up his hat and gloves, he turned to face Harry. 'You will convey my fondest wishes to Mrs Lockhart?'

'Of course,' Harry said, wondering if he detected a faint wistfulness in the young man's eye.

The two men proceeded to the hallway. As Aki appeared, ready to show Hargreaves out, the young attaché turned. 'I meant to say, Compton. I attended a meeting this afternoon at the Taotai's *yamen*. His Excellency gave me a message for Mrs Lockhart. Something about a mutual friend?'

'Fang Li-Liang?' Harry said quickly.

'That's right. The poor man has been very ill, I understand.'

'Yes,' Harry said, readying himself for the worst.

But it didn't come. Instead, Hargreaves smiled. 'Apparently, he is making a recovery – against all odds, it seems. What was the rather peculiar expression the Taotai used? He has "self-strengthened".' A baffled chuckle: 'Yes, that was it!'

As soon as Hargreaves was gone, Harry hurried upstairs to Clarissa's room.

'Well?' she said, sitting up in bed. 'What did Charlie say?'

'He brought a message from the Taotai,' Harry replied, unable to keep the joy from his face. 'Li-Liang is on the mend!'

Clarissa let out a little cry. 'Thank God!'

'And there's more,' Harry went on, removing the revolver from his waistband and shutting it into a drawer. 'My name is as good as cleared.' He took her radiant face between his hands and kissed her on the lips. 'It's over, Clarissa! It's finally over.'

Clarissa let out a shuddering sigh of relief. 'So you're safe now? You can go back to England whenever you like?'

He grinned at her. '*We* can be on the next boat, Mrs Lockhart – the moment your affairs are in order.'

Fingers flying to her mouth, Clarissa gave a little sob of joy, then reached out and took Harry's hand. 'I've something to show you.' Running to the door, she led him into her sunny dressing-room, where Harry saw something which made him catch his breath.

'I don't believe it,' he said, pulling the tray of icicle tree seeds towards him. Only the week before, he'd moved the tray into Clarissa's bedroom, hoping to make use of the light, and now . . . sprouting from the soil were five pale green tops! He caressed the tiny, fragile seed leaves.

'We ought to travel First Class to England, don't you think?' Clarissa said, tilting her head to one side and giving Harry her most persuasive smile. 'We wouldn't want them getting damaged.'

Harry chuckled. 'I think we can probably afford it.'

Then Clarissa drew him towards her, and kissed him, and Harry wondered if life could get any sweeter.

PART SIX
Seven years later

Chapter 33

Watering can in hand, Harry Compton moved around his father's old workshop. He'd converted the building into a working greenhouse back in the autumn of '69, and though the light was pretty good, there were still a few shady corners. One of the Chinese clematises looked like it could do with a little attention, Harry thought – *Clematis Li-Liangia*, as keen on self-improvement as its namesake.

Harry dragged the terracotta pot beneath one of the skylights, then sprinkled the soil with a little water from his can. Hearing the crunch of gravel outside, he turned to the open door, and saw Molly running towards him, her long auburn hair blowing in the breeze. 'Papa, Papa!' she called out. 'There's somebody coming!'

Harry felt a small prickle of alarm, as he always did whenever a stranger approached the cottage. This wariness was a part of him now, he knew, a legacy of all he'd survived.

Putting down his can, he stepped outside, limping very slightly, and saw his wife standing in the doorway of the cottage, hands on hips, slender as ever in her grass-green summer dress. Clarissa's face was a little thinner now – the lines between her nose and mouth more clearly etched, the planes of her cheekbones sharper — but Harry found her all the more beautiful for it. Taking her hand in his, they set off together towards the kissing gate.

A fly was trundling down the track towards the cottage. At the reins sat Davy Grigson, and sitting beside him . . . Harry caught a flash of greying red curls, and felt his stomach knot. But then Clarissa's hand was on his shoulder, steadying him, as she always did. 'You said he would come,' she told him gently. 'And he has.'

The fly drew to a halt, and Jack Turner jumped down. He handed a couple of coins to Davy, who peered at them in disappointment before whipping his horse onwards, back towards Pulborough Station.

Molly had already slipped through the kissing gate, and was tugging at Jack's sleeve. 'Who are you?' she asked, gazing up at him with her mother's clever green eyes.

'An old friend of your father's,' Jack replied. Then he looked over at Harry and smiled. 'You've been busy, I see.'

'Molly?' Clarissa called out, and the little girl ran back to her mother, burying her face in her skirts.

'Afternoon, Mrs Lockhart,' Jack said.

'It's Mrs Compton now.'

'And aren't I pleased to hear it!' Jack said. 'It's a lovely spot,' he added, thumbs hooked into his waistcoat as he glanced around the grounds. He'd grown a little rounder in the face, Harry saw, and the ruddy sheen of his cheeks suggested he was as fond of the tavern as ever.

'Would you care for a glass of cordial, Mr Turner?' Clarissa asked. 'You must be tired after your journey.'

'Go on then,' Jack said.

They proceeded into the kitchen, Molly still trailing Jack like a puppy, dodging away mischievously whenever he turned.

Clarissa poured Jack a glass.

'It's elderflower,' Molly said proudly as he took a sip. 'I made it myself.'

'Did you now?' Jack asked, smacking his lips. 'That must be why it's so delicious.'

As Molly beamed with pride, Jack looked about the walls, hung with those of Clarissa's paintings that Harry loved too much to let her sell. 'Now then,' Jack said at last, putting down his glass, 'I got your letter, Harry, and I have to say, I wasn't too sure what to make of it.' He canted his head. 'I mean, I understand you'd be curious to know when the icicle tree was going on sale, but did you really need me to drop everything and come down here the moment I heard the news?'

Harry and Clarissa exchanged a glance.

'Well, here I am' — Jack gave a mocking little bow — 'as requested. So would you kindly tell me what the—' He broke off, glancing at Molly. 'What in Heaven's name's going on?'

Clarissa laid her hands on Molly's shoulders, and they both watched as Harry led Jack out of the kitchen into the small conservatory he'd constructed at the rear of the cottage. And there, beyond the tangle of royal-fern fiddleheads and yellow weigela, was the Compton family's most treasured possession: a young ornamental tree with delicate pinnate leaves and branches laden with dazzling white flowers.

Jack turned to Harry in disbelief. 'But we made a deal, Harry! You said you'd sold me every cutting you had!'

'The cuttings, yes,' Harry replied. 'These I grew from seed.'

Jack frowned suspiciously. 'The big one there? You wouldn't have had time . . .'

'I grafted one of the seedlings on to the rootstock of a pistachio tree.'

Jack rubbed his furrowed brow with one hand. 'But I still don't understand . . .'

'Come on,' Harry said. 'I want to show you something.'

He led Jack across the courtyard to a piece of pretty grassland that lay behind the greenhouse. 'Are you still working in Cultivation?' Harry asked, as he unlatched the iron gate.

'Yes, but not for Piggott,' Jack said. 'I took a few months off after I got back from China. Spent all my money. Then Piggott said he didn't have room for me no more.'

They crossed the lawn, then stopped in front of two gravestones, and Jack crouched down to examine the inscriptions. '*Ada Margaret Compton*,' he read aloud. '*Born 7 March 1826, died 5 November 1857.*' Moving to the second grave, Jack read, '*Michael Compton. Born 9 October 1819, died 29 August 1867. Beloved Husband to Ada and Father to Harold . . .*' He glanced round at Harry. 'You found the body, then?'

'In the end,' Harry replied, feeling the bile rise in his gullet. 'It was hidden in the old ice house over there.'

'That sick bastard,' Jack said.

Harry nodded. 'I've a score to settle, Jack. It may have been Decimus Frith who murdered my father, but it was Josiah Piggott who paid him to do it. And he's still sitting pretty up there in Chelsea, about to be the toast of the horticultural world.' Harry glanced around and saw Clarissa walking towards them, Molly skipping at her heels. 'There are men like Piggott everywhere,' Harry went on. 'Men who think they have to dominate in order to succeed. Men who will do anything – lie, steal, even murder – to get what they want.'

Molly ran over and pushed her hand into Harry's, and they walked together, Jack at their side, Clarissa watching from the gate. 'While I was travelling in Guizhou,' Harry said, 'I came across some poppy fields.'

Jack looked at him in bewilderment. 'Poppy fields?'

Harry nodded. 'White poppies. You see, the Chinese had come to realise that the only way to end the stranglehold of the British was to grow the opium for themselves. That's what planted the idea in my mind.'

'What kind of idea?' Jack asked.

'Of how to ruin Piggott.' Harry turned and looked at Jack. 'When's he planning to unveil the icicle tree?'

'Thursday next,' Jack replied. 'He's got a big song and dance planned. Invited anybody who's anybody.'

'Thursday, you say?' Harry exchanged another glance with Clarissa. 'Then we'd better get started.'

Chapter 34

It took them three days to get to London. Davy had strapped a canvas canopy over his wagon, and Harry, Clarissa and Jack sat in the back, Molly on her mother's lap as they all kept a close eye on the terracotta pots, making sure they were secure. Fifteen icicle tree specimens, along with twenty of the more conventional prizes they'd collected on the expedition. It was a hoard valuable enough to make a highwayman's eyes water, Jack had said – should the brigand have the wit to know what he was looking at.

On their first night, they stayed at the White Hart in Crawley. Clarissa and Molly shared a room, but Harry chose to spend the night in the stables, sleeping on a straw pallet with Frith's revolver under his pillow, determined to protect the plants at all costs.

He slept fitfully that night, tormented by strange dreams. First, he found himself shivering in his cabin on the *Redemption* as the storm raged outside; then bantering with the wretched Mr Dancer on the balcony of the Bubbling Well Guesthouse. Then he was at the British Consulate, sinking into a chair under Charles Hargreaves's sceptical gaze; then sweating in his bed at Celestial Heights, Clarissa flitting in and out of his room like some ghostly angel. Then the magic lantern turned again, and the comprador and the Taotai, Aki and Zhang each appeared in turn, until Harry reached the Yangtze, and then it was Li-Liang smiling benevolently upon him, followed by a procession of pirates and mercenaries and children throwing stones. Then Harry was walking past those dead Miao men in their execution cages, then marooned on the wrong side of a ravine, watching Wilberforce die, before clamping his hands around the killer's throat, squeezing as hard as he could, until suddenly it was Piggott's neck he was throttling, and the man was winking at him — 'You're no better than me, Compton, whatever you might think!' — and Harry woke up, finding himself drenched in sweat.

The next night they spent at Epsom, and Harry asked Davy to keep watch over the plants — for a sensible sum, naturally — whilst he slept in the same bed as Clarissa and Molly, and caught up on all the hours of sleep he'd lost the night before.

They set off again before dawn, the sun just coming up as they passed through the village of Balham, and on into Battersea. Rolling up the canopy, Harry was fascinated to see how much London had changed over the years. There was a new bridge spanning the Thames — they'd named it the Albert Bridge, Jack said — but as the toll was ruinous, Davy took the more familiar route over Battersea Bridge, its creaking wooden planks antediluvian now compared to the octagonal, cast-iron towers of its younger, prettier sister.

The river had been embanked, Harry saw — its mighty breadth trammelled by high stone levies, and the idyll of

Cheyne Walk ruined by a new avenue built on the southern side of Chelsea. A monstrosity, Harry thought, lit by electrical arc-lamps, and already swarming with hackney cabs and pantechnicon vans making deliveries.

'I barely know the place now,' Harry said, a little sadly.

'You'll know Chelsea!' Jack replied.

They drove up Beaufort Street and turned on to the King's Road. And then Harry could see that Jack was right — for there was the Man in the Moon, entirely unmolested, with the Cremorne and Mr Wimsett's stovehouse behind it; and then came Paultons Square, with the squawking cacophony of Mr Baker's pheasant dealership beyond.

'What a lovely street,' Clarissa said, and Harry swung round and smiled, pleased to see her respond to the place just as he had. She wouldn't be the first artist to be drawn to Chelsea, he thought, seduced by the charms of its riverine light . . . Molly was asleep in her arms, and for a moment Harry was tempted to wake her — until he remembered the demanding day that lay ahead, and felt his mood darken.

'How far up d'you want, Harry?' Davy Grigson called from the front.

'Just past the dogleg, please,' Harry replied, glancing right into Mr Little's nursery, then left into Markham Square, which had two terraces of houses upon it now, as well as a brand-new tavern, the paintwork still fresh. 'Just about . . . here.'

Davy drew in the reins, and they stopped opposite JM Piggott's Plant Emporium. Harry could see now the preparations that had been made for the big launch. A huge placard hung above the usual signage marked, 'World Exclusive — Thursday 20 May — icicle tree!!', and gaudy pavement signs stood on either side of the stovehouse door. *'Most Beautiful Tree in Existence!'* screamed one, whilst the other held a colour print of a familiar image – the illustration that Clarissa had created of the icicle tree, all lacy green leaves and startling white flowers. At the bottom, however, were the words, *'Pigottia sinensis'*.

Shaking his head in disgust, Harry looked round to see a grimy-faced man dragging a barrow of cut flowers up the road towards them, snarling to find Davy's ramshackle fly parked in his usual spot. Jack hopped down from the wagon and intercepted him. The two men clearly knew each other, and whatever Jack said seemed to appease the flower-seller, as he turned his barrow around and began looking for a pitch elsewhere.

'We're golden,' Jack called to Harry, so loudly that Molly yawned and opened her eyes.

Harry pulled out his pocketwatch, and winced. Almost eight o'clock – there was no time to lose! Quickly, they unloaded the trestle tables from the back of the wagon, placing the less valuable plants – campanulas, lilies, meconopsis – on the first. The second table was more awkward to dress, as the mature icicle tree was to be positioned in its very centre, with the smaller trees grouped around it. The terracotta pot containing the mature tree was extremely heavy, and they needed Davy's help to lift it down from the wagon, with Molly flitting all the while about their feet, getting in the way.

As soon as they were done, Harry covered up the table with the canvas canopy. The grand revelation must be saved for the right moment.

Just as they had finished, Harry heard the squeak of hinges, and looked up to see the front door of Piggott's stovehouse shudder open. It was Rex Barrington, his hair a little thinner, his Van Dyke beard so jet-black now that it could only have been tinted. Barrington frowned in puzzlement at the gimcrack operation setting up opposite him, but he didn't seem to recognise Harry, and Jack made sure to keep his back to him until he had moved away.

Piggott was in there too, Harry knew, having caught a glimpse of his stout frame bustling amongst the tropical foliage. Unheard of for the master to arrive at his stovehouse so early – it must be a red-letter day indeed.

'I'm hungry,' Molly wheedled, directing her entreaty to Harry, always a soft touch.

'Could do with a bite meself,' Davy Grigson added.

'There's Ecclestone's on the corner,' Jack said. 'I could . . .'

'I'll go,' Clarissa sighed, taking Molly's hand.

Harry watched his wife and daughter walk away towards Lincoln Street, then started marking up the blackboard, setting out their prices. Lilies for a half-sovereign, campanulas for ten shillings – expensive, but not outrageous.

Soon, their first customer approached the table, a young lady with a lapdog on a lead and an older, bespectacled companion in tow. 'Is that a tiger lily?' she asked.

'It is indeed, miss,' Harry said, flashing her a charming smile, instantly back in salesman mode.

'I'll take one. Mrs Bream?'

Her companion reached into her reticule for a pocket-book.

'When does the nursery open?' the young lady asked.

'Eight o'clock sharp,' Jack replied. 'After an icicle tree, were we?'

416

'People have spoken of nothing else since that article appeared in the *Illustrated London News*.' The young lady leant in closer: 'There are rumours that the Queen herself will buy one. Apparently, she plans to confer a knighthood on Mr Piggott, then relocate the Great Spring Show from Kensington to Chelsea as a reward for . . .'

The stovehouse door flew open, and Rex Barrington reappeared carrying a blackboard of his own, the prices already chalked upon it. Harry screwed up his eyes, trying to make out the numbers: '*Icicle tree: Seedlings — 10 sovereigns; Saplings — 45 sovereigns; Mature trees (grafted) — 100 sovereigns . . .*'

'*A hundred* sovereigns a tree?' Jack hissed to Harry. 'That must be a record!'

'Are you open yet?' the young lady called to Barrington.

'Sorry, miss,' Barrington replied. 'Give us ten minutes, would you?'

The girl huffed impatiently, then moved to the side of the stovehouse door, her companion close behind. Moments later, a queue began to form behind them, a group of elderly women, then a gentleman carrying a dry-plate camera, accompanied by a weasel-faced man clutching a notebook.

'Price our icicle trees the same as Piggott's,' Harry said to Jack. 'But we'll ask for pennies, not sovereigns.'

Jack chuckled to himself as he carried the blackboard behind the wagon and went to work with his chalk stub. Clarissa, meanwhile, was making her way towards them, holding an Ecclestone's paper bag. Molly was skipping beside her, sugary smile suggesting she'd had her breakfast already.

'Everyone was talking about the icicle tree,' Clarissa said, handing Harry a Chelsea bun. Then she looked up

417

and frowned, shading her eyes from the sun with one hand. 'That's not him, is it?'

Harry swung round, heart lurching as he realised that Clarissa was right. It was Piggott, out to greet the crowds! He was a little less tall than Harry remembered, those mutton-chop sideburns almost completely white now. But his chest was as puffed-out as ever, his gold-knobbed cane still swinging imperiously from one hand.

'Welcome, friends!' Piggott bellowed.

The reporter broke out of the queue and hurried towards him.

'All in good time,' Piggott snapped, holding up a hand to halt the man's progress.

The queue was even longer now, Harry saw, and Piggott waited a moment for the babble to quieten before embarking upon his speech. 'Today,' Piggott began, 'you shall bear witness to the culmination of my life's work. I have dedicated all I have, and all I am, to hunting down and cultivating the most beautiful tree in existence. This is the only place on Earth where you can buy one, and when you see it' – Piggott paused, porcine eyes raised Heavenwards – 'you shall know of what wondrous miracles our great Creator is capable.'

Seeing Piggott wipe away a crocodile tear, Harry let slip a snort. The man had some cheek . . .

'And so,' Piggott resumed, 'without further ado, I present for the delectation of the good denizens of Chelsea and beyond . . . the world-famous icicle tree!'

Flinging out an arm, Piggott stepped aside, licking his lips to see how the queue surged forward, pushing and shoving to get into his stovehouse. The journalist tutted, furious not to have got there first, and as he passed close to their table, Harry shouted to Jack, 'Now!'

Jack whipped off the canopy to reveal the table of icicle trees, stopping the reporter in his tracks.

'Get your icicle trees here!' Harry yelled. 'Tenpence a seedling!'

'What's all this?' the reporter said.

'Icicle trees,' Jack beamed. 'The best to be found in England.'

'For tenpence a pop?' the reporter scoffed. 'You must be having me on . . .'

'See for yourself, sir!' Clarissa threw in.

'Ambrose?' the journalist called to the man with the camera. 'Get over here!'

Davy had just completed his first transaction: one of the icicle tree saplings, sold to a man with a luxuriant horseshoe moustache. As soon as he was gone, a woman took his place. 'But they're exquisite,' she said, stretching out her fingers to stroke the flowers on the mature tree, unable to believe they could be real. 'And such a *fragrance* . . .'

'Yours for twelve and fourpence,' Harry said.

'Really?' the woman whispered, looking up at him in wonderment.

Harry nodded, and she bit her lip. 'I'll take it!'

'No, I will!' said an older woman, trying to elbow her aside.

There was a scrum at the table then, and Clarissa took hold of Molly's hand and led her behind the wagon. As the photographer stooped down to his tripod, Harry spotted Piggott standing behind him, straining to see the cause of the commotion. Suddenly, seized by frustration, Piggott pushed past the photographer, sending his tripod flying. 'What the Devil's going on?' Piggott barked.

'We're selling icicle trees, mate,' Davy said with a smug grin. 'Same as you!'

'But that's . . . impossible,' Piggott stammered. His eyes fell upon the mature icicle tree and widened in horror. Forcing a customer out of his way, he examined it up close, breathing heavily through his nose. Then he looked up and saw Jack. 'You!' Piggott roared, his face puce. 'I'll see you hanged, Jack Turner!'

Barging aside an elderly woman as he pushed his way through the crowd, Piggott suddenly found himself face to face with Harry, so close that Harry could smell the kippers on his breath. Piggott stood there, staring at him, snorting like a carthorse, cheeks striated with broken blood vessels.

'Harry Compton, sir,' Harry said pleasantly. 'At your service!'

Piggott opened his mouth to reply, but then his body gave a sudden jerk, as though he'd just been stuck in the back with a knife. He remained rigid for a moment, mouth opening and closing like a guppy.

'Mr Piggott?' Harry said, unsure if this was all part of the man's performance.

'Can't . . .' Piggott gasped, beating one fist against his chest, 'breathe . . .'

The crowds were pressing in on them now, and somewhere in the background Harry could hear the odd stray remark — 'Don't waste your money at Piggott's . . . bloody conman . . .'

'Piggott?' Harry said, as he watched his former master fall to one knee, his lips turning blue. Turning, Harry yelled into the crowd, 'Someone fetch a doctor! Quick!'

420

'Compton . . .' Piggott hissed as he slumped on to his side.

Kneeling next to the dying man, Harry put an ear close to his mouth. 'What is it?' he whispered.

'You . . . *bastard thief*,' Piggott exhaled, then his eyes glazed.

To his surprise, Harry found that he was holding Piggott's hand. 'Is he . . . dead?' Jack asked, crouching down next to him.

Harry nodded, then withdrew his hand from Piggott's weakening grasp. 'Don't let Molly see,' he said, his mind a curious jumble of shame, triumph and sadness.

'Doctor!' Harry heard in the distance. 'Doctor coming through . . .'

Harry straightened up, then extracted himself from the growing crowd of people gawping at Piggott's corpse. Further down the King's Road, he could hear the plant-sellers and flowermen calling out their wares, the rhythmic clop of hooves, the bark of a lapdog, the clatter of the great city going about its business.

Clarissa was standing behind the wagon, smiling as she watched Jack Turner on his hunkers in the dirt, distracting Molly with some silly game that involved them knocking knuckles. Seeing Harry, her face lit up, and for a moment all the noise, all the dark thoughts and unsettling memories, receded, and there was only her.

Harry smiled back, then pressed on towards his wife.

By the time dusk fell, the little crew was once again nestled beneath the canopy of the wagon, as Davy Grigson drove them out of London.

Exhausted by the events of the day, no one spoke much. But then Clarissa broke the silence. 'He won't have suffered,

Harry,' she said, seeing him staring blankly into the middle distance. 'It all happened so fast.'

'Never knew what hit him,' Jack ventured.

Harry pictured Piggott's raddled face and bulging eyes, and was not so sure.

'Papa?' came a quiet, cunning little voice.

Harry looked down to see Molly pointing at the Ecclestone's cake box that was wedged between the folded trestle tables. 'You'll have to ask your mother, Mol,' he said. 'I've had enough troubles for one day.'

Molly sat back and stuck out her lip.

'Wonder what'll happen to the nursery?' Jack said, as the wagon rattled past the old Kingston turnpike.

'Piggott's wife will probably auction it off,' Harry replied glumly.

Everyone fell silent again, but then came Clarissa's thoughtful voice: 'I wonder what price it would fetch?'

Slowly, everyone's eyes lifted — apart from Molly's, which remained fixed upon the cake box.

'Not that much, I reckon,' Jack said. 'Rumour has it Piggott had run up a hell of a lot of debts.' He winked: 'Had a soft spot for diamonds, so they say!'

Clarissa looked over at Harry, and saw the smile forming in the corners of his mouth.

'Turner & Compton,' Jack said. 'Decent name for a nursery, that.'

'Compton & Turner,' Clarissa corrected. 'There are two of us, don't forget.'

Hearing Molly let out another slow, agonised sigh, Harry chuckled. 'I suppose a small slice wouldn't hurt.'

The little girl's face brightened, and Harry reached for the cake box, opening its lid to reveal a massive Victoria sponge, heavily dusted with icing sugar and oozing with raspberry jam. Jack passed him a penknife, and Harry cut the cake into five giant pieces. The first he passed forward to Davy, then let everybody else help themselves.

'To the future,' Harry called out, raising his slice of cake.

'To right now,' Molly said, sinking her teeth into the soft sponge.

Everyone laughed.

'You got any more back there?' Davy called from the box seat, wiping the icing sugar out of his whiskers.

'Afraid not, Davy,' Harry replied, throwing an arm around Clarissa's shoulders. 'But you never know, we may be back in Chelsea again before too long.'

And the cart rolled on, kicking up the dust behind it. Full of laughter, hope and possibility.

Acknowledgements

Huge thanks to Broo Doherty at DHH Literary Agency for believing in this book from the start.

Thanks also to the team at Welbeck for publishing it so wonderfully: Jon Elek, Rosa Schierenberg, Rachel Hart and Matt Tomlinson; Annabel Robinson and Rob Cox; Sam Matthews for her excellent project-management and proofreading; Hayley Shepherd for her eagle-eyed copy editing; Alexandra Allden and Adele Leyris for the beautiful cover; and Oliver Holden-Rea for helping get the show on the road.

Further thanks to Tara Loder, the Boyles, Gerald and Geraldine, Jeremy and Hilary Mogford, Sophie Bathgate, Alison Warshaw, Nicholas Maddison, Lewis Crofts, Dr Jennifer Rea and Haafiz Suleman.

Tip of the bowler to the real-life plant hunters and adventurers who inspired this tale.

And, of course, thank you – for everything – to Ali.

WELBECK

PUBLISHING GROUP

Love books? Join the club.

Sign up and choose your preferred genres to receive tailored news, deals, extracts, author interviews and more about your next favourite read.

From heart-racing thrillers to award-winning historical fiction, through to must-read music tomes, beautiful picture books and delightful gift ideas, Welbeck is proud to publish titles that suit every taste.

bit.ly/welbeckpublishing

WELBECK

ANDRE DEUTSCH

MORTIMER

MORTIMER

WELBECK